D1460750

Daniel Pascoe was born and educated in London, and worked in the north-east of England for twenty-seven years as a consultant oncologist in the Health Service. Now retired, he plans to devote much of his time to writing.

His first novel, *The London Sniper* (2015), was a chilling contemporary thriller, a story about revenge, with the patriotic heady times of the London Olympic Games 2012 as a backdrop.

He still lives on Teesside with his family.

DE AD END

DANIEL PASCOE

The Book Guild Ltd

First published in Great Britain in 2016 by
The Book Guild Ltd
9 Priory Business Park
Wistow Road, Kibworth
Leicestershire, LE8 0RX
Freephone: 0800 999 2982
www.bookguild.co.uk
Email: info@bookguild.co.uk
Twitter: @bookguild

Permission to print original song lyrics is gratefully
acknowledged from the following publishing houses:

Glad All Over
Words & Music by Dave Clark & Mike Smith
© Copyright 1963 Chester Music Limited trading as Ivy Music.
All Rights Reserved. International Copyright Secured.
Used by permission of Chester Music Limited trading as Ivy Music

Green Green Grass of Home
Words & Music by Curly Putman
© Copyright 1966 Warner/Chappell Music Limited.
All Rights Reserved. International Copyright Secured.
Used by permission of Warner/Chappell Music Limited.

Please Release Me
Words & Music by Eddie Miller, Dub Williams & Robert Yount
© Copyright 1954 Sony/ATV Acuff Rose Music, London.
All Rights Reserved. International Copyright Secured.
Used by permission of Sony/ATV Music Publishing (UK) Ltd.

Typeset in Adobe Caslon Pro

Printed and bound in Great Britain by CPI Group (UK) Ltd, Croydon, CR0 4YY

ISBN 978 1910878 859

British Library Cataloguing in Publication Data.
A catalogue record for this book is available from the British Library.

Thanks to Sandra for her faith and advice

Dedicated to the memory of Ruth and Lucy,
two beautiful women taken in their prime

Contents

Prelude

38 Shepherd's Way, Rickmansworth, North London NW16 8DS.

April 4 2010

Alison Blunt,
Tippling & Blunt,
Literary and Theatre Agents,
94 Great Russell Street,
London WC1 4BZ.

Dearest Alison,

Please find enclosed my debut manuscript, in 12 point and double spaced as instructed, with a single page synopsis. I would be most happy if you were able to peruse it and like it (hopefully) and help me with finding a suitable route to publication.

Since my father died just before Christmas, I have been clearing through some of his stuff and found a box-file full of his lectures, seminars and various other essays on a host of things (including such gems as his theories of gender difference in public toilet queuing). There was a copy of the speech he made at Annabel's wedding, which was as long ago now as July 1997, can you believe, just after New Labour had come into being and just before Lady Diana was killed in Paris, you will recall. Remember, that notorious wedding speech, in which he wooed the audience with humour and honesty, perhaps too much honesty. Well, there it was in full in black and white type with some of his notes scribbled around the text. And it got me thinking, how wonderful it would be if I could finally pull the whole story together and create a novel; after all, the complete saga is a rather extraordinary one.

Hence this manuscript, which I started some years ago when Dad was alive and after I had interviewed Sophie about her experiences. I have put it together in sections, in chronological order, but with some back story. So I am the narrator, written at first from Dad's point of view, using a lot of his original words in the speech and from many long talks I had with him later; and then from Sophie's point of view, mostly from her own words. All in the third person, past tense. Lots of show and tell (it works, you read it). The final section of the manuscript concludes the story, full circle as it were, again from Matthew's view point. You may like to be brought up to date with what happened to Sophie, poor thing.

So pleased to see that you have created your own agency at last. I know that you are looking for clients and are sympathetic to debut novelists. As you can imagine I would be absolutely thrilled to become one of your new treasured authors. I really look forward to hearing from you.

Hope all is well with you and yours,

Best wishes and my love,
Roger Crawford.

(PS – would love to meet up some time if that were possible, catch up with old times and so forth!)

Tippling & Blunt,
94 Great Russell Street,
London WC1 4BZ.

April 17 2010

38 Shepherd's Way,
Rickmansworth,
North London NW16 8DS.

Dear Roger,

Just because we were once married a long time ago, does not mean that I will show you any favouritism with this work. But I have to admit the story is good and well told and I think with a bit of editing we could knock it into shape. Cressida Sharpe, our well-trusted senior reader and editor-in-chief, will be in touch to fix up some work sessions and then we will see. I have a couple of publishers in mind, but this is only preliminary, you understand.

As for meeting up, I think it would be best for both of us to put that idea completely out of your mind.

Yours faithfully,
Alison Blunt.

ONE
The Wedding Speech

July 1997

1

For Matthew Crawford, the moment he had been waiting for for so long was at hand. Caldecott had called time.

This was Matthew's chance to impress and reassure people, not so much to show off, that was not his way, but to firmly demonstrate that he was in control of his life once again. He had overcome his recent difficulties and he was ready to 'move on'. He wanted to draw a line at this point, to admit mistakes and to tell the truth. After all, he was a senior member within the family; not the most senior of course, but he had been around long enough to have earned their respect. Surely he was entitled to say what he wanted and set the record straight, without having to worry too much about their feelings. For Rachel's sake. She would have expected honesty.

He would surely have told Rachel the full story by now, if she had been there, if she were alive. And at that precise moment, Matthew so wished she was alive, with him and beside him. In fact, he was daydreaming about her, had an image of her soft pretty features in his mind, could even feel her warm breath on his cheek and cool fingertips on his neck, just then, despite all the distractions of noise and bustle around him. He was looking forward to the next half hour with some nervous excitement.

It was late afternoon, a disappointingly wet midsummer weekend, and there must have been well over a hundred snappily-dressed relatives and friends and assorted hangers-on, all settled inside the marquee sheltering from the drizzle and thoroughly enjoying themselves. Matthew rose up from where he was sitting among the top table guests and sauntered over the slightly uneven matted floor to the music-stand placed precariously to one side of some trestle tables that supported the weight of a multi-layered white icing-sugared cake. Amid the discordance of noise of excited people talking loudly and laughing, waiters clattering hither and thither with plates and cutlery and glasses clinking, Matthew confidently clutched a heavy black microphone and pressed its cold metallic grid to his lips. In his late forties, comfortably attired in the essential dress for such an occasion, grey flannel tails, white stiff wing-collared shirt with grey and pink silk cravat, black patent leather shoes and a buttonhole, he looked every bit the proud father on his daughter's special day.

A moment earlier, Caldecott, a thick-set man with shovel-like hands, dark jowls and bushy eyebrows, who looked anything but comfortable in heavy black tailcoat, white stiff collar and grey silk cravat, promoted especially to be head butler and master of ceremonies, had banged on a table and prayed for silence for the bride's father. Caldecott had worked on the surrounding farm for countless years and, knowing the young couple concerned, looked especially proud of the honour placed upon him for this day and this day only.

Since Annabel's mother was no longer alive, it had been decided to hold the wedding unusually at the groom's home. And so a rectangular off-white canvas enclosure, guaranteed thankfully against all weathers and designed to accommodate one hundred and fifty guests comfortably seated, was pitched earlier that week on a patch of damp lawn adjacent to the Stirling's family house, which nestled almost unseen in the heart of wooded farmland south of the River Tweed and sufficiently close to the border to justify the extra expense of hired bagpipes at the entrance.

Extracting his notes on folded white paper from inside his jacket pocket and spreading them over the angled surface of the stand, Matthew coughed for attention. He heard an echo-like electrified response, which satisfied him that Roger had plugged the jack into the right amplifier socket behind the scenes and out of the way at the back, where the catering staff ran in and out with their laden trays. Sitting in a line next to each other on the far side of the top family table were three elderly ladies, in brand new colourful and overlarge outfits, with matching headgear and plumage. A combination of the excitement of the day, the comforting meal with plentiful champagne and the warmth in the marquee had conspired to inflict all three with doziness, their heads nodding forwards in various attitudes of sleep as befitted their great ages. No one seemed to be taking any notice, except for some friends sitting at the front under Matthew's nose, who were making shushing noises to no one in particular but themselves. Matthew coughed again into the microphone, clearing his throat a little louder, and the three elderly heads with their multi-coloured hats jerked up in unison at the sudden noise and wobbled awake, eyes blinking at the brightness of all the lights.

As a distinct lull in the noise levels settled around him, Matthew drew breath and with a barely detectable quaver in his voice, began his confessional.

'Ladies and gentlemen, Auntie Mary, special guests, friends, boys and girls, if I could have your attention, please.' All sounds subsided to a quiet hush. 'Annabel has given me seven minutes to deliver what is normally of course the highlight of any wedding – namely the bride's father's speech.' He studied the guests closest to him, trussed in their smart suits and tight dresses, their neatly cropped and salon coiffed hair-dos, their flushed cheeks and wet eyes from the swirling cigarette smoke, and paused for a second or two. 'I am the bride's father, by the way,' and a barely-concealed look of pride lingered across his pouting lips. He spoke with a clear voice that was easy on the ear, in plain English without accent. The deep navy of his eyes contrasted with the cream rose-bud in his lapel, and with an unruly wave of blond hair flopping over his lightly tanned clean-shaven face, Matthew looked foppish and handsome.

He smiled his perfect smile. Excited and happy, like everyone else seemed to be, he looked around at the sea of freshly-painted shiny faces, young and old, all turned toward him, their mouths open in hope of hearing the best wedding speech ever. Matthew was not particularly famous for them. He was known to be a quiet man, private, of even temper, averse to any form of showmanship. But, as a university professor, he was often speaking in front of audiences, at lectures and seminars, even at public meetings, and was actually quite a dab hand.

'So this is the moment you have all been waiting for, the most exciting bit to the day's programme.' Matthew spoke with measured certainty, which disguised his slight feelings of trepidation that the one glass of champagne he had allowed himself had not completely settled. He could feel the tight elastic of his new jockey shorts and became deeply conscious of wanting to scratch at his crotch. 'The give-away speech, the never mind losing a daughter, think about gaining a son speech.' He slithered long fingers unobtrusively into his right-hand trouser pocket and clawed through a thick pile of curly hair to reach the itchy area; relief was instant.

The main area of the marquee was closely packed, twelve guests to each white linen-topped round table, and on each a miniature flower arrangement and silk ribbon decoration matched the chosen colours of the day, gold, cream and purple, and coordinated neatly with the bride and bridesmaids' dresses. Hundreds of candles and tea-lights were placed everywhere on tables and ledges, hanging from arrangements across the vaulted ceiling, slung on strings from one stanchion to another, producing flickering light which inconveniently added to the heat already generated by the dozens of energetic souls jammed into the confined space. They also gave off a lovely summery scent, which helped counter the fetid waft of wet grass trampled underfoot. Raindrops could be heard gently pattering over their heads and to one side a flap in the canvas had been folded back to allow some cooler air into the place, through which the rain could be seen darting at an angle from the darkening skies.

This was not his first wedding speech, if he counted his own wedding twenty-five years ago, nor did it feel like it would necessarily be his last, but it did feel most special. He had begun to prepare for it well in advance. In fact, he had rehearsed it a hundred times in his head over recent years, starting long before Annabel had even met Douglas. In anticipation of just such an occasion, waiting for the opportunity to say certain things, to get them off his chest, and had even refrained from speaking about them in other settings among the people that mattered to him, on the off-chance that one day he would be able to offload all these things all together, when he would only have to say them once, as everybody who needed to hear them would be present, as a captive audience, trapped in a giant tent with no escape. The audience would be listening as he spoke, solemnly or humorously as the moment took him, and this way he could get it all over with at one go, and not have to keep repeating himself. And by being there in front of them, standing up at a podium, with a microphone that conferred a degree of authority to his words, he would gain in confidence and the meaning of his speech would gain in importance. No one would answer him back and he would be able to hold the audience in his spell. He was feeling good in elegant tails and buttonhole; who was going to challenge him when he looked just the part?

'First of all, are you all having a good time? I hope so. I would like to welcome you all to Arthur's seat here in Upsetlington; and to thank him and Margaret and all the Stirling family for their organization and hospitality in letting us use their grounds for this reception in this marvelous setting, and for this impressive erection.' By raising both hands upwards and looking towards the roof, he indicated he was referring to the huge tent enclosure that surrounded them, obviously. The youngsters in the audience were in particular high spirits, whistling and jeering, ready to roar with laughter at the least little thing, and duly obliged. He could not make out all of the people at the back who were probably forty metres away and was glad of the microphone effortlessly throwing his voice around the whole space, into every corner.

'It really is a lovely setting, for a lovely occasion. Pity we couldn't fix the weather as well, but we cannot have everything. I would not be surprised to find Bel has organised a little focus group work or facilitated workshop for us later on, just while she's got us all here and to keep us all occupied. Look at how the tables have been arranged; and I'm sure I saw a lot of flip-charts by the entrance when I came in.'

Matthew had rehearsed this speech while showering each morning, while getting dressed and while driving to and from work, imagining the warm response, the smiling faces, the applause and the admiration for a man who they had never realised was so perceptive, so sensitive and open, especially after what he had gone through. That was special, they would think, that took some courage; what a lovely man, shame he does not have anybody with him just now. Matthew did not quite realise it, but he was seeking approval, from the whole gathering and, most of all, from Annabel.

He began putting the words together on his computer screen only just recently, digging deep in his memory for some stories to tell that would make them laugh, some of the usual jokes; some sad moments that would make them cry. He felt like a scriptwriter or a stand-up comedian trying some new, and some not so new, gags.

'I wanted to bring my laptop, but Bel said no, you cannot give your speech from a PowerPoint. If you see my right hand twitching, it's because I'm still feeling for the mouse.' And he stretched out his right hand and flexed the fingers, trying to rid himself of a slight tremor.

Matthew knew that the key to a good speech was making it sound like an ordinary conversation, having a collection of jokes and stories that he could relate with a sincere and intimate tone, but equally sounding off the cuff and spontaneous, whereas in truth every word and comment, every pause and hesitation had been rehearsed endlessly beforehand. Rather than reading the carefully composed lines from a sheet of paper, he made them sound as if he had only just thought of them, and his notes were more of an aid to his task, which he merely had to glance at from time to time.

That morning, when he had woken quite early alone in his strange hotel bed, the weather had been fair and sunny, just some light cloud scudding across the feeble blue sky. As the morning progressed, after lingering over a protracted breakfast with his family and some of Annabel's friends who were staying at the same hotel, he found time to rest up in his bedroom, on the third floor with views over the sprawling gardens, with distant fields and rolling hills beyond. Sea breezes were blowing a summer freshness in through his open windows, and half dressed, propped on an elbow on the bed, he went through his typed words yet again, making last minute pencil notes in the margins. He found himself falling back onto the pillows in reflective mood, staring up at the moulded architraves around the ceiling, while images from his past powerfully chased each other across his mind, reminding him of how his life had been years ago, when Rachel was alive, when the family was intact. His lovely Rachel kept appearing, shaking and lying half-conscious across a grey bathroom carpet, with spittle at her lips.

He felt the pain of being alone and imagined Annabel's anguish at not being able to share her life's moments with her mother. He was no substitute, however hard he tried. A father-daughter relationship was quite different anyway. Based more on protective loyalty, Matthew was always going to be challenged by a stream of young virile boys hovering in the wings, waiting their chance to commit acts of fornication with his little darling and to steal her away. Matthew had to cope with that alone, and most vital of all to make it clear to everyone including Bel that he was perfectly capable of doing so. It should not have been a problem, but however symbolic the moment of separation, of declaring the end of an era, it was certainly going to feel to him like losing his daughter. And another poignant reminder of Rachel's absence.

Bel and Rachel were so alike, both generous personalities, pretty to look at and fun to be with, to hug and to hold. Bel had always made friends easily and had a loyal group of them around her. They loved her supportive nature, the way she managed to be sensitive to their needs. Matthew worried that her very kindness made her vulnerable to accepting the first offer that came along, that appeared to provide the family warmth and closeness that she craved for to replace her loss.

This was always going to be a special day for Matthew and Annabel, a day of joy and of tears. Perhaps of revelation, but most of all a day when he could return his love for her, visibly for all to see, which would make up for the times past when he had not been able to show her how much she really meant to him.

'A few months ago a young man with a soft Northumberland accent phoned me at home, early on a Saturday morning, I was still in my pyjamas. Asked if he could marry my daughter. Just like that! Well, I fell over, didn't I? Hardly knew the fellow. I called back down the phone: "You on your knees, Douglas, 'cos I'm flat on my back here?" My concern was immediate: "Bel's vegetarian, you live on a beef farm," I offered.'

There was some knowing laughter among the guests. And it was true that Douglas's family had been cattle farmers in the Borders for decades. Arthur Stirling oversaw a large dairy herd and was also breeding ostriches and trading the meat, which was processed on site, packaged and made ready for supermarket delivery. Ostrich skins were popular for shoes and handbags especially in Japan and the Far East, and the plumes were used to decorate hats, some examples of which were probably on display on the previously mentioned top table.

'Of course I was pleased. What nicer fellow than Douglas could possibly come along and take my little girl away?' Mathew knew that he could have been gritting his teeth at this moment, but he was not, he was feeling genuine, he liked Douglas. Everyone could see how he and Bel were suited to each other and so many had told Matthew as much over the last few days. 'I am really delighted to have Douglas as part of the family.'

'I have known Bel almost half my life and we have many things in common: a love of nature, rambling through Hampstead Heath or walking in the Lake District; being at a live concert in the Albert Hall or at a Stoppard play in the West End; we love cuddling cats, curling up in front of a roaring fire on a winter's afternoon with a Dorothy Dunnett historical novel. We both have plentiful blond hair,' and Matthew paused slightly between each phrase to slow the recital, 'we combine casual good looks with cutting edge intelligence and wit,' and a bit longer this time, 'and we are both surprisingly modest with it.'

Some of the loud-mouths roared, the university chaps, the slightly tipsy girl-friends, all trying to show how chummy they were with the hosts, with some over familiar gestures and shameless pouting. The atmosphere in the marquee was turning decidedly stuffy and little trickles of sweat were starting to tickle Matthew's temples.

'A long time ago when Bel was about five, we were in one of those huge stores like aircraft hangars, that we see nowadays, looking for beds. Bel went off on her own, playing quietly in and out of the furniture, into an area where imitation bathrooms were laid out on display. She came back after ten minutes when we were talking to a salesperson in the middle of this store, with her knickers down at her ankles and her hands held out in front of her, whispering urgently to Rachel, for all to hear, "I can't find the loo paper, mum; the toilet's broken!"'

The guests hooted: 'Oh, no,' exclaimed the row of elderly widows on the top table in unison, incredulous, 'I don't believe it, not Bel.' Matthew's mother was there, in a nice navy blue twin set, sitting side-ways and cross-legged, leaning forward on a wooden walking-stick, stick thin herself. And Muriel, Bel's other grandmother, in a pink suit and flamboyant bonnet to match, was next to her. She was silently masticating, her bright red lips massaging at something imaginary in her mouth, dentures clicking, uncomfortably rubbing on her gums. And next to her the third octogenarian, the formidable Auntie Mary in olive green, which made her look sallow, with matching hat and shoes, and a huge clasp in the shape of a bird of paradise pinned prominently on the down-slope of her impressive bosom, constantly shuffling to try to find a more comfortable position on her hard wooden chair.

'Bel once grew her hair down to her bottom, but had it all shortened at university. I had mine trimmed some years ago, but some of you will recall our heyday (or hair day) in the late Sixties, when shoulder length locks were *de rigueur*, for the fellers. And we all wore flowers in our hair.' And Matthew's fertile mind uncontrollably filled with the pop soundtrack of the time, as a vision of a dark-haired beauty lying back topless on her parents' double bed blowing blood-red rose petals into the air and singing, "If you're going to San Francisco, be sure to wear some flowers in your hair", all such a long time ago at the end of his school days.

The background noise level had drifted upwards again but was manageable, as the neatly dressed waiters discreetly slipped between tables, this way and that, bringing clean glasses, extra bottles of wine or cups of coffee to insatiable guests, some of whom seemed intent on chatting and making comments throughout, clinking their glasses, banging plates or thumping on the tables.

'As a child Bel had always shown promise, she was bright and quick, conscientious; always doing her homework on time, always a smile on her face,' Matthew continued. 'She took to music early on and weren't we proud, Rachel and I, when she won her scholarship. That love of music was reflected in the church service earlier today when Imogen played so beautifully that clarinet solo for us. Thank you, Imogen.' A round of applause and a few cheers went up, and somewhere in the crowd Imogen blushed demurely. 'There are many stories I could tell you about Bel, about her love of the natural world, her religious instincts and other achievements; but I am not here to embarrass her, but to tell her how much we love and care for her.'

Since Matthew had been on his own, Annabel had been

good at keeping in close touch, over the phone or with little cards in the post. She always remembered his birthday and sent him a present, unlike her younger brother, who never remembered and needed reminding, often by Bel herself. Even then if he did send a card, it would arrive inevitably late with a little apology and a "something to come later" note, only there never was with Roger.

'And how delighted we all are for her on this, her special day. As you well know, Bel has developed into a wonderful woman, caring, thoughtful and always willing to help others.' A few 'hear! hears!' went around the marquee and Matthew's voice dried with a little tremble. 'I am delighted to say, she takes after her mother.'

And it was on the word 'mother' that the sound from the microphone suddenly stopped and Matthew's voice disappeared in the general melee. He was trying to say, now that Bel had a new man in her life, the rest of them were going to have to spread her more thinly in order to get their share of her. 'Roger, my boy, this seems to have gone dead,' he mouthed into the audience, pointing at the microphone in his hand and seeking out Roger's flushed face across the tables. He wondered if anyone had noticed, but then realised that quite a few were now gesticulating towards him to speak up, 'can't hear you'.

Auntie Mary, sitting near to Roger on the top table, was grasping at his upper arm, and in her croaky voice, was trying to tell him above the general noise, that something was amiss and his father needed his help. Caldecott was moving through the crowds, weaving between tables toward Matthew, feeling hot and bothered. Matthew spotted Roger, tall in his grey tails, moving swiftly towards the rear entrance close by the kitchen access. He quickly found the sauce of the trouble: the amplifier cable had been pulled out of its power socket, probably by a passing waiter accidently kicking the flex, and he replaced it. With a thumbs up and a 'try that now, father,' he returned to his seat among the elderly widows next to his new girlfriend, Alison, whose nipples Matthew could plainly see imprinted through her skin-hugging golden dress, with plunging neckline and no obvious boob support that he could make out. 'She leaves one with quite an impression,' Auntie Mary had whispered to Matthew earlier, as they were settling at their places.

2

Georgina Maria Hayhoe-Beatson earned her title of Auntie Mary, universally used by all family, friends and anyone else who came to call, and ever since anyone could remember, through her autocratic and commanding, not to say bossy, personality. Not for her some quiet unnoticed backwater as she gently ripened through old age, but a vibrant and busy presence at all family occasions, large gatherings at Christmas and Easter, and frequent summer vacation parties at her Eastbourne flat, were the order of the day.

Married to the promising dancer Barney Hayhoe for only a short while in her twenties, she became the centre of media attention after his untimely death, and secretly loved every moment of it. Potential suitors hovered around her London apartment, falling over themselves to be noticed as she flitted to a waiting taxi for a shopping trip in the West End or a train journey from Waterloo to visit a friend in the Home Counties. Later married to Stanley Beatson, a second-rate professional tennis player and first-rate *Daily Mail* sports editor, Georgina managed to maintain the media interest with her film-star looks, colourful dress sense and tendency to frivolous comments about Valentino's new spring collection, Mrs Simpson's real motives for upsetting the public or the failure of English lawn tennis to flourish since Fred Perry.

For a second time widowed early and unexpectedly, after the Second World War, she regularly and for years invited her favoured cousins, nieces and nephews to free seats at centre court during the Wimbledon fortnight, where she fraternised frightfully with the minor officials and an occasional sports personality, and then lavished strawberries and cream on her young devotees. Where once Georgina excelled as the ill-fated romantic heroine, Auntie Mary adapted the more comfortable role of indestructible dowager, and like a comic matron she bustled about, organising people and persuading them to her point of view, whether at a local branch meeting of The Women's Institute or a gathering of the Eastbourne Conservative Club, where she indulged in fiendishly competitive bridge.

By the time Matthew had first met her, when she was well into those comfortable years of discretion that were never defined exactly, when he was probably about six, she had become unashamedly overweight, wearing shapeless printed dresses that hung like tents over her bulky frame, and had long retreated to the warmer climes of the south coast. She always smelt of a mixture of Chanel, lavender and moth balls, and was forever dipping her pudgy fingers into lavish boxes of chocolates. As her looks faded with age, she so powdered over the cracks in her face that when she laughed or shook her head, a cloud of fine particles would be caught in the light as they erupted all around her and slowly settled as dust. Matthew once remarked on how wobbly were Auntie Mary's exposed upper arms, like the loose flesh around her cheeks and the bags under her eyes, and was memorably scolded for being so thoughtless towards someone so generous at heart. With each holiday visit that Matthew saw her, her double chin and big nose became ever more pronounced. In the summer months, family gatherings usually included walks along the windy promenade and ice-creams in crispy cones, but Auntie Mary had to sit down to rest so frequently that she barely covered more than a few yards from her front door.

As part of Auntie Mary's pedigree, she was blessed with a booming voice that gave her authority. Although there was also quite a pleasing and sweet soprano that she used in a staccato fashion to join in the singing voices of any show or opera on the radio, whether she recognised it or not. She mostly did, she seemed familiar with the words to *South Pacific*, *Oklahoma*, *The Sound of Music*, *My Fair Lady* and all the rest. She laughed a lot, often in memory of better times past, and was always generous when she visited the family home, usually slipping a half-crown into one of the children's palms before she left and whilst their mother was busy in the kitchen, shaking her head and saying with a winking eye 'don't spend it all at once'.

Nowadays she was extraordinarily large, sadly plagued with ill-health, like diabetes, high cholesterol and blood pressure, and at eighty-six and nineteen stone, she found it hard to get about, so that she would pay for others to do the heavy lifting, cleaning, shopping, fetching and carrying. She spent most of her time frustratingly cooped up in her flat and confined to a sofa designed for two, watching television and getting bored by it, as there was never anything worthwhile on, although she did have a soft spot for David Attenborough. She would read more but her eyes too were failing her. She was just able to see the English Channel, from her ground floor flat, which was a godsend.

There had not been a 'do' at Auntie Mary's place for some years, not since Margaret Thatcher resigned as prime minister, and so everyone was delighted that she would be at Annabel's wedding. Getting her there from the south coast was another story. She was now heavily slumped on a folding wooden chair that looked absurdly tiny and unsafe under her broad bottom, in a place of honour on the top table close to her beloved Bel, the bride, and, she had insisted, to Bel's equally lovely brother. Roger had spent most of the last hour during the meal making small talk and amusing the elderly ladies, which he was good at, with his mix of cheeky charm and youthful zest, making them cackle or gasp with his stories of the various carry-ons at Cambridge these days. Auntie Mary had never had any children of her own.

'Two television aerials on a roof fell in love and got married,' Roger informed his elite and dedicated audience, 'the wedding wasn't great but the reception was fantastic.' Roger's shoulders shook with amusement.

In reality Auntie Mary was some sort of distant cousin of Matthew's late father and by virtue of her exotic early life, meeting celebrities and travelling the world, she commanded a senior leadership role among the other elderly ladies, none of whom were actually related to her but were happy to pay deference to one of such worldly experience and physical size. 'Had this marvellous fellow, drove me all the way from my door, only stopping at Newport Pagnell, where we had a light meal, before retiring early,' Auntie Mary was saying, retelling the tale for the second or third time in her breathless way to no one in particular. 'Up at the crack of dawn, made it to the church, with five minutes to spare. Harry, his name, he must be here somewhere.' Noticing lots of bare flesh around the shoulders: 'Don't catch your death, dear, will you,' she said to Alison when they first sat down.

Matthew's mother, Minnie Crawford, was quite the contrast to her broader companions, her thin frame hardly seemed big enough to occupy the chair she was perched on. She bent forward with a crick in her neck, leaning on her stick, with both wiry hands holding on tight, and her chin resting on them.

'Didn't vote for that Tony Blair, I suppose?' Auntie Mary bawled above the noise into her ear earlier on. Minnie shook her head from side to side, 'Oh, Heavens, no; that awful man, wouldn't dream of it,' she said, 'never trusted a man who wore suede shoes.' She hoped that would put a stop to the conversation as the speeches were about to begin.

3

'That was close, thanks, Roger,' Matthew was saying, when the microphone crackled back to life and sound returned, relieved he would not have to shout the rest of his speech out into the distant recesses of the marquee. 'I've never given a daughter away before,' he said with a touch of irony and a bare squint of his eyes, his gaze on some distant face in the crowd. 'It's a bit like a swap I suppose, losing a daughter, gaining a son, you're definitely swapping one set of troubles for another set of troubles. It's appropriate I think that we are up here in the Borders, where traditions and customs have remained unchanged for so many centuries. Many a man still sleeps with a battleaxe by his side. Local farmers are apt to feed their chickens with whisky in the hope they will lay scotch eggs.' Matthew hoped Caldecott was busy with other duties rather than listening to him, because he was sure he would have taken offence by now.

'I heard on the news this morning that there was a warehouse burglary last night near here in Berwick; more than fifty thousand pounds' worth of Viagra tablets were stolen.' Matthew had heard this joke from Roger last night. 'The police are looking for a gang of hardened criminals.'

With his straight expression and deadpan voice throughout, Matthew was beginning to enjoy his experience;

his tremor had subsided and, although there was a stickiness to his underarms and a slight sheen to his perspiring face under all those burning candles and spotlights, he felt comfortable. It all seemed pretty easy, plain sailing. Until he started to think about bits of his speech that were still to come, when he wanted to talk about Rachel and how she died, the impact on the family and their relationship; how he and Annabel had struggled to maintain a normal life and had seemingly drifted apart; how he had turned to drink and how he wanted to say sorry for all that and to be more a part of her life again.

He told himself not to get distracted. He needed to say something complimentary about his daughter's job, knowing her boss and many friends from her work were present. Annabel was in the management training sector and did corporate leadership seminars; phrases like 'business re-engineering', 'empowerment' and 'benchmarking' were frequently scattered through her lexicon, although he remained uncertain as to how she actually earned her living. He imagined her working with teams on 'away days' helping the employees explore their strengths and weaknesses, redesign their work patterns and make lists of the most irritating habits of their chief executive. Flip charts were always part of the proceedings.

Yesterday in the late afternoon, wanting to stretch his legs and shake off some of the tiredness from his long car journey from London, he had taken a walk in water-proofs with Roger and Alison, out over the damp hills behind Arthur's farm, through heather and fern to the higher grassy slopes. From there the marquee, with coloured standards flying, even at half-a-mile away, looked a pretty size in the distance with its vaulted crenellated roof and funnel entrance. Erected by the main house in neat gardens, it was enclosed by trimmed box hedges and tall conifers, standing like sentinels around the four corners. If you wanted a big marquee that left a big impression, Arthur had clearly chosen well; it was almost certainly visible by satellite. To Matthew, it looked like something out of the Middle Ages, England at the time of the Crusades, and he imagined a dozen horsemen thunderously riding over the ridge behind them fully armoured with funny pointy helmets with nose tabs, their bearded faces hidden and unrecognizable. "In the name of God and good King Richard!" they would shout, the ground trembling under them, with noises of rattling bridle and clashing sword.

'Remember to keep the speech short and to the point, Alison said to me yesterday, when I asked them what I should say. My family all seemed to have opinions as to content and length and Bel came up with seven minutes. Don't get sentimental, she said, it'll make your buttonhole droop! Why bother with a speech at all, Roger asked.' Matthew paused as he created an indulgent smile. 'Well, there are one or two things I would like to say, and I believe they are worth saying. First of all, I must thank you all for coming, especially those who have travelled some long distances to get here. I think you are all privileged; to be friends of Bel and Douglas is a privilege. Thanks also to a lot of family friends, real best friends who I've known for a long time, for coming all this way, it is really lovely to have you here.'

Matthew pressed on. 'Weddings are such lovely things, aren't they really? They bring family together that don't normally bother with each other, friends from years ago meet friends from today, a lovely excuse for a get-together. And putting everyone together in a way that fits is like doing a jig-saw puzzle, slotting each person into their rightful place.' He left a good three seconds pause before going on, looking across at his mother, who seemed to have dozed off again. 'My lovely mother over there, she loves jigsaw puzzles. She was very pleased the other day when she finished a puzzle after three months. It said "4 to 6 years" on the box.'

Minnie Crawford nodded benignly, almost certainly missing the point. With hardly a glimmer of a smile himself, Matthew paused for only a few moments here for some audience laughter before continuing. 'It's good to see Auntie Mary here as well, after a bit of an absence from family gatherings.' And here he smiled broadly across towards the top table. 'Hope she won't mind me telling you this – erm, it's personal – she's had a bit of trouble recently with her... piles, (he mouthed the word 'piles' with soundless exaggeration, an apologetic expression wrought around his mouth). 'She went to her doctor who gave her a suppository for the... back passage,' (and he did the same with these two words, mouthing them without actually speaking them, with over-exaggerated lip and mouth movements) 'but, you know, she lives in a ground floor apartment, it doesn't have a back passage, so for all the good it was, she may as well have shoved the suppository up her bottom, frankly.' This last with a bit of a camp indignity, his jaw dropped behind the flat of his hand, as if he was sharing a secret with the audience and Auntie Mary would not be able to see his face properly, although his wide-eyed stare was directed across to her, whose face had crumpled like a deflated soufflé.

It was a testament to the easy relationship he had with Auntie Mary that he could have told such a story without causing offense, if indeed she had heard it properly. They had always enjoyed each other's company with a similar sense of humour, and over the years Matthew had developed considerable affection for the old girl, still enjoying trips to her flat from time to time to confide in some little family tale or two over a conspiratorial cup of tea or something a bit stronger. The other two ladies definitely looked a little shocked and frowned at each other with twisted smiles, as if to see whether they had heard Matthew correctly, and whether it would seem improper to show that *they* had understood the joke by laughing with everyone else.

Matthew had to pause for the cackling laughter to rise and fall. 'My parents of course brought us up in the Fifties and Sixties to believe in our Lord and to open our bowels regularly.' He spoke with his usual calm almost expressionless voice. 'But I'm an atheist, thank God!' Almost without pause, raising his voice above the laughter: 'I love all the hats as well, don't you? Just look at them,' and Matthew turned again towards the three elderly ladies perched at the top table like targets at a coconut shy, indicating with his nodding head the row of ornamental exhibits on show. 'Impressive or what?' A few affectionate cheers and whoops went up as Matthew mockingly toasted them with a raised glass of champagne that he had swiped off the tray of a passing waitress, taking a big sip. He raised his voice, 'I frequently wear a hat,' turning back to the audience again. 'I have a hat for every occasion actually, as all gentlemen should – a furry hat for the winter, a woolly hat for skiing, a floppy white cricket hat for the summer, a baseball cap for golf, a deerstalker for I don't know what exactly, even a flat cap for country walks. But I couldn't decide what hat to wear for this wedding. So I asked a good friend of mine, Patrick, what hat I should wear for a weekend wedding up north in hunting country near Upsetlington, and in a broad Irish accent, he said "wear the fox hat". Somewhere up on the Borders near Berwick, I replied.'

After some hesitation, while that one was fully appreciated, spluttering laughter and clapping broke out. Matthew had forgotten how good applause sounded, how addictive it could be. It was what made actors and comedians and politicians come back time and again, he supposed, treading the boards, getting the audience to react the way they wanted; it was seductive and powerful. He went straight on this time, with barely a pause: 'I make no apologies for not wearing a kilt, by the way. Never has truer Scottish blood flowed through the veins of the Crawfords, but if you had ever seen me in shorts you'd understand.'

The throng of eager faces were mostly turned toward him, giving him their full attention. 'Actually I was a little worried, you know, about this weekend, all the arrangements, the organization, meeting all you people, many of you I hadn't seen for ages; I thought I would ask Maurice to be *my* best man for the occasion (why should only the groom have a best man?), after all, he's done it for me before. Dr Maurice would come and hold my hand, check my speech over, give me a joke or two, I thought, make sure I was wearing clean underpants.'

4

Sharing a table close to the front with a number of their crowd was Dr Maurice Wellwood, red-faced and a little tipsy. Described by friends and patients alike as solid, reliable, dependable, Maurice was a long-established GP in Richmond in a long-established marriage to solid, reliable and very dependable Pauline, with four lovely children and a large Dulux wallpaper dog. Although not the brightest, he had done pretty well for himself, and so had Maurice incidentally; they were living proof that the longer a dog lives with its owner the closer the two come to look and behave like one another. Maurice, unruly greying hair and loosely trimmed beard, always pronounced his surname, especially to any visitors to the practice, in rhythmic tones: 'double u, e, double l, double u, double o, d', that tripped off his tongue, with a straight face.

In his early university years, Maurice had his sights set on a surgical career at a prestigious London teaching hospital, craving the kudos and status that that would bring him, to say nothing of the potential income. But he had struggled to overcome the closed professional culture and vigorous competition, and had eventually settled instead for a life in the easier environment of general practice. Nurse Pauline had been solidly behind him all the way, and together they had built a strong reliable partnership, less glamorous perhaps than they had at first envisioned, but satisfying nevertheless in its own right.

Matthew and Maurice had developed their friendship when naïve eighteen-year-old first-year medical students, carefree in the big city, when all that worried them was who to take to next Saturday night's hop. Maurice had been best man when Matthew and Rachel married all those years ago, long before the middle class traps of mortgages and children and responsible jobs closed in on them. Maurice and Pauline missed Rachel almost as much as Matthew did.

Matthew could recall them playing croquet on the evening before his big day, in warm late summer sunshine that cast strong shadows across the back lawn of their hotel in Cheltenham. Maurice seemed entirely *au fait* with the rules and went to strike confidently his ball placed up against Matthew's, with his left foot positioned firmly on the top; but he mistimed his stroke and whacked his own foot so hard that he leapt away in pain, grabbing it in both hands, hopping on the other foot, while his mallet arced away through the air over his head landing in a distant flower bed. His annoyance, somewhat overplayed for effect, increased even more when he saw that Matthew's ball had not ricocheted off into the shrubs where it was supposed to be unplayable, but was now perfectly placed for a shot through the next hoop, whereas his own ball was half buried in the soft grass before him where his left foot had been. He had yelled rather loudly and fellow hotel guests apparently complained to the manager about rowdy behaviour and unsavoury language on the croquet lawn.

Matthew and Maurice had shared much of their growing up, their worries and joys during those formative years, being regular supper guests or weekend visitors at each other's houses, and frequently attended over the years the major family events as they unfolded: the birthdays and anniversaries, weddings and new arrivals and the rest. They had holidayed together with their young families in Northern France in the summer time or the Alps for a winter's skiing; they had laughed and cried together, and supported each other during house moves or the birth of their various children. Rachel and Pauline became close friends, seeing eye-to-eye on most issues and both so down to earth and such straight-forward characters. Last summer, Matthew, Annabel and Roger had enjoyed a wonderful day celebrating Maurice and Pauline's daughter Nancy's wedding in Richmond, which had included a trip across The Green in a long trail conga-style of all their well-heeled guests, well-heeled in designer shoes and best outfits, a couple of elf-life university friends playing clarinet and flute leading the bride in glittering white with four little bridesmaids in matching dresses tripping in her wake while trying to keep up and hold onto the edges of her train at the same time.

If grown men in their forties really had best friends, Maurice would be Matthew's and probably *vice versa*. And so it was only natural that the Wellwoods should be at the wedding of Matthew's first born, the lovely Annabel, whom they had known intimately from the moment of her arrival.

'Maurice was busy, as usual, but he is here today with the delightful Pauline; and the big dog (Pete) is out in the car. He's an enormous English sheepdog that dictates life in their household. When Maurice comes home late from work, he usually cuddles the dog and sleeps with the wife; or, if he's *really* late, tries to cuddle the wife and ends up sleeping with the dog.' There was laughter, and the loudest guffaws emanated from Maurice himself.

'Maurice first introduced me to a pretty girl at the university sports ground, when I was coming off the tennis courts. I always tucked the extra ball in fashionable style into the pocket of my shorts when I was serving. I had forgotten to remove the last ball and we went into the bar, where this attractive brunette was having a drink with some friends and she stared suspiciously at the bulge in my shorts. Somewhat embarrassed I explained that it was only a tennis ball – to which Rachel replied, 'Gosh, that must be so painful; last year I had a tennis elbow'.'

Further bursts of laughter slowly subsided. 'Ah, I love the romance of it all: I remember when we had just got married, we were driving up to Blackpool from Gloucestershire, and I reached over and shyly caressed Rachel's bare knee. She smiled and blushed demurely and said, 'We are married now – you can go further if you want.' So we drove on up to Glasgow instead.'

Matthew needed to pause, just for a few vital seconds, to draw breath, to achieve the calmness he required before navigating through the next phase of his task. He perceived that so far everything had jogged along fairly well, even though he was way over his allotted seven minutes. Most of the shiny faces out there were apparently happy, the drinks were still flowing and nobody had shouted out any objections or heckled him with abuse; no one had got up to leave.

'But lest we forget that weddings can also be tinged with sadness,' and Matthew scanned the sea of faces again, roving across the assembled groups, as if looking for someone, 'as we realize that certain people are missed, people who cannot be here or who are no longer with us.' He wanted to settle his gaze on one person who could represent the entire audience, a friendly face that could act as a sort of surrogate funnel for his emotional contact, so that some kind of understanding could be achieved, preferably a friendly stranger to whom he could speak directly, someone who would sympathize with what he was saying, about not having that key person beside him.

'There are of course two people of especial importance to me and to Annabel who are not here, but whose influence on our lives remains immense. My father, who died last year, would have dearly loved to share this occasion with his family. He loved Rachel very much and Bel was dear to his heart.'

Matthew settled his gaze finally on Annabel herself, logically the person he was really addressing. She was sitting upright close to the top table, with Douglas next to her and her hands grasping his in her lap, tensed in anticipation of some personal or embarrassing remark. Today her blue eyes and salmon-pink lips radiated a joyful bliss, and with honey-blonde ringlets tumbling over bare shoulders, she had that French seventeenth-century look, delicious in her creamy-white flowing dress with contrasting purple ribbons. She had been laughing as much as anyone so far, an infectious warbling sound.

Matthew felt the pricking sensations around his eyes that he so feared and had promised himself would not surface in front of everybody. He paused to swallow and lowering the microphone away from his lips, inhaled deeply through his nose. He managed a beseeching smile at Annabel, before raising his hand and insinuating his lips around the wire mesh. Conscious of a quake in his voice, he spoke quietly: 'And so logically that brings me around … to Rachel.'

5

Rachel Huntley had appeared shimmering on Matthew's narrow horizon like an apparition, viewed from some way off. He, a boy of eighteen, timid and nondescript among the crowd; she, a woman of eighteen, a sparkling perfection who stood out in the crowd. He simply could not touch her, but satisfied himself by watching dolefully from the sidelines, dreaming what seemed like the impossible. He would catch brief glimpses of her during the day, darting between lecture theatres, striding across the grass quadrangle to the residents' canteen in spirited conversation with other girls, passing purposely along corridors or dashing down the main stairs to the meeting hall, and he would record that moment in his mind's diary, adding it to the few others and calculating an accumulative whole, which represented the pathetic sum of his romantic activity during that winter term in London, 1968.

While all the other blokes in Matthew's year seemed to have found girlfriends within days of arriving at College, he was slow in coming forward. Somewhat bruised by recent experience, his natural sense of reticence held him back from jumping in with the first female he bumped into. He was biding his time, still in the eyeing-up stage. But he found himself on more than one occasion sitting at the top of the residence stairwell, listening to a light soprano practicing Bach or Handel behind the locked doors of the female shower-rooms or from along the fourth floor corridor. Matthew, shy and uncertain, became so acutely aware of Rachel, so attracted by her sophistication, that it was driving him to distraction, and yet feeling so out of her league that he was unable to approach her; and particularly over quiet interminable weekends, when Rachel would often be away and he was left feeling morose and stupid, imagining her singing the Mamas and Papas.

After a colourful childhood spent in East Africa, her colonial parents landed up in Gloucestershire when she was about eleven, where she flourished at the local school. Arriving in London from the countryside at eighteen, like a porcelain figurine thrown casually in among the bigger rough-and-ready dolls and stuffed animals in the toy box, she appeared at first naively out of place in the noisy city. But she was polite, delightfully deferential, hesitant even, before moving forwards with confidence and so quick to learn the art of survival in the male-dominated world. This was the Sixties in London and Rachel came to personify the exciting expectations of her generation, young people being seen as the future, grabbing the high ground wherever they could. She eagerly contributed to student magazines, wrote about the new music and poetry and the anti-war movement and went to local rallies in Trafalgar Square to shout the slogans with the best of them. She took in folk music, poetry readings, the theatre, whatever was going and whenever she could. She enjoyed intimate groups discussing politics over coffee, late into the evenings and sang in the college choir, Bach's Oratorio to be performed in St Paul's Cathedral over Christmas. She worked hard and played hard, often out late in clubs, in Soho and Theatreland, till one in the morning, yet would be up in time, coffee and toast in hand, cheerfully ready for the next day's lectures by nine o'clock. She did not smoke and avoided drugs, never over-drank and slept soundly, usually alone. Out of a full year of 120 students, with the competition especially intense among the eighteen girls, she routinely came out in the top five when test results were posted on the college notice boards. And still she partied and faultlessly managed the burning of her particular candle at both ends without any apparent hiccups.

Matthew for his part threw himself into various sports and had been selected to play football in the college team, which meant training under floodlight during the week in the darkening winter evenings on the small grass pitch in the middle of college grounds, often watched by a thin crowd on their way back from the afternoon's activities, mostly girls eyeing up the local talent. Matthew attracted some attention, with his careless blond hair flopping over his face, his handsome looks and athletic body. Some of the girls would lean over to each other and whisper behind their hands about which blokes they fancied, and Matthew was regularly picked out as having the best backside and ironically was everyone's favourite.

At the end of their training games, hot, sweaty and breathing heavily, the boys would tramp through the watching crowd, stripping their shirts off on the way to the changing rooms, and a few of the girls would secretly swoon. Catriona (imaginatively nicknamed Cat) reached out once and pretended to rake her clawed hands over Matthew's chest and back, much to the other girls' delight, crying out that she was feeling horny and what was he doing later. Matthew laughed with the rest and shrugged her off, and they all went "Phooaaar". But not Rachel, who, if she was there at all, would stand to one side, smile to herself and keep her dignity, although she actually fancied Matthew, just as much as the others.

Matthew seemed never able to pluck up the courage to approach her to start a conversation. He noticed that she was going out anyway with a dozy redhead, called Rob, who smoked a lot of all sorts and was often spaced out in classes. Rob was always short of money and borrowed off his mates all the time; whether they ever got to see their money again, Matthew was never sure, but his were a tolerant circle of friends. Matthew was not too sure what Rachel saw in him, except that he was gentle and casually good looking, and played acoustic six string, singing Tim Hardin and Bert Jansch, country and folk stuff that Rachel often accompanied, sitting among friends late into the evenings. Rob was so obviously the opposite to her, untidy, disorganized and always in trouble for not studying enough to get through his exams, that Matthew was mystified – maybe Rachel viewed the experience as a challenge.

Rachel was pretty; Rachel was clever. Rachel was, Matthew decided, everything he ever wanted in a girl and he could not take his mind off her. She was bright, fresh, capable and in control. She had a small compact figure, often dressed in elegant cotton with colourful tank tops and waistcoats and tight miniskirts in flat shoes. She shone like a beacon above all others and seemed to move in a different circle to Matthew, attracting an elite group of female friends around her, while male predators circled a little further off. Everywhere he looked he saw her neat symmetrical face, under a boyish brown crop, soft cheekbones and sensuous lips, so easy on the eye. His dreams were bursting with the imagined feel of her silky skin, the pout of her wet lips against his, under the scrutiny of her sparkling acorn brown eyes and she would laugh as he traced with a trembling fingertip her wide dimpled smile.

In mid-December the week before the Christmas Ball, always a big event at the college to which everyone attended, grabbing partners wherever they could be found so as not to be left out, Matthew found himself quite by luck standing directly behind Rachel in the mid-morning coffee queue. He inhaled deeply her scent and spoke, saying 'Hi' in as casual a manner as he could, with his dry croaky voice, that she apparently failed to hear. Next thing, people behind him were shoving forwards and he could not restrain from barging into her. He put his hands up instinctively to cushion the effect, as she was turning to find out what the fuss was, his hands straying across her chest for an instant. 'Oh, hello,' she said, unperturbed, 'how are you?'

They chatted hesitantly about this and that and nothing in particular, and then he mentioned the coming Ball and would he see her there? He was praying that she would say no one had yet asked her, but no such luck: she would be there with a crowd of people, she said excitedly and it would be fun if they all met up; and then she dropped into an offered chair with her cup of coffee at a table of her friends and Matthew was left standing alone; he moved on.

As it happened, Rachel brought her younger sister, Helen, up to London, introducing her to Maurice, who didn't have a girlfriend at the time. Rachel partnered an older bloke who Matthew had never met, clean shaven, short-back-and-sides, called Alan, who had just got a BSc in biochemistry. Matthew felt cool and suave in an Edwardian high collared black velvet dinner jacket that he found the week before in Portobello Market, with ball-crushingly tight black trousers and black Cuban heeled ankle boots, all of which served to be quite warm on an icy cold evening and outrageously different to all the other conventional evening outfits around. It also helped to calm any sense of jealousy that kept rising as a bitter taste in the back of his throat, as he knew he looked rakish and attractive, and that Rachel would surely notice sooner or later how irresistible he was and redirect her attentions his way.

Matthew spent most of the evening with a chummy public school girl in full length flowery dress called Fiona, who had dodgy skin and danced crazily all evening, with wild gyrations to the Rolling Stones, swilling down large glasses of warm beer while sweating profusely. He had hardly seen Rachel all evening and was wondering whether the whole thing had been in vain. While everyone else seemed to have discarded their jackets and ties as the evening had warmed up, the girls dancing in skimpy tops with acres of bare flesh on view, Matthew kept his prized jacket on for fear of losing it or getting it damaged, despite becoming hot and sticky.

Late on, feeling disheartened while queuing for yet more drinks at the packed bar, just able to hear the background strains of the Nightingales Steel Band, Rachel, out of the blue, pushed her way through the noisy crowds over to his side and shouted unexpectedly up into his ear that Alan was a complete bore and they could go into the ballroom next door for a dance, if he wanted. Matthew was so flummoxed by her surprise advance that he lost all powers of speech but was able to track eagerly behind her, watching closely her bare back and the way her glittery full-length dress hugged around the curves of her bottom, as she threaded her way through the throng of hot moving bodies. Past the loud and the louche and the mostly pissed, they pushed into the middle of the dark discotheque crowd, where the beat was thumping and the music was Mony Mony. Rachel swayed and gyrated to the rhythms with an easy freedom that had Matthew mesmerized. Flashing strobe lights caught the whites of her eyes and her teeth in lurid phosphorescence while she writhed and twisted, uninhibited and free-flowing, dancing for him to appreciate. When the pounding beat was replaced by slower songs of the Bee Gees and the Hollies, he was rewarded with the sensation of her hands on his shoulders, as they smooched close together, her thighs and hips moving hotly against his, his cheek coming to rest on her damp forehead, the intimacy electric and terrifying. Matthew was drawn into a powerful swoon by her warm adjacency, her smell and gentle touch, while he gazed blissfully at close quarters upon the textured flesh of her modest unsupported bosom.

After what seemed like an hour of sheer pleasure, with perspiration trickling in little streams down his face and back, his shirt clammy tight and his legs starting to tire, he suggested they should go outside for some fresh air. Rachel indicated an open tall window at the far side and they climbed through together, laughing as he helped her down from the sill, into the car park road that ran along the side of the building. They dashed away holding hands around the corner in the dark, feeling the chill of the December air, their shoes clacking on the gravel. He caught her round the waist and they were breathing hard as she put both hands up to his chest, holding the edges of his velvet lapels. She accepted his offer of the jacket, which he readily discarded for her bare shoulders, and she felt seduced by its warmth and the raw smell of his body wrapped around her.

He said Fiona was only interested in dancing and drinking and that she had exhausted him; they had hardly exchanged a word all evening. She muttered something about Alan being an utter disappointment and how lovely it was to get away from all that smell and noise. They surmised that the others would be wondering where the next round of drinks had got to and that they did not care one little bit. They giggled and shivered, their breaths mingling in clouded puffs, and both agreed how strange some people were, but that it took all sorts.

'I'm sure they'll be having a good time without us,' Rachel pondered.

'Probably won't have even noticed we've left,' said Matthew, plucking up his courage to ask: 'Why did you not come with Rob?'

'He didn't ask me,' she replied matter-of-factly. 'Not his thing. Anyway, I think we have just about had enough of each other; we will remain friends but we have agreed to go our separate ways.' He detected a slight regret in her expression.

Rachel turned her face up towards his. Her short hair was sticking across her forehead and the sides of her face, while the rims of her ears peeped through at the sides. Her shiny bright eyes fixed on his and as he coyly lowered his face toward hers, her smile changed into a pout and their cold lips touched. She closed her eyes, blue painted eyelids sinking like shutters. Awareness of everything around him evaporated, nothing else mattered, as they merged themselves into one, their very breathing put on hold.

Elated, in the end it had been so simple: they had not recoiled from each other, with the shock of it. They relaxed, smiled, laughed a bit, which broke the spell, unafraid. Eager for the magic not to end, Matthew fanned his fingers around the small of her back inside his jacket, arching her close, her thighs hard against his, her flat belly nestling into him.

In those precious moments of first discovery, forgetting completely their freezing cold surroundings, while she gave the clearest signals of wanting him, he joyfully realized he had the best catch of the whole college, of the whole year! Just as Dick Emery started his midnight cabaret set, they held hands and artlessly bumped into each other as they slipped back through College Hall, dashing between the milling boozy couples unnoticed, and ran up to her fourth floor room, to spend the rest of that memorable night innocently cuddling on her single bed, where they slept fitfully into the next hungover misty morning.

From then on, Matthew and Rachel became an inseparable pair. Inseparable indeed for the next twenty-four faithful years.

Rachel qualified with ease as expected and soon moved into general practice as first choice, sharing much of her career worries with Maurice, while Matthew, having found clinical activity not entirely to his liking, had moved into a more academic world of science and mathematics. Rachel was a partner in practice in West London when she died.

As such poignant memories of her flooded his brain, he could still recall the taste of her cloying lipstick on dry lips as they lingered over their first kiss, he could still feel her body shape, hot and close.

'It is not hard to imagine what Rachel would have felt at this time – if she were here,' Matthew Crawford intoned to the attentive guests, who seemed quite happy to indulge him. 'She would be pleased, I know, she would be proud and deeply grateful that God had steered her daughter to safety. Like me, she would be saying how nice that after so much struggle and hard work one's children can turn out to be so richly rewarding.' There was some applause at this and murmurs of 'absolutely' and 'hear! hear!', but the audience was partly subdued, sensing the tension in the speech and uncertain where that was going. Matthew's mind was in danger of being overwhelmed with myriad memories that would distract him from his script and tempt him to reveal more emotion than he intended, or could handle.

Undaunted, he continued, softly and with surety. 'Rachel died suddenly one Bank Holiday weekend, the result of overwhelming myeloid leukaemia, her bone marrow and liver and spleen bursting with a prodigious uncontrolled growth of tumour and white cells, which resulted quickly in brain haemorrhage. She was with me on the Friday and gone by the Monday. She was forty-two.'

That had been three tortuous years ago, and the sick empty feeling in Matthew's guts that reminded him so vividly of those events suddenly returned, and with it a bitter taste, that he tried to swallow away. Everyone was quiet, many of Mathew's friends looking at him with love and sympathy, even if not quite understanding the shattering effects of the events he was relating, or the painful feelings he had gone through. Some were wondering if this was going to turn into an embarrassment, if Matthew became unable to control his emotions; yet others, why Matthew felt the need to reveal some of his most personal feelings at all.

6

It all happened at the Easter weekend in May, when Rachel decided she could not go out to a dinner party they had been invited to, as she felt too extraordinarily tired. Her periods had been heavy recently, she explained rather petulantly, which were unusual for her, and she put the tiredness down to that. The next morning, Good Friday, she collapsed in the adjacent bathroom shortly after waking and Matthew heard her throttled cry and then the thump as she hit the grey carpeted floor. Dashing into the room he found her lying on her back, shaking and frothing a little at the mouth, a trickle of spittle emerging from one corner. He managed to half-lift half-drag her back to their bed. She did not seem to be focusing her eyes properly. They waited a couple of hours for the local emergency doctor to come round, during which time Rachel dozed.

Their GP, Dr Robin Pallington was a man they both knew and liked. He was ushered up to the bedroom, where with his gentle voice he extracted answers in a series of questions, relating to the sequence of events, while Rachel had her swollen abdomen examined, which made her flinch. Robin had a concerned frown on his face as he phoned consultant colleagues direct at the hospital, to get Rachel admitted. Apparently she had been feeling unwell and excessively tired for a few days and had even fainted after work two nights previously when she was out with a friend. She had recovered, told herself it was nothing, did not want to worry Matthew. Rachel would not have wanted any fuss and believed wholeheartedly that she was super fit, she did not become ill, it would pass.

In Charing Cross Hospital the next day with the diagnosis in the open, Rachel typically was facing up to things in her matter-of-fact way. She was making entries into her diary, surmising when therapy might start and how long before she was back home and at work again. Matthew tried to go along with her, although deep down he was terrified. He went off to a supermarket with a shopping list. He phoned Annabel who was away at university but due back Sunday and would need to be prepared for the shock of her mother's illness, her robust mother who was never ill.

The weather was awfully dull and the skies drizzled depressingly all that weekend, which expressed aptly the feelings of everyone who had become aware that Rachel was bed-bound and in hospital and seriously unwell.

Matthew imagined the worst and dreamt wildly of a life alone. He tried to shut the possibility out of his mind. He painted more attractive images in his mind's eye, of lazy days caring for Rachel, recuperating from unpleasant hospital visits and debilitating treatments, sitting in sunshine in the garden next to their pond with its worn lilies and bedraggled fish. He would take time off work; he would speak to her in hushed tones, unhurried and devoted, gently holding her or reading to her from the newspaper, and they would share memories of better times together. They would whisper tenderly how much they loved each other. She would clutch at him, telling him that she would never leave him, they would always be together. He would show his complete devotion to her with kindnesses, helping her to dress or move from bedroom to sitting room, to manage the stairs; he would prepare her meals and do her washing.

But of course none of that ever happened, she never got out of the hospital, alive.

'We had no time to prepare or say goodbye,' Matthew continued quietly to his receptive and hushed audience. 'It was a bit like a car crash, so sudden. Which was good for her actually, she did not have to go through some ghastly and prolonged process of treatment, chemotherapy or whatever with endless hospital trips and all that agonizing and discomfort. She didn't really know what had hit her. She slipped into a coma slowly over Sunday and passed away that night unaware of the reality, peacefully. We were all there, Annabel in a state of shock, Roger seeming to take it in his stride, sister Helen and me, fussing around everybody, fetching coffees and snacks, needing to do things.' Matthew was having to take these sentences slowly, to control the level of his voice. 'The agony was on our side, watching Rachel go down, not being able to do anything, helpless and useless. And ultimately we were left alone. We had to painfully live each day with the memories, wanting to share so much; and especially today, so angry that dear Rachel is not here among you and with Annabel, and sharing in the celebration and excitement of this lovely event; angry that poor Annabel has only her sad old sod of a dad to share it with.'

There was no denying, there was a sting in Matthew's eyes and he felt the need to blink, with moisture starting to well up. Turning away from the microphone, he wiped the sides of his nose with thumb and forefinger of one hand, sniffing for a moment.

Matthew counted slowly to five, braced himself, before resuming his narrative. 'Facing life alone filled me with dread. So I decided I would try a different lifestyle altogether, one of unbridled and wanton mischief. I would stay out late, drink too much and mix with women of the night. I would do precisely what I wanted. I would get up when I wanted, eat what I wanted and fart in bed whenever I wanted. I would wear my tight black jeans again, watch adult material on television and play Led Zeppelin really loud.

'The main obstacle of course was that I had spent so much of my adult life attached to one other person that, although Rachel was no longer there, I was unable to flourish in any independent fashion. She influenced my every move. I scurried about the kitchen, folding tea towels and tidying the cupboards. I cleaned inside the drawers and dusted along the top shelves. I rearranged all the paperbacks in height order, placed chairs neatly under tables and hoovered under the bed. I ironed my socks and underpants. I pottered around the garden, pretending I knew what I was doing.

'More recently I took stock of my life and counted up my successes or rather lack of them, since Rachel died. I had not been short-listed for a literary prize or learnt to speak Russian. I had not been elected to parliament or won an FA Cup medal, or managed a marathon in under three hours. Although I had won a box of Terry's All-Gold at the university's Christmas raffle, which I suppose was something.'

Matthew swallowed, his dry throat leaving his voice croaky, introducing a calculated pause. And still looking straight ahead of himself, with a slight upwards glance towards the ceiling, he called softly: 'but, oh Rachel…we do miss you.'

7

And now, he realized his big moment had indeed arrived. All that had gone before was obvious, known to everyone really; nothing new had been revealed. But now, this was the real moment he had been waiting for and for so long. His confessional.

'What Rachel never knew was something that I have not told anyone for thirty years. I have kept it to myself, without ever forgetting what happened. But more importantly, I never shared this with Rachel over all those years and now unfortunately she is not here to learn about it. But I feel she would approve of my telling you.'

Matthew was asking himself yet again whether it was appropriate to be using this family gathering, this celebratory wedding day, as a vehicle for his personal issues. Was that the right thing to do, to continue with his deeply personal account of past events and to foist them onto Annabel? What did he expect her role to be afterwards? And why the big audience? Was he expecting applause for his courage, weeping for his pain and plight, sympathy for the difficult events he had had to cope with? Everyone knew that he had turned to drink after Rachel's death and that it had been difficult for him to overcome, but that was behind him now. He encouraged himself with the thought that problems shared were problems halved, even if the truth turned out to be uncomfortable. What he wanted of course was approval and understanding, to assuage the guilt he had felt in his heart over the last few years. He needed forgiveness from the audience, and most of all, from Annabel herself.

Anyway he had started, so now there was no going back.

'It happened in the summer of 1967, towards the end of my school days, when I had barely turned seventeen. Thirty years ago and a year before I first met Rachel. Some people say "if you can remember the Sixties, you weren't there", but I was there alright, and I remember much of that summer of love as if it were yesterday. It was not exactly love that was in the air, not in the dusty streets of North London anyway, but there was a sense of expectation, that things were changing and that anything was possible. This was England after World War Two, rationing had only just ended, everything was grey and dreary. Life was drab, uninspiring, there were no luxuries about. People were generally at a low ebb, but the staid old customs and taboos of the day were being challenged. The young preferred to loaf about, grow their hair long and play weird music; they meditated in the open parks while listening to 'Piper at the Gates of Dawn' and Jimi Hendrix. The new flowery symbols of gentleness, love and peace were everywhere. We sang along with Scott Mackenzie: you had to be sure to wear some flowers in your hair if you were going to San Francisco. The message everywhere was the same: "let it all hang out".'

Matthew's eyes glazed over for a moment and a look of wry amusement passed across his handsome face. His pause lasted several seconds. 'I had a short-lived love affair with a gorgeous black-haired girl from a nearby school and she had a child, a love-child, a girl that was born in April 1968 and who is twenty-nine years old and has never met her real father.'

Matthew remained perfectly still, his left hand resting on the music stand, his right still clutching the heavy microphone, nervy tingling feelings wriggling over his skin, making the hairs down his legs stand up. With a melancholy aspect he stared ahead over the still crowd in front of him, feeling the silence in the marquee like a cold clammy hand down his back. The fetid damp of the grass and sticky heat of all the guests was almost too much for him and all he could think of then was to leave. He wanted to be on his own, striding out over the hills with fresh air to breathe and his own thoughts for company. He wanted to talk to Rachel, to feel her hold on him, giving him strength.

Everyone was staring with eyes fixed on Matthew, like they had stopped suddenly doing whatever they had been doing, thinking whatever they had been thinking, caught in a freeze-frame tableau and were now waiting breathless and expectant, to be told what was coming next.

Matthew spoke with passion, rapidly, the words pouring out from his innermost recesses. 'We were kids in short trousers, raised on a diet of cabbage and boiled potatoes, playing on the street, our dirty faces peering through the fog. We were happy with Popeye and Blue Peter, with our Meccano sets and Dinky toys. And then, all of a sudden we were adolescents discovering facial hair, the smell of girls and the fun of falling in love. We swapped Pinky and Perky for Pink Floyd, and pretended to be grown-ups. The cool sound then was Sergeant Pepper, a blend of music hall and psychedelia, that gripped our imaginations and hopes. Friends in beads and Afghan coats gathered in cheap cafes to smoke whatever was going, to listen to the new music, to get involved with student politics and civil rights. These groovy people, with their dope, their colourful clothes and their rock 'n roll, believed society could be changed for the better; they were on the brink of social revolution. By hitching a ride to the West Coast, taking drugs and getting laid, they could bring an end to the Vietnam War. "Make love not war" was the slogan of the time: it was a mesmerising and idealistic time.

'But it didn't last of course: the hippies did not save the world, they did not end racism, communism or imperialism. And it now all seems such an anti-climax, looking back.'

Matthew felt clear-headed and dry-eyed now. The sheer moment of revelation was over and it did not feel as bad to him as he had expected. 'Except I had met a beautiful girl called Stephanie, who I honestly thought had breezed in from paradise.'

TWO
The Summer of Love

1967

1

The media-christened 'summer of love' was when Matthew Crawford began to grow up, in more ways than one. Matt, most people called him, was seventeen and miles away from his parents' London home at a boy's boarding school in the country, with enough activities to fill his time, oblivious to what was happening in the outside world. He was more concerned about his batting average than spending time with girls. He had met a few before, but he was not overly concerned and had other things on his mind.

For a start, he had three tricky science subjects to work at for a university place, which was by no means assured. It was expected that he would be putting in extra effort this term. All the boys, from first entry at thirteen to senior sixth form, selected for their academic abilities and sporting skills, had to perform to a certain level, that was the culture of the place. Failure to achieve their goals was rare and unacceptable. Everything was designed to prepare them for what lay beyond the safe confines of their existence. The school prospectus described the atmosphere as disciplined, reasonable and fair at all times, with pupils fully aware of what was expected of them, with living conditions as perfectly suited to youngsters in the Sixties preparing for the harsh realities of the world outside. Most of the boys however thought of their school days as harsh, rigorous and Spartan, devoid of anything domestic or homely.

Somewhat to his surprise Matt was to be a house prefect this coming term, with tedious extra duties, like organising team games, supervising prep periods and having a dormitory full of squirts under his responsibility, all of which he could have done without, frankly. Many of the first year sixth formers, the oiks with attitude and skin problems who resented that they were not quite at prefect level, would mercilessly take advantage of any perceived weakness, so a slip-up would be disastrous for self-esteem and survival; they would undermine his authority whenever possible, to make him look silly, especially in front of the juniors. Another problem for Matt to pay attention to.

Matt was at the phase of growing up in that strictly male environment where he wanted to impress; he needed his audience to look up to him as their hero; it felt good to be admired. His fine athletic body and sporting prowess gave him leave to walk tall through a crowd of boys. And in matters of discipline, school rules and all that, his approach was always one of common sense and fairness, while trying to be decisive. All good qualities that he expected the little ones to worship. Careful of course not to take any advantage, although just an occasional glance of a peachy *petit derriere* in the younger boys' showers gave him unexpected guilty pleasure.

Matthew was certainly not planning any escapades along romantic lines. His experiences with girls had been limited. There was that hurried peck on Priscilla Jones' lips in the dark behind the school chapel last term (and she was one of the masters' daughters); a quick feel of Angela Littlejohn's cold inner thigh in the holidays when she needed help climbing down from the tree-house at home; and a silly grope down Christine's blouse that she forced him into while putting up decorations in her house next door last Christmas, to discover she had nothing covering her puny breasts; all of which had been fairly objectionable at the time.

Despite this deplorable dearth of action on his part, he had an inner feeling of confidence about girls, which helped to give the average teenage boy swamped by erratic bursts of testosterone the impression of considerable worldly knowledge of the mysterious opposite gender. With weary familiarity, he would explain about girls' monthlies, where Dutch caps were fitted, how lads should use French letters to avoid VD and reassured his absorbed audience that lots of sex would not make them go blind. Even when his mother during the holidays at some idle moment in the kitchen had made oblique references to the growing man within, he had managed to give the impression that girls scared him not at all, and that he could handle anything they threw at him.

Where that pretentious and misconceived confidence came from he had no idea, but he was always cool was Matthew, knowing what he was doing and that he would succeed. He would win the heart of the right girl at the right moment, he knew, when the time was right. He just did not know when that moment might be, but then, who did at his age?

He felt no particular desire to discover it either, at the start of that summer term 1967. Which turned out to be a momentous period for him, every detail of which lies etched into his memory.

Picture him, a fresh-faced, energetic good-looking lad with blond hair, a clear complexion and sharp blue eyes, keen to make the right impression, eager to please, stepping through his formative adolescence with all its mysteries and uncertainties, with a trusting and carefree approach. An exciting yet nervous time, not knowing what was to come, but ever so cocksure that his destiny was just waiting for him around the corner. He was ready for whatever it was. And whatever it was, he did not really care, just that he knew it would be a life-changing experience; each day he felt more excited and expectant, like being in a waiting crowd ready for the highlight act of the show to make their appearance through the stage curtains at any moment. As the term progressed, he thought more about the time soon when he would be leaving the confines of the school, to make that leap into real life, to discover an independent, free-thinking chaos beyond; he couldn't wait.

When in the first week of school it was announced that the next theatre production was to be a shared effort with one of the nearby girls' schools, his heart had surprisingly skipped a little at the prospect. There had already been a few joint activities with some of the nearby girls' schools, science and language classes, field trips, debating societies, that sort of thing, in recognition that girls (yes, girls for Heaven's sake) were a good and maturing influence on boys, if kept under strict control; and that co-ed was the future. He never heard the case that boys were a good influence on the girls, maybe they weren't, it was just that the girls were desperate for male company. Anyway Matthew, without telling any of his friends and without any expectation of success, took the chance of an audition for a part in "Romeo & Juliet", to be directed by Miss Robinson, a loveless creature lacking any sense of humour, who would certainly quash any possible desires that may be kindled between any of the boys and her girls. However, that it was to be the first time ever in their history that a boy and girl would kiss on stage in a school play, well that caused a little thrill of excitement to buzz around the upper school studies and dormitories for some weeks, make no mistake.

Matthew was not a natural on stage and had to work hard to overcome his fright on the day, but was rewarded for his effort with the minor part of Sampson, a Capulet servant. It was to give him plenty of free time while waiting around the edge of the rehearsals practicing his lines mostly in Act One to chat up the few girls that were there, whenever there was an opportunity. And there weren't many, but he managed a quick and easily forgettable hug with a mousy-haired lass with gap teeth from Birmingham called Geraldine, who spoke with a thick nasal accent and was playing an insignificant Nurse in the production with only occasional entrances. Unfortunately, he never got close to Juliet (otherwise known as Teresa), who was truly gorgeous and sexy and firmly attached and probably in love with the leading man, a swarthy sixth former named Christopher da Costa. Matt found himself looking upon these two with some envy, they seemed the perfect match, their charisma and humour in unison with their obvious physical attractions. She was a language scholar and star netball player by all accounts, da Costa was into history and politics, had first eleven cricket colours, boxing and fencing cups, and was deputy head boy to boot. Their talents flowed with everything they did, light sparkled in their eyes, with equal amounts of good looks and virile ambition, and Matthew eagerly elevated them as his number one role models, both seemingly so clean-cut, passionate and transparently untouchable. It was silly of him, really, but that's what boys did, idolised their seniors.

Ironically they were destined soon to part, Chris and Teresa, not to meet again, each going their own separate ways after the end of term. Which just goes to show: celebrity, who needs it?

During the Easter holidays Matt had discovered rhythm and blues on the radio and started buying Paul Butterfield and John Mayall records when he could rustle up the money. Once or twice a week he would bus into Soho to hear John Baldry or Spencer Davies at the Marquee Club, where he would meet up with a few like-minded friends, who drank a lot of beer in the pubs after the show, long after Matt had left them to walk home alone empty-pocketed along the Finchley Road, feeling sweaty, foot-sore but elated.

Back at school, music was increasingly a means of expression for these young guns going through their scary adolescence, a powerful ingredient in their daily lives. How they sang, when Tom Jones came on the radio on a Sunday afternoon, everyone hanging out of their studies into the corridor, starting quietly and building up with each verse, and absolutely at the tops of their voices for the chorus, "Down the lane I rode with my sweet Mary, hair of gold and tits like cherries, it's good to touch the green, green grass of home." The other favourite was 'Glad All Over' by Dave Clark. Just before the punch-line was the characteristic double drum beat, to which they all stamped their feet, slammed the doors and thumped their desks, between enthusiastic singing. "And I'm feeling," stamp stamp, "glad all over, Yes I'm," slam slam, "glad all over, Baby, I'm" thump thump, "glad all over, so glad you're mine".

Late Sunday afternoons were a more relaxed time, when everyone was back in their houses, lounging around before evening meal time and prep, just a short break from the stresses of work. Kids played table-tennis in the common room or listened to records in the corner, read the papers or wrote letters home in their studies. The older boys had Top Gear tuned in from the radio and played cherished new LPs (the Rolling Stones' 'Aftermath', The Who's 'A Quick One' or Nice's 'Thoughts of Emerlist Davjack'). Most of the sixth formers, self-conscious about acne, armpit hair and unwanted erections, tried to experiment with style and appearance within the limits of strict school rules about dress and hair length, as they climbed painfully the last few slopes to the summit of their adolescent life before being let out onto the wider world, only for them all to be knocked off their perches quickly enough, usually by the first class Monday morning.

Although Matt was not exactly in the thick of it, he felt the changing mood among his peers, some with strong desires to do their own thing, slightly anti-authoritarian without recourse to obtaining permission. Part of that was predictable teenage rebellion towards school and parents, but there was also a growing sense that real freedoms were there to be taken. The mates he met up with in the holidays, in their leather jackets, smoking with blondes hanging onto their arms and every word, were showing off how they had broken free of old society's programming that dictated everything that was expected of them. But they were not planning to plug away at some mundane job working nine to five, just to marry the girl next door, have two point four children, buy a second-hand Vauxhall Victor and settle down to the daily grind for the next forty years. That was not what those boys had in mind, and nor did Matt, when he really thought about it; he did not want to follow the predictable drab pathway of his parents' life, no way.

He had things to do, places to visit, people to meet, he was not going to be part of the regimented, stale and out of touch way of life of past generations. He would do the unexpected, differently. He would wear his own choice of clothes, velvets and corduroy, colourful loafers and leathers. He would join the protests in the streets if he wanted. The world was opening up, easier travel meant going abroad was becoming a possibility, getting away from England, for holidays or work. He knew of a few school leavers who had even ventured across the Atlantic to America.

There was a sense of expectancy, waiting and ready for something to happen, and when it came, whatever it was, he was going to make his mark, leave an impression. Life was short, time was short, and they were there to achieve, to leave things better shaped than when they arrived. Matt wanted to go to university, he recognised the need for qualifications if you wanted to get on, he was no drop-out; but he craved to be part of a different set of modern thinkers and doers, people who wanted to change society, change the way they thought about things, and experience some free love and sex along the way.

He knew he would accomplish things his parents' generation would never have dreamt of, like… Well, he was not exactly sure what, to be frank, but they would be different and exciting for sure. Matt's sister Jennifer in her own idiotic way was going through the same sort of revolutionary emotions, only three years ahead of him, muddled and unsure and still in love with Cliff Richard. She had shown him a thing or two, rather too literally as it happened, with her take on the swinging Sixties and how to let it 'all hang out', dashing out of the family bathroom one evening, heroic bazoukas bouncing erratically while she hurriedly pulled on a dressing gown. The site of bright nipples and dark woolly bush, so shocking against milk-white skin, stayed with him disturbingly as a mildly stimulating image, like peeking at pictures of women with no clothes on in some of those filthy magazines that Roberts had at school.

'Fancy a bit of these then, do you, boy? What do you think?' She was preparing to go out and pouting obscene expressions into her dressing table mirror, to get herself into the mood, while applying bright red lipstick and thick black mascara, and thrusting her chest out.

'I think you're indecent, and if you're not careful you will land yourself in trouble,' Matt had protested, while secretly admiring her boldness. He was a little embarrassed by the episode, but did not want to make anything of it.

'Oh, what sort of trouble?' she pleaded, but he was out of there quick, he did not want to see or hear anything more. His sister was nuts. She was going out with a tie-dyed twit she called Buzz, on account of the vibes that passed through her body 'when they were close', she told him once; he called him Fuzz, on account of the silly patch of hair growing on his chin. Actually, his name was Barry and he was probably a perfectly nice bloke underneath his unwashed hair that was longer than hers and his dirty feet, but he was so often in a smoky haze under some influence or other that Matt just found him repellent. Until the following year when he wanted to look and dress just like Buzz, when he thought it was cool. And he loved some of the records Buzz left for her to play, like the Doors, Jefferson Airplane and Frank Zappa, West Coast US bands everyone was talking about.

2

Matthew was not prepared for the stunner that was bowled his way, a sneaky spinner that bruised his middle stump that he failed to see coming, despite his air of misplaced confidence. It was the force of it that knocked him over, and knocked all other thoughts and activities over the boundary. He carried on acting his usual cool, with an easy familiarity, but inside he was spinning around erratically, in danger of losing control; and sometimes he had urges to leave and make a run for it. He was not sure where to, but he became gripped in a way that he had not experienced before. A girl, it had to be, like an obsession – a special girl who filled his mind day and night with alluring breathy sounds and intoxicating scents, a mysterious presence, aloof and yet tempting.

She was his first discovery, his awakening, who personified a crudely defined and sought-after freedom. He wanted to share his excitement with her, to experience with her the revelations he sought that were so close, yet out of reach. He wanted to travel through their discoveries, exploring all the mysteries that life had to offer, a leap towards the mature world of the grown-ups that had been kept at arm's length from them. This was both something physical that clawed at his insides, unfamiliar and teasing, and something more ephemeral, a desire for her to open up his mind and pore over his hidden feelings, upending his little secrets. All of which served to throw him off balance, upsetting his appetite, his sleep, his whole physiology.

The first time he saw her, she was pointed out to him at a distance on the boundary line of a school cricket match, slouched in the unbecoming brown of her uniform, tall, indifferent and just to one side of a small crowd of Upper Wycheside girls and nobody knew her name. Apart from noticing her good legs, free of hideously thick brown stockings, he paid little attention, but a couple of the boys sniggered behind their hands and seemed to acknowledge her as something special. And then one weekend, Jolyon Hunter persuaded Matt to cycle with him over to Wycheside for afternoon tea, about four miles of winding steep road that traversed the ridge of hills that separated their two schools. Jolyon, a large and cheerful chap from his house, enumerated the simple rules that were involved: having obtained agreement from your housemaster, with a written invitation from a named girl in hand, you signed out on a Sunday afternoon, you never went alone, you had to wear at least an identifying school blazer, you stayed strictly in the girls' common room throughout and quietly drank tea and ate cakes, and you never stayed more than two hours; you signed back in on return to your house. Under no circumstances would you ever be alone with any girl and a physical distance of at least three feet between was advised and strictly adhered to by the female teachers who prowled the Upper Wycheside grounds and buildings throughout the afternoon. Matt wondered what it was all for, but never got a really convincing answer from Jolyon, except something about relieving the boredom of house life on a slow Sunday afternoon. And the cakes were usually jolly good.

Jolyon, it turned out, had a sister in the final year at Wycheside who facilitated many such trips and he had the required letter to hand, open and above board. Jolyon appeared quite the adventurous one and seemed to know all the sixth form girls, although he had his beady eyes on one particular lass, called Sarah, apparently. Matt sensed that it was all rather lightweight and jolly hockey sticks, probably nothing more advanced than a snog behind the bicycle sheds. Of all the girls to choose from, Jolyon had said that he had found Sarah willing and that she had a fabulous little bottom, but whether that was gleaned from outward appearances, direct inspection or wishful thinking, Matt was too polite to break protocol and enquire.

Anyway, on a blustery Sunday afternoon in early May, Matt was persuaded to join Jolyon on their bike trip. Jolyon was not in Matt's usual crowd of friends, as he did not play cricket and was doing languages not the sciences, but was a decent sort for all that. He was broad and strong, with a short back-and-sides blond mop-top, combed forward and wetted flat, so it jutted out over his forehead. And he was a surprisingly nimble athlete for someone so over-sized. He had proved that more than once in the squash courts where he had won many a house match and was a notoriously difficult opponent to get around. As a cyclist, belting along difficult roads and country paths, mostly up hill on the outward journey, he was well-balanced and energetic, presumably driven by the promise of that little bottom, which made the heavy straining seem somehow mundane in anticipation.

Upper Wycheside School for Girls was a sixth form college, a sort of finishing school in the country, where sixteen, seventeen and eighteen-year-olds would learn all the skills they needed to get a head start and catch an eligible man as soon as possible, namely domestic sciences and deportment. The boys pictured them as frustrated nymphomaniacs, but Matt was not expecting anything too wacky. There were three separate old red brick Victorian buildings arranged close to each other around landscaped gardens, nice lawns, flowering shrubs and blossom trees, which were all out in their pinks and creams when Matt and Jolyon rode through the open gates, everything looking prim and pretty.

The plan was to meet a few girls in their common room, including Jolyon's sister, Beth, and his Sarah, have some tea, stay for an hour or so, and then enjoy the fast ride back down to the house, to tell tales of drunken naked orgies to the circle of envious lads who would be waiting for their return.

And so they did. It was harmless and gentle, with tea and cakes taken in a big oak-lined room, with tall sash windows and a huge open fireplace with marble in-lay surround at one end. The flooring was dark-stained wood and boards of past winners of school prizes embossed in gold print and heavily framed, hung around the walls adding to the whole sombre feel. The numerous girls lounged on aged leather sofas pushed back around the perimeter of the room while the few boys occupied the free space in the cleared centre. Jolyon hugged his sister on arrival with some forced jollity but otherwise the conversations were rather strained, about nothing in particular. The girls were smart, polite and sweet in their own ways, but Matt felt pretty much detached from the whole arrangement, and certainly did not fancy any of them. He settled on the fat arm of one brown leather settee, from where he could overlook the gardens outside. Nearby was a cumbersome lacquered box record player the size of a trunk standing on four wooden legs, and a low table strewn with piles of well-used and scratched black plastic 45s, the only sign of the modern era and personal character in the place. A selection of half a dozen discs were regularly grabbed and fed onto the central pole of the turntable, to be dropped heavily one by one with each short play, the arm and needle swinging automatically up and out at the end of each song to crash down again onto the edge of the next crackly piece of plastic. 'Puppet on a String' was played repeatedly with the Tremeloes and Bee Gees and the Walker Brothers. From time to time, Matt would pick a disc to be played, but his style was his usual cool, a distant but amiable look on his face, a smile on occasions that would neither offend nor attract anyone.

'I saw Sandie Shaw on television singing this in the holidays,' a little waif of a girl with tied-back mousy hair was saying, 'she won the Eurovision Song Contest for Britain, don't you know.' To which Jolyon adopted a quite obviously envious expression, disappointed with himself that he had not been up-to-date with such dynamic information with which to impress his audience. 'She wasn't wearing any shoes, was she,' commented Beth, and her hand went up to her mouth, as some cake crumbs tumbled down her front, as if she had said something rude, and she blushed.

Jolyon, flushed as always, introduced the girls that he knew; he was enjoying himself as the centre of attention. And so Matt met Sarah, his rather plain flat-chested friend, with reddish hair and freckles, who also blushed whenever she had the conversation and felt that others were watching her, but laughed at all Jolyon's jokes, and had eyes for him alone. Matt could not make any comment as to the aforementioned bottom, as she wore an unflatteringly baggy pink checked summer dress.

So they stood around in small groups swapping tales, then pausing for short periods before thinking of the next topic, and carrying on again with more giggling as everyone started to speak together. Matt was remembering what he had seen in the headlines of Saturday's newspaper, and asked what people thought about this old chap who had just got back to Plymouth, after sailing around the world on his own. 'Francis Chichester?' he enquired.

'He must be very brave,' said one of the girls.

'Mad old turd,' said Jolyon, with much tittering

'Or just crazy,' Matt murmured under his breath, thinking it was truly a fantastic achievement. 'And he's been knighted by the Queen. I wonder if any of us will be making the headlines in ten or twenty years' time with some remarkable story.' There were a few nodding heads, quizzical frowns but no one volunteered any suggestions.

The afternoon wore on rather tediously and just as Matt was thinking it must be time to leave, he caught sight of someone quite different, a lanky girl in white, blouse and tight jeans, who slipped into the room through the heavy oak door and established herself in a nearby single leather armchair, having helped herself from the sideboard to a cup of tea. She kicked her shoes off and sank elegantly, curling cat-like onto the cushions, balancing her saucer on the arm of the chair as she watched the assembled crowd with unconcealed boredom. She had jet black hair drawn from her forehead and bobbed untidily at the back. A long nose and fine high cheekbones gave her an aristocratic look, he thought, while her sharp edged jaw-line and thin mouth suggested a serious demeanour, that spoke of an uncompromising vanity. A slightly olive shade to her skin made Matt imagine her a diplomat's daughter from southern Europe. It appeared that even the boldest of the boys was afraid to get too close or to speak directly to her, as having to throw their voices over the heads of her supportive cast of girls that formed a ring around her, rather deterred them.

Matt recognised her as the girl he had seen watching the cricket a couple of weeks before. Most striking was her make-up, painted eyelids, caked lashes that curled like forks, bright pink lipstick that was surely not permitted, in pointed contrast to the other girls who barely showed any signs of grooming. A cool rebel, a bit anti-authority and so self-assured; she seemed older than the others too, more sophisticated. The girl was making a point, that she was special and able to flaunt the rules right in front of everybody just to show what she thought of them. She did not converse with anyone in particular, but made occasional comments that Matt could not hear from where he was standing and nor could lip-read, as each time she would bring a slim hand up in a rather demure fashion, straight fingers pressed over her lips, her wrist cocked slightly, and showing off her glossy painted nails as she whispered an aside to the loyal little group around her, who nodded and giggled like sycophants.

Ironically this girl looked like an authority figure herself, a prefect perhaps, the way the others rather deferred to her. Matt did not catch her name while they were there, or speak with her, although he strained his ears to pick-up her voice and he was sure that she had looked at him once or twice with a more than quizzical half-smile, tilting her head to one side while fixing him even if only for a few seconds with a languid stare. Matt needed time to think of an approach, preferably in more private circumstances, without the giggly audience listening to his every word.

Jolyon had spent his time trying to be entertaining with quips and poor jokes, but soon faltered. He managed a few stolen moments with Sarah, outside the room in the corridor, which was risky with the Upper Wycheside mistresses always on the prowl; he risked being banned from future visits if he was caught transgressing the agreed rules. On the ride back, Jolyon sang Sarah's praises, telling Matt about the way she kissed with her moist tongue. Matt casually asked Jolyon who the girl in the white trousers was, and he shouted, 'Stephanie,' across at him through the noise of the rushing wind and crunching gravel, 'but she is a bit of a minx, I would steer well clear of her, dear boy, if I was you.'

'Like bollocks,' thought Matthew keeping his quiet.

They cycled back to their house, freewheeling down the

long hillside roads, their rosy faces whipped by the wind and tears streaming across their cheeks, but their minds respectively on wet kissing and minxes in tight white trousers. Matt realised he wanted to meet with Stephanie and that that had quite suddenly become a top priority.

He had to wait five frustrating weeks.

His second visit to Upper Wycheside was two weeks later and followed much the same pattern as the first, with the same bunch of people turning up, the same boring cups of tea and McVitie's ginger cake. At first there was no sign of the girl in tight white trousers. He slipped his blazer off and crouched on the floor by the record player, running through the piles of singles and a few LPs, pretending to take little notice of what was happening in the rest of the room. Someone placed a cup of tea on the table for him. The records varied a bit, and he studied some of the sleeve notes. He was surprised to find a John Mayall LP among the usual pop stuff, and saw that a name had been written in black ink on the back top right corner: 'Stephanie Patek'.

He stacked a collection of six singles on the central pole, pulled the arm up and to one side, which click-started the turntable and allowed the lowest disc to drop onto the rubber mat. He lowered the heavy arm and stylus over to the edge: 'Love Me Do' (The Beatles).

By the time 'Reach Out, I'll Be There' (Four Tops) started playing, the girl in white had arrived, slipping in as before, sinking into her armchair and folding those long legs away under her. She spoke little, drank black tea and observed the scene from her distance. And Matthew realised that she must be there on behalf of the school, an infiltrator to be their eyes and report back later the details of the other girls' behaviour; she was a sort of spy, he decided, working for the opposition. Matt wandered away from the record player nonchalantly edging closer to her side of the room towards her retinue, as 'Brown

Eyed Girl' (Van Morrison) came on. He was determined to say something, but everyone seemed to be joining in with the chorus. He started talking eventually about cricket to one of the boys standing close, but that elicited little interest, so he moved on to his last family holiday in Brittany, 'A' level biology and how his older sister had obtained Scott Walker's autograph after a concert in Leicester Square. There was some general chatter but Stephanie only offered brief comment under her breath, taking little notice of Matthew. A couple of unfamiliar boys from other houses were sitting nearer to her with their tongues hanging out, almost salivating at being so close, exchanging their personal life stories in pithy and witty little packages and then laughing precociously.

As Bob Dylan warbled his 'Homesick Blues', Matthew, stealing ever longer glances towards Stephanie, came to witness a quite perfect specimen. Classic bone structure and facial symmetry was offset by the black hair again stretched back casually from a high forehead, the bob skewered behind, with a lazy central parting. She had creamy unblemished skin that was darker than the others and close-up Matthew picked out her matching green eyes, the colour and pattern of pear skin. And she exuded class. When she relaxed her face, a hint of a smile undulated along her lips, softening her cheeks and providing some sympathy to an otherwise stern expression. She had a way of wrinkling lines along the ridge of her nose between her eyes when she said something funny, accompanied by that little twist of a smile, when clear white teeth would appear. Her posture alert, shoulders pulled back, she moved with silent agility. Even under a loose blouse Matthew discerned a goodly bosom, and with her tightly rounded backside and narrow waist clamped within a broad belt, he imagined her classic hourglass shape and appearance.

Matt was relieved to leave with Jolyon after the usual hour and a half, because he was not going to make any progress with Stephanie that day. She did not seem interested in any of them, and Matt was feeling sorry for himself on their return, avoiding meeting up with any of the regulars to swap stories. He went into dinner feeling grumpy and antisocial, got through his portions quickly and left to shower and head for an evening of work in his study alone.

The Sunday afternoon visit to Upper Wycheside that rewarded Matt for his perseverance was later in the term, when he had acquired a healthy tan from playing much cricket in the sunshine. Under a sparsely clouded blue sky, he and Jolyon found themselves once again straining hard to cycle up the hilly roads, their hearts pounding with exertion and expectation in equal measure. With their hair ruffled and their blazers open to the wind to cool off their bodies, they approached the wrought iron gates and neat gravel paths of the now familiar girl's school, breathing hard. Everything in the gardens was looking lush after a night's rain. Sounds of giggly girls' voices mingling with the Monkees playing on the record player came to them through the open windows of the first-floor common-room. Jolyon had dark stains down the back of his shirt and wet patches under his arms, but that was not going to deter him, and full of himself as always, he whipped off his ankle clips and pressed firmly on the door bell.

When they were let in and led upstairs, they found two other boys from the school were there already scoffing sponge cake and drinking lemon squash. There was a jolly set of girls this time and conversation seemed easier than usual. Matt chatted away as he munched on cucumber sandwiches. The room was stuffy, despite the open window. Sarah was there, forever flicking a hand to comb hair behind her ear, while idolising her Jolyon. There was no sign of Stephanie and Matt felt ominously sure that she had been collared by a cunning sixth-form scruff who had whisked her off to an upstairs bedroom where he was at that very moment having his way with her.

Some of the girls were playing records while others, probably English 'A' level students, were reading bits of TS Elliott and Roger McGough from well-thumbed paperbacks. It was 'Release Me' (Engelbert Humperdink) that seemed to get all the plays this time.

Eventually, the delicious lithe all-in-white Stephanie Patek minxed into the room to take up her routine position, curled into the small sofa at the back, with various younger girls arrayed around her. Whereas they were mostly in school pink blouses with navy skirts, Stephanie wore a sleeveless shirt with a rounded collar that was loose and enticing. She was slightly tanned with only a hint of mascara and glossy lips this time. She behaved with an easy maturity, didn't giggle at the silly jokes or when answering to the boys, and was entirely comfortable in her role. With her head tilted to one side as before, she caught Matthew's eye more than once during the afternoon, when each would quickly turn away with a coy smile, to murmur to someone else.

Matt assessed his position. It was then or never. Stephanie appeared aloof and Jolyon had warned him off, but that only made her more desirable. And she was the most desirable creature he had ever come across. Her separateness and difference from the others, in dress and behaviour, said that she was prized, which tempted Matt to drive on. With his eyes firmly targeted on the only prize in the room worth striving for, he was preparing to launch himself towards her retinue, when Jolyon came up behind and pushed him forwards, with his hands on his shoulders.

'And this is Stephanie, everyone's favourite dolly,' Jolyon was saying with good humour, nudging Matthew in the back. Matt managed a confused twist of his mouth, his blond hair flopping over his forehead as he nodded towards her, mumbling hello. She made a surprized face at Jolyon and then, Matt would have sworn, fluttered her spidery eyelashes at him, at Matt, while sending him a knowing smirk. Then she stretched out in his direction a long bare arm, elegant and fragile, the wrist bent downwards for him to grasp her hand courteously while planting a dry kiss on the back, as he bent forward. His homage to the princess, and there was much giggling among the other girls around him. 'I'm Matt,' he croaked, 'how do you do?'

'Oh, very well, thank you,' she breathed huskily, withdrawing her hand slowly with an understanding look. Matt sensed she wanted to talk to him, but there were too many people around for either of them to feel comfortable. So close now, Stephanie appeared beautiful and real. She rarely smiled and it was a demure movement easily missed, that briefly widened her mouth, sometimes revealing the lower edges of upper white teeth. From time to time she worked her tongue along the edges of her lips to catch a crumb or drop, the tip flicking out and then disappearing to leave a glossy trail behind, that kindled a swoon through Matt's body. The bright afternoon light imparted a lustrous sheen to her clear skin, whereas all the other faces in the room were made-up to cover over teenage spots and were dull by comparison.

As his fingers encircled her delicate hand for that introductory kiss, his tense lips squashing against soft lemony skin, his keen eye wandered beyond the cotton edge of her cut-away sleeve, glimpsing a smooth armpit and a swell of soft white flesh, which he craved impulsively to scoop up in his hand, like a fresh-baked dumpling. He blinked and looked away guiltily, fearing he would blush at the indiscretion, while realising her innocent look belied an obvious knowledge of the sensuous. She was sucking in her lower lip, chewing it with two large front teeth. He was totally entranced.

'And what do you do, Matthew,' she asked lazily, with a breathy voice that sounded aristocratic, 'when not working away at your books?'

He stood back, looking down at his feet, feeling a flush coming over him. In order to win her over, he had already concluded, he needed to impress her, to rise above himself, to excel in something extreme; he could not just rely on a posh accent. But he felt inhibited. He wanted to recount his hand-gliding adventures in Wales last summer, the details of the facial punishment he had taken in the boxing finals for his house last term from a much heavier boy, before flooring him with a left upper cut or draw a laugh with his tale of how he had caught his foreskin in a trouser zip last week and nearly committed auto-circumcision; or perhaps he should describe in Dickensian tones his family's poor downtrodden home life, so she would recognise how clever he was to have reached so far, with Oxbridge beckoning? But then again, she might be easily bored.

'I play lawn tennis, sometimes,' was all he could manage and before he could launch into an explanation of the finer points of returning a backhand top-spin down the line, she had passed her cup and saucer over towards him. 'Might you fetch me a top-up?' she asked.

Later the general talk turned to the forthcoming school dance that was to be held at the Boy's School on a Friday night in three weeks' time, under strict teacher supervision, for the senior sixth form. It would be a disco apparently, and boys wanting to invite specific girls had to sign up with their housemasters by next weekend, stating the name of the young lady in question and the school she attended. And it was free, which probably meant it would be rubbish, but hey, there was a chance to be mingling with the opposites, so what the hell, everybody was getting excited.

The afternoon wore on with more 45s played and endless

tea and cake. Stephanie stood up at one point and wandered over to the open window to watch some girls down on the lawns outside wrestling each other. There was undignified cheering from the gathering spectators watching the ungainly site of two hefty blondes rolling over and over in the grass, with skirts riding high, large floppy bottoms in baggy school underwear exposed, grunting and screeching. It was only when they started trying to pull each other's hair out that some friends stepped in to separate them. Stephanie remained detached from the situation, but, when everyone's attention seemed to be fixed on the outside gardens, she caught Matt's arm, and cleverly signalled with her eyes and face to follow her quietly out the big door which she left ajar, without anyone else noticing. Trying not to show undue haste, Matt casually stepped backwards to the door and slipped out into the hall after her, ignoring his missed heartbeats.

He stood in his shirt-sleeves, hesitating for a moment to check no one was following or watching and saw her light shadow and bare feet disappearing around the curve of the stairs going up to the next floor. He followed rapidly and nervously, trying not to make a sound on the wooden stairs. She was in a bedroom, a small pale blue room at the top of the house, which was stuffy with summer heat. Her door was half open and she was sliding the windows up to admit some cooling air. He stood at the door trembling, trying to look casual without appearing afraid, but he was out of breath and needed all his concentration not to choke. 'Hi,' he croaked.

'Come in, shut the door,' she breathed. She had let her hair free, so it tumbled from the back of her head to her shoulders as she ruffled it out. She cat-walked towards him, her hips swaggering with confidence. 'You're a quiet one, young Matthew,' she said, remembering his name, which he liked. Stepping closer, head tilted fractionally backwards, her green eyes fixed on his, she lifted her arms up and slid her hands slowly over his shoulders, fingers squeezing the muscles and spreading up over his neck each side. 'Those girls can sometimes be such bores, so bourgeois, don't you think?' She played with the tufts of hair on the back of his neck, caressingly. His hands had automatically found her waist, sticky palms feeling her soft sides.

His brain was bursting with confusion and string orchestral sounds, his balance wobbly, his heart fluttering and some uncertainty in the nether regions, as their bodies collided. 'Stephanie, wow, I never thought you, erm, wow …' He trailed off feebly as she tugged him forward, their faces coming close. So close her eyes seemed translucent and Matt stared into their glistening depths as their lips touched. Hers were wet, his were dry. The contact was electrifying. Her eyes closed and mouth opened as he pouted his lips, tasting her sweetness, smelling her warm scent as cascades of suppressed desires erupted like waterfalls tumbling inside his head. He could not fathom their intimacy, how he could study the very pores of the skin over her cheeks, the quivering of her painted eyelids, the arched brows plucked to perfection. Her thickly blackened lashes tickled his cheek as he felt the breath through her nose caress his face.

She suddenly pulled away, opened her eyes wide again and giggled triumphantly, flinging her head back and shaking her mane in the breeze. Her taste was on his lips, he felt breathless. She was unbuttoning her shirt.

'I just had to get out of there, they can be so catty and jealous. So predictable. But *you* are lovely,' looking intensely at his face again, lifting a hand up to Matthew's chin with that challenging smile on her lips. 'So are you going to take me to the dance, mister?' She was teasing him with her husky whisper, or was she being serious? He could not tell. And then she pulled her shirt off, completely, tossing it aside; and fell backwards onto the bed with a wild flourish, showing off her bare chest with pride.

Matt was lost for words, his mouth dropping open, gawping at her bare bobbling breasts. Then he was side-tracked towards a deep shadowy perfectly rounded belly-button positioned exquisitely in the middle of gently undulating flesh, that had it been coated with a light covering of icing sugar he most surely would have mistaken for a ring doughnut and taken a delicious bite.

He grunted something about how pretty she was, and yes he would love to take her to the dance, and what in heaven's name did she think she was doing with all those people downstairs and the teachers on the prowl. 'Oh, sod them,' she said with a laugh, pulling her arms up and tucking her hands behind her head, puffing out her beauties. 'Well, what do you think?'

Matt's eyes were wide open. 'I think, I think, wow, how perfect can they be?' He was hesitatingly polite, embarrassed, but drawn forwards he scrambled on all fours over her, staring at her rounded ripe flesh like a child being handed a dripping ice cream on a hot summer's day. 'Can I, can I touch them, can I kiss them?' Christ, was that a question?

'Kiss me, properly,' Stephanie urged, pouting her glistening lips and showing the tip of her tongue. 'Then you'll have to go.'

So there he was, our novice of seventeen, in a moment of nervous bliss kissing the pouty lips of a dusky half naked maiden, pressing forward against her, painfully aware of the hard swelling that had started to bulge awkwardly in his underpants, both shocking and delightful.

Then somehow he was walking slightly uncomfortably down the grand wooden staircase and passing through the small gathering of girls saying their goodbyes in the hallway, feeling they knew all about his secret indiscretion, out through the front door into the sunlight, where he regained his breath again. He retrieved his blazer and bike and ran on to catch up with Jolyon, who was at the front gates offering his farewell to his less than impressive gazelle. As they hurtled back down the hills, freewheeling dangerously and swerving this way and that to avoid the odd pedestrian, child and dog, Jolyon and Matthew sang at the tops of their voices: "Please release me, let me go, for I don't love you any more", emulating Engelbert's finest hour, and then roared with laughter. But Matt was secretly thinking about bouncing boobs and Stephanie's consent to go to the dance, and the paper note that had the house telephone number written on it that she had slipped into his trouser pocket from behind, where she had calmly stroked his softening erection, as he was reluctantly leaving her bedroom. Aware of a gnawing ache in his crotch, squashed and crushed as it was on the hard narrow bicycle seat, he felt as if he had been kicked between the legs. But, with the air rushing through his hair and billowing his blazer out behind, nothing could dislodge from his exhilarated mind, even the knowledge that they were returning to the drudgery of their house routines, a miserably sparse evening meal, and a work-packed week ahead with those dreaded exams looming ever closer, exquisite images of the beauteous Stephanie lying bare-topped on her bed.

3

By the following Wednesday Matthew was able to leave it no longer. He had been working hard in the cricket nets all afternoon, trying to take his excitable mind away from dark haired minxes in white, although he imagined her watching him from every angle and saw her everywhere, leaning in the shadows of the great willow next to them, over by the pavilion on a visitor's bench, walking along the upper path.

Soon after six o'clock, with the remains of the day's sunlight arcing low across his face, he left the grounds by the southern entrance, heading down the lane, under the railway bridge at the bottom. He slipped surreptitiously and unseen into the only red telephone box for miles around, which had always been reliable, never out of order. Hereford 4459: a young girl's voice answered the phone, after several rings.

He spoke quietly into the black mouthpiece. 'Can I speak with Stephanie, please.'

'Stephanie who?' she asked innocently.

'There can't be many Stephanies in your senior school – she's dark haired, wears white trousers.'

'Oh, I don't know.' She had a slow way of pronouncing things.

'Erm, Stephanie Patek.'

'Stephanie Patek? Oh, I don't know. I'll go and ask, shall I?'

'Oh yes, please, if you wouldn't mind. Don't make a fuss.' He tried not to sound irritated.

'I'll go and find her then, shall I?' she repeated slowly.

The telephone box was chilly inside and smelt of dog's wee and cigarettes. A few choice comments had been etched in the grey metalwork of the set, along with arrows drawn through hearts and lover's names, long forgotten. The directories hung forlornly from their metal hinges, torn and bent in all directions.

'Hello?'

'Stephanie?' Pause. 'It's Matt, from the tea party on Sunday, remember?' There was silence at the other end. 'You know, last Sunday, you slipped me the note…'

'Yes, Matthew, hi, I know who you are. Managed to phone without any trouble? Well done.'

She sounded all different, harsh somehow and distant. 'I thought you might like to meet me in town on Friday,' she continued, 'pretend shopping etcetera, I'll be in WH Smith at half past two, can you make it then?' Then she put on an extra special posh voice: 'we could have tea and cakes somewhere,' and laughed.

'Yes, wow.' Matt's heart was in his mouth again, dry and tongue-tied. He was surprised by the immediate offer, without any preamble. She knew he would concede. They quickly agreed, venue and time checked; they said hurried goodbyes.

Matt was on edge the rest of that nerve-wracking week, as he searched his brain for ways that he could impress Stephanie and ultimately clinch the deal, as it were, as her new dashing boyfriend, with the cool looks, the athletic figure and sporting physique, the dry humour, her obvious choice really.

He could not quite reason why she had been so brazen at the school, on the spur of the moment, after such calm detachment. They had hardly talked; it had been mostly eye contact. Was it just raw instinct on her part, based on first impressions and physical attraction? But to be so bold, so forward, taking her top off, touching him. He was stunned. She was stunning. Should he be suspicious? For a first attempt, for Matt, that was triumphal, utter vindication of his approach and choice. Was there nothing this boy could not achieve? He kept his counsel, not sharing with anyone else his thoughts, especially not Jolyon, who fancied Stephanie like everybody else but knew she was beyond his league, and who would have been insanely jealous.

Friday afternoon came round hideously slowly; he could not eat properly, he felt sick with apprehension. He needed the John a few times before he set off. He signed out in the exit book outside the housemaster's study – reason: personal shopping; expected time out: two hours maximum – and scuttled into town, walking, skipping, jogging hands in pockets, open blazer, tie loose, scuffed shoes, hair dragged back and stuck under a straw boater.

He was reading the titles of magazines in the stationer's rack, trying to avoid the naughty ones, and she was ten minutes late, when he felt a hand slip inside his palm and a sweet husky voice whisper into his earlobe, 'Hello. Sorry.' They pecked hastily at each other's cheek, heads down.

After he helped her find a birthday card and a paperback, *The Carpetbaggers* (Harold Robbins), for her big sister, they walked side by side, shoulders knocking against each other, keeping their hands to themselves, along the main shopping street, ignoring all the other passers-by, chatting about their activities in school and their friends, class work and his cricket. They sloped down the steep hill in front of the Abbey, its dark, forbidding shape looming above them, all pillars and buttresses and old stained-glass catching glancing sunlight, surrounded by a narrow area of graveyard, with grass and flowered borders swaying in the breeze. They chose a distant bench by a laurel hedge and in shadow under a massive cedar tree that obscured them from street view. Stephanie lit a cigarette and even in her school frock and little white cotton socks and scuffed brown leather regulation outdoor shoes, she looked rebelliously pretty.

The mood turned serious, which worried him for a moment. She sat with bare legs crossed, deeply inhaling and blowing smoke away through her lips, watching Matt intently while he told her about his home and his sister, his parents and the cat. Then she suddenly interrupted him: 'Have you ever seen your Mum and Dad making love to each other?' Matt was a bit horrified, not only by the thought of his parents with no clothes on, but how he was supposed to answer the question in a way that would constitute a cool reply. For a moment he suspected a trap.

'We all used to share a bath together actually up till a few years ago,' he laughed, 'my parents were quite free and easy about that sort of thing.'

'My parents are separating, I think,' she interjected matter-of-factly, although Matthew sensed she was holding back some tears. 'My Dad has some other woman, apparently, she's not much older than my sister. He's moving out, going back to live in Switzerland.' He did not know what to say. She waited a while fiddling with her cigarette before continuing. 'Daphne is twenty-two next month; she's designing clothes and things for this bloke who works for some film people, in Carnaby Street, or the King's Road, or wherever, in London. She went to Los Angeles last month, for some important film production.' She smiled brightly, enjoying dropping the names of cool places into the conversation.

'Is that what you want to do, go to London, the fashion scene and all that?'

'Love to, God. My dad is so against.' She made a face

at some recollection. 'I want to get into it, selling, to the stores and abroad and things, and maybe design, I love that. Trouble is Dad wants to take me off to Lausanne, to help in his business. He thinks I can count and understand numbers. Just because I once converted pounds into Swiss francs and made a little profit selling home-made jewellery at an arts and craft fair!'

'That must be his name, Patek?'

'Yeah, he's Swiss.'

'I'm sorry to hear they're separating. That must be awful.'

Stephanie sat huddled in the shadows, head down, picking at her fingernails, even as she held the cigarette between her long fingers, the smoke rising up past her face.

'You're not happy, are you?' He looked at the top of her head, and waited for those big eyes to flick up to his face, hoping for a smile.

'I'm happy now, with you.' And she responded as if he had asked her, lifting her gaze to his face, her bright eyes glittering green in the light and a smile flickered momentarily below. She bit a corner of her lower lip, and reached out a hand that squeezed the top of his thigh.

'You don't mind the smoking, do you? I know I shouldn't here, it's a bit public.' The afternoon was quiet by the row of old grave stones, the traffic noise some way away and few people walking by. 'It makes me feel more grown up, daft, I know. I really hate being cooped up at Wycheside, can't wait to leave this summer.'

'Oh, wow, I won't see you after the dance, then?' It was sort of a plea, and she responded by knitting her brows and screwing up her eyes but then she smiled beautifully.

'No, no, I will call you, in London, right, give me your home number. I am not going to Switzerland straight away, I will be with my Mum some of the time and so we should be able to meet up. We will have some fun. You can meet my sister. And Mum, and of course, Wellington.' She was writing her home telephone number down on the WH Smith paper bag, and he did the same with his number and then she tore off little strips that they swapped and pocketed. To Matthew it felt so sweet; he decided at that moment that he loved her.

'And who is Wellington?'

'Wellington is the goldfish, silly.'

'Ah. Of course.' She looked so pretty in the shadowy light, her creamy complexion so smooth, her contrasting black hair pulled back into a ponytail, but with many loose strands waving free in the breeze either side trickling over her cheeks. He was just so happy in her presence, his eyes tracing the lines of her perfect features; he could stay there forever without a care, thinking she must be a star. 'Is Wellington as beautiful as you?' Soppy idiot. She pouted and gave a little shake of her head, while the tip of her tongue curled out over her upper lip.

'And what about your sister, is she as beautiful as you?'

'Now that *is* a leading question and you can make up your own mind when you see her. Come on. Let's go down to Carter's and see what the latest is? Shall we get a drink?' And with that, Stephanie dropped her cigarette butt on the paving, stubbing it out under one of her shoes and bounced off the bench. She reached down for his arm, and they proceeded at a sedentary pace to leave the churchyard and join the people in the main street along to the next row of shops. Carter's was the local electrical store, and the only seller of records, music sheets and instruments in town, as well as light-bulbs and kettles. There were lovely Spanish guitars and Fenders hanging by their necks like chickens in the window, and inside were rows of stand-up pianos and drum kits. He always had a tinkle on the keyboards whenever he went in, although a one-handed Fur Elise was about all he could manage. At the back of the store were racks of records, in classic, pop, jazz or trad collections. On the far counter were the singles in crude cardboard boxes, and pinned to the wall were the week's charts scrawled in felt-tip, keeping everyone up to date with the latest sellers.

They were sharing a coke through a single straw. Matt spent a quick five minutes rifling through the singles' collection, choosing two for Stephanie – 'Whiter Shade of Pale' (Procol Harum) and 'Got To Get You Into My Life' (Cliff Bennett and The Rebel Rousers), which he thought were great, selling for five and nine each. 'Have you got these, Steph?' he called back to her, holding up the discs, while she was sitting at a piano quietly playing Chopin.

He stared admiringly across the shop floor at Stephanie hunched over a white Yamaha in her sloppy blazer, black ponytail draped down her back, her head slowly nodding in time to the nocturne, as she played her long fingers convincingly over the keys with a delicate touch. She later admitted that she had been playing pianoforte for ages and had reached Grade Eight this summer.

Later, just before they had to part and say goodbye, he pulled her over to stand against a massive plain tree in Avenue Road. He held her round her waist, their cheeks pressed together and then he kissed her on her lips fleetingly, mumbling, 'I don't want you to go,' and she tasted a little of cigarettes. The tantalising feel of her warm body pressing against him wiped his mind clean of any other thoughts. 'I just want to make love to you,' he murmured recklessly into her salty neck with new-found confidence.

'Quite,' she said, kindly, 'but not here, darling, you will have to wait.' And she slid away from his grasp, touched his pouting lips with the tip of her finger before skipping across the road to the far railings, from which was a long view out over many rooftops to the eastern valley, still basking in the late afternoon sunshine.

They stood and stared at each other across the road for

a while, oblivious of the few cars that passed, before moving away slowly in opposite directions, until they had turned different corners and were out of sight. Matt wandered back through town to his house, Stephanie climbed back up to the main street, to catch her bus back to Upper Wychside. 'See you in two weeks' time,' she had called back to him, and blew him a kiss, leaving him with one of her most generous of smiles. 'Can't wait,' he mouthed with a sickly ache in the pit of his stomach.

4

The date chosen for the school summer dance was fixed in every sixth former's feverish mind weeks in advance and targeted on their wall-planners with coloured circles and broad arrows. Scheduled for the night after the last of the university entrance examinations, it was considered to be at the pinnacle of the social calendar for any sixth former worth his salt, stealing so much attention as to endanger their concentration and preparation levels for the said examinations, which so defined why they were at that school in the first place. Matt would be involved in his finals the following year but the junior sixth formers still had mock exams to get through and much was expected of them.

The chance of a close encounter with a girl, a grope of female flesh or a snog in a dark corridor, drove the boys to a frenzy of post-pubescent anxiety. And none more so than Matt's study mate, Tony Felton, a Liverpudlian with a pretty face and dark mop of thick hair, which he combed incessantly in front of any piece of mirror he could find. He liked the look of himself and was always prepared in case an opportunity to chat up a girl should arise: out would come his comb from his back pocket, a quick pull through with his free hand following to ensure perfection, a charming smile in place and he was ready. Tony had invited a girl from one of the colleges in town to the dance and Matt was looking forward to meeting her, having heard endless stories of her sophistication and good looks.

Tony was a cool character, a good looking self-interested lad and he knew it and did not mind who else knew it. He was bright too, modern languages, acted a bit and played a nice guitar; a boy of many talents that he developed without fanfare or showing off; but it was his prowess with girls, with his Scouse accent and Beatle appearance, that he was most proud of and keen to develop further.

Real excitement started to build up during the day, a Saturday with irrelevant lessons scheduled for the morning and sporting activities in the afternoon. Matt was involved in an invitation cricket match from midday played on the senior pitch against the Country Falconers, a local team of builders and farmers' lads with a few ex-school boys to make up the numbers, a team that were generally strong and canny at dominating a game. The bowling was different to what the boys were used to at this level, relentlessly accurate with more bounce and with fewer loose balls that gave runs away. Matt batted at number four and with both openers out early, he and Duffield struggled for a useful partnership of fifty-five, before Duffield was caught behind off the edge to a nasty ball that cut away late. Matt was sticky and tired in the summer sun but held on for another half-hour before being caught at mid-off, mistiming a drive to a disguised slower ball, having made a respectable 46 and the applause was nice if short-lived as he trudged back to the pavilion.

Sweat ran off his face and liberally trickled down his back. In the changing rooms he stripped off, slurped cold water from a tap, splashing it over himself, quickly dried and pulled on a clean white shirt and a pair of brown brogues. Someone murmured something about Wycheside girls watching the game at the far end, under the willow trees. Names were mentioned, but not Stephanie's. He slipped away from the team room via a wooden balcony that led down to the upper path that ran along the high side of the pitch boundary, feeling inwardly pleased with his performance. He wandered the full length of the perimeter, behind thin lines of spectators sitting on benches or lying on the grassy edge, chatting, occasionally clapping politely at runs made or wickets taken. There were several spectators in groups in the shade of the overhanging willows. He could see some girls in the drab brown of Upper Wycheside, uniformed boys milling around them.

There were three girls standing together, Sarah among them, but no Stephanie. He had not seen her for three weeks and was trembling at the thought of meeting her again. They had only spoken briefly on the phone to each other last week. She had sounded a little lost and downbeat, as if she had forgotten their afternoon meeting or the coming dance. It was all he had been thinking about day and night, and he couldn't wait for the evening. She was due at the school on the hired bus, expected at around seven o'clock.

Matt stopped to speak to them and Sarah said that he had only just missed Steph, her mother had turned up unexpectedly at the far gate and dragged her away to go off into town in an open-topped Mercedes to meet with her father. Apparently she had seen his batting to the end and thought he was truly brave and wonderful. Matt looked suitably coy, but inside he was delighted at the thought that Stephanie had taken the time to notice what he had done, but disappointed at the mention of her mother and father being in town; she had said nothing about them being around this weekend.

Matt waited in a state of nervous anticipation in the foyer of the sports hall, but Stephanie failed to appear among the gaggle of giggling girls that clipped and clopped across the tarmac into the entrance from their hired bus, which had arrived still in daylight just after seven o'clock as the shimmering sunlight began to sink behind the hills. They all tripped along to a toilet designated for the ladies as Matt talked to Sarah, unsure where Stephanie was, she had not returned from her afternoon outing. Matt was told other buses would arrive in a while but they were from other schools, so he did not hold out much hope that she would appear. He paced around at the entrance, a mix of anger and frustration building up, of hurt and annoyance at looking such a fool. Perhaps with her parents here they would drive her down themselves. But she never showed up all evening.

He went in and drank a diluted shandy, listened to the live disco music, chatted aimlessly with people he had no interest in. Tony Felton was there with Joyce and Matt did think she looked rather nice. Jolyon danced with Sarah all evening, a satisfied expression on his increasingly flushed face. At least Sarah was loyal to him, even if she was not much to write home about, he thought uncharitably, but Matt was sure Jolyon would be secretly pleased, after all, he had warned him repeatedly about little minxes.

Matthew ached with hurt pride and dejected misery in the remaining days of that term, missing completely his batting in two matches and barely managing to keep his cool in the house with the irritating younger kids that he had responsibility for. He had a sore head for days and thought endlessly about Stephanie, asking unanswerable questions. Why could she not come to the dance? Could she not have sent him a message? Why did she not contact him later, through Sarah perhaps? He dared not ring the Wycheside number for fear of finding out that she did not want to see him again, for whatever reason. Then all he could think was that something untoward had happened.

Then on the last day of term, with half-packed open trunks lining the dusty corridors and blocking doorways, studies being stripped of their contents and rubbish strewn around the floors, and sixty rowdy boys clambering constantly up and down the narrow staircases dragging stuffed luggage down to the back door for loading onto transport for the station, Bill Stubbings himself wandered into Matthew's study unannounced with a letter. There was a tense air of nervous excitement all around, everyone about to depart for the long summer holidays, and the considerable noise from shouting and crashing furniture had disguised his housemaster's arrival. Matthew stumbled up to stand politely in front of the burly man in his Harris tweeds. He had a pipe in one hand, but it was not alight.

'Ah, Crawford, there you are. Look, I think we can safely say that we had a pretty good term, what! We can feel proud. I look forward to seeing you next term with some extra vigour, after a refreshing summer vacation, and remember, we might be moving you upwards soon, play your cards right, what! School prefect and all that, how does that sound?'

'Er, fine, sir.'

Stubbings was fingering a black-and-white photograph of Matthew in cricket whites, pads and bat, making a nice cover drive in a senior match that a boy had taken and printed for him, pinned to the front of his wall-cupboard. 'Good batting, yes, first rate. Well done.' And he held a small white envelope up between his first and second fingers, as if he was an umpire signalling 'out'. 'Letter delivered this morning by hand, only just had chance to bring it down.'

In spidery blue ink "Matthew Crawford, School House" was scrawled across the front. There was no address or stamp. It was from Sarah, who kindly informed Matthew that as far as she knew, Stephanie was alright but had had to return early with her mother to Maidstone and would be spending most of the summer in Switzerland with her father. She was really sorry she had missed the dance and hoped to see Matthew soon, she would call him at his home when she could.

5

The first weekend after term and Matt was off to Ricky's leaving party. Ricky Ballone was having to leave school a year early, something to do with his father being posted to Washington, and so had arranged a gathering of his best mates at his home in Gerrards Cross, while his parents were away. He promised girls, music and cheap food, and a stay-over if wanted. Not everyone was going to be there, many lived too far away, or would be away on their family holidays, but for Matt, coming up from North London was easy.

Ricky was Italian Jewish with a delightful aptitude in socialising. At school he was always having get-togethers and parties, in his study or a meeting room, or up in the hills for a picnic when the weather was fine, any excuse. Habitually he would produce hampers with pastas and lasagne, with bread and cheeses, Tiramasu, ice creams and wine, ordered locally; how he did it, no one quite knew. He daringly smoked cigarettes whenever he could get away from the school grounds, and womanised something awful. He was quick to share stories of his latest conquest, usually involving heroic moments of pursuit, passion and reward, liberally dotted with knickers and knockers. He was a bit of a lad, in other words, but always well turned out, never short of spare cash and generous to a fault.

He loved playing cricket, especially the away games against local opposition, because he could drink beer and smoke freely and without fail would find some curvy female soft enough to pop behind the pavilion with him for a quickie, before he was due 'in', elsewhere, as it were. Once Matt had to search desperately for Ricky as he was next in to bat at a crucial stage of a match, and found him hidden away behind a low fence in long grass, bonking a half-naked girl from behind like a dog, panting and grunting with his pads on, bat and gloves within easy reach, ready for his turn. His batting was usually atrocious, but by striking out adventurously at every ball, he would score some runs, have some fun, before likely being caught dramatically on the third man boundary after attempting yet another cow shot.

Matt found his way from the station in the early evening with a small overnight bag, and met Rick and a small gathering of friends in the back garden of the big house. 'Is agood to see you, my friend,' he called out with arms aloft. He had a prominent bent nose, small brown eyes and a ruddy complexion, offset with black curly hair. Ricky would often talk in a joke Italian accent for effect, but normally spoke the perfect English. He and Matt hit it off from the moment they first met and had been friends for the last four years. 'We 'ave some girls 'ere today for you, including the lovely Christina.' Ricky indicated a short, well-endowed girl in perfect white, struggling to keep her balance on the edge of the wet lawn some way off.

Christina was just one of Ricky's many girlfriends, at least twenty years old with a narrow waist and an impressive bosom, which at that moment, was tightly squeezed into a clinging low-cut dress. She was wobbling dangerously on stiletto heels which kept sinking hilariously into the soft lawn every time she tried to step back onto more solid ground nearer the house. Some lads were laughing from the safety of their dry stone path. And each time she stumbled forward, her shoes left stuck in the grass, her wobbly breasts seemed ready to break free from their tentative moorings and the small crowd of testosterone-infused lads with their eyes and mouths wide open jeered in expectation. Even some other girls were laughing and Matt began to fear for her safety, thinking she might end up head-long in the petunias. 'Hello, Christina,' they all chorused, moving cautiously backwards to avoid being caught up in an accident. As the light of the day began to fade, they drank more beer from bottles, made more ribald comments and drifted indoors, where music emanated from the conservatory.

There must have been thirty or so and girls aplenty, as Ricky had promised. There were packs of food, piled on all the available table space, mostly take-way fish and chips, pizzas and crisps, and stacks of coca-cola and beer. A couple of girls in aprons came through from the kitchen with a huge bowl of steaming chilli con carni, with French bread on the dining table. They drank, they ate and drank some more, and sang the choruses of all the pop songs while eyeing the local talent sprinkled around the room.

Sergeant Pepper was played endlessly over and over on the gramophone, well into the early hours of the morning. By midnight they had all learnt the words and sang along heartily about Vera, Chuck and Dave. Snogging couples were settling down on settees and sofas, on chairs and the stairs, groping each other on cushions thrown around on the floor, and some sneaked out into the hall or found spaces in other rooms, including upstairs in bedrooms.

Matt found himself with a short dark-haired girl called Vicky, who wore round black-rimmed glasses, had an obvious gap in her top front teeth and tried to look terribly serious. She wore something knitted and close fitting on top, but had an unremarkable chest. She drank wine continuously and had been kissing him on and off all evening; around midnight, when everyone had paired up in the darkness and wondered off to find comfort in quiet corners or other rooms, they had snuggled up together uncomfortably on a small settee in the shadows of the main room. His head rested across her chest and her legs were crossed over his lap with her skirt creased up to her thighs. He stroked the warm skin of her upper legs as she lay bleary-eyed and in need of sleep with her head thrown back on cushions. Matt was thirsting for a drink of water, his lips dry from all the kissing. When he thought she was asleep he edged his fingers further up inside her skirt, feeling his way between layers of soft sticky flesh, trying to touch her spongy white knickers, but she suddenly nudged him away and folded herself defensively. He sensibly withdrew his hand. Sleep came fitfully and awkwardly during odd moments in the night. When he bumped into Vicky the next morning in the bright light of the kitchen, he could not help noticing an angry spot on her lower lip and was revolted by the grotesque thing, imagining that he had been licking at it all night in the dark without knowing. He made excuses, avoided her completely and left at the earliest opportunity with a sore head and aching crotch, accepting a lift in a Vauxhall from another friend's family.

Back at home in West Hampstead, secluded in his attic room with views over roof tops and leafy trees, and not confiding in anybody, he longed for the secretiveness of the dark evenings alone, when his imagination brought Stephanie to him, late in the night, calling his name, wearing nothing but see-through white cotton flapping in the breeze that dropped from her tanned shoulders at an easy touch, to show off her firm rounded young body shimmering in the moonlight, her doughnut belly lightly dusted with icing sugar. And he would reach forward to bring her into his arms, and to lick her, but she would howl with laughter and back away fading into the night cloud, never letting him touch her. He pretended she stayed to caress him through the night and pleasure herself on his rippling physique, leaving him perspiring, panting and gasping for more. It usually ended too soon, but sometimes helped him to sleep, only to wake the next morning feeling more bereft than before.

6

A few days later there was a phone call, in the middle of the afternoon, and he was totally unprepared. His mother answered in the kitchen and then called him in from the garden where he was lounging miserably in short trousers in the sunshine pretending to read Albert Camus. He dragged himself up feeling hazy, wiping the sweat from his forehead. She said it was a girl, Stephanie she thought the voice had said. Matt's legs went weak, his mouth suddenly dry. He took the call in his father's study at the front of the house, almost in a state of panic.

'Hello?' he whispered into the black telephone.

'Hi, Matt. It's me. You OK? Your mum sounds nice.'

She sounded miles away and he was trying to picture her face as she spoke, wondering what she might be wearing. She obviously wanted to sound chatty.

'I'm at home, in Maidstone, but I have to be quick,' she said. 'I am going to be in London next week and was hoping we could meet up. My sister has a show in the King's Road, in Chelsea and I'm going over to help her prepare, and I thought if you could come over too, we'd have some fun, I'm sure we'll enjoy it. You'll meet some interesting people, and it will be cool.' She paused a fraction: 'And I'll be there.' He was having difficulty getting sounds out of his mouth, they were caked up somewhere at the back of his throat.

His mind was racing, next week should be fine, where could they meet, what should he wear, where would Stephanie be staying, what was her sister like? Was she going to say anything about missing the dance, or did they just forget that. Though he was desperate to see her, he tried to sound calm and interested without being overly keen. They agreed a set of arrangements and he was suddenly deliriously happy, everything else irrelevant, realising that she had obviously missed him and could not manage without him and was desperate to get him on his own so she could ravish him as soon as possible.

They met on a scorching hot day, outside a shop in Chelsea that Stephanie had mentioned. Dressed in a white T-shirt under a blue denim Ben Sherman, with tight Levis and brown ankle boots with crisp leather soles that clipped along the pavement, he felt hot and cool at the same time. Not relaxed, but cool. He would play the boy she had met at school, a friend who had come along for the hell of it, who could take it or leave it, who probably had a handful of girlfriends back home to choose from.

The moment he saw her, he melted, lost his voice again and started to stammer. She was brightly dressed in red tights and green miniskirt, a pink shirt with dark green suede waistcoat and plunging neckline filled with dangling necklaces that rattled with every move. She had bangles around her wrists and huge earrings with coloured stones and feathery attachments. Her face was brilliantly painted around her eyes in emerald, crimson and sky blue, contrasting effectively with her perfect complexion and crimson lips. Somehow he recognised her, with her tied back black hair cascading down her back, those few wispy strands escaping at the sides. She looked stunning, a wild transformation from the sullen schoolgirl in dull brown and heavy scuffed shoes that he was more familiar with, into this raunchy sex kitten.

She was laden with piles of clothes in both arms, almost obscuring where she was going, as she trailed behind a group of young trendies in Old Church Street, coming out of a big doorway. They were all chatting busily as they shuffled along the pavement towards the shop front where Matt was standing next to a pub. An extremely thin dark-haired young fellow in a snazzy tight blue suit with navy velvet collar, four buttons at the front done up, winkle-picker leathers and a fag hanging out of the corner of his mouth minced along beside them aiming his Pentax at the group from the side of the road, calling for smiles as they passed.

When Stephanie spotted Matthew, standing alone wide eyed, her face lit up, she sprang forward, dropping all the clothes she was carrying on the pavement, to throw her arms around his neck and to plant a wonderful squelcher full-on, with a satisfying "mmm" for all to see. 'Darling, Matt, how lovely, alright? Lovely. How do I look, darling?' Her thick hair was tied with a long green silky scarf. 'You must say hi to Daphne, and then I'll introduce you all. Help me with these, darling, will you, and then we can go inside and we'll get some drinks. Oh, it's so nice to see you, don't you know.'

She kept on talking, not giving him any space to answer as they struggled with the clothes, colourful tops and miniskirts on plastic hangers, out of the bright sunshine through open doors and into a large and cool bare space of wooden flooring and tables. The shop windows were papered over and it took a while to adjust to the darkness inside, but someone switched some strip lights on that were high above them among heating pipes and ducting.

Stephanie flustered about, nervy and excited and Matt's eyes were fixed on her. She called about to lots of people, running through names and sometimes commenting on what they did in the group, but frankly he could not remember any of them, even moments later, except lovely Nigel the photographer, and Jonathan, who seemed to be the leading design manager, and of course sister Daphne, who was busy and bubbly, bigger than Stephanie with strong Mediterranean features, wearing colourful loose fitting clothes, with bundles of silk ties around her waist and neck, and a scarf tied tightly around her forehead holding back a mass of unruly black hair. She had a prominent mole on her left cheek and a delightful smile, showing lots of upper white teeth. She welcomed Matt with a tight hug, pressing her soft bosom against him and pecking at both his cheeks.

Daphne proceeded to tell him how stressed they all were, because she had to have her collection ready by tomorrow afternoon, and they were all helping get the material right, and the textures and of course the colours. There were a couple of flat-chested waifs standing about in their underwear and high heels at the back under lights, being used as models as cotton and silk materials were shaped over them, pinned and cut, in experimentation, as the drapers created folds and sashes and borders, with endless directions shouted at them from various designer types watching. Then the rough and ragged shapes was slipped off, wriggled out of, with squeals as sharp pins pricked delicate white flesh, and everyone around the room stared across in sympathy, seeing the models again down to their little bits of underwear, before the next creation was tried on. Matt had his arms around Stephanie's shoulders, leaning against her and watching proceedings from behind and felt pleased that he had come, whatever her motives.

After a long slow session, during which Stephanie had helped shift piles of materials and clothes from one place to another, and occasionally had offered comments and advice among the general mayhem, they all had a break when a tray of drinks was brought in. There were paper cups of steaming tea, some cans of lager and biscuits. Daphne and Jonathan seemed to be close, lovers even, from the way they sloped away together, touched each other and spoke into each other's eyes.

Matt and Stephanie wandered away from the main area of activity into the darker recesses of the space, and found some chairs to perch on. 'I am so sorry about the dance, and not turning up, I feel so guilty about it. Was it good?'

'Oh, forget it, it's alright…'

'How was it? I bet you had a lovely time without me.'

'No, I certainly did not, I waited for you, but no one seemed to know why you had not come. I was left thinking that you didn't want to be with me and, you know…' his voice trailed away into nothing.

'I am sorry, Matt.' She reached forward to squeeze his hand. 'It was my fault, of course, but actually it was my parents, they both turned up on Friday, I had no idea they were coming, they were arguing, and I had to come down to the school; I watched you playing cricket, you were so very good. But my mother found out where I was and came down in the car, she took me off to town, where they were staying in the Abbey Hotel.'

'But I thought they were separated?'

Stephanie looked worried and knotted her brows together in an adorable way. She shook her head. 'They were trying to make it up, you know, get back together, but they argued most of the evening, mostly about me and his other woman, Dad obviously hadn't sorted her out. The long and the short is that he wants me back with him in Lausanne in a couple of weeks, while Daphne stays here with mother, because she's got a career, sort of, although Dad thinks it's pathetic, what she does. I said it was good, she's been to Art College and so on, she should be allowed to use her skills.'

She sat back in the shadows of the room, resting her chin on her hands, elbows on her knees, perched on the edge of some wooden boxes. Piles of unwanted clothes and material were stashed all around, while Matt sat at her feet on floor cushions, and relaxed in her presence, relating the pathetic events of the night of the dance. She listened with pretended interest, trying to concentrate on what he was saying, her mind probably elsewhere.

'It's so important for Daphne, this show, because Jonathan is trying to sell their designs for this film company and it means trips to Los Angeles for the team if they win. And Daphne has worked so hard. Apart from the money which should be good, you know, reputation-wise, recognition-wise, it will help Daphne, could set her up really.'

They had finished their drinks and were thinking about the arrangements for the evening, when Stephanie was called out to the front once again, further work required, with more pinning and some changes, and reruns to design. Over to one side there were three dress makers with sewing machines and they were heads down rattling along seams and sewing edges and folds, frantically trying to keep up with Jonathan shouting for the items back again once they had been modelled.

Much later in the day with most of the work done and a more relaxed feel in the place, a group of young people were sitting around smoking and Nigel was explaining why he was looking so dandy. 'In the photo business, mate, you have to be clean, with it, smart but at the top of the fashion, and this is what all the pop stars are wearing now. I mean last month, you know with Pepper and all that buzz, I went out and bought a kaftan, got a perm and stuffed flowers in me hair. It was beautiful.' He posed and pouted his painted lips at Matt. 'Unfortunately my girlfriend thought I had turned homosexual, cried a lot and left me. I've been a bit queer ever since. Ummm.' There was some naughty laughter and Nigel placed a hand on his forearm. 'You don't think I'm a poofter, do you, Matt dear?' and mimicked blowing him a kiss. He cackled outrageously with all the others.

'Mind you, I think we have been missing a key ingredient, over here, I mean. In the US of bloody A, they are all fuelled by marijuana, darling, weed, hashish for God's sake, something, but we haven't been able to get hold of the fucking drugs for love nor money.' More laughter and another girl slid over to Nigel, running a hand over his shoulder, pulling his face round toward hers, saying 'Listen, love, any time you feel like you want me to blow your little trumpet, you know where to find your Lola, yeah?' They smacked lips full on and Nigel squeezed her big bottom with both hands.

'Did you hear about the students in Totteridge Road last week,' another boy with wispy facial hair was saying, 'having a bit of aggro with the fuzz; it was a sort of anti-war demo, with placards and things, were they Israelis?'

'We got arrested a couple of months ago,' two nice looking boys arm in arm said together, 'for possession. A tiny amount of weed, it was ridiculous. Same day that Mick Jagger was arrested. We all spent June in The Scrubs together.'

'Something else in common with the lads,' called Nigel in triumph, 'public outrage with the police harassing our rock n' roll heroes.'

The sun was cooling outside and dipping below the heights of the buildings opposite, when Stephanie came over with Daphne and they started to clear up for the day. They were going over to Luigi's for a meal later. 'And then we can go back to Daphne's place,' Stephanie whispered hoarsely to Matt, with a little smile. 'She shares with some other girls, a flat near here, Jonny will be there, and other guys will be dossing down, but we can find somewhere; I was sleeping there the last two nights. Alright?'

Matt sounded as enthusiastic as he could, but was by now feeling a little frustrated. He was besotted with desire and was impatient to get Steph alone to himself. Her loveliness was obvious, to him and to everyone else, and he wondered jealously how many of these boys she had been with. He wanted to stick with her, although at one point he was thinking he would be better off going home and arranging something else with Steph for another day.

'And then it's an early start, but I was thinking at the weekend, the house should be free, my mother is going to be away, so we could be down in Maidstone and have some fun. There's a pool, and nice walks and things.'

'And Wellington,' he remembered.

She squeezed his hand tenderly and smiled at him. 'Precisely.' She pulled him into a soft embrace with a lingering wet press of the lips and he immediately changed his mind. Stephanie was obviously feeling the same way as he was and so, why not stay with her for his reward later, although he might regret it by morning? He started to worry that he had not brought any rubber johnnies with him – he should have bought some from the machine in the gents in the pub next door, but it needed a half crown and was too embarrassed to ask the man behind the bar.

It was a balmy evening and nearing midnight by the time Daphne, Stephanie and Matthew stumbled wearily up stone steps to the main door of a big Edwardian terraced house, close to where they had been working all day. Matt had his arm around Stephanie's waist, and she in turn had squeezed the flat of her hand into one of his back trouser pockets, squeezing his buttock as he walked; he trembled at the thought of what was in store and shivered momentarily. They had had pizza, soup, cheeses and puddings and had drunk a bit in the Italian, so were feeling warm, full and pretty relaxed. They could hear the sound of Joan Baez playing somewhere as they climbed up to the third floor in the dark, as quietly as they could.

It was dim everywhere, but Matt could make out a number of doors leading off a corridor, and a high-ceilinged main room with settees and heavy curtains undrawn overlooking the King's Road. There were other people wandering around half-dressed, or in pyjamas and bare feet, nipping into the bathroom or back to their beds, while others slept. Daphne showed them how to pull one of the settees out into a divan, found some sheets and a blanket, and after ten minutes of whispered sisterly chat left them to it, while she went off to find Jonathan. Matt made the bed up as best he could in the dark, while Stephanie went off to find a bathroom. Then it was his turn; afterwards he tiptoed back to the darkened room with just a towel around his waist. Stephanie sat hunched in a silk dressing gown, her black hair free and trailing luxuriously down over her shoulders, catching the eerie mix of light from a silvery moon and yellow street lamps that angled in through the gaps in the drapes, her face shiny with cleanser, her lips bare.

'I'll need a shower in the morning,' she whispered, offering him a glass of water as he perched himself next to her, 'I need to wash my hair.' Nervous but outwardly relaxed, Matt reminded himself of the bravado with which he related tales about girls to the innocent boys at school. He took some initiative right away, reaching for her neck and slipping long fingers inside her thick curtain of hair; he started kneading her tired muscles at the nape and she closed her eyes and sighed, tilting her head back.

'You are so lovely,' he whispered.

Their young faces turned towards each other and they kissed with a gentleness that suggested meaning. He felt light-headed, as the wetness of their tongues collided. He chose to lose his sense of awareness, allowing his body to float in a sort of elevation, like bobbing along on a warm ocean wave, while his hands wandered free to explore. His fingertips stroked along the ridges of her neck, which gave him a sense of direction as he splayed his hands out over her shoulders, spreading them down her bare upper arms, inside her gown, peeling it open.

She bowed her head and in one easy movement, rose up naked before him, her gown crumpling silently to the floor around her feet. Stepping aside, turning, posing purposively, her chest proud, one knee angled in front of the other, she tilted her head to one side, fixing her eyes on the shiny pools of his, while chewing one side of her lower lip. Then her slim arms arced above her head in slow-motion, stretching and shimmering with wave-like motions. The slanting light daubed weird patterns over her textured skin, casting dark moving shadows, as, like a fragile ballerina, she slowly *pirouetted*, for Matt to feast his gaze on her perfectly moulded form, as if in a dream. She held the *demi-pointe* for a second or two on the balls of her feet, her silken fleece gilded in yellow flame. A waft of her pungent scent filled his distended nostrils, propelling him lustfully, instinctively, breathlessly.

Suddenly fearful of impending failure and unable to restrain himself any longer, our naïve teenager in the guise of experienced Lothario, made a voracious grab for his goddess. Standing upright, his towel tumbled from his waist and in that glorious moment of triumphant anticipation, he realised she was there for him, to surrender for him, completely.

Without taking her eyes off his shining face, she laid herself down on the rickety divan, guiding him to lie with her. He descended trembling between her thighs, rushing in, as if suddenly there was no time to lose. His lips and tongue sucked and licked at her clumsily, growing more urgent, as he prodded his way forward. She held hard onto his shoulders, consoling him with comforting words of restraint. He paused, but only for an instant, the power in his loins so eager for penetration and soon she succumbed to his thrusts and gasped sharply when he slipped magnificently and with no great resistance into her deeper recesses and inner warmth.

He watched her rounded breasts bouncing in rhythm and tried to catch the smooth nipples between his lips. Their bodies locked together, as he bombarded her, while she encouraged him in her husky whisper, her hands gripping his solid buttocks, the sharp fingernails digging into his flesh. Their thighs slapped together and the divan squeaked in complaint. Sweat broke out over his face in giant droplets as he became increasingly desperate to complete his task, thrusting with even more gusto, as yet unashamedly unaware of any of the subtle components involved in sharing and making love; and then he exploded with breath-taking release and uncontrolled high-pitched grunting.

The moment of his joy was spent almost before he realised it. He shifted his position to lessen his body weight on her, and his breathing slowly returned to more normal levels. He dreamt of blissful sleep, lying forever gloriously cushioned in the warmth of her nakedness, inhaling her smell. For a novice that was surely not bad and he wanted to laugh at his success. Everything this girl held dear and private had been opened to him, which mistakenly he took to mean her heart and soul. In his innocence he assumed her beauty was the truth and the truth was love.

It was only in the bright light of the early morning that Matt and Stephanie with hilarious embarrassment realised that others had shared the comforts of the huge bedroom, presumably all through the night, in other made-up divans and a mahogany Victorian double-bed, as they watched horrified from under their covers a number of bedraggled, unwashed and long-haired figures in crumpled pyjamas or less emerge sleepy-eyed from under their own covers, looking for the John and asking if breakfast was ready. It was hard to tell which were girls and which were boys. They laughed about it later.

7

Over the following few dreamy days, Steph (nobody called her Stephanie any more, except her father) and Matthew repeatedly and without shame consummated their desire for one another more times than either could keep count. In various beds, in a bath, in the back of a car, in a clothes designer's waste bin behind the Chelsea studio, even in the back row at the Criterion cinema watching *The Graduate*. And when they transferred for two glorious overnight stays to her parents' home in Maidstone, they cheekily used the master bedroom with its presidential-sized bed and black silk sheets and mirrored walls. It was a wonderfully liberating experience, to run around the top floor of the large house with no clothes on, the warm summer breezes wafting them through open windows. Steph would dress loosely without underwear for him to catch glimpses of her, while doing ordinary things, like cooking or washing up. She would emit a saucy giggle when he peered up her trembling skirt as she climbed the stairs ahead of him and then they would tumble into any number of different bedrooms, to endlessly explore their young bodies, fascinated and obsessed. Matt had never seen or touched a girl so intimately before or used his own body to achieve such acts of passion. And it was Beach Boys ('You're So Good To Me') and Small Faces ('Itchygoo Park') booming from her father's stereo system that formed the accompanying soundtrack that he remembered so well.

After little sleep during the nights, they would awake slowly towards midday, finding the outside day already deliciously warm with golden sunshine. Matthew would wander outside with a bowl of cornflakes and lie on the grass, Steph would shower and join him fresh and shining. One morning she cut a basket load of red rose blooms and placed them in her parents' bedroom that had been claimed as their love nest. That afternoon during an inevitable process of foreplay, with Scott Mackenzie warbling about wearing those flowers to San Francisco, Matt shook the blood-red petals free from their stems and scattered the velvety cups over her naked body as she lay across the ruffled sheets, arched and posed like Marilyn Monroe.

They showered together, lathering each other before having sex under the warm water jet; they had sex at the top of the carpeted stairs, on a soft rug in the sitting room, and once outside in the garden under moonlight. He could not believe how much time he must have wasted in his earlier years ignoring the glories of such coexistence, or indeed how lucky he was now. Nor did he ever contemplate being without Stephanie, not together to share their intimate freedoms as on those hazy lazy days. Or that he could physically miss her so much, when, like all good things, it eventually came to an end.

Stephanie's mother returned in the open topped Mercedes earlier than expected, unannounced at ten o'clock one morning as they slumbered in the master bedroom. Startled, Steph must have heard the crunching on the gravel drive and pushed Matt still half asleep sideways out of the bed, whispering urgently to get all his things together quickly and to dash for it. He wrestled with tangled sheets on the floor as he watched his naked girlfriend desperately trying to get her legs into a pair of jeans hopping on one foot while pulling a loose top over her head, and then brushing her messy hair, apparently all at once!

'You need to jump out of the window at the end of the corridor onto the garage roof,' she was saying urgently as she pulled the sheets straight and tried hopelessly to make her parents' bed look neat. 'Then wait till Mum is in the house and jump down the side and across the lawn to the fence. Climb over and you're at the side road – at the main road you can get a bus, they all go to Maidstone, main London line, every twenty minutes.'

It was his turn to run around in circles grabbing at underpants and socks, pulling trousers on and finding a shirt. He stubbed his toe on a bed leg and emitted a half-suppressed 'shit.' Steph managed to contain her giggling as she left the bedroom to ward her mother away from the stairs. Matt stumbled along the corridor and struggled to open the sash window quietly. He shoved everything through the opening, including himself still in bare feet, onto the sharp flat roof below. Steph looking furious suddenly appeared with his overnight bag, which she threw out to him, shaking her long hair, black and bedraggled. 'Be good, my angel,' and she pouted a pretend kiss for him. 'I'll call you in a day or so, when I can.' He pushed everything he could into the bag, dirty T-shirts and socks, underpants, a pair of shorts, swimming trunks, a denim jacket, a spongebag and a cheap paperback, holding back the disappointment of their sudden parting, before dropping his shoes and the hold-all onto the grass below.

The window closed after him, as he dropped down off the roof onto soft grass. He frantically dressed himself properly, found his socks and put his shoes on. Then he crouched carefully behind a rhododendron bush, made sure nobody could see him before making a silent dash across the lawn away from the house through the bushes that ran alongside the garden and to the fence beyond. He threw the bag over and scaled it easily himself, even as he watched through the foliage Stephanie's mother unloading shopping bags or something from the boot of her car, walking to and from her front door, which finally was closed with a thump, which to him ominously signalled the end of his dream.

He landed on the verge of a pavement and glanced back over the fence one last time, up towards the closed window he had climbed out over the garage, but there was no sign of Stephanie, no face at the glass anxiously peering out. He mouthed "goodbye" towards the house and set off for the main road and a bus journey back into Maidstone and the railway station.

For the rest of the holidays Matthew mooched aimlessly about the house and scuffed miserably along pavements, whistling tunelessly with boredom, while nothing seemed able to grab his interest, apart from listening to music, familiar tracks being played loud, over and over. Vivid memories of his intimacy with Steph filled his head day and night and partially sustained him, but he felt bereft and nothing would heal his fraught heart other than her presence. There had been no contact for days and the Maidstone number remained unanswered. As far as he knew, his black-haired beauty had withdrawn to Switzerland with both parents and there was no contacting her.

They did manage an obscure meeting the day before he was due to return to school. Steph had phoned him, said she was on a rapid London visit with her parents and would have a short moment when she could get away from them. It was at Marylebone Station where they both had trouble suppressing their tears, hanging onto each other, kissing each other's wet faces. But it only lasted a few unhappy minutes before Steph was dragged away be sister Daphne, to return home with their father in charge, demanding that Stephanie spent time earning her keep abroad.

Despite some glorious autumn weather, Matthew returned to school for the Christmas term full of gloom. The other boys were quickly involved in all the daily hurly-burly, while Matthew reflected on his grief with mature solemnity, spending too much time staring at his image in the mirror, adjusting to the habit of shaving his chin, and staring out of windows into the middle distance, seeing nothing and wondering how he was ever going to get through the term. But of course he had to join in and was soon involved in the challenge of sixth form, house activities and playing football. He found himself promoted to Head of House, Mr Stubbings sticking his neck out to place his trust in his choice, which meant regular meetings and a formal weekly lunch together in the house, and on every Friday night after supper, he would walk through to the housemaster's private residence to take coffee and indulge in dreary conversation in his sitting room with his wife Goethe in attendance. His sixteen-year-old daughter, Isabel, who always wore skirts far too short for her beefy legs, was also usually there saying nothing, together with their soppy old Labrador, which sprawled across the floor at his feet, making grunts and smells and was frankly of more interest.

He declined the Upper Wycheside Sunday afternoon bike run again, despite Jolyon's urging. And apart from one untidy letter, postmarked from London, chit-chatting about nothing consequential, declaring how she was becoming used to her routine life in her new home in Lausanne and mentioning without much conviction how much she was missing him, to which he immediately composed an amusing reply that burst with frustrated anxiety and grief at not being able to be with her, which he sent off at the earliest opportunity, he had no other contact with Stephanie at all throughout the term.

Just a few days before Christmas, at home after returning from school and seriously trying not to get too irritated with his sister for playing some of his best records without asking, a letter arrived in the midmorning post with a bundle of other family cards, addressed to Mister Matthew Crawford Esq., which his mother handed to him at the bottom of the stairs with an interested smile on her face, when he came down from the seclusion of his room. Written in ink on a single blue Basildon Bond page, folded once, the note was short and to the point. Stephanie was expecting a baby in April, was living permanently in Lausanne, would not be returning to England and would not be contacting Matthew again. It was dated: 12th December 1967 and was signed: Rosemary Cross. There was no address or telephone number. That was it.

A baby. A baby? Crickey, you mean, Matthew's baby?

After hours of complete loneliness lying on his bed, he changed into jogging clothes and ran out into the Hampstead streets, heading powerfully up through the rising avenues and along pathways that lead to the Whitestone Pond. The air was bitingly cold and he jogged with vigour. He crouched by the roadside and watched distractedly the ducks being fed chunks of bread by some small children. He found a bench to perch on for a few moments peace. He wanted to be entirely alone, to see no one, to wallow in his private misery. Stephanie Patek had left the country and had gone out of his life, forever it would seem. He felt as if a giant hand had ripped out a chamber of his heart. He was totally depressed and had no one to share his despair with.

And she was going to have his baby.

A bedraggled collection of small donkeys, mounted with children sitting sullenly in their duffle coats, woolly hats and scarves, were being lead slowly along a dirt pathway towards him. The sky was overcast and darkening and he wondered whether it was cold enough for snow just then. Where he sat on a rise, the highest point on the Heath, was a place traditionally used by idiots on skis, or anyone on a bin liner or dustbin lid after the first snowfalls of winter, for a five second adrenaline thrill sliding down the steep slope in front of him, something he recalled he had done in years past.

Matthew's thought processes were freezing over with the falling temperatures. He was never going to be able to find a substitute for his dark-haired beauty, he was doomed to be forever single. Stephanie was going to have his baby. Mrs Cross had felt the need to inform him and gave him the expected date that confirmed he was likely to be responsible. Why had she done that? To have greater impact, he supposed. She had used her maiden name, which Matt took to mean she had probably separated from Stephanie's father. Cross by name and cross by nature, she had obviously taken control and would be looking after her daughter with her new child. He was excluded; he was wiped out of their lives; he would never see his baby. But what was this: was he actually relieved? When he thought it through properly, how would he have coped with his school life, having a girlfriend with a baby? He could not possibly imagine it, it had no reality for him.

Matthew thought that he had better share the news with his mother; she would understand and offer him some solace. He was having trouble containing his calm, his emotions were of loneliness and the unfairness of it all. How did these things work? Would the authorities come for him, cart him away, make his parents pay astronomic sums of money to put things right. He was numbed but in pain, knowing simply that he could not live without Steph, even more so now that he knew she was pregnant. He felt sure that Steph would have fought angrily to be reunited with Matthew, somehow, but had had to concede to her mother's wishes. 'I miss you desperately,' he almost yelled, looking up at the dark skies overhead and a yellowy-looking moon rising over the flat pond. 'If you can hear me, send her a message: wish her well. God, wish her well.' And he could not stop himself, his chest heaved and the tears that had been threatening came, as they had to, overflowing down his cheeks and tasting sharply of salt. There was a stinging along his recently shaven chin.

He cried silently into his hands for a few minutes.

In that Chelsea flat Steph said she had just had her period so they would be alright, and that she was starting on the new contraceptive pill, had found a doctor in London to prescribe it for her. Matthew had been lazy with precautions and was pleased to hear that she had everything under control, which on reflection he realised was stupid of him, and they were paying for the mistake. Perhaps they had both been irresponsible, but it was Steph suffering most; she must be suffering more, surely she would not be pleased one little bit. Would she have wanted a termination?

Back home he went upstairs and showered and then once again hid himself in his attic room alone, confused and heartbroken, not sure what he should do. There seemed no way he could get in touch with Steph. He was suddenly uncertain whether she would have wanted him to. There were no hidden meanings between the lines in the letter, which he read again and again. Her mother was in charge, which he knew would be hurting Steph, losing her independence the worse possible way.

* * *

Around June the following summer, in his final year at school, Matthew was contacted by Sarah, Jolyon's Sarah from Upper Wycheside. There was a written note and an arrangement to meet one afternoon along College Road at a distinguished bend in the road by a bench seat under an old oak tree. Sarah explained that she and Stephanie had remained friends, they wrote to each other from time to time and that Sarah had received a recent update from Switzerland. Steph had had her baby a few weeks ago and they were both well and healthy. She had a new boyfriend and they were soon to be married. Steph said she had not wanted to involve him when the pregnancy happened, as she thought it would spoil his chances of finishing school, getting into Oxbridge, achieving all those things he was destined for. She admitted to it all being her fault. She hoped Matthew would be happy, that he should not worry about her and she wished him well for his future.

And that seemed to be that.

Matthew never saw her again. Except in his mind's eye and in his dreams, she kept popping up everywhere. So their meeting at Marylebone Station last August turned out to be their last. Did she know then, Matthew wondered; she gave absolutely no hint. Then her one and only letter to him, which suggested that she was not coming back, at least trying to let him down gently. She must have argued with her parents but her mother had won the day. He recalled the sighting of Steph's hurriedly departing figure in the underground lobby of the station, slim in tight brown coat, half turning towards him, a little wave of one hand before being swallowed up among the crowd of other travellers, his last forlorn memory, as they moved away in opposite directions.

Stephanie never tried to find out how he felt about being the father of her child. But then she never came calling either to press him for any financial support or to take up a father's responsibility. Instead she had flattered some other poor sod and started a new life with him, no doubt some wealthy Swiss national, thank you very much. She had reassured Matthew about the pill; her pregnancy was surely a sorry mistake; she had to live with the consequences and she had gone through with it. Her family had probably felt ashamed that a daughter of theirs could disgrace them so and with someone like Matthew, a nobody, so they had retreated back to Switzerland where she could be kept out of the way until the baby was born, and a replacement beau found for her. It did occur to Matthew once that maybe that was all she ever wanted from their relationship, a child, that would totally depend on her and love her, without the complications or mess of having to live with a man, although deep down he did not really believe that.

According to Sarah, the baby had been christened Sophie.

* * *

Thirty years passed from the end of their summer of love, without Matthew meeting Stephanie again. Thirty years for his unknown daughter to grow up and develop her own life, during which time Matthew had himself married and fathered two more children and had hardly thought about Stephanie or Sophie at all. But for some reason, a sudden curiosity, a creeping guilt, something had infiltrated into his thinking and Matthew felt compelled by a most persistent urge to meet her, his Sophie, to see what she was like, and to share with her the truth. Inexplicably. Even after thirty years.

And he felt the need to tell everyone about her at his daughter's wedding.

THREE
May All Your Dreams Come True

July 1997

1

The rain had stopped.

Outside darkness had engulfed the marquee; the atmosphere inside was uncomfortably warm, with that persistent background smell of damp. All eyes remained on Matthew Crawford, alone on the podium, standing tall, elegant in grey behind the black microphone stand, still looking in control. Nobody dared let their attention drift, for fear of missing something. Even the waiters had stopped moving about; a few were standing around the periphery, like statues, caught up in the tension of events. The level of background noise was strangely subdued. It appeared as though all the wedding guests were stuck in their positions. Until a baby in its pram gave out a feeble cry in the distance that broke the spell and a few felt the need to clear their throats.

Annabel had her gaze fixed firmly on her father, with a slightly pained and uncertain expression in the way her brows were wrinkled and her mouth puckered; she wanted him to finish.

After a long pause, since telling everyone that thirty years ago he had fallen in love with a girl called Stephanie, Matthew had come to the point in his oft-rehearsed speech, where he needed to wind down and draw to a close, so that the younger

121

characters in the ensemble could be allowed to do their turn. Douglas' best man was a red-headed Scot called Fergus with some funny tales to tell. Douglas himself would bring some reality into the proceedings with the usual mix for any newly-wed man of effusive gratitude to everyone for being there and complete astonishment at realizing the enormity of what he had just done.

'A lot of water has flowed under a lot of bridges since 1967.' Matthew needed to get away from the solemn mood that had pervaded the gathering and offer some frivolous advice on marriage. He had chipped an enormous chunk of heavy baggage off his chest and dropped it in the middle of his daughter's wedding, surprising and astonishing everyone. Annabel for one was probably feeling that this had neither been the time nor placc. He had to make amends.

'Today we are here to celebrate marriage: the triumph of hope over experience (Samuel Johnson called it); or of imagination over intelligence (as Oscar Wilde put it). A triumph, certainly. I've often wondered why the girl always wears white at her wedding, the standard answer being that white on the bride shows that this is the happiest day of her life. Sad then that the boy on the other hand so often wears black. Although I am pleased to see Douglas in his more colourful kilt.'

There was an ironic sigh among the guests, a sort of collective twist of the mouth into the semblance of a smile, but more in relief that the moment of confessional shock was over and that they could all now move more freely. There would be no more surprises; they could all relax.

'Auntie Mary always used to say whenever a girl feels like marrying a man, she should go and have lunch with his ex-wife. Most marriages are not actually made in Heaven, although *this one* probably was.' And he smiled hugely across at Annabel, mustering what he hoped was a look of sheer love but that Annabel probably took as an apology. 'We know that most marriages are the result of complete chance, like the throw of a dice: two young ideals coming together by chance to share a common dream. For a girl, marrying a man is like buying something you've been admiring in the shop window for some time – you may love it when you get it home but it doesn't always go with everything else. There is always that unpredictable sense of optimism and of hope. Marriage is an alliance between one person who never remembers a birthday and the other who never forgets one.'

Matthew paused, softened his features and smiled once again at his beautiful daughter. 'I think we are all witnessing the best day of Bel's life so far, and with Douglas, it feels natural and easy. In years to come, we will look back at this day with fondness, knowing that Douglas and Annabel made the right decision on their way to fulfilling their dream.

'Never have I doubted that Annabel would achieve what she wanted in her professional life and in her private life; that one day she would make a good wife and a terrific mother… just like her mother before her.' There was general sighing all around at this point. 'And in Douglas, I feel sure she has found her spiritual partner. I wish her and her new husband every success in all that they do – no one deserves that success more. I would therefore like to conclude with my most official duty and something that I am most proud to do: I would like to propose the toast.' And with that, Matthew rescued his recently topped-up glass of champagne from a nearby table, raised it in traditional fashion and said with a shake in his voice, 'To Annabel and Douglas, may all your dreams come true.'

His throat was sore and dry. Everyone stood with a great clattering of chairs and feet stamping, relieved to able to stretch their legs, and they raised their glasses, calling out the names proudly in unison. They sipped generously at their drinks. Matthew took a couple of sips himself and smiled broadly, before gulping the rest of the cool bubbly liquid. He turned away and approached Annabel with open arms. They embraced, their faces close and Annabel smeared a thin film of tears across his cheek, unsure whether it was her father's or hers.

And then someone at the back clapped their hands together and a few more joined in slowly to applaud, intermittently with no general coordination, but as Matthew moved from the place where he had stood for the last half hour, tired by the effort and emotional strain, but relieved and triumphant at what he saw as his success, the applause grew in strength and enthusiasm. He walked back to his seat at the top table near the old ladies, relishing the support from the guests, which was now developing into a genuine ovation, as they showed how they appreciated what Matthew had put into his effort.

Over the next half hour, he relived every moment in his mind, and could feel the laughter and clapping ringing in his ears. He hardly heard a word Douglas or his best mate said, his mind replaying over and over all of his own best moments, with the pauses and the inflections, for him to analyze from every angle, from every side, like the slow motion action replays of a televised football match.

He joined in with the laughter and clapping around the marquee as Fergus left the centre to return to his table, giving Annabel a kiss and a hug and Douglas a man-hug and punch on the shoulder on his way. They seemed to have relaxed again, and there were lots of happy looking people now milling around the marquee, although Caldecott at the entrance was asking people to wait for all the ceremonials to finish before leaving.

The wedding cake was to be cut, and the photographers had further work to do, flashing away at the happy couple wielding a huge carving knife in their hands over the white icing. On the top table, everyone was awake, and some were starting to push back their chairs, stand and stretch. Roger continued to study Alison's open cleavage and marveled for the nth time that afternoon how she managed to develop such deliberate nipples and whether he would get away with giving each one an impulsive tweak.

A head waiter was overseeing the distribution of small squares of cut cake to every table, whilst more champagne and coffee was served. Douglas felt in need of a breather and set off to check on further arrangements, grateful for the chance to involve himself in something different for a while. There were transport issues, some people looking to leave early now that the main events were over and wanting taxis to the station, furniture needed moving and he would check the disco team were happy with their set up.

Roger looked across at his father and caught his eye. With an urge to say something to him, although unsure what exactly, he managed a little smile. He had a deeply-felt regard for his father, his achievements and professional standards; he respected his cleverness, his intellect, his integrity, and was totally free of jealousy. Roger was relaxed about his family, happy for any of them to do whatever they wanted. He never spent any of his formative years conducting the teenage rebellion, rejecting his parents' values or trying to copy or better his father. He felt all that was so much a waste of time, when there were countryside pubs and walks to explore, music, clubs and girls to discover. His mother he missed, and today that missing affected him hard.

To Roger's way of thinking, he and his father had a good relationship, comfortable in each other's company and honest with each other's feelings, easily expressed. Partly this was down to Matthew's easy way with his children, his affability. Matthew had from an early age allowed them to express themselves as they wished; they had been able to develop their ideas in their own way without gross parental interference. There was discipline, but sensible and negotiable. And Roger liked that.

But his father had clearly confessed to something pretty major in his past life that he had kept to himself, which he had never felt the need to share with his children, and had presumably kept secret from Roger's mother. And which he could only find the courage to reveal in the somewhat protected environment of a family gathering, after she was dead. Roger was thinking that perhaps his mother had been betrayed and he was sure Annabel would be feeling the same. He had a slightly unpleasant taste in mouth as something close to anger bubbled inside.

And to do that on Annabel's wedding day, how selfish was that? He needed to talk to her before confronting his father. He got up casually, started to light a cigarette, and stepped over towards Matthew, still seated, patting him on his back muttering well done, good speech, very funny. He signaled to Annabel, who was standing with her bridesmaids hovering around her like a phalanx awaiting instruction, while she finished some wedding cake, and he headed out for some air. Alison seemed occupied, leaning over towards Auntie Mary to hear what she was saying.

Annabel was stunned, like Roger, feeling betrayed in some way; this was something she rightfully felt she should have known about before, and not something to learn about at her wedding reception. She slumped in her chair, for a moment, lacking drive or energy, unsure how to respond. She felt speechless, as the meaning of her father's words were sinking in. The noises and movements going on all around the marquee were muffled and dulled so that nothing registered, like listening to a piece of music under water.

Then she stood up, dismissing her entourage, and tried

to focus on the affable figure of her handsome father, while he was listening distractedly to other conversation across the table, and whom she might now need to assess in a different light. She lowered herself awkwardly in her bulky dress next to him.

'So what now, Dad? Any more surprises?' Her voice was solid, although that was not quite how she felt inside, and sarcasm was not her usual tack. Matthew, still in a little world of his own, was drinking gratefully a cup of coffee and clicked out of his reverie at the sound of Annabel's voice. He leant affectionately toward her as she placed a hand on his arm and then manoeuvred herself and her chair around so that she could look straight at him. 'That was lovely and really good, but why the surprise?' She was controlling her feelings, whatever they were; she did not really want to show any emotions or have a row, especially not here and not now. Matthew looked tired, his face was shiny and he stared deep into the cup held with both hands, pausing, before looking at her. Annabel's two grandmothers were struggling up together, and they were clinging onto one another as they set off towards the toilets. Annabel could see that they would have to negotiate the step down from the dais and so sprang up to help them across. 'You okay, Grannies, need any help?'

They both murmured lovely, dear, yes, absolutely fine, how are you, you do look wonderful. 'Your father is an exceptional man and he is so very proud of you, well done,' Minnie said with genuine affection, giving Annabel her best toothy grin and patting her bare arm.

Matthew twisted around to watch his beautiful child, innocent, angelic in cream silk and purple touches, slightly flushed, cascading ringlets, helping the old ladies safely down steps; always helping others, that was Annabel. He was thinking how Rachel should have been here, God damn it, to see their daughter, she would be heaving with pride. He would talk to Rachel later, giving her a full report of the entire day's events, when he was alone, which was something he was pretty much looking forward to. He would tell her everything about Stephanie and his surprise first daughter. It was what he wanted, had planned for really; he had got so much off his chest today and out into the open, but still had not spoken directly to Rachel. He might have overdone it a bit, and presumably that was what was making Annabel look so agitated. He half stood up himself and realized he was feeling a little drunk with the pleasure of his performance if not the champagne.

'Yes, good speech, Dad.'

Annabel returned to her chair, sinking down carefully among the folds of her dress. There were other people hovering close, wanting to say things to Annabel, to kiss her, congratulate her, impart words of wisdom, and a small queue was forming, which included her boss, some friends from work, old school mates, cousins.

She leant towards him. 'It was really good, thanks for those things you said; you know, it was quite funny. And brave.' She smiled with a little irony. 'I miss Mum so much and I know you do too.' Now her eyes started to prick and she had to wipe a finger nail carefully along the under edge of her lower eyelids, in danger of smearing the mascara. She realized there was no time for conversation now but Matthew started to move his lips and was saying something.

'I'm going to find her.'

'What?'

'I want to find her.'

'Who, who do you mean?' Annabel was beginning to feel indignant but remained aware of the need for calm and understanding. She was trying not to judge him, but just the whole issue of honesty within the family over the years, and honesty with her mother, this felt big to her, and today was just not the best of occasions to start telling everybody. Why had he waited until this moment to reveal this most personal of memories, and in front of so many people, some complete strangers?

'Sophie. Sophie, my daughter. Your step sister. I need to find her and meet her. Wouldn't you like to meet her?'

2

It was much later on in the evening, when a complete blanket of darkness had descended over the valley, that Matthew and Annabel were able to have a more fruitful conversation. Father and daughter had taken a turn arm in arm around the garden, following the lantern-lit paths, the night air damp and pungent with verdant freshness, carrying the scents of jasmine and wild honeysuckle. She had found a woolen shawl against the night chill. His silk cravat hung loose around his opened shirt collar and he was still wearing his grey tails. They returned to the Stirling house through a side door and found themselves alone in a small sitting room. The house was quieter now, many of the guests having left and an evening meal was being prepared in the big kitchen for the few that remained. The happy couple were not flying off to the Canaries for their honeymoon until tomorrow. They could still hear disco music coming from the marquee and imagined a few strong-minded revelers remaining to dance and drink the night away.

'It has been so long, what, thirty years since you last saw this woman, and you've never seen the girl.'

'Sophie.'

'Yes, Sophie, so why would you want to see her now, after all this time? She doesn't know about you, does she?

What makes you think she would want to see you? Have you been in touch?' Annabel was trying not to get emotional, controlling her voice which tended to squeak at the end of all her stuttering questions. Matthew was shaking his head, mostly giving no as his common answer.

Annabel prized her tight shoes off and aired her stockinged feet. She was feeling oddly deflated, the excitement of her day spoiled by his revelation that she had an older sister, that some other child had preceded her. She presumed her father thought that she would be excited by the news but she was not, and was now worrying that this was going to spoil the start of her honeymoon holiday. Just out of the blue, your father tells the world that he actually fathered another child before you ever existed, and sorry, but he forgot to tell you, and he wants to find her and introduce her to you, and expects you to be nice and friendly to her.

'Dad, this is ridiculous, you don't know anything about her. She presumably is under the illusion that her father is someone else. You can't just walk into someone's life and turn it upside down. Where does she live, anyway?'

'I don't know,' he said quietly after a moment's pause, with a slight shake of his head.

There was silence between them. Annabel was looking at her hands clasped in her lap, fiddling with a stray purple ribbon. She was chewing her lower lip, something Matthew had not seen her do since she was a small child worrying about school. Matthew's expression was serene, untroubled, a heavy weight lifted from his shoulders. He had made up his mind, a decision had been taken and he knew precisely what he was going to do. Nobody was going to shake his resolve. He had lived for this day over the last few months and had planned to use it as a starting off point. He could not proceed with the plan until he had got this day out of the way, his second daughter safely married.

'I met your mother over a year later, when I realized obviously that I was not going to be seeing Stephanie again. I had blocked out Stephanie and the baby from my mind, I had worked fiercely hard at everything after that summer to take my mind off the events, so that I could forget. I told no one, my mother didn't know. And I met Rachel at college, by chance and found her to be so… so sweet. She swept me off my feet, literally, and we fell in love with each other, and we had two children, and there was never a time or a cause for me to tell her about Stephanie or Sophie. Why would I ever have told any of you, the circumstances never warranted it. It never came up, it was in a past life, if you like, there was no overlap. I hadn't had an affair with some bit of fluff, and then got her pregnant. These were consecutive events and I was caught up, in love, in the circumstances which controlled everything.' He was pleading for Annabel to understand. 'Rachel didn't go into details with me about former boyfriends when we met. Neither did I with her.'

Matthew held his hands up in front of him like he was holding an imaginary object, delicate and in need of protection, trying to express to Annabel the powerful urges involved in his situation. 'Girlfriends, obviously, not boyfriends.' He spoke firmly, the pitch of his voice under complete control. He did not understand why she was having such trouble with the news, it changed nothing in reality. He wanted to talk to Rachel in private and clear his thoughts, and then gather his resolve for a re-start.

'But when your mother died,' and he went quiet again, his lips dry and quivering and his throat still sore from his extended earlier speech, 'and I was alone, again, and bereft and missing her, I started to re-live the loss I had felt before, it's almost a physical thing, you feel frightened that you might die alone, it's scary. Like drowning. I should have talked to someone about this, I admit, but I had no one really.'

'You could have talked to me,' Annabel pounced, harshly, 'at any time. Or Pauline, or Sue or Henry and Marcia, these are all your friends. Or Maurice, he loves you, he could have helped.'

'Annabel, I have talked to these friends, but not about the Stephanie episode, there seemed no point. I needed to work this out for myself.'

They both sat still for a while. The distant thudding of dance music and the clattering of someone next door preparing for the meal sounded more intrusive. And then the door banged open as a deep brown Labrador nosed its way in and flopped at Annabel's feet, enjoying the fuss of her hands around its soft ears. It was pitch black outside and the low brown leather couches and patterned carpet and small television in the corner were perfectly reflected off the uncurtained glass panes.

'You should appreciate the people around you, Dad. They expect it and they are upset when you bypass them. Did Maurice know about this before today?'

Matthew was shaking his head. 'I wanted so much to make amends today, for all the years I have failed you, Annabel. I just wanted to express how much I care about you. It seems I overdid things, or failed to get it right.'

'Dad, you have not failed me, ever; you've always been there for me.'

Matthew and Rachel had enjoyed being parents, together. They had worried endlessly about their children, like all parents, but were able to let go as they grew up, giving them more responsibility for the things they did and the decisions they made. The two children had arrived early in their marriage, so losing the advantage of having some dedicated time together, to get to know each other better as a couple; but as a consequence they had had to learn parenthood together, as they went along and found that both of them were good at it, sharing the chores and the duties and all the fun bits too. Matthew loved the smell and warmth of their baby skins, their cuddles at bath time and at bedtime were the best moments of all. He remembered so much they did together, watching games from the cold touchline of many a school pitch, helping with homework sitting round a kitchen table in the early evenings, with weekend trips when transport was needed. Matthew did not slope off to football matches with his mates on a Saturday afternoon or disappear to the golf course on a Sunday; when they went out they would all go together, to friends' houses, or walks along the river, or to the local gym and tennis club.

But finding the family time for activities became increasingly difficult, as later during the teenager stage, Matthew and Rachel both went through their own career pressures. Working lives become busier and children confide in their own friends often before their parents. But then later motherless and searching for peace of mind, Annabel had felt the need to seek his closer understanding. Matthew well remembered a wet afternoon in Cambridge, when she had poured her heart out to him sitting among the strong smelling coffees and sticky chocolate brownies in a corner café on Sydney Street.

She claimed that she never knew if Matthew was happy with her or was pleased with the work she had done; he never made her feel special to him. How could she please him, what did she have to do? She had just won a seat on the student's college council, after a week of heavy lobbying, which she felt was impressive, given that she was shy and struggled with public appearances, but Matthew had seemed indifferent to her success. Just like when she had won a music scholarship to sixth form he had said well done and all that, but was he really impressed? He should have been, this was Godolphin School, among the hardest scholarships for any pupils to get.

She didn't feel his pleasure, just more demands from him to work harder towards other successes.

'We always had to achieve. You drummed it into me and Roger that there was no point doing anything unless you did it well, to the best of your ability, better than the next person, and always striving to do it better still next time.' Annabel by now was fingering a small white cotton handkerchief, and occasionally sniffing and wiping the end of her nose with it. 'We never went on holiday without some challenge to achieve by the end, whether it was flying a kite or riding the beach donkey, composing a competition winning poem or whatever, we had to achieve something by the end.'

'So was that so bad?' Matthew was mildly amused, knowing that his children were natural talents and always obtained good results, and actually only needed a little prompting and encouragement from him. 'Is that not just learning good discipline? And did that not result in you and Roger succeeding in all sorts of things that you can be proud of, and maybe my nagging you just a little helped you in getting there, reaching fulfillment? No?' Matthew had wanted her to laugh, but Annabel, oblivious to the other customers bustling around their table in that little café, seemed about to burst, an overflow of built-up anguish.

And now, those feelings returned even on her wedding day. 'Dad, it continues into my adult life, I always think that I must do better so that my father will be impressed, but then you never are, or you never seem to be. I never know if I have pleased you, whether you thought something I had done was worthwhile. I sometimes have felt so useless, and now it is obvious that your real desire is to fulfill some other dream, for someone else, your first born you tell us; who no doubt when you find her will be lavished with all your praise and attention, to the further exclusion of Roger and me.' At which point Annabel was standing and turning away, to wipe her eyes. In mild surprise, the dog heaved himself up as well.

'Roger and I, Annabel, didn't they teach you anything in school?'

'This is no time for silly jokes,' she stuttered, stamping belligerently towards the door. 'I don't even know if you approve of Douglas or not.'

Matthew stood up as well and reached for her arm, but she had moved away, her chest heaving and with a feeble sob, she left the room with a swish of her dress. Both the dog and Matthew were disappointed, standing alone together in the dark room, with the conversation only half finished. He could smell the tired scent from the deformed rosebud at his lapel.

3

Matthew returned to Chiswick the next day in the Volvo alone, arriving in the evening after seven hours on the motorway, feeling stiff and somewhat deflated. He poured himself a large glass of chilled white wine from the fridge and stuffed his mouth with chunks of cheese, before slumping in a settee and commiserating with a fluffy tabby-cat on his lap, looking out over the garden in the fading light. The quietness in the house enveloped him. He remembered the times when the place was filled with people, young family and friends, with noise and laughter, music and fun. Instead his days now looked empty and solitary. He missed having someone who would be there for him when he returned from work, someone to welcome him home, to warm his heart and calm his brow, like those old days. Someone he could care for and love in return, someone to make him feel that his future life was worthwhile and had a purpose. 'Only *you* know how I feel, don't you, Rachel,' he croaked aloud.

Annabel had given him a warm-hearted hug that morning, outside the hotel when he left, and said clearly into his ear that she loved him and would support him in whatever he needed to do and that he should keep her informed on events.

All the way down the motorway, speaking openly,

tearfully with Rachel in his head, informing her on events, he felt as if he had had a companion with him and the time had passed quite easily. He frequently looked forward to being alone with her in his conversation, with some space and peace around him. And in this, he was sure she understood why he had never told her about Stephanie or Sophie. He had reached across to the empty seat next to him, imagining her fingers tracing over the wobbly veins on the back of his hand. He had whispered his thoughts and asked for her forgiveness, reassuring her of his complete devotion to her during her lifetime and since. They had had such a good life, hadn't they, with their family, their careers: why had it all come to an end at forty-two? It did not make sense.

His quest for Sophie would help fill in a gaping hole in his life.

A few months ago, fingering aimlessly through the bric-a-brac of his life, in old shoe boxes and files on his study shelves, stuff that he had collected piece by piece over the years from his earliest school days onwards, he came across the only photograph he possessed of Stephanie. Under a heap of old pamphlets, programmes, notices, exam results, and other memorabilia, even ticket stubs for concerts and museums, every little thing collected, nothing it would seem ever being thrown out, he found some colour prints, one of his sixth form school friends from their last party taken on Rick's sunny lawn, a team picture of the school cricket eleven with their coach in front of the pavilion, and, at the very bottom of the box-file, a flattened photograph that she had given him that summer, that he had not seen for years. The colours were well-preserved, the surface shiny and unscratched; and there she was, a raven haired teenager with long bare legs and smouldering eyes. It had been taken in the holidays by her father he guessed in their garden in Lausanne, distant hills and forests blurred in the background, bright sunshine catching the rim of her washed hair, all fluffed up and a little caught in a breeze, that framed her lightly tanned face. Looking self-conscious but determined in a pink loose shirt over a bikini, she was trying to smile but only managed a resentful smirk. The picture had been hidden away all these years and Rachel had never seen it, as far as he knew.

He trimmed its edges and found a wooden frame for it, covering another old photo, and had placed it on his desk. And as he had looked at it, every day these past few weeks, he was increasingly troubled by thoughts of responsibility, that he owed it to Stephanie to at least contact her and find out how she was, how life was treating her. And to his offspring, he owed her something, didn't he? He had no idea whether Sophie knew of his existence, most probably not. Had Stephanie had any more children, how had her life panned out? All his old memories had poured back across his mind, causing joy and pain in equal measure and these thoughts had started to nag him. He paid a visit to Auntie Mary a month ago in Eastbourne, seeking her impartial advice. She had been perfectly discreet when they met at the wedding, bless her, not mentioning to anyone about his clandestine visit.

It had been a useful afternoon and their conversation had helped Matthew with his thoughts. He had decided that day that he would reach back into these past events and mention them in his wedding speech, after Auntie Mary had given him some encouragement, albeit with a warning that it might upset certain parties, to tell his story. She thought it was perfectly reasonable however, and then the family could decide how they felt and how they wanted to play it; it was not up to Matthew to dictate that to them.

'I think you were caught up in the circumstances of the times, my boy,' Auntie Mary had said, shaking her great head gently and spraying her usual cloud of fine dust around her.

She was pouring shakily yet another cup of tea, from an old Staffordshire pot that had a beaming round cheeked country woman's face fashioned on it. 'I think you have behaved as you should, there was no reason why you would have burdened Rachel with this story. And certainly no reason why Annabel and Roger should have been told.' Matthew sipped his tea, looking out the window across the gardens and coast road, away over to the murky flat sea beyond. For a moment he wished that he could stay there longer, sharing his thoughts with the fathomless waters that washed the nearby coast line, and not have to bother about any of the family at all.

'It's not always as quiet as this, I can assure you, when those bitter easterly winds blow up the channel, the sea can get quite rough and waves thrash over the front terraces down there.' Auntie Mary was managing to stand next to Matthew at her little bay window, and she put a large arm across his back. He turned and kissed her on a cheek, 'Thank you, Auntie Mary, for your wisdom and advice. And for the tea. And I am really looking forward to seeing you at the wedding. I hope the journey does not upset you too much.'

'Taking it in stages, dear boy, we will be fine, I'm sure.'

Matthew drove away late in the afternoon, his belly swilling with tea, but pleased that he had had his plans reinforced by someone whose opinion he valued; notwithstanding that she had never had any children of her own and was not actually a blood member of the family, he reminded himself.

One morning, about a week after the wedding, Matthew spoke to Auntie Mary on the phone. 'And what was Roger's reaction?' she was asking, once Matthew explained that he had had a longer chat with Annabel and Roger the day after, before he left the hotel for the drive back to London.

'Oh, Roger was Roger, laid back as ever, apparently unconcerned. You know, do what you have to do, Dad, it's up to you, that kind of thing. He was a little upset that I used Annabel's wedding for the announcement, he didn't quite see the point of that. What do you think of Alison, by the way, I meant to ask you, did you like her?'

'Yes, a little cold, perhaps; I mean, not just the flimsy dress,' she laughed at her own humour, 'I mean she didn't seem too warm a personality, but I may be wrong. Are they close, are they an item, is that what we say?'

'I don't know, really, Roger never talks about these things, but they've been together as long as he has been with any of his girlfriends before, about six weeks now, I think.'

4

Matthew crossed over Richmond Green and the perimeter road, late afternoon sunshine bathing everything in a bright light. He approached one of the middle Victorian houses in a terraced row of four, which had a tall porch entrance, with pillars either side and black and white chequered tiled steps outside. Expensive looking cars were lined up along both sides of the road, but the empty off-road asphalted slot in front of the house indicated Maurice was not yet back. Shadowy movements could be seen beyond the leaded decorative glass door panels. He pulled at the bell attached with an old brass knob on the grand façade and heard the tinkling inside. A dog barked instantly and would not stop, despite the shrill voice of Pauline shouting at him. 'Pete. Shut up. Stop it, damn you. Down.'

The door flew open. 'Hello, Matthew.' They embraced tightly as usual. Pauline seemed larger than Matthew remembered and he had trouble getting right around her. Pete jumped up, placing his big paws onto Matthew's shoulders. He would have licked his face too, only Matthew did not fancy his wet smelly breath, so grabbed him by his ears and wrestled him to the floor, where the dog rolled onto its back, submitting completely with his legs paddling the air. Matthew could have strangled him and Pete would not have minded, probably would not have noticed, so long as he was being paid some attention.

'Sit yourself in the lounge there, I think Tom has got some school programme on, change it if you want. I will get us some tea; I think I've got some chocolate cake somewhere, left over from Billy's birthday party, and then you can tell me all about it.' Pauline disappeared and Mathew could hear her busying away in the adjacent kitchen. 'Maurice should not be too long tonight, it's Friday, so he's usually back soon after five,' she called out from the doorway. Matthew watched the view across the neat garden, where sparrows and a blue tit were pecking at a net-bag of nuts hanging from a wooden post, and out over the fields that ran down to the water's edge of the Thames.

He crouched on the floor with the dog in the lounge, spoiling him for a while, till the tea came with cake and biscuits. Tom and Billy, the younger sons, were nowhere about and Pauline turned the TV down, continuing her conversation almost without pause.

'You gave us a little shock actually last weekend, we thought we knew all about you, you dark little horse.' She sounded friendly enough, as she poured the tea and then passed the cup and saucer over.

Matt sat in a soft chair and smiled. 'It wasn't entirely deliberate, you know, it was circumstances.'

'So why did you decide to tell us at all, especially on Annabel's day?'

Although he had known Pauline a long time and was usually comfortable enough to talk to her about anything, today he was just not feeling up to it; he had not come over here to be interrogated, neither did he feel he had to justify his actions. 'I just felt I should, to legitimize her, to explain who she was if she was to appear suddenly, you know, everyone would have heard of her. And by telling the story at the wedding I had the best possible audience, so I won't have to repeat myself to every different aunt or friend I am going to meet over the next year.'

'So what are you planning, Matt, does Bel approve?'

'I am going to start by looking for Stephanie.'

'The mother. Any idea where she is?'

'No, not really.'

'Do you have a photo or anything? Will you know what she looks like after all these years?' Pauline peppered him with questions, giving him little chance with answering calmly.

'No, I never had a camera then. But Stephanie gave me this one from her house in Maidstone,' and Matthew passed the framed picture over to Pauline that he had been carrying in a plastic bag. 'No, I mean I still picture her as she was at eighteen – but I'm pretty sure I would recognize her if we met. I need to talk to Maurice, about the next steps, you know.'

'Are you staying tonight, for dinner, do you need a bed?'

Matthew said he would, if she didn't mind, for dinner, but he would go home to his bed. And within a few minutes after Pauline had left to prepare things in the kitchen, he was lazing back on a soft sofa, the TV quietly playing in the background and the *Evening Standard* draped like a tent across his outstretched legs, beginning to nod off. There was the distant rumble of traffic and children playing in the background. Pete was stretched out under his legs, occasionally scratching, or grunting as if chasing something in a dream, and letting off doggy smells which added to the soporific warmth of the room. Matthew had nothing else to hang onto in his mind, as he let the tiredness that had been building up over the last few weeks overwhelm him. The paper slid to the floor over the dog and the *Six o'clock News* came and went.

Maurice arrived nearer to seven o'clock, his key in the outside lock immediately alerting Pete, who suddenly scrambled up from his sleep, barking loudly in a frenzy of excitement. Maurice was swamped by the dog in the hall and it took him ages to get through into the lounge, retreating backwards into the room, and fending the beast off good humourdly. He managed to press the door shut with the animal on the other side, flattening his back against it, holding his body still as he tried to get his breath back. And listening intently, like playing a target on the run, so if he was quiet enough, his pursuer would give up and look elsewhere.

'Hi, Matthew, my friend,' and Matthew and Maurice came together in a bear hug with some added backslapping.

After a wholesome dinner of pasta and grilled chicken strips with an avocado salad, followed by something sticky with chocolate that Maurice devoured eagerly (being a definite pudding man), that Pauline tucked into enthusiastically (being a definite pudding woman), but that Matthew declined, saying he would just have some fruit and coffee, they all three wandered into the lounge and flopped onto various couches.

'So where are you going to begin, Matthew?'

'Good question. Sophie, who will be about thirty, could be anywhere in the world; she may be married, obviously with a different surname, I don't know. I need to find Stephanie first. Now I don't know whether she is still in Switzerland, or wherever. Her surname was Patek, but she sometimes used her mother's name, Cross. She did marry someone else in Switzerland apparently, soon after she left England, her mother told me in a letter once, but I don't know the name.'

'So you've not got much to go on really, have you? I mean Somerset House isn't going to be much use, you're not looking for births or deaths, are you? What about marriages, if she was married in the UK, you might find that, but not if she had been married abroad, they would not have any record. What about local registry office, in Kent, you said?'

'Yes, she lived in the family home in Maidstone, in 1967.'

'Of course that wouldn't tell you where she had moved to. You could ask the people living in the Maidstone house, I assume her mum's not there anymore.'

'Doubt it.'

'OK. So you could follow a trail from the house in Kent, and see whether anyone can identify where the Patek/Cross family moved to. The local electoral roll at the council, they list names and addresses. What about the last census, in the UK, when was that? Would that help?'

'Well, you might find her father, Patek; the census would be listed under the male name of the household,' Pauline said.

'Would her mother still be alive now, how old would she be?' Maurice probed.

Matthew sipped at his coffee, screwed his face up as he thought out loud. 'She was probably early forties, that was thirty years ago, so she must be seventy-two or three now. She could well be alive. So looking up Cross might lead to Steph's mother.' He pulled a bit of a doubtful face, 'But her mother would not be welcoming to me, I doubt; she would not help, I'm sure.'

'You never know. I could always go and see her, pretend to be someone else,' Maurice suggested, trying to be positive and he even managed to sound quite enthusiastic. 'She might have forgiven you after thirty years. No?' He glanced sideways at Matthew, his eyebrows ascending a notch or two up his forehead, with a little sympathetic smile just curling his lips. 'She wouldn't have to see you necessarily.'

'That's an idea, thank you, Maurice. Actually I may need to use some sort of professional agency, if I get nowhere. She had a sister, Daphne. Older by two or three years. She was clothes designing in London in 1967. Daphne Patek, she was but probably married, with another name now. Worth a try: she would know where Stephanie was. And then there was

Sarah, Steph's friend at Upper Wycheside, they might have kept up some correspondence for a while. And a girl called Louise, she was always hanging around her. I could try the school for addresses. Or the Old Girls' Society.'

Maurice wiped a palm over his facial hair and caressed his beard. After a pause, while staring hard at his friend, he persisted. 'Can I speak as I feel, Matt?'

Matthew smiled, 'Has it ever been otherwise?'

'Matt, surely you have better things to do than chase after this girl, whom you have never met; thirty years have gone by without you doing anything about it, till now. Thirty years is a long time. And for what? What are you going to gain? Some emotional satisfaction? Are you going to be able to develop a father-daughter relationship – like you have with Annabel? Or will you end up upsetting Annabel and Roger, disturbing what are really good relationships. Or are *you* going to be emotionally shattered: they might turn against you, these lost women from the past, mother and daughter, claim damages and costs from a wayward father, as some kind of recompense.' Maurice sat forward, genuine concern on his face. 'Listen, mate, whatever you want to do I will help if I can, but are you sure about all this?'

Matthew was nothing if not determined and once set on a course, he knew he had to follow it up. But he was comforted by Maurice's honesty. He had thought through all of his friend's doubts, had thought about them endlessly night after night, and could only conclude that the desire to own up to his responsibilities and the aching need to meet a child of his, however much time had passed, was overwhelming. 'Yes, I am absolutely sure.'

Pauline was unusually quiet during these exchanges, listening but saying little; she was probably thinking exactly the same as Maurice, about the futility of Mathew's quest, that Matthew was being selfish. But then she piped up:

'Maurice, you don't want to be getting involved with these family affairs, this is very personal to Matthew. Anyway you've got a busy schedule ahead, before we go on holiday at the beginning of next month. We're going to Gran Canaria, it should be lovely, this time of the year.'

'Um, that will be nice, the weather should be just right. You playing golf there, Maurice?'

'I'm sure I'll be taking the clubs, yes, if Pauline allows.'

'Or croquet, perhaps,' Matthew mused with a little chuckle.

5

About two weeks after his daughter's wedding day, with the happy couple still away on their honeymoon, Matthew was driving alone once again in the big Volvo up through the West Midlands, with numerous music CDs from the Sixties and Seventies to entertain him, returning after thirty years to his old school. His thoughts were scattered with the pleasant memories of the event, the delight at seeing Annabel looking so beautiful, the friendliness and relaxed atmosphere, the easy going nature of hosts Margaret and Arthur. And his speech kept returning in snatches, able to recall word for word all the jokes, the applause and laughter still ringing in his ears. One of Annabel's girl friends had touched his arm just afterwards, saying how moved she had been, how sensitive and funny he was, if only her own father could talk so openly to them like that. Others had approached him with warm sympathy and support.

It was at boarding school in Worcestershire that he had spent five formative years away from home, overcoming the anxieties and uncertainties of growing up, years that transformed him from child to young man. His mind was basking in a plethora of memories as he rediscovered the gentle countryside, with its meandering rivers and small townships, much of it hardly altered over the time gap. The place had preserved a timeless feel, with its wide tree-lined avenues and small colourful parks. He approached from the flat valley to the east, seeing the familiar line of grey hills rising up in the distance ahead of him, while dark clouds loomed overhead with a slightly forbidding look.

It was late July and warm, but a storm was brewing up for later. He was hoping to get to Upper Wycheside and his prearranged meeting with the headmistress by four o'clock, back at her school desk especially for him, but there was always work to be done, preparations ahead for the coming term, so she had said.

The main school buildings looked familiar, like Victorian workhouses, although much had been added on since, red brick and dull. He crept past the house he remembered the girls had lived in back in the Sixties, where they hosted their Sunday tea-parties, looking up at the windows, but he did not get to go inside. He was kept waiting a short time sitting calmly on a leather Chesterfield outside Miss Stokesley's office, in a shadowy oak-lined waiting area at the top of the main flight of stairs, with glass covered photos of past head mistresses and school governors on the walls, and the school crest and Latin motto fixed boldly above a cold stone fireplace.

Miss Stokesley had sounded pleasant and efficient on the phone. She came out of the office and called him quietly in, introducing herself with a show of pleasure, a large smile and a stiff handshake. She was well made-up with a fresh perm and wore a green two-piece and sensible shoes. She was quite intrigued by Matthew's visit, a little in awe of a Professor from London. She spoke with a plum in her mouth and looked every bit the school mistress spinster. Matthew had spun a yarn about a promising female student who attended the University College Mathematics Department in London at the end of the Sixties and had written several extremely advanced theses, which were undiscovered at that time, until recently when past works were being audited and several of the senior staff had selected her along with one or two others whom they would like to consider for a recognition award, as they were approaching the 250ᵗʰ anniversary of the founding of their college during the reign of George II. They wanted to trace this girl to interview her and invite her to take part in the celebrations next summer, which Matthew reliably informed Miss Stokesley would be a pretty lavish affair. They were inviting many of their past alumni, from all over the world, and Stephanie Patek was one person they wanted to consider. She had been at Upper Wycheside School in 1966 and 1967, and as Matthew himself had spent five years of his youth at the boy's college, it seemed appropriate, and an opportunity for him to revisit Wycheside, for him to pursue the matter himself, with Miss Stokesley's help and permission, naturally.

'Naturally, I would like to help. I think it's a wonderful idea, and will of course ultimately reflect on us here at Upper Wycheside School if she receives some sort of recognition.'

'Oh absolutely, Miss Stokesley, without a doubt, this would be a nice little bit of publicity for you and the school.'

'Although I am a little amazed that after thirty years this is still relevant.'

'Well, it's recognition of work done, over as many years and generations that we can find. The original contributions or even just a mention of the names would be worthwhile, but if we can trace the people involved then so much the better, so much more convincing.'

'Yes, I'm sure. But will you be able to find her on the basis of her home address of thirty years ago?'

Miss Stokesley had already been to the bursar's office to fetch the school diaries and registers, related to the years Matthew had suggested earlier on the phone. She was now standing over her desk, leaning forward and stooping, a pair of dark rimmed glasses on her nose, and a steady hand with red nail varnished fingers studying the old pages in a leather-bound volume that she had selected from the pile. Matthew was drawn towards her and found himself leaning forwards to peer over her shoulder at the list of names in the left hand column, as her bright-tipped forefinger moved slowly down the stiff pages with faint blue lines, while she pedantically read out the surnames line by line. He was surprised and a little repulsed to detect the smell of cigarettes about her.

In the Sixties, entries in the school register were all made by the bursar personally by hand, she explained, in black ink in lovely flowing script. 'As you can see, the bursar at that time was Mr. Arnold Hopewell and his signature after each terms' entries of new girls is clearly seen, with the date written in tiny Roman numerals just underneath the 'well' at the end of his name. He was a very tidy calligrapher. Although I was not here at this school at that time, obviously,' she quickly exclaimed with an in-drawing of breath and a stifled guffaw.

'Are you encumbered with children of your own, Professor?'

'Yes, er, two; they are older now, away and married and things,' Matthew stuttered as he became aware of the slight physical contact with Miss Stokesley's shoulder.

'So Stephanie Patek entered school in September 1965, you say? And she left in the summer term of 1967. Stephanie Patek?' Miss Stokesley was deliberately and slowly turning over the large pages.

'Yes, that was her father's name, he was a Swiss national. But I think she started with her mother's name, Cross; they thought it sounded easier, or something.'

The columns had names in alphabetical order, dates of birth and age stated, name of parent or guardian and home (or contact) address and telephone number.

'Here we are,' Miss Stokesley suddenly squawked with

excitement. Her finger had stopped half way down the list of names on a particular page, for the entry year September 1965, "Cross, after Crest and before Dane, Stephanie, born 18th February 1949, age 16, parent/guardian Mr Mathias Patek, Mrs Rosemary Cross, of 23 Woodside Avenue, Maidstone, Kent. Telephone MAD 6691." The old telephone numbers, but you should be able to get the code from the BT phone book.' She was clearly delighted with her find.

Matthew's knees felt a little weak for a moment by the sheer thrill of seeing her name in the entry, as an adrenalin rush hit his chest and muscles with an unexpected force. He pictured her wind-blown face in the town High Street the day they shopped together, and could almost hear her husky voice saying how much she enjoyed being with him, and how she wanted him to meet her mother.

'May I?' he asked, with a charming smile, reaching for the large volume as he edged his way along the desk, easing Miss Stokesley sideways. He sank backwards into the headmistress's chair and reached into an inside jacket pocket for a notebook and pen. He jotted down the details but at the same time quickly scanned other names, in the short list for that term. He was looking for a couple of Stephanie's friends: Louise, who had always been hanging around and Sarah, who was Jolyon's girlfriend at the time. God, it was Jolyon who had introduced Matthew and Stephanie in the first place and who had advised him strongly not to mix with her. Both these girls would probably have kept in touch and might be able to supply further help with his quest. And he found both quickly, Sarah Beal with an address in Chelmsford and Louise Lumley, living in Bexleyheath. He jotted down both names and addresses and telephone numbers and felt triumphant as he turned to Miss Stokesley, shutting the great volume of the book with a pleasing thud, 'Well, that has been *so* helpful.'

He was able to leave the headmistress's office a few minutes later, despite her protestations for him to stay for a well-earned cup of tea and a slice of Madeira cake, with profuse handshaking and head nodding, with all the details that he needed, his notebook tucked back into his jacket.

Matthew would start ringing around as soon as he returned to London tomorrow, and was prepared to visit those addresses if he needed to. But first he drove down to the town and parked by the big supermarket next to the Winter Gardens. He walked out to the main street, which sloped steeply upwards towards the Hills, with its lining of familiar looking shops. He went into the grounds of the Abbey to sit on the same bench that Stephanie and he had sat on to talk together that same afternoon under the giant cedar tree. Nothing seemed to have changed, although the laurel hedge was bigger, but even the flowering honeysuckle growing over the outer wall smelt the same. Then he tried to find Carters, but it had gone, replaced by a travel agent and a few other new shops, which saddened him, when he reflected on the role and fundamental influence that the old music shop had made on him and so many of his friends at that time.

He knew her details well: Stephanie's birthday, February 18, 1949, to her Swiss father Mathias Patek and English mother, Rosemary. By the time Matthew met her at school she was eighteen, and according to his memory her parents were divorcing, with her father returning to Switzerland where he had business interests and Stephanie residing with her mother at the family home in Maidstone. Which family home he had already visited, and where he had enjoyed a very dirty weekend, thank you, and very nice it was too.

In his pocket Matthew found the letter that he had received shortly after Stephanie had abandoned him, from her mother and signed Rosemary Cross; the blue paper a bit creased, telling him in no uncertain terms to forget Stephanie altogether now that she had returned to have her baby in Switzerland. Presumably the family had gathered together around her, her father non too pleased, Rosemary there to support her through her pregnancy, divorce proceedings delayed, their Kent home abandoned, perhaps for good. Stephanie would "not be returning to England and would not be contacting him."

The matter was closed.

Matthew sat turning the letter around in his long fingers, enjoying the memories of the day they sat on that bench by the Abbey in the sunshine, Stephanie openly smoking a cigarette in her frumpy school uniform. He could smell the freshness of the churchyard even as a few heavy raindrops began to splatter over the old stone path. Threatening cloud above had darkened the skies further, just as Matthew's eyes had filmed over at such compelling memory recall. Stephanie had gone off with another boy who had been willing to take her on with her new child and so she would have acquired another surname, he presumed. And had probably had a half-dozen more children since and was living God knew where. And Sophie at twenty-nine could be anywhere.

He had no raincoat or umbrella with him.

6

Matthew's search for his long-forgotten daughter was on. The numbers he had obtained from his Upper Wycheside School visit needed updating and British Telecom's Directory Enquiries were helpful. His first call was to the Maidstone address where a man told him firmly that he had bought the house about three years ago from a property developer and paid over the odds, don't mind telling you, and did not know of any previous owners and had never heard of Rosemary Cross.

It was mid-July, the long days and pleasant weather giving the impression that there was an endless amount of time available, plenty of time before the next academic term began at the end of September. He had soon sent off his first enquiries and knew that he had a few days to wait for the replies.

Early the following week, he attended his office, overlooking Gower Street, to go through some routine and set out his planned academic charts and agenda for the coming year. He had made his reputation in the early Nineties on chaos theory, much to his surprise, using it in mathematical algorithms to predict human behaviour, advising government departments of the day desperate to see into the future. The Government of John Major used him to look at traffic flows. They should have asked him to look at their chances of being re-elected. They lost to Tony Blair's lot only two months ago and already New Labour were looking to do things differently, to involve the 'people' in more development and standard setting in public services, schooling and healthcare mainly. They wanted to establish more of a customer choice culture, more opportunities to pick for themselves the school for their children or where they wanted to have an operation.

New Labour had some major plan that was to be published soon for the National Health Service and were pretty obviously set on shaking up one of the last bastions of independent union power, the notorious closed shop of the medical profession, which even Margaret Thatcher (Blair's mentor, apparently) had been reluctant to tackle. Mind you, Prime Minister Thatcher had been able to choose where and when she had her cataracts treated.

Matthew had established some kind of reputation as the guru of solving traffic jam black-spots, based on probability theory and these skills had been used to advise on the ratio of women's to men's toilets required at a single venue to ensure no excessive waiting for women (five times, apparently, whatever the venue type or function). He had even set up his own consultancy on the strength of it, predicting that New Labour would come round calling.

He was mildly excited to see the bundle of papers on his desk, that had arrived by mail last week from Whitehall, and which he had already half opened. It amounted to a Cabinet Office request for him to head up a small advisory group of experts and consumers to review the methods and potential benefits of introducing choice into the Health Service. But he put all that to one side, worked rapidly through other material and essentially cleared his desk; on departure that afternoon he explained to his secretary that he would be inadvertently indisposed over the coming week or so, and that she should divert callers to his deputy for the time being.

He returned home and lay back across the soft sofa in the lounge with a cup of coffee to hand and the cat over his lap. In his head he was planning his next moves, but just then he preferred to dream of lying on hot white sands of a Jamaican beach with Rachel beside him, under a cloudless azure sky, with the distant sounds of ocean waves tumbling along the flats and only the occasional squawk of seagulls to disturb their utter peace in the outlandish heat.

The names of the occupiers at the two addresses he had obtained were Sidebottom in Chelmsford, but he started with Baxter in Bexleyheath. A young woman answered the phone after several rings and to the background sound of an infant crying told him she had never heard of the Lumley family, sorry, can't help you. He phoned the second number and spoke to a kindly woman who said she was Doris Sidebottom, who remembered the Beals living in her house before she moved there some years ago. And after some rummaging around in a drawer in her kitchen she did find a scrap of paper with their name and address on. 'Here we are. I knew I had kept it somewhere and it would come in handy. Mrs Elizabeth Beal.' And she gave Matthew the number. He telephoned it straight away and found himself talking to Sarah Beal's mother, who was still living in Essex but in a smaller bungalow now that she was alone. She was only too delighted to provide Matthew with her daughter's number: she was married to a very nice man with three lovely children living in Crawley.

That evening, trembling with excitement, he spoke to Sarah Beal on the telephone. Her voice sounded completely strange to him as he tried to picture her. Within moments of mentioning Upper Wycheside and Jolyon Hunter, she started chatting and sounded pleasantly amazed to hear from Matthew, whom she said she could remember well.

'Whatever happened to Jolly Jolyon?' Matthew asked with a laugh.

'Oh, I'm not sure. We didn't go out together after school. His home was in Manchester and I think he went to university there, but I've no idea after that.'

'And what about you, has life treated you well?'

'Oh, I think so.' She sounded confidant and happy to real off all the achievements of her own middle-class comfortable late middle-age, with growing family and successful architect husband.

'Sarah, I was really ringing you about Stephanie, Steph Cross or Patek? I'm sure you'll remember. I'm looking for her, actually, I wanted to meet up with her again, and I was…' and Matthew's voice trailed off, just as he thought Sarah might think it odd after all this time for someone to be searching for his long lost girlfriend and might not want to be particularly helpful. But he need not have worried, as she seemed happy to give him as much information as she could about her old friend.

Sarah and Steph had apparently kept up their friendship after leaving school for a while and indeed sent each other regular Christmas cards for some years after they parted. At first it was to an address in Lausanne, then Zurich, and once to Milan, but in about 1976 she moved to London, she had left her husband. She did something in local government, the legal department, Sarah thought, and lived in Fulham. She was still there, as far as she knew, but they had not written to each other for a few years now.

Matthew was staggered. Averill Street, Fulham? A couple of miles from Chiswick. Over all these years. Ridiculous.

'I went over to Geneva in 1969, I think it was, I visited Steph and met her husband, Georgio, an Italian chap, and her little baby girl, they actually lived in Zurich.' Sarah was studying and then worked for a publisher in Covent Garden.

Then she married and started her family, life was hectic, so they only met occasionally after that; Stephanie had come over for the christening of one of Sarah's children and she brought her daughter with her, Sophie, a lovely little girl, must have been about six then.

Matthew had also been searching for Daphne Patek but had not achieved anything, with various Patek's listed around the London area, none admitting to being or knowing a Daphne at any time. But she was almost certainly married, maybe to that Jonathan chap, although Matthew never knew his surname. He wandered down the King's Road one day to see whether he might recognize the shop and warehouse where they had all met on that hot sunny day thirty years ago, pinning skimpy strips of cloth onto skinny models as if that might be the start to a brilliant career in clothes design. The trouble was he could not remember the exact street and the shops had all changed hands, with modern fronts and looked so different to how he remembered them. There was never going to be anyone around anyway who would be able to provide useful information, not from so long ago – his search was hopeless, more a nostalgic trip. He had no idea whether Daphne had managed to make anything of a design career, he personally found it easier to think of her as a geography teacher at a comprehensive.

Matthew decided to write: a better way to introduce himself again, to break the ice, to allow Stephanie time to reflect and react as she wished without him confronting her. Then the choice of replying would be hers, in her own time. He mentioned Sarah, that she had given him her address. He asked her if he might come round to see her, to catch up with old times. He didn't mention any other reason.

He delivered the thin white envelope himself by hand,

having parked a few streets away, and walked casually along Averill Street, his jacket collar turned up. Outside number 22 he took the couple of strides necessary from the pavement through an open wrought-iron gate to reach the blue front door, where he slipped the letter through the box. He glanced in at a bay window briefly as he turned away to proceed fifty yards down the street, before stopping to cross over to the opposite pavement and work his way slowly back, along the line of parked cars, passing the anonymous row of painted terraced houses. There was a non-descript tree of some sort by number 22. The dark windows were all sash and closed and he could not see anyone watching him from inside.

He had no reply for an eternal interval, during which time he did go into his office for short periods in the day to focus on departmental administration. There were teaching sessions to prepare, if he cared to put his mind to them, and three new PhD students were expected in the Autumn so their work programme and research projects needed structuring. He went out most days, running the streets: not long distances, down to the river and along the towpath, over Hammersmith or Putney Bridge, and then back, usually three or four miles. It helped him think and stay focused, although he remained poised for the rejection that he was certain would come eventually and thus put an end to his mission. His anxiety grew by the day.

He started to drive over to Fulham, in the early evenings, just when it was getting dark, to take a look once again at the house, quick sideways glances into the windows to see if she was there, to check this was the right address, and maybe to get a glimpse of her, to brace himself for what might turn out to be quite a shock. She might have grown a moustache or lost a leg or something worse, like her chest might have dropped below her waist; he felt he needed some warning. After at least three trips, he had only once seen a shadowy figure cross an upstairs room, before pulling curtains across the windows, and he was not sure who it had been. On his fourth visit he came over mid-morning on a Saturday, watching the road from inside his car for over an hour parked at a distance from the front door, hidden between other cars and some trees. He kept his eye on the people on the pavement, the comings and goings, but not much happened. Then he saw an upright woman in a light pink cardigan and slacks, returning with heavy shopping bags from the Fulham Palace Road end, walking steadily towards his position, elegant and trim with a firm stride. She tilted her head for a moment and the sun caught the concentration across her face. Even at a distance of seventy-five yards he knew it was her, her outline clear enough for him. He slumped back into his seat, shrinking out of sight, but remained with his eyes fixed on the woman, not blinking, as she turned into her house at number 22.

Then out of the blue the next day, there was a short and rather thrilling phone call, early evening, that caught him by surprise. 'Oh, hello,' said a hoarse voice that seemed to jog a few memories. It was almost a whisper and it was Stephanie, the way she used to talk to him, intimate and expectant. He was not ready for her, not expecting her to ring, although of course he had put his number on the letter.

'Hello, Stephanie, is it?' He spoke in a breathy, relieved sigh, and let a long pause develop. She made a small shudder, a laughing sound and he smiled and gave a little laugh too.

'Gosh, this is a surprise. You wanted to talk to me?' Matthew was unable to speak he was listening so intently. 'Why don't you come over here one morning, maybe this week if you can, come over for coffee; after eleven, give me chance to do some shopping and things?'

When Matthew arrived at her front door at the correct time, he had walked a good way from where he had had to park, which should have calmed his nerves a little but had made him perspire in the warm sunshine. Dressed in an open blue shirt and light trousers, his shoes were soft blue suede, brothel creepers his mother would have called them. His freshly washed blond hair flopped over his forehead as usual, a bit thinner at the hairline than when they were teenagers and with some early distinguishing grey at the temples. About to face his once lover, the girl he had adored for all of a few weeks, whose body and soul he thought he had come to possess, he found himself trembling slightly, in anticipation of the unexpected. A woman in her late forties now, but how would she look? How would she react? Would she be as beautiful to him as she was then? Would she want to talk openly with him? Would their old passions be rekindled? She might be difficult and obstructive, rejecting any idea of contact between her daughter and Matthew. They might be completely cold to each other, the time factor having eradicated all the feelings that they had once had, the thirty years' gap having destroyed any sense of connection. Or she might be willing to help. Could go either way, he thought, trying to be philosophical.

The door was painted a light blue and had patterned glass panels, which Matthew studied for some while before plucking up the courage to press on the door bell. He took in some deep breaths. From inside the small house, Matthew heard a chime and then a dog yapping.

He looked at the twenty-two in aluminium numbers on the side brickwork, mentally checking that he had the right house. He thought he could discern the rumble of voices, female and male, and started to panic that she had a man with her. Sarah had said she was divorced and not remarried as far as she knew, but that didn't stop her having another boyfriend, for God's sake, what was wrong with that, although he might resent Mathew turning up like this at her house.

The dog went quiet. A shadowy figure inside moved

across the frosted glass and reached up to the lock. He could clearly make out a small hand; and he watched transfixed as the hand turned at the wrist, and with a suction noise, jerked the door inwards.

In the shadowy hallway, Stephanie's elegant face appeared and she was standing in flat shoes before him, with a reserved smile and receptive eyes, her arms spread in welcome. The dog yapped. She was in an ankle length skirt with a tight belted waist and a soft orange cashmere top covered her full bosom. They stepped hesitantly towards each other, he raised his hands up to both shoulders and they dryly kissed each other's cheeks, one side then the other, barely touching, both muttering hellos, avoiding eye contact. Her hair was longish and still black, with a hint of greying at the sides; still with that olive lustre to her skin, her long face thinner than he remembered, which made her cheekbones look sharper, but as aristocratic as ever.

'Good of you to come,' she murmured. 'So how long have you lived in Chiswick?' He closed the door and followed her, the yapping dog hopping around his feet sniffing and half-heartedly growling, through to a lounge with big brown sofas and a bright coloured central rug.

'Oh, about twelve years.'

'And I've been here over fifteen years now, so all this while we were actually very close, would you believe?' She flashed a quick smile at him, tiny creases fanning out from around her eyes and he noticed the slight looseness of the skin around her neck, reflecting recent weight loss perhaps. She slid behind a marble-topped kitchen island, gathering cups onto a tray. Matthew could smell the pungent coffee percolating. 'Would you like something to eat, do you like shortbread, or chocolate biscuits?'

The house was modernized Victorian, with an old iron fireplace in the lounge, original covings and architrave patterns picked out in separate colours and the old mahogany staircase preserved, but some internal walls had been cut back, leaving an open-planned downstairs living area. The walls were all whitewashed with colourful splashes of modern art and rugs and cushions in turquoise and orange. Through French windows Matthew could see a tiny flourishing garden, with a wooden planked patio and a small grassy area.

Stephanie quietly brought the tray across to lay it down on a low table between sofas, calling to Jasper to heel. He complimented her on the house, the artwork, the garden and her looks, all in an excited burst of enthusiasm and stroked the little Pekingese that had fussed its way into the room and was again sniffing suspiciously around his ankles. They sat opposite each other, six paces apart.

'I couldn't manage with a bigger garden. It's a bit of a sun-trap in the late afternoons, it gets quite hot on the patio.' A short pause followed while they eyed each other with quick embarrassed glances, both thinking desperately of some small talk they could use to fill the gap. And then Stephanie stepped in. 'So tell me, what do you do, Matthew? And have you got a family and so on?'

And so in his mellow gentle voice Matthew brought her up to date briefly with thirty years of family and professional life, with details of his career, his university work, his marriage to Rachel, the birth of his two children, and what they were doing with their lives.

'Gosh, all sounds so very busy and ordered. Sorry to hear about Rachel, that must have been terrible for you all. And how did you meet Sarah?'

'Oh, I looked her up, phoned her and asked her about you, about where you lived. I didn't meet her, actually, we just spoke on the phone. She sounded fine, busy with her family. She sends her love, by the way.'

'Yes, we have not spoken for a few years now. I don't know

why, these things fall away after a time, don't they? We used to send Christmas cards.'

'You should contact her again, you could still be friends.'

Stephanie was poised straight-backed on the edge of her seat as she chose a ginger nut biscuit from the plate in front of her. 'So this is really nice, but why are you contacting me now, Matthew, after all this time?'

He was waiting for that, obviously. 'I was just reminiscing the other day, preparing for my daughter to get married last month. I had to make a speech,' he paused slightly, looking into his coffee cup. 'My second daughter, you know, and that made me think about our daughter, the one you never let me see. Sophie.' He could not bring himself to look at her at that moment, until Stephanie started talking.

'Sophie, yes, what about her?' She sounded so casual.

'You suddenly disappeared then,' Matthew stuttered, 'and I always wondered why.'

The room was extremely quiet. Matthew could not hear any sounds anywhere; there were no clocks ticking, just an occasional snort from the dog as it snuggled up close to Stephanie on her couch. She was looking down and he noticed her feeding the Peek with little bits of biscuit, and the dog in return licking her fingers. Then she leaned back and relaxed more on her couch, shrugging her shoulders. 'Is that what this is about, you want to talk about Sophie, after thirty years, someone you have never met?'

'Yes, Steph, is that so surprising? I want to meet her, I want to know what she is like, who she is. Is that not fair and right?'

'Yes, I suppose it is, even after all this time, but she does not know who you are. Her father, Georgio, I divorced a good while ago, she sees him from time to time, I think; he lives in Bologna. You can't go telling her what happened, not now.'

'She wouldn't want to know the truth? I bet she would.

She has a right to know, doesn't she?' Under the surface Matthew was feeling a little raw, he felt he could lose control quite easily if pushed. He had come all this way and had thought about his scheme for so long that it was a given in his own mind that he would meet Sophie, wherever she was. But Stephanie was appearing less than happy with the idea.

'Steph, you can't deny me the chance. Just let us meet and start talking, and get to know each other, I mean no harm. We can see where it leads, I don't want to change her life, whatever she is doing, I don't want her to move or anything; she's a grown woman with her own life. Is she married? What is she doing?'

'No, she has never married. And she lives in Spain, in the south, Marbella. Works for an estate agent. I hear from her occasionally, not very often.'

Matthew's mind was whirring: South Spain, that sounded easy, well better than South America or something. He could fly to Malaga, he had been there a couple of times before on holiday, the Costa del Sol, nice weather at his time. 'Do you have a photograph, a recent one? I would really like to meet her, Steph. At least once, to share some things with her, to know that she is… you know, ours.' He was feeling a little elated now that the subject had been broached quite easily. 'Steph, we had something together, didn't we, if only for a short time. And it meant something; and she embodies that. You can't deny me the opportunity, Steph, please.'

He was prepared to plead if he had to, he was not proud.

Stephanie looked tired, her face in a thoughtful frown, but she stood up and went over to a heavy mahogany sideboard and came back with a wooden framed colour photograph, which she handed to Matthew, who stared at it for some while, seeing the resemblance to her mother. 'She looks lovely,' he said.

'She's doing better now, I gather, but she had a difficult

time in London, as a teenager, a bit of a rebel. I had real problems with her. She wouldn't settle to anything, clubs every night, boyfriends, tried the drugs scene, goodness knows what. This was taken a couple of years ago in Marbella, she sent it to me. I think she has settled down, but I don't know about boyfriends. She's twenty-nine, she's plenty of time.'

Matthew studied her picture, seeing a young healthy woman, attractive, tanned, with short jet-black spiky hair, half smiling into the camera on a beach somewhere.

'I'm concerned for her, this would be a shock,' said Stephanie. 'And she would wonder why I have never told her the truth before.' Stephanie's face was alive and taught with clear skin and bright eyes that darted here and there, with a few faint lines around her mouth hardly noticeable, only when she smiled. She remained attractive in her elegance, a dignified and proud woman, he could see that, but he sensed she had lost real contact with her daughter. For some obscure reason, Matthew was wondering whether she was still smoking.

'Why did you have to go so suddenly? I assumed you were unable to contact me, but surely there might have been a way.' Matthew smiled sheepishly, remembering that cold evening sitting up at Whitestone Pond, the tears warm on his freezing cold cheeks. All of a sudden, he was filled with a desire to touch her, like a swelling in his chest. He crossed over to her side, bending down easily onto the sofa and reached for her hands. She looked at him warily under her brows, clasping both his hands but keeping them at a distance.

'Matthew. Dear Matthew, you were so sweet. So kind and innocent. And unworldly. My father was incandescent when he found out I was pregnant, he was like an angry bear, with a sore head. He would have torn you apart with his bare hands if he could. He bullied my mother, always had. He insisted we all left for Switzerland immediately; he wanted me to have an abortion and he would take me to Lausanne, but my mother and I managed to persuade him that we could rescue something from this. I had no choice, I could not contact you, they watched over me and the next day we flew out of London. They found Georgio for me, the son of a business associate of my father's, who had always fancied me apparently as a young teenager, and the poor boy agreed to marry me, even with someone else's baby. We stayed together for a few years, bless him. He even managed to love Sophie to his credit, but I could not stand him really. He works in agriculture in Italy now, he's doing alright, married a country girl, got three of his own children. Sophie has visited I think, once or twice.'

Stephanie had stayed in Switzerland, near Zurich, for a while with her growing daughter and returned to England some years later when Sophie was growing up and at school. Her mother fell ill and died in Switzerland a few years later. Her father was in a nursing home there, she said. Daphne was in the fashion industry despite their father trying to stop her and was working for a fashion newspaper/magazine as an editor. Stephanie took up the law after school and was now working in a solicitors' office part-time in Knightsbridge, 'Domestic affairs and immigration my special areas.'

They sat close beside each other for a few moments more. The house felt peaceful; the dog was quiet on the sofa. Matthew noticed a lonely thrush landing on the wooden table outside the window to peck at some bread crumbs.

Stephanie released his hands and slowly stood up. The dog jumped down onto the floor and yapped a few times. 'Anyway you must say hello to Richard, he's with me now. He's somewhere in the house, probably working upstairs. He's a writer.' Stephanie went to the door and poked her head out into the corridor below the stairs, calling his name. A few minutes later Matthew was shaking hands with a tall greying man, with receding hair and a slight stoop, who looked older than Stephanie by some margin, and wore a heavy corduroy jacket, despite the warmth. He was polite and seemed friendly enough.

Stephanie went over to the kitchen island and found an address book. She wrote some addresses and numbers on a piece of paper that she handed to Matthew saying she would contact Sophie to say that a family friend from England would be visiting soon and would like to meet with her. She would leave it up to Matthew to decide how he wanted to play the introductions and Stephanie said she did not mind what he said to her, the truth should probably be aired; she was silly to be afraid of it. 'But remember Sophie thinks Georgio is her Dad, she will have absolutely no idea who you are.'

'I understand, I do.'

Shortly afterwards, with Sophie's photograph out of its frame safely placed in a jacket pocket with Stephanie's piece of paper, Matthew left, a small and sweet kiss near to a corner of his mouth, his reward. He wiped it with his fingertips as he walked slowly away, toward his parked car, feeling a heavy sense of disappointment sagging across his shoulders. They had made no plans to meet again.

FOUR
Adventures in Spain

August/September 1997

1

Friday August 22

Sophie sat daydreaming, gazing through grimy windows out into the hazy fervid afternoon. The usual midmorning traffic clattered by, with chirping car horns and emergency sirens. Distant sounds of grinding pneumatic drills and churning cement mixers added counterpoint to the discord that rasped around the sluggish streets of Marbella during that sweltering August of 1997.

The humid atmosphere was clouded with dust, builders' rubble piled up at every corner. A fine dry scum, highlighted in the sharp sunlight, touched all ledges and sills and the slightest puff of breeze blew powdery particles into the few pedestrian faces that were out and about. Nearby was one of many boarded-off sites returning to slow action after a peaceful summer recess, where men in coloured round hats hung about at all levels of the rising structures within, while monster trucks rumbled in and out leaving congealed mud smeared across the tarmac in their wake. Gangly steel cranes reached precariously skywards, while tons of wet crunchy cement were tipped into the bottomless pits beneath.

Residents and workers collectively longed for some relief from the endless heat and prayed for cooling rain, even though that would inevitably bring more builders scuttling back to resume their never-ending game of property boom that played out so relentlessly along the shores of Europe's most popular coastline.

Inside, business was slow and the office air was still. The air-con was not coping with the excessive heat and humidity. Sophie had taken her bare feet out of their flat shoes, which made no difference. Even though she was hot, across her back and under her arms, and her neck under the collar of her white blouse felt sticky, she looked effortlessly pretty. Her thoughts easily turned to what she might rather be doing, like drinking something long and cool while lounging by the waterfront, soaking in a pool, meeting friends in a club. She was dying for a smoke.

Images of various past dodgy jobs she thought long forgotten reminded her to be grateful for the chance of something respectable. So there she was, sat in a large window-fronted office they all called *la tienda*, on the ground floor of a residential block on a corner of the main Avenida de Ricardo Soriano, the thoroughfare that sliced east-west through Marbella, selling over-hyped over-priced dream properties to over-excited punters, just as much part of the crazy property boom as were all the developers and speculators in languid search of bargains that crowded along that glistening strip of real estate like an overflowing honey pot. Only two other sales staff were in that morning, Clarissa and Alfonso, each sitting quietly behind their own desk and desk-top computer and telephone and printed gold name label on a wooden block and a personal note pad with Baxwell Properties printed dark green in friendly handwriting style across the bottom, each equally enthusiastic and uncomfortable as the hour of the lunch break approached. All the staff there were a nice bunch, smiling at each other first thing in the morning and calling *buenas noches* on leaving at the end of the day, dressed in routine uniform, navy trousers or skirts and white shirts with their names printed and pinned prominently to their left lapels: "Sophie Patek – Sales Consultant" hers read. And then a customer would flop in off the street, the glass doors buzzing irritatingly, and another gush of oven warm air would intrude on their solitude.

The windows were dotted with advertising stickers and posters and on the walls all around the office were colourful publicity photographs blown up large, of villas and apartments set in various tempting locations, a lush and empty golf course, an enticing sandy beach with arching palm trees, with unrelenting sunshine and pure blue skies, this being the Costa del Sol. The one behind Sophie advertised a new development coming soon to Marbella, a multimillion pesetas beachside scheme for a five-star hotel, top class apartments and retail space, called Projecto Al Este De La Linea De Costa (The East Shoreline Project); early enquiries and registration of interest in off-plan investments was encouraged at Baxwell's.

Sophie flicked through the address book that was on her desk, where she found the number for their office window cleaners, and picked up her telephone. The conversation that followed in Spanish was succinct: the boys would be round Monday first thing.

'*Odio estas ventanas sucias,*' Sophie exclaimed, with a look of disgust and a shrug. She delicately wiped her brow and upper lip with a perfumed tissue from her bag. 'The windows, they're so filthy, it's bad enough with this heat. We must get the air-con seen to as well.' She checked her face in a hand-held mirror, applying a quick touch of gloss to her strawberry lips, before combing her fingers through short spiky black hair.

The almost imperceptible scar, more an indent of skin at the end of the thin line of a black eyebrow on one side, reminded her of what might have been, dancing images across her mind, her expression distant. It had been six years since she had high-tailed it to Spain, a lifetime ago it seemed, escaping from boring jobs and broken relationships, bad debts, bad vibes and a wonderfully disreputable crowd in London. She had played the system as best she could, with spells at a respectable travel agent, showing clients around the sights of Marbella, working as a croupier in the casino for one season and serving behind many a late-night bar. She had even spent time behind bars of another sort, but the less said about that the better. Her desperation for a living had thrown up a few scary near-misses, like being a fixer in a transvestite bar, a drug runner for a night-club owner involving Moroccan contraband secreted about her person, and a few scrapes with local *policia*. Really trying hard to establish some sort of better life for herself, she had kept out of trouble and fallen in with Alex Baxwell. All of which escapades had at least taught her useful lessons in self-preservation.

One night in a backstreet joint some dipstick had groped her once too often and in the physical struggle provoked by her angry refusal, she had been hit in the face and the crust of diamonds on his fifth finger had embedded painfully close to one eye. And without explanation there was Baxwell muscling the jerk away and holding a handkerchief to her face until the bleeding had stopped.

He had later tried to seduce her, of course, which she found repulsive, but he persuaded her to join his team in the estate agents' business, promising her a rewarding future on the Costa del Sol where new developments were flourishing everywhere and lots of money was to be made. He liked the way she operated, her good-looks would be persuasive to customers and he seemed to know a good deal about her sometime drug running activities. She had agreed and in return he had provided training and a prominent position in his head-office, with regular pay and a car to show the punters around. She even rented one of his flats but a few streets away, which she swopped for her sometime squalid shag-pit in Fuengirola where she had spent her early time on the sunny south coast.

She had become part of the glitzy Marbella set, Sophie reflected with some irony. Along the southern coastline of olive groves and rugged rocks close to the warm waters of the Mediterranean, developers had been building endless clusters of posh white villas and swimming pools amongst what remained of the original Moorish architecture. Although missing the white sands of Ibiza, colonies of wealthy foreigners had created their own summer playground in Marbella, the in-place for the in-crowd. Celebrities, TV stars and high-flyers, they all came to Marbella to be seen, emblazoned with designer logos and not afraid to splash out a bit. Which meant there was plenty of money for everybody, if you knew how to work the system.

Sophie remembered when she first arrived seeing English women at the airport, expecting endless nights of clubbing, with hair rollers already in place. The men were concerned about the state of the golf greens, the women about where to find the best liposuction deal and which cosmetic clinic to visit. No woman sunbathed topless in case the scars of surgery showed. Size was everything: superyachts, supercars and supermodels with silicon breasts were always jostling for space on the marinas, designer labels still attached.

Sophie would hardly give these people the time of day; she was not intimidated into joining in with their consumerist lifestyle and habits, however inadequate they tried to make her feel. She was determined to exploit the situation for what she could and then move on to somewhere else, before inevitable trouble caught up with her again. Away from the office, she would bound around town by day in skinny white slacks and sleeveless tops with open sandals, by night black jeans, pixie ankle boots and leather biker jacket, always a serious look on her face where clients were concerned which easily relaxed in the right company. She had plenty of friends, while cleverly avoiding the trap of entanglement, keeping the keenest boys at a distance. Sophie was a gamine creature, always neat and trim, with dark brows and a husky voice, a mischievous elfin beauty that no man had tamed.

The desk phone rang and made her jump out of her reverie. It was Roberto. 'Hi, it is me,' and he paused for effect.

'Mm,' said Sophie quietly with a sideways glance around the office, a hand reaching up to cover the mouthpiece.

'Hi, *it is me*,' said Roberto again, a little louder from his end.

'*Yo se.* I know, dickhead, what do you want?' she whispered.

'I want see you, tonight, I have idea.' When Roberto had ideas, Sophie got worried.

'Oh, yeah. Like what?'

'I tell you later. It is good. I bring some beer, you want?'

They agreed a time and his voice disappeared. Roberto was a chunky, hirsute, salacious, greasy little Spaniard whom Sophie at first detested, but he knew how to tickle a woman's fancy. Sophie's current fancy was someone physical (Roberto had an impressive lean muscle-building body to rival any of the blokes she bumped into at the local gym), someone playful, who paid her apt attention (he did not waste time looking for her G-spot, for example), and someone who did not snore afterwards like a walrus with overpowering armpits (Roberto was not a man to fall asleep immediately after nookies). She had known men who fell asleep during nookies but that was another story. And although Roberto doused his underarms liberally with various alluring deodorants before and afterwards without effectively obscuring his pungent primitive odours, he generally fitted the bill. For the last few months they had been sleeping together, Sophie and Roberto, on and off, as it were, on quite a few occasions. He would come over to her flat late and stay till dawn, before scampering back to his wife in their little pad somewhere in the Old Quarter.

Sophie actually found his masculine smell a strong turn-on. After he had taken her slowly to the heights of ecstasy and she had screamed in submission, he would leap off the bed, leaving her panting, exposed, and start doing press-ups on the floor, grunting hard; and then turn over to do some stomach rolls, while his taut body perspired all over, leaving him looking like a perfect model for the front cover of a lad's magazine. And she would swoon appropriately, and probably reach out to stroke him in awe and wonderment. She presumed he wanted her to watch from the side of the bed and admire the physical prowess of surely her most impressive lover, and so she did. He presumed, wrongly as it happened, that she had numerous lovers to choose from, not just Senor Baxwell, and therefore he had to impress her if he meant to keep her attention. So he would be up off the floor again, shaking the dampness off his body like a dog, standing over her, shiny and aroused; and with a light touch he would rework the whole stimulation cycle, with surprisingly delicate hands finding their way into all her likely places. He would kneel over her and plunge between her thighs, having maintained his monstrous kingpin at its prime throughout this Herculean performance, piercing her with all the fine skill of a performing matador. Typically, it was Sophie who remembered the condoms.

And because he worked for Baxwell, had been with him for over ten years and knew how he operated and had his absolute trust, he was a useful source of all sorts of juicy information that sometimes made Sophie's eyes pop out of her head. Roberto was the odd-job man. He did courier work around the south coast for the estates, driving people or valuables, often cash, for wages or payments of some kind, or contracts that needed signatures, most often debt collecting.

Occasionally he did those discrete sort of jobs for Mr Baxwell that required no paperwork or records, often with backhanders and no questions, sometimes with the use of muscle. He had been over to Morocco on the ferry numerous times, to exchange cash parcels for cakes of hashish that would be stashed away in hidden compartments of his work van and passed on to known distributors for more cash, usually the Chinese these days. Street prices for fashionable drugs for the wealthy middle classes were buoyant along the Costa del Sol, and with their contacts in the local banks, passing the money through into legitimate accounts was easy enough.

This was just one of Baxwell's little side shows that Sophie had recently found out about, in addition to rental property, estate management and agency work, for which he had a list of well-heeled customers, mostly from abroad, Saudis, Russians and Germans. He bought and sold development property off-plan, and by keeping in with the local Council planning committees, he had first-hand knowledge, advance warning and first options, that cost him many thousands of pesos in bribes every time, but usually paid off handsomely in the end.

Roberto's arrival was announced by finger tapping on her door. By now it was dark outside and Sophie had been hanging out wet clothes on a makeshift line on her sixth-floor balcony, glancing at the town lights and listening to the street sounds rising from the warm duskiness below. She spotted his Suzuki parking in the shadows next to a row of scooters and delivery vans that worked for the fish shop on the corner. Her lights were dimmed and an aroma of espresso permeated through the warm rooms.

Roberto dumped a pack of Cruz Campo beers on her kitchen counter and stripped off his leather jacket onto a sofa, showing off his tattooed and bare upper arms. Rough looking and unshaven, Roberto came with a bruise on his cheek and grazed knuckles. He pushed past Sophie to her bathroom, where he ran hot water over his hands, washing dried blood and dirt away, moaning at the stinging. 'Some angry bastard thought he fight his way out of trouble. Ha.' Roberto laughed. Sophie fussed around him, dabbing his face, drying his wounds and applying anti-septic cream. 'Silly boy, he not do that again.' His crooked mouth showed off uneven nicotine-stained teeth.

They had not seen each other for some days and tentatively began to finger and touch and kiss each other, progressively stripping clothes off, leaving bundles in a trail through to the bedroom. Wafts of his working body odour pungently stoked her desires. Frantically they rutted for a few minutes on the big double bed, mercilessly thumping the wooden headboard against the wall. Then they lay naked side by side on their backs, sweating, panting in the dark, slowly cooling off in the night air that drifted through the open windows. Roberto fetched a can of beer and while sharing a cigarette, still catching his breath, he began to confide in her. He was ready to break away, he said, he had had enough of Mr Alex Baxwell. And now he had an idea. He was due to meet some unlikely Moroccan fellow off the ferry in Algeciras in a couple of days. The chap was new, replacing a regular driver and needed guidance; would be driving an old Citroen loaded with "merchandise", Baxwell had said. Some cakes and cash, Roberto presumed, although he did not know precisely what or how much. Roberto was to bring him back and show him around Marbella, help him find his feet, so he could stay for a few days and do some odd-jobs for his lord and master. Sophie could picture the potential chaos and dangers of a bewildered Moroccan tramping around the back streets of Marbella, secretly trying to find buyers for his dope among the tourists in that fiercely competitive local market, something she knew about from her past experience.

'It sounds bonkers,' Sophie said.

'We could hijack the car, steal the goods,' Roberto was suggesting, turning over to lie prone, propped on his elbows. 'You get good price for hash on the waterfront these days, especially Moroccan stuff.' Moonlight shining through the open window cast a silvery ripple over Roberto's uncovered shoulders and boulder-like buttocks. He looked for Sophie's approval with raised eyebrows. Sophie smoking quietly listened dumb-founded.

'Now you sound bonkers, Roberto. Have you turned criminal all of a sudden?'

'No, serious. We pull it off. Make it look like mugging, leave Ali Agra and me on side of the road, drive off in the car with the goods, hide it. No one find it. Then sell off the stuff little by little. Handy income, what you say?' He was smiling like a Cheshire cat, the black-eye making his face lop-sided. Sophie sat up and he carelessly started to stroke her bare back.

'Ali Agra?' she repeated sceptically.

'Ali, whatever, I don't know.'

Roberto needed to wait for the signal, then drive down to the safehouse in Algeciras to meet this Ali Agra fellow and bring him back, all quietly done after dark, park up in one of Baxwell's garages behind the office. On a deserted patch of hard shoulder on the coast road, Roberto was suggesting, an old car with bonnet up and a girl bending over to look underneath, could be in place. The girl in shorts, nice long legs, nobody else about; Roberto is thinking, she is alone, I fancy my chances. He stops the car just beyond the distressed woman and while leaning under her bonnet himself, he is set on by a couple of lads (who had been hiding in the dark) and he is thumped and overcome, hands tied behind his back and left in the gutter. The two lads dump Ali Agra out and drive off with the girl in Roberto's car, containing the money and stuff. 'How's that?' he asked proudly.

'Did you think this up all by yourself, you little *malvado*?' Sophie was teasing him, not really thinking that Roberto was serious enough to go through with something like that.

'I hate Baxwell, I want to get out of his job and set up myself. A nice car hire firm, looking after smart cars of executives, top end, make good money. Not this Baxwell shit.' He spat out the words as he swung his legs round onto the floor and walked to the open window, looking out over the shadowy city of grimy rooftops. TV aerials and dishes poked up everywhere into the skyline and by practically every window on every building was a rusted air-conditioning box, leaving discoloured streaks of rust on the white wash beneath, like dirty barnacles on the underside of a boat. He could smell fried fish and garlic in the air, vaguely aware of thumping disco music in the distance.

After a while Sophie realised that Roberto was thinking in much the same way as she had been lately: it would soon be time to move on. Baxwell was a creep, she had no sympathies in that direction. But she needed money and the initiative to plan her exit: maybe this could be it. 'You may actually have quite a good idea there, Rob.' She turned serious, pulling on a baggy T-shirt, with "I love NY" and a big red heart shape on the front. Standing behind him, her hair ruffled, she bent forward to kiss his neck, the tips of her breasts teasing against his back. He twisted round and pulled her close to him, but Sophie was having none of it; or rather she had already had a lot of it and wanted to tidy the place and send Roberto, badly overdue at his marital home, on his way.

She worked through his proposal in her head, wondering who she might recruit for the roles. Extra money would always be welcomed and could be shared out, but she tried to imagine what sort of ructions it might cause. 'Who's the hash for, there might be dealers expecting it?'

'Don't know, it was for Ali to pass on to Baxwell to get rid.'

'And the money, how much, did Baxwell say?'

'Is payment for something, I not sure. But I would expect a lot. Baxwell was excited, he spoke with eyes gleaming, secret to me, I think it important, there should be a lot. Baxwell is loaded, he will not suffer, much.' Roberto had a satisfied twist across his swarthy mouth and then sucked deeply on the last of their shared cigarette before tossing the stub out the window.

'I'll think about it. Look, I am supposed to going straight, keeping my head down, you're a bad influence,' Sophie mused kindly.

'Not long, we must move soon.'

After a little while she asked: 'Safehouse, what's that?'

'Lots of the boys use, they stay for shelter, swops and deals, safe, away from the watching eyes. It's in poor part, off from the port, among some apartment blocks. Baxwell own it, a few workshops and flats on three floors.' Roberto seemed to know all about it. 'Not for you to worry,' he reassured her.

With a thrill in her voice, she continued. '*Esta bien*. I think I know who we can use – three of them, we could pay them each, say ten or twenty thousand pesos, that should do it for them. I can talk to them tomorrow, before I go to work, I've got a late start. If you're serious?'

'*Si*. I am. And then we get away from here and *hacer el amor* every day with you.' Roberto was reaching for the hem of her T-shirt again and she had to tug herself away, holding the material down. She went round the flat picking up discarded clothes from the floor, thrusting them in a bundle into Roberto's hairy tummy. 'And you must get yourself off home, Roberto. You live with Luciana, remember? Go see her and make it up to her.'

2

Saturday August 23

By night during the season the popular Blue Ocean Club was a glittering place on several floors down by the sea front, packed with trendy punters throwing their money about with abandon. Down in the Dive, the DJs played their own music choice, up-to-date and loud, a continual body-shuddering throb that made the mirrored walls tremble and with a lightshow to match, that went on well into the small hours. There were bars on all floors and from the top away from the hubbub it was possible to imagine peaceful views over the glittering waters of the Mediterranean, with the marina just a stone's throw further along, with its array of white masts bobbing and swaying, caught in bright search lights.

Sophie had started early that morning with a visit to the marketplace to catch up with some friends, followed by another hot working day at the office, even though it was a Saturday. She had been home to change, and had been working her stint flat out in the bars with the rest of the team all in black, shirt and miniskirt. She had had fun; there were always people she knew popping in for a dance and a few drinks. Nursing a vodka cocktail and puffing a Marlboro, off-duty and alone, she perched herself on a stool in the Dive, after the crowds had thinned out, and the music and lights had been toned down. As the night drifted away, a few romantic couples smooched to the slower numbers. She was nearly ready to leave.

Out of the blue, through the cotton of her blouse, she felt a sticky hand slide around her waist fingering her flesh. A thick arm wrapped around her back from behind and she knew it was Baxwell by the smell of him. And by the look of him, he had had quite a few drinks.

Sophie always thought of Alex Baxwell as a bully, an overambitious underachiever, who took his failings out on other people. He was obviously making a fortune with his chain of estate agents along the Costa, but he was a nasty and brutish operator, making sales at any cost his mantra. He was a weak man always quick to blame his staff if sales fell through, who hid his faults behind a brash exterior. He was overweight because he could not control his eating habits and he drank too much to dampen the reality of his fractious marriage and to boost his flagging confidence.

He was a womaniser and a most unattractive one. He had flabby cheeks cratered from an acned adolescence, and reddish hair that was thinning and retreating along a sloping forehead, pale and freckly. The sun made his skin erupt in pink blotches so he had become obsessive about slapping on creams, wearing a fedora, and letting himself into the offices before the sun was properly up and creeping out after dark. Confined to the indoors, he had a chronic pallor that made him look unwell. Quite what he thought he was doing setting up his business in one of the hottest and sunniest parts of Europe, Sophie could only guess; the money was obviously seductive.

'*Hola*, you pretty little doll, drinking all alone?' he shouted above the music, his hot breath irritatingly ruffling the hair across her ear and cheek. Baxwell wobbled onto the empty stool next to her, in his usual expensive Italian silk suit and hand-made shoes, with a wafer-thin gold wrist-watch and various gold rings on his fingers, sweating profusely. 'You are looking particularly appealing just now, if I may say so.' Whereas you might expect someone who meant what he said to accompany such a remark with a smile, even a lascivious twist of the mouth, Baxwell managed a mean tightening of his pale lips and a Scottish lilt that sounded aggressive. Sophie was unsure why Gloria had put up with him for as long as she had.

'I'm glad I caught you. I have a job for you.'

Baxwell was definitely the last person she wanted to talk to. There was no one about in the club that she knew, who might be looking out for her. She was unsure why she had stayed so long. Baxwell was drinking freely from his glass. 'Listen, finish your drink and we'll go outside. It's too noisy here.' He leant over the wet bar surface and downed the remains of what looked like a whisky. Sophie still had to shout to be heard, but she kept a distance between them.

'What is this about?'

Baxwell just indicated to tip her glass back. He threw some peseta notes onto the bar top and reached for her hand. Pulling her off her stool, she just had time to grab her jacket and bag before wobbling towards the back exit. They awkwardly climbed some unlit metal stairs outside up to the back alleyway of the Excelsior Hotel, still and oven-like between the close buildings but with a welcome quietness. Sophie could smell the pungency of fish and cooking oil, mixed with human sweat. Baxwell's shoes clipped on the paving as he pulled her along flat-footed with his arm around her waist again, while she tried to play cool with her hands well away carrying her jacket and bag.

His dark green Range Rover with his company logo painted on the side doors was parked under a lamp and he pushed her in eagerly onto the back leather seats, pulling the door closed behind him. He started to fondle her around her neck, pulling at her shirt, his big body crowding her, rising above her. She was saying, 'Stop it get off,' and was about to slap him as he continued to paw her, but he was persistent and for all the drink inside him, was strong and determined. 'Come on, Sophie, come on, don't be such a prude, you know you want it. Just give me a feel. A quick one before we get down to business.'

He was clawing between her legs and crushing her under his fatty load, but she twisted painfully sideways and so his soft flesh, and some not so soft, dug uncomfortably into her bony hip. He heaved and humped and somehow managed to undo his fly and was rummaging around inside his trousers, trying to yank something out that he would not be proud of in the cold light of day. He started to pull her face down, saying, 'Come on, Sophie, give a man a good suck. I miss you, damn it. Crank my shank, you know you want to.'

'No, I bloody don't,' she screamed into his lap.

He slapped her cheeks and grabbed her face, clutching her hair either side, pulling her up towards him. 'Now you listen to me, young Sophie. You owe everything you have to me. I gave you your job in the first place, trained you, promoted you. Remember? Your apartment, your car, it's all down to me. Just don't tempt me, don't bloody tempt me, make me drop it all, you would have nothing, you realise, so just don't be so smug that you... you... you think you can ignore me for ever.' His anger was getting the better of him, and the embarrassment of the situation made him relax his grip. 'I just want something back for all my help.'

Sophie twisted and wriggled free; shouting at him and turning onto him, she managed to dig a knee firmly into his groin. 'For Christ sake, just put it away, and we'll say nothing more of it.'

Baxwell was breathing fast. He could not reach properly around his belly or even see to zip himself up, but just pushed everything out of sight, turning on Sophie with a menacing growl. 'I have a job for you to do. And I'm perfectly prepared to drop you overboard if you don't do it properly. Or even set one of the boys onto you. Now listen, damn you.' He paused while he readjusted himself best he could. 'I need the Mayor on my side, Senor bloody Nestor, he has the casting vote on this development I am bidding for, the East Shoreline Project.' He waved a hand vaguely, still breathing heavily. 'Just producing a fucking bribe is not enough. We're getting to the stage in this town where money no longer secures what you want. The man's a rogue, but he is always persuaded by a bit of female charm.' Sophie sank back into the soft leather, running her hands through her ruffled hair, panting a little as she buttoned her shirt and pulled her jacket on. 'I need you to deliver a package into his hands, discretely, for no one else to see. It will be at his villa, there is nowhere else to get to him these days, but I cannot go there myself. It would be disastrous if I was seen there, it would completely blow my chances just now. But if you went there, no one would know who you were, or that you were associated with me.'

'Fuck you. You have no right.'

'Listen, I need this project. It will mean a lot of money, the firm would really take off. I would get sole estate rights, and a proportion of all profits – we would all benefit, knock-on effects. This would secure a really great future. For you as well.'

On the spur, Sophie turned to him. 'OK, but I want to see some of this money you keep talking about. We don't see any of it at our end. I want a promotion and a proper pay rise. That you have been promising me for ages.'

'Yeah, no problem, we can talk about that. Sophie, you know it makes sense, do this for me and we will all profit, believe me.'

Sophie remained quiet, suppressing her anger. Calm

reasoning told her she needed to cooperate, resigned to being used. She looked straight ahead through the wide windscreen of the car, noticing the beauty of a silver crescent moon staring back at her low along the narrow alleyway. 'When?'

'Monday. I've made a midday appointment for you.'

* * *

He had explained the routine to her. She was to go to OpenCor along the road, buy some loose fruit and vegetables, enough to half fill a plastic carrier bag. Then upstairs in his office he would hide two packages at the bottom under the groceries. She would drive up to La Zagaleta, up to the security gates, they would search her at the hut, they would look in the bag, don't worry, they had done this before, then she would transfer into a chauffeured car for the short drive to the Mayor's villa. She would stay maybe a half hour, be polite, flatter the man, take some refreshment, food whatever, deliver the packages personally with explanation, and then return; the reverse would happen and she would drive back to town on her own, job done.

Only, when she had left Baxwell's office and walked casually along the steaming pavement to her Renault parked around the corner, she had an irresistible urge to look into the bag and examine the packages herself. She had watched Baxwell retreat with a bunch of keys into his back office space where he kept the safe, a heavy square box of steel on the floor under some storage shelves, and then returned with the plastic shopping bag, rearranging the contents to his satisfaction, which he then handed back to her. It felt no heavier than before; she had smiled, told him not to worry, she knew what she had to do. She was heading home first, to put on some different clothes. Be a bit daring, Baxwell had said, make the Mayor open his eyes and take notice. 'A smile, put on some charm, like you know how, flutter those eyelashes, a bit of cleavage and leg,' he suggested helpfully, his tongue wet at his open mouth, his accent rolling in anticipation. 'Flatter him. You want the Mayor to think that he is special and that he might meet with you in different circumstances at a later time.'

About forty minutes away from her *rendez-vous*, depending on traffic congestion, Sophie had time to change. But the urge to peek into the bag was too great. There were the apples, the loose oranges and the lemon and the few brown paper bags of radishes, mushrooms and carrots, and the smell was fresh and earthy; a lettuce and a cauliflower were at the top. In her stuffy kitchen, she removed everything carefully onto the table. At the bottom of the bag were two brown paper packages laying innocently side by side, each was rectangular, 14 by 8 centimetres, about four centimetres thick. There were no markings, just brown sticky tape round the edges. She picked one out. It was soft, not heavy, less than a packet of biscuits. Along the top edge was a slit, cut to allow you to see inside: to see that the pack contained a thick stack of money and not cut newspaper or recreational drugs or explosive.

She carefully pulled out all the notes from one bundle, mostly crisp and new, brown *cinco* notes with some boring old explorer drawn on the face, and counted them with a trembling relish. She had never had so much pure cash in her hands before: 1000 and 5000 peso notes, a few hundred of them. Two million pesetas in all, she reckoned, which was about nine thousand pounds in her old currency – and that was in each packet. That seemed a steep bribe, even for the Mayor, to encourage him to support Baxwell in a property deal. Baxwell obviously expected to make a lot more than that if he was awarded the Project. Sophie quickly made the assumption that the Mayor would not know how much he was getting – that it would be the person committing the bribe to decide the minimum that would convince (a whim, really, although there was obviously a going rate, whatever that might be) – and that he should be satisfied with two million pesos, in cash. And Sophie would be ever so happy with the other two million, thank you very much. Just think of the debts she could pay off and still have enough for tickets out of there, to Athens or Cairo perhaps, and with some spending money. Liz would be astonished, a birthday present for her. She was breathing more rapidly than usual in her excitement and combined with the heat, a film of perspiration was glistening across her forehead.

She fingered the crispy paper money, running her thumb down the edges like a card player before dealing. Carefully replacing all the notes in their brown wrapping, she stared at the two bundles for a little while before putting one of them back at the bottom of the shopping bag, covering it with the groceries and fruit, the lettuce and cauliflower at the top. The other she left on the kitchen table. If the Mayor was insulted by such a paltry sum as one million pesetas, he might strike Baxwell off his Christmas list and bye-bye as far as the Project was concerned, but then so what? Baxwell would survive.

She downed a full glass of cheap Spanish plonk for courage. And then as if someone might catch her unexpectedly, she snatched up the innocent-looking package from the table and stuffed it away next door under a loose floor-board, her secret place, positioned under her bed and covered over by a dull coloured rug. She stripped off and in the bathroom made sure her legs were smooth. She selected a push-up bra and negligible briefs for underwear and a colourful sleeveless dress in stretch cotton that conformed neatly to her body shape, with matching heels, no stockings. She mascared her eyes and applied minimal foundation, soft earthy colours over her cheeks with an outrageous cherry lipstick. A gold necklace chain with tiny dangling scimitar (a gift from a grateful Moroccan trader she had helped a couple of years back) nestled brazenly between buoyant breasts and she completed the ensemble with a few haphazard sprays of *eau de cologne* and a perfume drop behind each ear lobe. Pirouetting in front of the bedroom mirror, drawing in firmly the muscles of her stomach and patting the flattened area, she generally admired the effect with a confidant pout at herself.

It was blisteringly hot again around midday, 38 degrees recorded on the dash, as Sophie headed west for the hills near El Madronal with all the windows open. La Zagaleta, shimmering on a hillside above Marbella well away from prying eyes, was a recently-built secure villa complex, a hide-away favoured by the well-known and the wealthy from all parts of the world and boasting some of the most expensive real estate on the south coast. Here you might run into an ex-England football captain, the dancer wife of a late well-known bullfighter, a German diplomat. Baxwell Properties had purchased a relatively small villa with six bedrooms and infinity pool for a Russian client last year, a deal that Sophie had been involved in, with her best commission earned, so she knew the area a bit. But the Mayor's villa was altogether a grander place, standing well apart from the others in a protected area for the really special people among the special people, that looked deserted; absolutely nothing was moving. She pulled up outside a high whitewashed wall and manoeuvred into some shade under an olive tree. A security man in uniform appeared and hustled her into a hot guard house, where another uniformed man, bulky and silent, with wet patches under his arms, frisked her inexpertly and rummaged around in her shopping bag, with a little smirk on his shiny face, when he turned to her. She thought he was going to give her a wink, complicit in her treachery. She had a crisp 1000 peseta note poised between two fingers that she flicked in front of his eyes as he straightened up. 'I'm sure this will be OK, the Mayor *is* expecting me.' The guard went cross-eyed before snatching the note quickly from her grasp. Sophie wanted to laugh at the farcical nature of the whole process which was clearly not an unusual occurrence.

She was transferred into the creamy leather air-conditioned interior of a black Mercedes and chauffeured through the gated area, along a broad empty strip of perfect tarmacadam, lined with white-painted borders and immaculate lawns. Serviced and catered for around the clock, these massive villas were hidden by further screens of bushes and fences with discrete security, a level of privacy much favoured by retired politicians and Middle Eastern arms dealers. Turning into a curved drive they crunched across gravel through landscaped gardens to the side of a magnificent three-storey residence that from its high vantage point commanded panoramic views over the southern coastline far below and the blue-grey Mediterranean shimmering beyond. The Mayor was well known for using his little pad for party gatherings and council committee meetings, to which only special members were expected, preferable to the stuffy traditional and publicly obvious town building in Marbella.

The sun shone from high in the absolute blue sky giving everything a blinding glow. Behind tinted glass, Sophie felt rather special herself and surprisingly relaxed, neat and chic as she was in her Raybans, even with the grubby plastic bag of groceries at her feet. But she was kept waiting over two hours in a side-room in one wing of the villa, with comfortable settees, glossy magazines and a tray of coffee, water and fruit to help herself, becoming increasingly frustrated whilst the Mayor presumably was completing his morning's business. She was finally led outside along a tiled walkway, down steps away from the house through a tropical area towards a kidney-shaped pool, surrounded by columns of stone and palm trees. She had not expected a crowd, but here was an air of casual indulgence: overweight business groups in business dress, smart people in casual clothes, lazing around the water's edge, sipping and smoking, bursts of laughter erupting between quiet murmurings, many shaded under striped umbrellas. All their heads turned suspiciously toward her in sequence as she passed, walking with measured care behind her guide in pressed black trousers and white shirt who had been sent to fetch her.

Standing a little apart in a shaded area on the far side of the pool, with drinks in hand and eating with their fingers, were a group of tough-looking men in suits, huddled together in quiet conversation. One man, in particular, slightly smaller in height than the others, with a thin black moustache and black hair creamed flat and swept straight off a bronzed forehead, seemed to be staring at her, facing her straight, unflinching, legs apart. She had become aware of him, watching her, as soon as she had started to promenade by the outside pool. He was in neatly-pressed trousers and shirtsleeves and when at last he turned away from her, she could see in profile a splendid hooked nose; a man of distinction at the centre of his group of business cronies, their jackets discarded in the heat.

At the far end of the pool, Senor Jesus Nestor was slouched in his outside Jacuzzi like a portly Roman Emperor, with his gold chains of office shining around his ample breasts, smoking a cigar, drinking wine. His assistants in neat shirts and short skirts sat around at small tables ensuring he had done all the necessary paper work for authorising contracts or planning permission, obtaining his signature on various dotted lines. While a small army of attractive young bimbos waited on the assembled officials with food and drink and anything else they might care for. Sophie passed along this unfamiliar path into unknown territory, approaching the Mayor with some trepidation.

For one terrible moment she thought she might have to strip off and join the man in the water. Earlier she had felt confident and good about herself and the smell and touch of all that money in her hands in her kitchen had given her a cynical feeling of success. She had dressed seductively because she had been strongly advised to and her plunging neckline and short hemline had obviously drawn the attention of the assembled audience. But now with all that waiting around and her dress creased and her armpits sticky, her perspective had changed and the ridiculous power of wealth that was staring her in the face was making her feel nervous and her confidence was draining away with each step into the lion's den, where perhaps her true self would be exposed and she would face humiliation.

The Mayor was waving her over to him, she could see his dark head and bare shoulders emerging above the foaming water, sunk into the paving. A minion dressed bizarrely in black slacks and bikini top was bending down at the edge to speak discretely into his ear, to introduce her. Senor Nestor stood up boldly out of the water, disregarding the waves he created and the water splashing all around him, all smiles. Solidly built, bloated body covered in white curly hairs, over his shoulders and chest and down his back, where they were darkened with the wet, he was easily in his sixties, clean-shaven, impressively sun-tanned, his dyed black hair neatly parted. He stretched out a generous hand, all urbane charm, and welcomed her loudly. 'Ms Patek? Please. You like English, yes? I am sorry for keeping you waiting. Enjoy the view.' He waved his dripping arms in a vaguely all-embracing way across the horizon and of course everyone nearby stopped to admire from their position around the pool the glorious sights on display on such a lovely day: the shimmering of light in the distance over the flat unreal sea spreading southwards far below towards the thin grey hazy coastline of Africa. Marbella was sprinkled below them like a collection of gravel stones, with its few short stretches of beach, while lush golf courses carpeted the valley floors between grey rugged outcrops of rock, with groves of olive and wild cypress. She thought she would have caught a glimpse of the Rock of Gibraltar but it was obscured by the mountainous coastline.

'Patek? Do I know this name? Perhaps you would like to join me, Ms Patek?' the Mayor was asking mischievously, indicating the bubbling surface below him. Sophie looked doubtful and in fairness the Mayor said no. 'How silly for me,' and indicated to a maid nearby to bring him his robe. He ascended from the depths sloshing more water around him and was wrapped in a gold coloured towelling robe. 'So nice of you to visit us at our little enclave.' He retreated to some shade under an awning where there was a glass table with drinks already prepared. There were bite-sized meats, fruits and cakes on small plates. He discarded his cigar stump. 'Help yourself, have a cool drink, plenty of ice on such a hot day. Then we can sit over here and talk, away from all this business.' He was only a little taller than Sophie.

With a tumbler filled with something like Pimm's, with boulder ice cubes clunking inside, in one hand, clutching her plastic bag in the other, she lowered herself carefully onto the edge of a low couch, next to the puffed out fluffy figure of *el Mayor*, who was eyeing her lasciviously. 'To be young again! Eh?' he called out, laughing with some colleagues standing a little way off. And seductively, 'You look beautiful, my dear,' he said, leaning forward to place a large palm on her nearest bare knee, from where he started to indent the soft inner flesh of her thigh with stabbing circular movements of his stubby fingers, while his eyes fixed on the bobbing convexities of her breasts and the deep space between. 'And you look tired after all your hard work,' she replied, lifting his heavy hairy hand off her knee and placing it firmly back into his lap, with a sweet smile that dimpled both her cheeks, her eyes fixed on his from under fluttering lids.

He smiled sardonically. 'Tell me everything about you, don't be shy!' he cooed. 'How long have you been here and where have you come from and why have I not met you before?'

And so she talked about herself, a little falteringly, about her arrival from England six years ago and something about the jobs she had done, painting them in the best light she could, omitting any real detail, whilst answering the little questions he kept putting to her. She related the story that Baxwell had taught her, finding it surprisingly easy to open up to Senor Nestor, who had an almost cuddly fatherly aspect to him. While talking at a hushed level that no one else could hear, she glanced occasionally across the pool at the short authoritative figure who had been staring at her before, to see that he was still there and watching her; and that once he smiled faintly back at her. 'Alex is convinced he has the most innovative plans for Al Este De La Linea De Costa. He has two of the best building contractors on the south coast in his consortium and their architects and designers have come up with some brilliant plans for a five-star hotel with its own shopping mall, landscaped parks and high-end villas. He needs to win your support for his bid and looks forward to receiving the Mayor's backing for his planning permission.' Sophie smiled once again, glancing sideways into the Mayor's face from under her thick eyebrows and leaned closer towards him, placing a delicate hand deliberately on his arm and speaking more softly into one of his large flabby ears, for his hearing alone. 'And as a small measure of his gratitude, Alex would like the Mayor to accept this gift.'

With that she delved down into her plastic bag at her feet, wriggling her hand through the vegetables, inducing a state of near apoplexy in the Mayor with his front row view of her tumbling bosom. She straightened up with the flat book-shaped package of plain brown paper and adhesive tape in one hand and placed it discretely on the cushion between them, wedged between their thighs. Mayor Nestor, slightly flushed and unable to tear his popping eyes away from her chest, snatched it up, squeezing it, testing it, making crinkly sounds with his fingers, pretending no doubt in his own mind that he was fondling her lovely puppies.

'I'm sure Alex is professional at all times. His will be an excellent entry. I look forward to seeing the fruits of his labour, excellent, I know he has been working on this for a long time.'

'Day and night,' added Sophie with a tired smile.

The Mayor casually stuffed the money behind the cushions, saying nothing else about it. He did not question how much there might be, but stood up suddenly taking Sophie's hands. 'Come, let's dance,' he simpered, as if the most natural thing in the world, as music started playing, over an outside sound system with speakers hidden among the foliage around the gardens. He pulled her into a swirling movement in the shade at first and then out into the sun and around the pool, his loose robe flowing out as he waltzed in his bare feet. He was nimble for a big man. Sophie did a few inept turns with him and soon claimed that she needed to rest and have a drink. Then he wanted to introduce her to his friends and colleagues and she smiled sweetly at all the various faces, shaking hands with some, as they circulated around the pool with the Mayor reeling off name after name.

'And this is the most powerful man on the South Coast, after your illustrious Mayor, of course, Mr Juanito Robicalon,' and the Mayor roared with laughter, but whether at his irony or in fear or disbelief it was impossible to tell. The staring man with the distinguished nose and thin moustache had turned towards her with his image set in charm mode; close up she saw how handsome he was, with his swept back black hair and aristocratic features. They had barely touched palms in greeting before Senor Nestor had moved her along. Shortly afterwards she started to give her excuses, and when the Mayor retired inside to dress for a late lunch, she slipped away to the front entrance with her plastic bag of vegetables in search of her limousine ride for the return journey. She drove out of La Zagaleta, down the twisting roads with their hair-pin bends, feeling as if the whole episode had been make-believe, and was relieved to get back in one piece to the coast road, where the steaming heat of the afternoon had not lessened one bit and the breezes were too few to cool anyone down.

3

Sophie was at her desk soon after nine o'clock feeling intermittently pleased with herself and immensely guilty, although she justified everything she had done on the basis that Baxwell was a turd and probably was using stolen or laundered money with his bribe anyway. Although at intervals that annoying modern day maxim of her mother's kept cropping up in her mind: two wrongs seldom make a right.

Roberto's anger at Baxwell was understandable, which was why she had decided to help him in his ploy. Roberto had been loyal for many years but had actually gained little for himself for all that. He picked up his wages each week, which were always the same, had never varied week in week out, whatever Roberto was involved in. Baxwell was not given to moments of generosity, that was for sure. His promise to her to review her pay was probably all wind, just to appease her the other night when he was feeling sore and compromised. He was a tight-fisted tight-arsed self-serving bastard and Sophie did not trust him at all. Baxwell was also heavily in debt, according to Roberto, with commitments to a number of building projects, borrowing money wherever he could and deeply worried about deadlines. Every payment out of the business was questioned and delayed to the last minute and every creditor was hounded from the start. Gloria was also keeping the pressure on him with their own villa construction in a new estate on the hillside near Benahavis, which would have lovely views over the coastline from their sloped plot, if only they could see it finished, but it was proving ever increasingly expensive as she demanded her luxury additions, including sauna/pool complex, all of which she so thoroughly deserved; and there had been delays of one sort or another. Recently Baxwell had had to swallow his bile with more payments to fund some extra structural additions that were needed and he had nearly blown a gasket.

Mid-morning Sophie found herself daydreaming again, between demanding customers and repetitive phone calls, staring aimlessly for a while with a cup of coffee in her hands, through the shiny glass windows at the world outside, the hooting cars and rushing pedestrians, some of whom stopped for a few moments to make faces at the property advertisements in their window. From her handbag, she retrieved the postcard that she remembered had been delivered to her post-box that morning: a view of the River Thames in London, from her mother, who only occasionally got in touch these days, birthdays or Christmas time and not much else. It made her shiver, reminding her of the cold visit home two years ago. She read the short message on the back written in customarily round style, about an old friend of the family who was coming out to Malaga to visit soon and wanted to get in touch; and she wished her well. It served to remind Sophie how fast the years were passing, the best years of her life, slipping away almost unnoticed, and that she would soon be thirty and had she thought seriously about what she wanted to do with the rest of her life?

The door-buzzer sound made her glance up. A heavy man in a black suit and lumpy shoes had stepped in, leaving the glass door to swing shut with a bump. He stood in the middle of the office, looking around at all the desks in turn, before deliberately striding in Sophie's direction. He looked hot and his shirt collar was loosened around his fleshy neck. Up against her desk, right in front of her, he stared at the name on her label and placed heavy fists down onto the middle of her workspace, leaning forward so far that his ugly face came close to hers. Sophie looked unmoved, '*Puedo ayudar*? May I help?'

The man's leathery face was lived-in, the skin faintly pock-marked. He was clean-shaven and his head was meanly cropped. He had no eyebrows worth mentioning, which looked odd, and a flat broad nose spoke of a former boxing career.

'The boss, he want speak with you, with coffee, over the road,' he spoke with a gruff accent in English. 'JR,' he added when Sophie looked confused.

'JR?'

'Senor Robicalon, Juanito. He insist.' And the black-suited man stood up straight, stepped back and sideways, indicating with an arm the front door. His look was one of worry, with cracks either side of his mouth and further deep lines between his eyes and he was in no mood to argue.

Stepping across the road to *El Capricho*, which she frequented herself from time to time, Sophie, in her navy and white uniform with medium heels, passed from blindingly bright sunlight in the street to cool shaded darkness inside and, taking her sunglasses off, it took her a few seconds to adjust. She followed the big man in black and noticed how the ordinary customers were clustered at the front of the shop, well away from the group of three men looking awkward on the cushioned seating at the back, with white china cups on the low table in front of them. Sophie caught site of the outline of the man from the Mayor's villa yesterday, with his long nose and swept back hair, who sat in the middle of the group. He wore a fawn linen suit, with open shirt and gold chain, and shiny brown leather slip-ons. Robicalon stood up when he saw her and reached out to shake hands when she was within touching distance. 'We meet again. Please sit, my dear, thank you for coming.'

'I had no choice, your man…' Sophie perched gingerly, her knees clamped tight, in the space reserved next to Robicalon.

'Can be persuasive. This will only take a minute. You will take coffee, cake, no? I'm paying,' he added with a faint smile, his line of moustache curving ironically along the mean upper lip, a delicate hand placed across his chest.

More a statement than a question, Sophie decided to be sociable and to take the coffee that was already placed in front of her, and to be prepared to listen to whatever the man had to say. He was clicking his fingers and giving commands to his team before sitting heavily, shifting his position so he was close up against her and she could sense his hot thigh against hers. He whispered conspiratorially into her ear that this was a conversation for them and nobody else, did she understand? She was hemmed in by the broken-nosed goon sitting close on her other side. She nodded her agreement, staring at the frothy coffee and the congealing cocoa powder spinning on the surface as she stirred smoothly.

'You work for Alex Baxwell, yes? You are his confidante, you know his thoughts and his movements, yes?'

'Well, I wouldn't say I know all his movements, but I do know a little about him. So what?'

'You are his lover perhaps, his mistress?'

Sophie turned instinctively to Robicalon with a genuine look of horror on her face, her brows furrowing furiously. 'No, absolutely not,' she urged.

'So what was this bringing bribe money to the Mayor's residence yesterday, what was that, eh? Baxwell's money, yes?'

Sophie was taken aback and hesitated. 'Well, I, yes. How did…? I was under instruction, it was a payment Baxwell owed the Mayor, I do not know the details. You would have to ask Alex.'

'Yes, but we both know it was bribe for the Mayor to choose his plan for building permissions, don't we?' Robicalon was leaning against Sophie's shoulder and his piercing black eyes were perpetually scanning her face. She felt disconcerted and her cheeks began to colour. That close the open pores around his nose were like giant pock marks. She could detect skin foundation and carefully plucked eyebrows failed to disguise his age, the loose sag of skin and array of plentiful soft lines around his eyes giving the game away. She was aware of a rather manly perfume about him.

She was desperately trying to think what the hell Robicalon was after, when he placed a warm hand firmly across her arm. 'I want you,' and he squeezed her flesh tightly, Sophie suddenly feeling queasy in the pit of her stomach, 'to get some informations for me. You not tell Mr Alex, or you be in trouble, believe me. But you tell me informations about the Baxwell bid for the East Shoreline Project and to know I need by Monday, next. Yes?'

Sophie's brows looked worried, and she was about to object.

'No excuses, you work for me on this. I reward well if you do as I wish. If not, I not happy and that not good for you.' He ran a long finger around the front of his neck, tracing over his sharp Adam's apple. 'Yes?'

Sophie thought he needed to trim his fingernails. 'What's in it for me, then, Senor?'

'Ah, always wanting something for herself, always the same. I don't know, I think of something, yes?' he smirked.

Sophie decided she had had enough. She sat unmoved for

a few moments more, holding her cup with steady hand. On the spur of the moment, she stood up, dropping the hot drink into the lap of her minder next to her, and stood purposely onto his foot, digging her heel into the top of his shoe. She shouted, 'You creep, get off me, you're trying to touch me up, *ayuda!* This man tried to assault me…' Sophie hopped away from the back of the café towards the counter, away from Robicalon whose mouth had dropped open in total surprise, while the scalded man was screaming about the hot soaking and the pain in his foot. She repeated her accusations for all to hear; a couple of young women who had been operating the coffee machine and the till came round to stand protectively by her, as she continued to complain loudly. Customers in the front of the café were turning round, some were standing. The manager came out of a back office to see what all the commotion was about and then started asking the men to leave, probably not recognising who they were. But Sophie had squeezed herself through a cluster of people standing about at the entrance and slipped out onto the hot street; she crossed over to Baxwell's agency, where she darted into the cloakroom at the back to powder her nose and calm down.

4

Wednesday August 27

Behind large rounded sunglasses Sophie sat outside, restlessly swivelling her eyes back and forth, scanning the crowds that wandered along the lanes of the Old Town. She drew deeply on a cigarette and forced on herself a moment of calm, while reflecting on yesterday's incident, with the priceless image of Robicalon standing in surprise and trembling with anger at the back of the café playing across her mind. He must have seen the package hand-over with the Mayor, and added two and two. She managed a rueful smile. Perspiration was wetting her back and the sticky heat made her pink cotton top cling uncomfortably. She was regretting the black slacks and leather ankle boots. Everyone else out that lunchtime was in loose lightweight clothes and open sandals, trying to keep cool in whatever shade they could find, out of the full glare of the overhead sunshine that burned and bleached sharp patterns around the open square.

The narrow streets were bustling with tourists on foot searching for bargains in jewellery and leather; or local office and shop workers grabbing a bite and a drink before scuttling away for their siestas. Young men with girl-friends on scooters occasionally buzzed by tooting their horns at unsuspecting pedestrians. Noise was subdued as the main traffic was down the hill some blocks away. Sophie liked to lose herself sometimes among these people in their labyrinthine alleyways, often discovering a quaint old church or a crumbling row of cottages she had not seen before, around another corner or down some hidden steps.

Perched upright with a ready smile for anyone, she waited at a small outside table in the middle of the Plaza Los Naranjos, with its hanging geraniums and decaying sixteenth century buildings. Protected under the orange trees, she was growing increasingly impatient, desperate to tell Liz about what had been happening in her life. She vaguely wondered if she was entering a troubled world of uncertainty and danger, but then, rather than making her back away, it excited her, attracted her. How else to explain her extraordinary reaction to yesterday's encounter; she was actually feeling sorry for that poor man with the hot coffee and sore foot.

But what the hell was it that compelled these men to pick on her. One day it was Baxwell with his oozing complexion (a prize creep who made her flesh crawl), then the randy Senor Nestor, with his ogling eyes and wandering hands, who asked her outright when she was at his villa to stay for the afternoon for some more private play after a spot of lunch, which she had declined sweetly, flabbergasted. And then she had to deal with Robicalon (JR indeed), a smarmy creature with mean eyes and not to be trusted, she reckoned.

She puckered her brows together, pulled at her stubby nose and wondered how she was going to get the information JR wanted about Baxwell's bid for the East Shoreline Building Project, something that was driving Baxwell at the moment and probably the most important piece of business he had ever been involved with, its potential rewards way beyond anything he had achieved so far. JR must be competing against Baxwell to win the project and she knew that closed bids had to be submitted in the next couple of weeks to the Council offices. To win you had to pitch your price correctly and get it right on the night. Half a dozen other competitors were involved, desperate to gain any advantage through spying or passing bribes to all manner of people. Baxwell had aimed for the top man, the Mayor, but maybe all the others had passed bribes to him as well. The cheating among the Marbella Council members must be something else. She could see the whole thing was a farce, the only winners likely to be the Mayor himself and people like Robicalon.

If she could somehow play Baxwell and JR off against each other, the bastards might cancel each other out. For a moment she remembered her old friend, dear Hernandez Cagigas, the Deputy Police Chief and wondered where he was in all of this? He had tried to tackle this sort of corruption before but had never got far; he was still in his job, so she concluded he must have given up like all the others. Maybe Hernandez could offer her some protection, if she needed it. She laughed, thinking there must be something more in it for her, other than stealing a paltry two million pesos from Baxwell. She was going to stow that cash away somewhere else the moment she got back, probably up into the attic two floors above her, and then she would feed small cash amounts into her bank account.

As the minutes ticked away, she began to suspect that Liz had been kidnapped by JR's men or something. She felt she was being watched. She was seeing potential spies everywhere among the bustling crowd: the young man looking at her intently as he slowly passed by on a scooter, perhaps; or the man with open white shirt and grey shorts holding a camera to his eye that he kept fixing on her from across the square; or the middle-aged man in a crumpled cotton suit and panama two tables away peeping at her over his coffee cup that he sipped at audibly. Even the waiters looked suspiciously sideways at her, perhaps irritated that she had been at the same table alone for a while during such a busy period with an empty cup in front of her and had ordered nothing else. She saw a man walking among the crowd whom she was sure had been loitering outside the agency that morning.

She wiped her moist upper lip. Over the weekend, she had easily recruited the help she needed to support Roberto's plan, Jamie and his friends among them, who welcomed the excitement and the chance to earn a few thousand pesos. She and Roberto had sealed the details on Sunday night, looking at maps of the coast road. All was set for tonight, and Roberto would be driving down to Algeciras later that afternoon. Sophie needed time to persuade Liz about the scheme and to enlist her help. It would not be necessary to tell her quite everything, that would only put her off, especially if she lingered too long weighing up the potential dangers. Nor was she going to reveal her fling with Roberto. That part of the whole adventure was more fortuitous than necessary, although obviously proving useful. Although distasteful at first, she found it had become, well, quite desirable.

She was looking forward to a quiet night alone, actually: with a mug of hot cocoa and a long soak in the bath, and no shagging her tawdry Don Juan. An image of her mother suddenly came to mind and who was this bloke from London she was on about, who wanted to meet her in Spain? Presumably, some old crony from her mother's past. Sophie was thinking of where to move on to, she rather fancied Italy or Greece, although back to England was also a possibility. It had its drawbacks but would be safer than staying in Marbella. Unfortunately, she only realised the other night one important fact, that Roberto, although infatuated with lust for Sophie, was not an idiot, and knew exactly what she wanted. In fact, he said he was planning to go with her, wherever, the little devil.

'Fuck,' she kept thinking and well she might, imagining Roberto's muscular shape glistening with sweat lying next to her. She had to adjust her annoyingly tight trousers, wondering not for the first time how she was going to manage without him. 'Fuck, fuck,' she murmured again, feeling the time ticking on.

Then she suddenly saw Liz in big sunglasses wending her way shakily between the tables and milling customers towards her. She was swaying on her heels, trying to avoid knocking into people, while holding her shopping bags up above her head before swinging round to face the next obstacle. 'Liz, thank God you're here, I was beginning to worry.'

'So sorry, darling, oh God, the people,' and she reached out with both hands towards Sophie's shoulders, the crinkly bags hanging from her wrists bashing against them, bringing her close so she could kiss both cheeks, while their plastic glasses clashed. 'I couldn't get away and I got caught up in the crowds – you know how it is at this time of day.' She was puffing heavily and sank gratefully into the chair Sophie was holding for her, disposing of her burdens either side of her onto the stone floor and managing to order an American coffee from a passing waiter at the same time. She closed her eyes for a moment and took some long breaths. 'Thanks for your call last night, this is such a good idea.'

A blonde English woman in her thirties with a passable Spanish accent, Elizabeth was slim and tall, with an even suntan to complement her sea-blue eyes. Loyally, she had worked in the same insurance office nearby on the Calle Huerta Chica for some years and she lived mostly alone in a small apartment on the Calle Juan Alameda, overlooking the park, on the edge of the Old Town. She and Sophie had been friends from the moment they first bumped into each other when they were both being interviewed for a bar job at the Marbella Blue Ocean Club, way back. She was Liz to all her friends and she and Sophie were generally as thick as thieves, which clearly was something Sophie wanted to talk to her about. Liz was mumbling something about a trip to a garden centre to buy a gnome, so Sophie, stubbing out her cigarette and looking directly into her friend's lovely eyes, had to cut her off.

'Look, Liz, I know you've only just got here, but I haven't much time, actually I have to be back around two.' She was leaning forward, making room on the small table for the coffee that was to come, and creating an earnest look to emphasise the importance of their meeting.

'What happened to the Spanish siesta?' Liz loosened the buttons on her cotton top and puffed her breath out between loose lips, where a few fine hairs were caught in the glancing light. Her reddened face and perspiring forehead indicated that she was hot and she was asking for water with ice.

'I need to talk to you. I've got things going on, in my head. I have a plan, to get us out of here, but I need your help, Liz.'

'What on earth are you talking about, darling?'

'Well, it concerns Baxwell and Roberto, you know. He works for the business, on the transport side, heavy lifting, takes trips around the Coast or over to Africa, carrying things, merchandise, whatever.'

'Yes, yes, that randy little bugger.' Roberto had once gone off with Liz for a night of raw hot sex, but they had not hit it off, Liz preferring the wealthier tourist type, who would treat her generously to expensive dinners and designer gifts, before returning home to champagne and soft sheets. 'What about him?'

'Well, he's away down to Algeciras tonight, due back in the morning. He was telling me: he's picking up a Moroccan courier, new to the business who needs some help. And I've organised for them to be hi-jacked on the motorway tonight after dark and left to walk back to Marbella together. The car will be stolen with all the stuff on board and dumped in a car park in town. We need to go there and empty it –

early tomorrow morning, well later tonight, really.' Sophie's explanation faded away while Liz adopted a strange expression on her face.

'You're kidding, what have you been up to, Sophes?' sounding less than enthusiastic.

'Listen. Liz. We've talked about this before. We've not made this a great success here, have we? Really? I'm in trouble with Baxwell again and you know the story of my boss, so I won't go into any more of that.'

'He's a bully, Sophie darling, I don't know why you put up with him.'

'OK, the point is, we need to get away from here, get back to England perhaps, or move along to Italy or wherever, restart things. Right? You said you had no particular bloke you would stay for. And I think I have found a way of doing that, with money and with sweet revenge on Mr Alex Baxwell.'

'Sounds interesting. Does it have to involve breaking some laws?' Her smile was quite mischievous.

'Well, I ran into a man called Juan Robicalon yesterday. Heard of him?' Liz was nodding slowly with a thoughtful expression as the name sounded familiar. 'Calls himself JR. Wants me to spy on Baxwell and find out about a bid he's making for a development project. This Robicalon fellow is smooth as you like, he's a big shot around town, advises the Town Council and has his fingers in lots of pies as far as I hear. The Council does what he wants basically. And what he wants at the moment is to win this bid. It's called the East Shoreline Project, worth millions. Robicalon wants inside information so he can outbid the opposition and win.' And Sophie, with her hand on her chest, took a deep breath with a hurt look and recounted the episode of the hot coffee in the café and the implied threat from JR if she did not comply.

Liz was laughing at her tale, 'My God, Sophie, you poor thing. These men sound horrible, they're all bullies.'

'Maybe. I've been asking around about this JR. He seems to control all the planning consents, that the Mayor signs; nothing happens without JR's say so… the two of them are in league together. The corruption there, Liz, you would not believe. Almost certainly he will have his own consortium of builders and suppliers lined up for this Project – it will be one of the biggest developments we have seen in Marbella for a long time, along the Playa on the East side, along the Camino Pescadores. Alex has talked about nothing else for weeks.'

A waiter in black and white with a long red sash around his waist arrived at their side delivering the coffee and water and a plate of *mariscos* from a round tray he had perched at the ends of his upturned fingers. Liz quickly ordered two brandies in addition. '*Dos aguardientes. Gracias.* You need a little something, darling, to perk you up. I need a little something, after hearing all this. I mean, this is disgraceful behaviour, what have we come to in this country? Can this man get away with it? Go on, sorry,' and Liz shrugged, 'I'll just sip my coffee and my water while you talk. Have some of these.'

'This is one powerful dude, Liz.' Sophie was looking straight at her friend with alarm in her eyes. 'I mean, if he wants something, he gets it. Get in his way, he cuts your throat.'

Liz raised a hand to her neck with a look of mock horror. 'Are you going to tell Alex? How will you find out about his bid, without him knowing?' And she lighted two cigarettes, passing one with her pink lipstick stained around the butt across to her friend. The clock was moving on and Sophie was aware of the passing time, but grateful for the extra smoke.

'At the moment the plans are locked in his safe in head office, at the shop. He has meetings at the developers, David Silverteria, and they have Fahlenhangar, the building group, on board. He is keeping everything close. There is a huge application – I've been helping with the paperwork and documentation, filling in forms, about staff and facilities, we've had to beef it up a bit, you know, a few embellishments. The plans are well advanced but I have not seen the details of the offer. Presumably JR sees Baxwell as the main competition and wants to be offering a knockout bid. We need to get Baxwell's keys, for his office and the safe…'

'We?'

Sophie was looking thoughtful. 'Oh yes, Liz, I need you.'

'Anyway, you said JR gets whatever he wants, he will have the Council planning committee sewn up, won't he, what does it matter what Baxwell bids?'

'Ah, but on this occasion, the draw is to be in public, with the press and TV there, in two weeks' time, so there is no going back or changing the bids later. The whole idea is to ensure that the bids would be high and the Mayor wants the glory of the occasion to improve his flagging esteem, as there have been so many suspicions lately of corrupt decisions. So JR can't take any risks. Anyway it won't be his money.'

Sophie was shaking with nervous excitement, dying to relate her visit to the Mayor's villa in La Zagaleta, how she had seen him wallowing like a hippopotamus in his Jacuzzi. 'I was thinking, we could get the keys on Sunday at the welcome party Baxwell is staging, in one of his new villa complexes: it's for General Ishmail Willie Nassif and his Moroccan tribe. Baxwell's son George has been handling all the security, and he will have the safe keys on him. We just need to distract him, for a little while.'

Liz had settled in her chair, feeling more comfortable, eyeing the people moving around them while trying to follow Sophie's complicated plot. She was listening with care but liked to give the impression of nonchalance, as if all this talk of stealing things from safes was normal behaviour. 'Wow, you are wound up by all this. This is serious, yes? You're not kidding me?'

'No, this is the real thing. Baxwell is organising a grand party to impress this stonking rich Moroccan drugs lord, calls himself The General. He's coming over with his entourage. There will be drinks, girls, swimming in the pool, tomfoolery in the bushes, drugs probably and free sex in the bedrooms, fireworks etc. It's the Mijas feria and a big gambling week in Marbella, remember, and racing, they will all be over here, big money around. And Baxwell is cashing in as best he can.'

With the prospects of free drink and sex, Liz perked up, giving Sophie her full attention, with eyes widening by the minute. 'Willie Nassif what?' Although she was established locally by all intents and purposes as a decent hard-working expatriate English lady, the truth was that, despite her best efforts over the years with limited resources, Liz, rather like Sophie, remained somewhat frustrated that she had so little to show for it all.

Sophie laughed, head thrown back, 'That's his name, Ishmail Nassif, everybody calls him Willie.' They both laughed.

'Even though he's a general,' Liz observed dryly.

'I just need you to seduce Baxwell's son,' Sophie said straight-faced, reaching for the glass of water in the table.

'What!' Elizabeth spluttered.

'George Baxwell – at the party – I need those keys, for access to the office and the safe.'

There was a moment's silence between them, although the general noise and bustle of customers and waiters passing their table continued. Sophie met Liz's eyes, a luscious blue against her browned skin, and decided to race on: 'I have been so busy at the moment, I was working most of Saturday. Baxwell's on a knife-edge, balancing his money: between his own borrowings to fund someone else who needs the money he's borrowed to pay somebody else, and so on, it's complicated, more than you could realise. Baxwell is desperate to be part of the scene and to keep up appearances – he needs this to be a success.'

'And Roberto, where will he be when I'm supposed to be using my powers of seduction?'

Sophie sipped at the last of her coffee. 'Oh, he'll be well away doing Baxwell jobs, ferrying people about, don't you worry.'

Liz was thinking ahead. 'So you plan to pinch this car from Morocco containing what, money?'

'Someone else will. Tonight. It's all set up. The heist will be on the coast road, about one o'clock. Roberto will stop to help a young woman on her own with a broken down car. You know, damsel in distress, long legs in shorts, big chest.'

'That's Roberto, suits him to a tee,' exclaimed Liz perhaps with a little sense of regret.

'He'll be jumped on by a couple of lads hiding in the bushes, and they'll leave him up there with Ali Agra to walk back.'

'Ali Agra?' Liz queried with puckered eyebrows.

'That's the Moroccan courier, apparently. My team will steal the car and drive it to the McDonald's car park on the Ojen Road. We can go over there later around 3am and recover the haul.'

'And Roberto will walk into town with this Ali bloke and explain to Baxwell that he was mugged? And that he didn't see what hit him? All the money in the abandoned car gone?'

'And the hashish,' added Sophie, nodding.

Liz spluttered into her coffee, fine spots of brown appearing on her skirt, which she frantically wiped away. 'Hashish? You said nothing about hashish.'

'Ssh, quiet. Don't panic. We'll pay the gang, 10000 pesos each, whatever. They'll bugger off, we will rip out the hidden money and stuff and hide it away. Nobody will know. I'll find a buyer, probably through Hsui Long Long and his Chinese mob.'

'Sounds as if you've thought of everything. Who are all these bods that you use? I didn't know you had kept up with these kind of people?'

'You'd be surprised, don't ask,' Sophie joked. She left a pause in the conversation, to let what she had said sink in.

Liz was still feeling hot and her normally sharp senses were a little slowed. 'So where does that get us, Sophie, I mean, I know we'll have some extra money, what are we talking about, a few million pesos?'

'Roberto was unsure, but he thought it was quite a size, I don't know, a few million, yes, maybe; OK, not enough to change the world, but cash for us to use, enough to buy travel tickets and move on. It could be a start?'

Sophie had been talking rapidly, eager to get onto the bits that would involve them, without Liz asking too many questions. Frankly Sophie did not care where the money was from or what it was for, she understood it was illegal and she saw it as an opportunity for them to help themselves to some of it. If anyone was going to be hurt it would be Baxwell, who would be short of cash; and Roberto, who needed the wits to appear convincingly the ignorant unwitting driver and not an accomplice, but might end up seeking alternative employment, which is what he wanted anyway.

'Sorry, Sophes, I am beginning to get a little lost, what has this Moroccan General got to do with it?'

'He's a marijuana drugs lord, with a lot of money and power and runs his empire from the Rif Mountains. This guy has been laundering his drugs money through Spain for years, buying property and big cars in cash, and then selling on using local banks; most often the money comes over with a courier on the Algeciras ferry – bold as you like, cash stitched into the fabric of car seats, that kind of thing. His cronies come over and ride up and down the Golden Mile in brand new Mercedes, and spend most of the money on his behalf – mostly on women and drink. He's using Baxwell for the arrangements, they met a couple of times last year and Baxwell did some good deals with the Moroccans. The Spanish authorities are a bit pissed off apparently at this guy coming here with his dodgy money, and have put some pressure on the Moroccan Government, but it won't stop; it's usually American dollars and the Spanish economy is thriving on it, even if it is black market and laundered.'

Liz was looking thoughtful. 'So Ali Agra is part of his mob. Still if it's all unmarked, this money and hash can't be traced back to him. Roberto might get into trouble, I suppose, but he can look after himself.'

'Oh yes, he'll be fine. Listen, I need to be getting back, Liz. Can I call you later? Come on over to my place early, we'll get some sleep before we set out in the morning to collect, around two o'clock. Alright?'

The two of them left the café shortly after agreeing that something needed to be done, that they had no qualms about relieving Baxwell of some dodgy cash, that the Sunday afternoon of the party would be good for getting the necessary keys and the information that JR wanted because everybody would be distracted and probably drunk; and that they needed to agree about what to do with Roberto, so he would not become a liability.

Sophie was the first to dash off on her own but it still took her a good fifteen minutes to weave her way out of the Old Town and get back along the Ricardo Soriano to the shop, where she quickly settled behind her desk making calls, talking to clients, organising visits by repair men or bills to be collected. Baxwell always wanted to be in control and would complain endlessly when any of the office staff had long lunches or left early, so she tried to look as if she had never been out.

Late in the afternoon Sophie took a call at her flat from Roberto. He was near the Playa Rinconcillo in Algeciras apparently and sounded a little fretful, a long way away. The line was crackly and he was shouting in fast agitated Spanish that Sophie struggled to fully understand. She had to slow him down. Ali Agra was nowhere to be found, he was saying, had chickened out in Ceuta and had given everything to a different fellow called Bruce, who could not drive and was alone at the safehouse. And his driver was sick. So Roberto would be driving a different car, a Skoda Estelle Estate, an old green thing trailing a horsebox, stuffed with bags of fertilizer and compost. These needed to be dumped somewhere out of the way, could she think about that and make her team aware of the changes before they were in position. A green Estelle estate, he repeated, and gave her details of all the hidden stashes. He would be leaving well after dark, around midnight. She must get her team ready with their plan.

If Sophie suspected anything at this stage, she was not saying, but she did sense that something was not quite right. A Moroccan courier unfamiliar with the routine, crying off as he was too scared. A different car, trailing a horsebox. Another driver claiming to be sick, accompanied by a co-driver who could not drive. Called Bruce?

5

Thursday August 28

Roberto's masterplan was acted out in the early hours of the next morning, in the end exactly as he had envisaged. He had made his call to Sophie from a box outside a café up the road from their safehouse, while Bruce was taking a leak. Ali Agra had cried off in panic apparently, he had lost his nerve at the Ceuta border control and Bruce and his driver had stepped in, with all the extra merchandise loaded into their Skoda Estate. A diversion had been organised at the dockside customs, with some asylum seekers and stowaways in a truck ahead, young boys really, Sudanese, Bruce thought, seeking a better life; and they occupied the customs officers and Guardia for so long that a restless queue of pedestrians and cars had built up and were becoming impatient. They were ushered through quickly and the Skoda with its horsebox in tow was only paid a cursory glance. And then at the safehouse his driver had become sick and went upstairs to a bathroom to puke his guts out. Bruce could not drive and so Roberto would take the wheel and that suited him fine. It meant he had to leave his Baxwell company truck in Algeciras but it could be picked up at some later date by one of their boys. The old road they would take ran all the way from Gibraltar eastwards along the coast mostly, through Marbella and on to Malaga, and Sophie's friends had arranged to be in their position at the end of a long slow uphill section just before the laden Skoda would reach the summit, a stretch of carriageway chosen for being remote and totally unlit.

Roberto did not tell Sophie all the details until they caught up with each other much later on the Thursday, in the evening, after Roberto had taken Bruce to Baxwell's office and they had together tried to relate in some detail without getting heated to an increasingly putrescent Alex Baxwell exactly what had happened. Roberto was soaking his bruised body in a hot bath in her flat, Sophie ministering to him once again with oils and soft flannels. At the top of his back between his shoulder blades, against his left hip and in the small of his back were deep red weals and darkened patches that were looking angry. His face was bruised under the left eye to match his old black eye from Friday, and his feet were swollen and blistered at the heels.

'I expected Baxwell to be angry, but these are a bit much, aren't they?' Sophie said, straight-faced gingerly touching his wounds.

'This was your team, bloody hell!' Roberto croaked between his moans and screwed-up facial expressions. Sophie could see how the acting of her team in Roberto's assault must have looked convincing to the watching Moroccan but she half apologised for their enthusiasm.

They had trundled slowly in the filthy old Skoda across stretches of empty dockside tarmac following the '*salida*' white road markings, Roberto driving, pulling the grey horsebox behind, and then joined their route that meandered through Los Cortijillos and San Roque with only the occasional car or small truck to distract them. They barely noticed the Gibraltar turn and the Rock over to their right in the dark gloom, as they found their exit off the causeway onto motorway A-15. The estate car was many years old with its counter stuck on 999,999 miles and was noisy, belching out dark smoke from the exhaust every time the accelerator pedal was pressed hard. It was an uncomfortable ride, the seats thin and worn. The inside was so stuffed with unmarked cardboard boxes that Roberto could not see properly out of the back window. Bruce, a tall long-legged African, settled as best he could in the front seat, explaining that the boxes were filled with souvenirs, typical things that black African men ply the sunny coastal beaches and restaurants with: wooden carvings of giraffes and lions, coloured plastic lookalike Elvis Presley dolls, pathetically cheap bracelets and watches, leather slippers and purses, pouches, little bags and rugs. As they motored further eastwards over more rugged and deserted landscape, with the occasional decrepit roadside shack or bare olive tree breaking the rocky skyline, Roberto started feeling weary and struggled to stay awake. Bruce had already closed his eyes and his head nodded against the side window, despite the rattling noises from the back.

It was after a good hour and a half since they had set off and well after midnight, when Roberto was struggling with the lack of power in the old estate going in lowest gear through a slow climb along a rising section of the lonely carriageway, that at last he came alongside the old Cortina that he was looking out for. Picked out by convenient moonlight that had emerged through a sparsely clouded sky, it was parked at an angle on the hard shoulder. As they came alongside, Roberto pretended to ogle at a woman in shorts with bare legs bending over the open bonnet and remarked suggestively about the shape of her bottom, wondering whether they should stop and help. Bruce, who only spoke a halting English and no Spanish as far as Roberto could tell, was coiled up in his seat half asleep and seemed to grunt his approval. The young woman stood upright and waved sheepishly at them. Roberto parked up a little way past the Ford and told Bruce to stay in the car as he jumped out, taking the keys with him.

He jauntily walked back and engaged in a conversation in Spanish with the shy-looking woman, who seemed ever so grateful for his offer. Once Roberto was leaning under the bonnet next to the girl, two figures in dark combat clothes and white masks emerged suddenly from the shadows and jumped him from behind. Another figure in black wearing a white plastic mask hopped into the Estelle brandishing a baton that was prodded hard under Bruce's chin. He turned round to watch the scene with horror and was unable to do anything. Roberto had taken several heavy blows across his back, a kicking to his side and a punch across his temple. Bundled to the ground, he had his arms pinned back and wrists tied behind him with some thin rope. The car keys were forced from his grip and one of the attackers came over to their Skoda. Bruce was pushed out to the ground at the side of the road and his wrists were similarly tied behind him. The old Skoda with the horsebox in tow departed jerkily with two of the masked figures while the third man and the woman followed in their Cortina, which had started up perfectly well. As the sound of their engines gradually faded in the distance, dark oily smoke and diesel smells were all that was left by the roadside to remind them of their treasure-packed chariot.

Bruce tried to remember the Spanish number plate on the Ford and was reciting out loud letters and numbers in ever changing versions as he ran over to Roberto lying on the grass verge. Working back to back, they were able to free their ties after a while. Roberto was shaken and bruised, with a cut over his left eye and struggled to stand up straight at first but they trudged their way back along the deserted highway, about twenty-five painful kilometres to Marbella, taking them over six hours. They managed to cadge a lift at the end, the last four kilometres into Marbella, and they were dropped off at Roberto's flat, sore and weary, arguing how they would explain to Baxwell that they had been mugged and that the Skoda with all its hidden booty had been stolen and that they had no idea who did it or where it might be.

* * *

At around two hours past midnight, Liz and Sophie were awakened by the bedside alarm and quickly prepared for their adventure. The early morning air was surprisingly warm and they travelled together in Liz's VW hatch with the windows open, calmly negotiating the deserted streets onto one section of the Autovia, before taking the slip road at the Parque Comercial exit that curved round almost in a semi-circle to a roundabout, right by the big yellow 'M' of the McDonald's, the deserted restaurant still dimly draped in neon. Its long car park had no barriers and extended away among bushes and cypress trees, neatly hidden from surrounding roadways and chosen by a mate of Jamie's for not having any CCTV cameras or security guards on night patrol – quite how he knew those details, Sophie was unsure but was prepared absolutely to believe him and it looked as if he had it right. It was a simple drive in, an unlit area with the solitary Skoda Estelle Sophie had heard so much about, thankfully without its horsebox, tucked away at the far end among the leafy shadows. The boys had agreed to unhinge the trailer and leave it in fields adjacent to Jamie's father's place, just outside town, where nobody would notice it. So far everything seemed to be going right.

Liz parked up beside the dirty estate car, switching off the engine. They sat still for a few moments, listening to the silence of the night, before easing open their doors. They moved in soft shoes, both wearing gloves and whispering to each other. Sophie examined the dirty Skoda with sandy dust over its sides and a Moroccan number plate (4889-45|2), with an MA sticker on the back. She retrieved the keys that had been left for her on the front tyre passenger side.

Unlocking each of the doors of the Skoda with the key, they slid into the back seats on either side with two zip-up bags, pushing cardboard boxes filled with junk out of their way as best they could to work on the door panels. Once the wind-up handles were removed, a screwdriver inserted under the edges easily levered them off their clips, and fingers completed the job. The inside door spaces were packed, just as Roberto had promised, with dozens of hard brick-sized packets taped in brown paper wrapping, rather like Baxwell's bribe money had been, and other square heavier packets in cellophane and cling-film. These were hashish cakes, wrapped well and covered in a slippery cream to prevent the sniffer dogs of the Spanish border patrol detecting them. That was all Ali Agra's stuff destined for Baxwell, but of course they now had two consignments and Sophie knew about the false compartment under the chassis, that Bruce had been nursing: by pulling up the floor carpet behind the driver's seat, there was a cut-out thin metal flap that when lifted, allowed a hand to pass into a narrow space that ran alongside the central drive shaft. Roberto had explained it all to her over the phone.

Suddenly there was a piercing wail of an alarm and the sound of squeaking coming from inside the car in the boot space behind them. They both jumped out of their skins, frozen and wide-eyed. Liz rummaged around frantically pulling open box after box until she found the offending doll, a little Elvis with black sideboards and white satin trousers, that had somehow been set off, complete with flashing lights and unreal laughter. She viciously broke it in two and twisted the base off, when the piercing sound stopped; she puffed out her cheeks in relief. Sophie returned to the narrow compartment below her and found a mass of crisp notes in paper bundles inside see-through plastic bags, all dollars these, which surprised her, and she stuffed them all into her hold-all. Liz filled the other bag with the cakes and packages from the doors.

Intently aware of the magnitude of what they were doing, Sophie was focused on the job, of getting the full haul out of the Skoda, back to a safe hiding place and the two of them returned to the comfort of their own apartments. They hauled the two zipped bags over to the boot of Liz's car, closing the lid quietly, both wondering to themselves what the contents were worth on the street and exactly how much cash they had acquired?

Liz asked, 'That it? No more?'

Sophie had to suppress a desire to laugh. 'I'm sure that's the lot.'

'Shame,' added Liz under her breath.

They abandoned the Skoda with its stuffed boxes of silk slippers, wood carvings and ridiculous dolls, leaving the keys in the ignition and unlocked, for some lucky punter to find later. Liz drove cautiously out of the carpark the way they had come, their hearts racing, while Sophie imagined a patrol car waiting for them around the corner with armed police at the ready, informed by one of her insider friends. She held her breath until they were back on the Autovia and heading west. There was nobody waiting to stop them, all the roads were clear and they were unobserved. How could she ever think that any of her friends would give her away? While the journey was uneventful and they passed no more than the occasional taxi on the roads, they were both anxious enough to keep quiet until they arrived back in the Calle Nuestra.

Liz parked outside Sophie's block in the dead quiet darkness and switched off, and only then did they breathe more easily. 'Roberto and this Bruce bloke will be still on the march down from the coast road, I bet they will have sore feet.' Sophie sounded genuinely sympathetic.

'So how much money do you think there is, then?' Liz twittered, feeling quite like a naughty schoolgirl. They stared intently through the front windscreen at the other cars parked along the roadway, both slightly shocked at their own actions.

'God knows,' Sophie laughed, 'a lot; more than I had expected. Especially all those dollars – wonder who they were for? We'll count it in a few days, when all is quiet. You better go. Thanks Liz, you've been great.' She leaned across and put an arm round her neck, kissed both her cheeks. They smiled at each other. 'The boot's unlocked,' Liz commented and Sophie got out to retrieve one of the bags from the back, the one with the money, as agreed, and took a small hash cake out as a sample from the other bag, which she left in the boot. After closing the lid gently, she whispered through the open window, 'Good-night and sleep well. I'll be in touch,' and waved a hand.

As the Polo pulled away, Sophie scuttled along the shadows close to the buildings, conscious of the weight of the bag she carried, admiring some new graffiti on the wall opposite. She could smell the drains and a couple of cats darted down a side alley as she turned into her entrance, wearily pushed inwards on the heavy glass doors and climbed her dingy staircase to the sixth floor. Her legs felt heavy and she was in need of sleep. Much of her skin felt stiff with dried perspiration. Once inside the front door, she placed the full bag on the floor and leaned backwards, closing her eyes, resting her head against a plastered wall, feeling mightily relieved. In the kitchen she drank a glass of water; then she took a shower, cleaned her teeth and gratefully slipped bare into the coolness between her cotton sheets where she slept fitfully through the rest of the night. Waking early with dreams of Roberto beaten by Baxwell into telling him where she had hidden the money, she lay restlessly turning this way and that, disturbed by the bright early morning light intruding through the flimsy curtains. She needed to be up doing things but her legs were heavy and would not move for her. She heard no sounds from within the building or activity outside and dozed a bit longer.

Eventually the recurring violence in her dreams woke her again and she forced herself up, found a pot of yogurt in the back of her fridge and some bread and made a coffee. Then she left the flat, in some rough clothes thrown on without thought. Downstairs she peered out into her shadowed street and started to walk around the neighbourhood, feeling the warming sunshine pleasant on her face, constantly looking out for potential watchers and unusual parked cars but found nothing untoward. She had convinced herself that JR would have some men watching her round the clock and reporting back to him, but having found none she felt mildly disappointed that he deemed her not important enough, silly man. Now she could visualise Baxwell himself storming over in a stew, puffing and sweating in his anger, with some heavy muscle in tow to beat the truth out of her. When she returned to her apartment once again and safely acknowledged that there were no signs of any unpleasant thugs hiding around corners, and that she was alone, she proceeded to secure a good hiding place for her bag of treasure.

* * *

From first thing in the morning, Alex Baxwell had been pacing nervously around the agency, wandering from desk to desk to see what the staff were up to, staring at their computer screens; sometimes he would be smiling profusely as he shook hands with a passing customer, leading them to a desk for further attention, or be retreating back up the inner staircase to his sanctum, mumbling under his breath. He could be seen looking out over his shop, his belly pressed against the internal glass panels, hands poking into baggy trousers, wiping sweat from his forehead or working a cigarette nervously between his thin lips.

At her desk Sophie heard his footsteps behind her and not for the first time felt his stare on the back of her neck, making her feel uncomfortable. He leant down on an elbow beside her, looking at her screen.

'I'm worried,' he grumbled under his breath into her ear. 'I've still not heard from Roberto, he's not reported in this morning – the van's not out the back. I've just phoned his flat again, it's not ringing. It's after eleven, so where is the little shit?'

Sophie looked up casually from the paperwork on her desk and glanced at Baxwell's over-flushed complexion with its signs of lack of sleep. 'He's just sleeping in, I should think. He was probably late last night. What job was he on?'

'Don't you worry about that – he had been down to Algeciras to pick up some stuff, some important merchandise – from Morocco. He should have called in last night, whatever time.' He straightened up to leave, but then bent down quickly on second thoughts bringing his face almost in contact with her hair. 'You sure you delivered my parcels to the Mayor properly, um?'

'I did exactly as you asked,' she replied through pursed lips.

As the morning wore on, the still air in the office became increasingly stuffy, the air-conditioning unit working no better than last week. Baxwell became increasingly agitated, with more pacing, more cigarettes and some loud telephone calls which ended with him slamming the phone down.

Around midday Baxwell called for coffee and sandwiches from the café over the road, for a group of developers and planners in their summer suits, that included a couple of friendly Englishmen who chatted with Sophie, that arrived *en masse* for a meeting in the upstairs office. Among them was

Baxwell's son George in open necked white shirt and pale slacks, a thinner version of his father, thank goodness, still heavily built but taller, with pale freckled skin and reddish hair, who breezed in with a woman in a green suit carrying a box of leaflets about the East Shoreline Project. In the boot of her car outside she had a scale-model made of *papier mache* and chicken wire, with wooden cut-outs and pieces on a wooden base. There were miniature plastic trees and plastic people walking about between apartment blocks, swimming pools, roads and the sea painted in with rocks and sand, tiled roofs and artificial grass. George and Sophie helped carry it into the shop, where they made some space for it on a table, to one side of the front lobby so customers could walk around it for inspection. A plastic cover like a lid was brought in to enclose the model. All the suits from upstairs came down with glasses of bubbly in their hands to talk about it and congratulate themselves on a good looking piece of work. On a card was a list of the particulars and the green suit lady was able to proudly reel off the unique collection of high-end specifications and design firsts on display. Sophie had to admit that it looked rather impressive, the right combination of scale, style and originality.

Baxwell was now in triumphant mood, the problem of Roberto forgotten for the moment. With less than a week to go until submission, there was nervous and excited laughter in anticipation. They all looked satisfied that the hard work had been done and that there should be no last minute glitches. Hands were shaken, backs were patted and more champagne poured and sipped. With arrangements to print more posters to gain maximum publicity agreed, they planned to meet at the Town Hall in Malaga next week for the presentation. Their model and its details would be transported there next Monday morning for the judges to study for a day, before the announcement at midday on Wednesday.

'Sophie is working on the papers now, they will all be ready on time, I'm sure,' and Baxwell gave her a condescending smile from the other side of the room and all the assembled people clapped at least a little, turning their gaze onto her while she had the sense of timing to blush demurely, to smile but to say nothing.

A little while after they had all departed, Baxwell came to the top of his stairs and called for Sophie to come up to his office for a moment. He sounded stern. Her heart sank. What had he found out?

With the door closed, the air felt tense as she stood upright in front of his desk while he fidgeted behind it, finishing off the last of his bubbly drink in a flute. Baxwell placed the empty glass back onto his table top and seemed to be studying the marks around the rim, which had suddenly become of interest.

'I spoke to the Mayor just now. He rang to see how the preparations were going.' He stared hard into Sophie's face with a severe expression, a headmaster about to remonstrate with a wayward member of staff. 'He said he was phoning all the candidates. He had heard that popular opinion was in favour of the Baxwell Properties Consortium bid. I thanked him for his courtesy and hoped he would look on our bid with particular favour.' Baxwell rose and stalked around his desk towards Sophie, not an inkling of amusement on his flabby face. 'Senor Nestor told me two million pesetas would come in handy.' Baxwell paused beside her, studying the miniature gold earring that drooped from one pierced lobe and the smooth line of her chin that he admired so much. He could see a pulsing in her neck that he was tempted to touch. Besotted by the beauty of her satin-like skin, a faint blush over her cheeks conferring an innocence to her expression, his suspicions seemed intensely aroused. She could smell the warm alcohol on his breath.

Inside her stomach lurched, but she remained impassive,

looking straight ahead trying to avoid his eyes, even though he was now poking his face right in front of hers. 'So what happened,' he asked between clenched teeth, 'to the other two million fucking pesos in cash that I gave you, Sophie, dear?' The outer third of his right eyebrow rose and fell farcically as if controlled by string. Flushed anger was beginning to erupt across his face, reddened in blotches, his thin hair standing up more than usual.

'I was going to tell you,' she started, swallowing hard, still looking straight ahead, 'Alex... but I thought it would anger you and that you would not find out anyway... and that perhaps it did not matter.'

'You're damn right it would anger me. So what have you done, you little...' He was close to screaming but unable to say the word 'tart'.

'I had to listen to the Mayor pontificating about his democratic council and how he wanted this project to be a special landmark of his ruling time into office, something for the ordinary family and not just for the rich people. He said it would be important to get Robicalon's support. And he was there, with some of his cronies around the pool. JR. He came over and challenged me directly, he said there were others on the judging committee. He was so rude and threatening. The Mayor suggested that you should make the same offer to both of them. So I said that I had come prepared for that and had two packages, one for the Mayor and one for Senor Robicalon. They took their bundles and smiled and slipped them out of sight. Without the slightest shame. They thanked me for being so sensible. They then talked about other things and ignored me completely. I was soon dismissed. I had no choice really.' Sophie managed a wet tear in the corner of her eye and Baxwell was convinced.

'My God. The bastards.' Baxwell backed away, his face softened into a look of slight surprise and then he tried offering sympathy without much luck. 'You know that JR is secretly funding one of his own bids, under another name of course, and he's judging so bribing him would be useless, which is why I was not going to bother.'

'I'm sorry, I had no choice, Alex.'

'Alright. Let me think. Under the circumstance you did well, Sophie.' Baxwell retreated to his side of the desk and sank into his leather swivel chair. 'The Mayor seemed happy enough with his two million on the phone. Let's pray it works. Anyway our land bid is a killer; no one will top it. We've been quite clever. It is conditional: depends on the agreed type of building, use and quality.' He was smiling now, more of a smirk, contemplating his own tactics. 'On a sliding scale, the higher quality we are allowed to build the higher becomes the bid. The Council will be tempted to allow better quality, which will earn me more in rent and fees, and the Council a bigger capital payment. Win-win. The others won't be doing that.'

'So long as it's specifications remain within the aspirational goal for the ordinary family, was the Mayor's point,' added Sophie, sounding horribly like an estate agent.

'Oh, absolutely,' Baxwell cooed in his Edinburgh burr.

'And, er, what's our total bid for the project, then?' Sophie asked with such boldness that it seemed to be totally without ulterior motive.

'Oh, now that would be telling. Anyway we have not finally settled on our cost base; Trevor and a couple of the others have still got some work to do.' Baxwell was chewing a pencil and making some notes on a pad of paper on his desk. 'I'll decide next week, before we submit,' he added as an afterthought. 'It'll be a killer.'

Feeling relieved that her story had got her out of trouble, Sophie listened carefully to Baxwell's ramblings while trying to look contrite for her error and innocence.

Towards the end of the afternoon, a sense of languid calm had settled around the shop, as staff with cool drinks or teas from their cramped back kitchen, settled the day's inventory, closed books and prepared for tomorrow's schedules, chatting quietly. The air was possibly a little cooler now that the sun had moved off the front and the street door had been left open to encourage some airflow.

Baxwell came heavily down the wooden stairs once again and stomped over to Sophie's desk in a state of obvious agitation.

'Still no word from Roberto,' he hissed into her ear, but not caring any more who else might hear. 'Something must have happened to him, for sure. It does not make any sense to me. There was a whole lot of stuff he was picking up and a man was there waiting for him, he was supposed to bring him back, for some exchanges here. Did Roberto not tell you about it? Or anyone else?'

'I had no idea, why would I know about it. Nothing to do with me,' she said defensively. 'I haven't spoken to Roberto in weeks.' Sophie rather enjoyed on reflexion seeing Baxwell squirming with worry; it served him right, she thought.

A couple of hours later, before Sophie was ready to leave around six o'clock, with the fiery sun glancing across the opposite side of the avenue, the desk phone rang yet again and she was sorely tempted to leave it alone. There were still three other office staff present and they would be listening. Slowly she reached for the handset, speaking rather wearily into the mouthpiece: 'Baxwell's Estate Agency, *por favor* – can I help?'

'Sophie, is me.' Roberto's voice was croaky and quiet and Sophie had difficulty in making out what he said. 'We are back, sore feet. *Estoy cansado.* My back is bruised – those boys were rough. But it worked OK. Bruce was taken in. We have slept at my place.'

'Good. Excellent news, Senor. You may want to come in and look over the contracts, maybe later this week.'

'What you say, is Roberto. We will see Baxwell soon, then I come round.'

'*Si, Senor*. That would be fine. *Gracias. Adios.*' And with that, Sophie put the receiver down, leaving the tired and slow-witted Roberto a little confused but keenly anticipating a night with Sophie.

That Thursday evening Roberto struggled to drive over to Sophie's in Calle Nuestra and stumble up her stairs but soon came to be soaking in Sophie's hot bath. While he excitedly recounted again the details of his adventure and all the night's travails, she soothed his wounds the best she could, massaged his great shoulders and rubbed creams into his sore feet.

'We got to see Baxwell, I left Bruce with him. He went berserk, use lots of rude words. His face went purple,' and Roberto chuckled. 'You should have seen.'

'Tell me about Bruce. And what happened to Ali Agra?'

'Ali Agra had kittens on Ceuta side, refused to come over; persuaded Bruce and his driver Nabil to take consignment over in Bruce's car, the Estelle. Then in Algeciras flat Nabil become sick, stomach pains. Probably swallowed some marijuana in wax, the covering ruptured inside, Bruce had seen it a few times before. He look ill. We left him, someone will get him to doctor, if he lives!' Roberto seemed quite buoyant in mood, despite his sore injuries and wearisome feet.

'And Bruce, who is he, who does he work for?'

'Oh, I not know him, he comes over for Moroccan drug baron, El Mougrabi, who loves the racing. This man he buys a Spanish race horse and Bruce is to take it back to Rabat with him in the box, so the dollars was payment, I think.'

'I met up with Jamie earlier and he drove me over to his

Dad's place, it's along the Istan Road from Nueva Andalucia; it's lovely up there and he's got an old villa and some fields next to it – we found the horsebox, full of heavy plastic bags, fertilizer and compost. We opened some of them: hidden inside were big chunks of pure hash resin, 2kg each, wrapped in cling film and plastic, we thought about 150 cakes, that's 300kg in total. Or more, I mean, we didn't rip them all open; but that's ten or twelve million pesetas purchase cost, would sell for ten times that, once it hits the streets of London. I mean, that's more than I have ever dreamt of in my life. And there were lots of dollars in the Skoda, I mean a lot.'

'But that's good. Two consignments, millions of pesetas, dollars and hashish. We're in luck, just stay cool, sell off slow, bit by bit, we have time.' Somehow Sophie did not feel quite so confident as Roberto, but maybe the racehorse purchase justified those dollars, although she wondered who was selling.

'We need to talk to the Chinese to arrange some deals.'

'Yes, I know, I have it in hand, Rob. I just don't know how much we have to deal with and what sort of leverage we can apply, yet.'

Roberto chuckled. Sophie fed him and listened to him some more and laughed with him; and then coaxed him eventually back to his Suzuki to drive home, no night of canoodling just then. She dressed in tight black jeans and T-shirt, and with biker jacket zipped up and only faintly made up, she went off in search of her friend, Hsui Long Long, to persuade him to buy a ton of hash.

In the middle of town, she found John without difficulty as usual at the back of The Peking Duck, among the waste bins eating some leftovers from the kitchens with a few other Chinese blokes, ragamuffins all, using their dirty fingers, sticky with soy source, washing down rice and meats with bottles of beer and wiping their hands on their stained overalls.

Hsui Long Long, a Chinese lad somewhere in his late twenties, was treated as the local gang leader's son, and everyone except his family called him John. Ho Sup Ping was the elder statesman among the growing population of Chinese in Marbella, known as The Magician for the clever ways he managed to evade the taxman and other arms of law enforcement, and nominal head of the legitimate family business, mostly restaurants and launderettes. John always giggled incomprehensively whenever anyone asked him about his family or ancestry, so whether genetic or adopted The Magician was certainly the closest he had to a father. Nevertheless, he did not seem to receive any special treatment over anyone else. He was always dressed appallingly in the same ripped and worn clothes, usually unwashed like his hair, lanky and spiky black, over-long down his back. Scrounging for the day's unwanted food was typical of John and his friends, although he always had ready access to cash; and hash. He rarely seemed to sleep and could usually be found after dark around the narrow alleyways at the back of the Chinese restaurants, among the strip joints and the sleazy bars with their gambling and late night shows, mooching, smoking, sharing weed and playing dice.

He was respected though, by his family and friends, who recognised his intelligence, his quick mind, his languages and his arithmetic, extra sharp in money transactions and dealing. He was frequently used in negotiations for his father, his broken English and scent for a bargain working to their best advantage. Hashish, marijuana, cannabis, weed, what the rich European kids often called pollen, this was his specialist subject. He knew the latest prices, what was going down and who was involved. When new faces appeared on the scene he initiated investigations, always looking to disqualify them for inadequate finances or unsavoury background, for the Chinese were protective of their hard-won territory. He knew how the game worked and his father entrusted him with many a serious deal.

He was a user himself, undoubtedly, but always seemed in control. Everybody did business with John and he was easy to find with various brothers and cousins hanging about the kitchens. How he kept out of jail nobody on the right side of the law could understand, but then Marbella was well versed in mutual relationships between its authorities and its underworld characters, always some leverage, some connection and Sophie felt sure John was no different. Sophie had known him since her arrival some years ago when she was dealing with the low-lifes around town; smoking marijuana in groups was a pleasant way to obscure the reality of their sometimes meaningless lives. Sophie and John had worked together, hunted together on and off, identifying potential punters, collecting payments, picking up stuff for other clients, and so they knew each other's ways. Sophie trusted him. She had kept away over the last six months pretty much to avoid trouble but she still had friends in the area and she still hoped that Hsui Long Long was one of them.

John was looking a mess as usual and smiling a lot, showing off his discoloured teeth, fiddling with cash in his hands, rubbing coins between his grubby fingers. He wore a thin strip of leather around his scrawny neck and the usual plain T-shirt that was once white pulled out over a pair of black slacks that were too long for him, the frayed hems covering his bare feet and catching on the ground. His wrists had plenty of coloured and leather ties, which trailed untidily.

She sat down with the others and started chatting in Spanish and broken English for a while and even shared some chopped sour duck and a palm of rice; John gave her a fresh bottle and then they wandered alone along the back alleyway in the steamy darkness, softly talking.

'I have access to quite a bit of good stuff, Moroccan and

wondered whether we could use one of our old networks for a sale?'

'You not into hash business no, Sophie, you tell me,' and John snorted, baring his front teeth.

'This is special.'

'So who is source, this new?'

'Oh, I can't tell you that John, but it's verifiable stuff, the real McCoy, came in last night – about 300kg. Should fetch a hundred million on the street.'

'That's lot, very lot. Where you get, Sophie, is legit?'

'John, it's legit, OK. So you ask your Big Daddy if he wants to buy the whole package, yes?'

John looked sceptical and stopped to study Sophie's face, while he chewed some gum. She placed a hand on his arm and smiled back, 'It's important for me to make this sale, and you were the first port of call. But if you feel… '

'No, no, I talk. Magician, he be velly intested, I sure.' They wandered on slowly, John and Sophie leaning against each other, remembering some old incident from years ago, laughing under their breath. The alleyway opened onto a small square with trees and bushes in the middle and crammed with parked cars and vans; and a police car hovering on one side, its lights quashed. They retreated into the shadows of a doorway, where they stood closely together for some while. They made an agreement to meet the following night. John leant across Sophie and planted a kiss on her nearest cheek, and with a big goofy grin, an index finger over his lips, he slipped back silently along the way they had come. Sophie waited a few minutes before sloping off to find her car parked a couple of blocks away.

6

Friday August 29

Following another night of intermittent vivid dreaming, about bundles of money bursting out from the upholstery in the backs of cars and groups of Chinese warriors invading her apartment, orchestrated by an angry JR, grabbing her bag in one hand and throwing US dollars down the stairwell from her hiding place in the roof, she was dozing heavily when her morning alarm rang. She lay on her back for a while, pushing the sheets away to expose bare flesh to the cooler morning air, not wanting to get up, with one hand cradling her head, the other fingering stale underarm stubble, watching the early sunshine playing patterns across the ceiling. After coffee and toast, she stumbled into a lukewarm shower, assiduously cleansed and shaved and made ready for the outside world. In turquoise eye shadow and a pale apricot lipstick, she headed for the office, smart in her uniform, anticipating Baxwell on the prowl and beside himself with fury at the loss of his money and merchandise.

She worked herself tediously through a typical morning with a stack of paperwork, customers in the shop and a few established clients over the phone. Early afternoon her phone started to ring for the umpteenth time.

The voice was friendly, male, sort of American accent but almost certainly Spanish. 'Hello. I was calling in your office earlier? You showed me the new development in Santa Clara overlooking the golf course, I am interested in buying apartment.' Sophie pictured a good-looking man in a lightweight suit who came in that morning showing interest in a two-bed apartment only just been completed on a nice site golfside. He had decided he wanted to look round and would she be able to meet him there, maybe in a couple of hours? He was looking for a quick purchase at the right price and had the cash, he said.

She acted keen, he sounded genuine and they agreed a time, checking the address and best access route in question. Time enough to finish off a bit more paper work, which included more additions to the Project proposals; and then after the viewing she planned a supermarket shop before going home to prepare for her co-conspirators' catch-up meeting down at Jamie's place, for serious feedback and discussion.

She drove out along the coast, thinking how she never tired of the sparkling sea views and atmosphere; and fingered the second postcard from her mother inside a week, that was on the front seat of the car, where she had left it. It was another London scene, with an apology for forgetting to mention on the last card the name of the family friend who was visiting Marbella the coming weekend: Matthew Crawford. He would be contacting Sophie by telephone at either work or home. Once again her mother hoped she was keeping well.

She parked outside the new row of two and three-storey blocks with their terracotta sills and roofs, built on the hillside running along one edge of the golf course up at Santa Clara. There were strips of landscaped gardens in front and behind, giving the place already a mature look, and colourful bougainvillea spilling over from outside pots. Only a few of the apartments had been sold and were occupied but she knew there would be no trouble finding buyers for them all in due course. She checked her face in the car mirror. With the keys and sales details, she opened up the ground floor apartment, which was empty and airless. She watched the man arrive by foot and step up to the front door in his cotton suit and loafers, open collar, appearing fresh despite the heat, presumably having parked his car some way down the hillside. 'Harry Ferdaste. Thanks.' He spoke in English. With a sticky handshake he seemed unduly nervous. She recognised him from earlier when he had chatted to her in the shop and had taken her personal office number. He paid little attention to what Sophie was saying as they trailed around the empty rooms, their footsteps echoing on the dusty floors: master bedroom, another small bedroom, galley kitchen, air conditioning, terrace and the rest. He seemed to be stalling and wandered back through the rooms for a second time.

They had been there about ten minutes, when through the open front door unannounced burst two burly shaven-headed men in sharp suits, who stomped over and grabbed Sophie's arms, one man on each side, before she could react, lifting her bodily. 'Hey, what you doing?' she shouted. '*Que pasa?*' They marched her backwards struggling across the hall and dumped her into the empty walk-in clothes cupboard. She was thrown against the back brick wall and bumped her head. The door was slammed shut and she heard the key turn in the lock. It was dark, there was no window or air vent, just big enough for two people to stand side by side. She could not find a light switch. She screamed loudly, using choice Spanish words, but the door was shut firm, despite hopelessly shouldering against it. For someone who prided herself on being able to look after herself, this was exasperating, but after a few moments, a man shouted through the keyhole to be quiet because the boss was coming. The door opened a moment later, light flooding in momentarily before the two heavy minders squeezed themselves in, clasping Sophie's arms again, thrusting her backwards against the wall, where she bumped her head again. 'Do you mind… telling me, what the hell…?'

Another man appeared calmly at the entrance in a fawn linen suit. Standing with the light behind him, it was hard to see his face properly, but the greased back black hair, hooked nose and thin moustache told Sophie instantly that this was the staring man from the Mayor's villa, JR from the café, smelling of perfume. He stretched out an arm without a word, gripped her round the throat with bare fingers and squeezed. Which hurt and made her panic; she thought he was going to make her choke. She looked back with alarm into the man's face as it came up close in front of hers and she could taste his warm smell of garlic and cigars. For a moment the intensity of his eyes convinced her that her life was in danger. She wanted to kick out at him but was pinned back and her feet were almost off the floor. Frightened and nauseous, she was hurting, her arms, her neck, her head; her face was swelling up, her eyes were popping, she was probably going blue.

'Miss Sophie,' said the main man at last with heavy Spanish accent, 'you should stop struggle, shhh, quiet, quiet. We meet again, I think. You in great trouble. If I tell my police chief friend about you and everything you get up to, with your druggy friends, your dodgy habits, you would be locked away for long time. You know. Yes. Yes?' He released his grip a little on her throat and waited while she croaked and coughed. 'But I will refrain from tell Mr Executive Police Chief about that or what you do in spare time. Shall I? Yes? On one conditions.' He paused again and this time gripped her hard by the chin with his stiff fingers like pincers. His face drifted even closer to hers but the teary smears across her eyes made him look thankfully blurred. 'You supply me with the informations I need. Yes?' Sophie was sure he was smiling but his voice sounded mean.

'My name is Juanito Robicalon, you know. JR. Nobody not does what I say, understand, Miss Sophie from England. I am top advisor to Mr Mayor. The Town Councils do what I tell them. Nobody defies me, you understand?' She tried to nod her head. He looked sideways at each of his two bald headed monkeys still gripping Sophie's arms like iron clamps. Their body odour was clogging her nostrils. There really was not enough space in the cupboard for all four of them. 'And if there is any disagreements, my boys see to it.' At which, they squeezed and twisted her arms some more, so she cried out. They rammed her backwards against the wall behind and her head knocked against the brick wall, again. JR leered and his pincer grip squeezed her mouth out of shape, forcing her lips into an ugly pout, smudging her lipstick. Some tear drops spilled over onto his large hand. 'You know about this highway robbery two nights gone. Your man was mugged, his car was stolen, in the night, on the road from Algeciras. You know about these things?' This time she looked surprised, her brows high and eyes widening; she tried a frown and managed a shake of her head. The heat and smell of hot masculine bodies and bad breath was overbearing, but Sophie still had the wits not to be confessing but playing the innocent. 'I think you know,' JR continued, pressing against her, keeping the squeeze on her chin. 'The car had good stuff in it and money, cash in dollars. All this belonged to me. Not your man, Baxwell. This is highway robbery, like bandits. I will not have, not in Marbella. This is my town. And I will have what is mine returned. You know who is involved: your druggy friends from the marina, the Chinese maybe. Find out. There will be talk on the streets, in the clubs, where you work; you will find out and report to me. Not to tell anyone else, bitch. I will come for you. Yes? You understand JR?'

Sophie felt her eyes were bursting, as she tried another look of surprise and innocence, but he yanked her towards him. 'You will tell me. No one must know that you tell me. I will come for you, soon, you will have informations on Baxwell bid for East Shoreline Project as I ask you before, no mistake and you will reveal to me the perpetrators of this outrage, this car robbery. Clear? You understand?' He was hissing through gritted teeth, his nostrils flared. He squeezed her mouth some more, until she nodded and grunted, and then blinked the tears from her eyes. She felt his thigh pressing between her legs. 'I want that informations, or you will be in deep shit. *Mierda*. No misunderstandings, Miss Sophie from England. I want to know these questions. Let me down…I cut your legs off.' He discarded her with a flourish and turned away. The two thugs dropped her like a stone and also backed away. They left in a line one in front, one behind JR, the original customer scuttling out after them, closing the front door. Sophie was whimpering with the pains: her head, her mouth, her arms, her crotch. She managed to wobble round to the entrance, to watch a shiny black limousine with tinted glass pull away from the curb, with all four men inside, she presumed, which moved quietly along the service road and out towards the Autovia.

She had been fooled and crushed and now she felt nauseous. She managed a pathetic laugh which made her swollen cheeks and mouth hurt more. 'Sodding hell,' she said aloud, wiping her eyes with her finger tips and holding the sore patch on the back of her head, which left a reddish smear across the pulps of her fingers.

In the slowly receding heat of the day, feeling the need to cry, her bruises rubbing in her sense of humiliation, she somehow managed to return safely to her apartment using all the familiar roads, blurred with fast-moving traffic. For her the Golden Mile had lost its glitter that day. She parked in her usual place along her narrow pot-holed street and sat motionless for a while. A jumble of muddled thoughts was hammering away inside her head. She took a quick look at herself in the car mirror, at the smeared mascara over her cheeks; the turquoise eyeliner made her look cheap. She grabbed her shoulder bag and twisted gingerly out of her seat, locked up and moved slowly towards her entrance. A brown dog of some sort started barking at her from a balcony above. Although the sun was still catching the upper floors, her block looked dull and shabby, with its paint peeling, its windows dirty, some of the balconies uncared for, even the geraniums on resident's ledges looked lifeless. The surrounding buildings were the same, the whole run-down area making her feel depressed.

A man in overalls was fiddling under the bonnet of his car; a young lad was sitting opposite without his shirt on, smoking and leaning against the wall, with his head back and eyes closed. Two ladies with pushchairs walked slowly away from her along the opposite pavement side by side. Nobody was apparently paying her any attention. Everything appeared as it always did, harmless and domestic. There was no one around who cared that she had been assaulted.

Her step up the cold stone staircase to her landing was more of a trudge than the usual sprint. Normally so strong and resourceful, she was beginning to feel sorry for herself. As she applied her front-door key to the lock, she noticed a fan of fine scratches on the surrounding metal ring that were not there the last time she looked, like this morning. The key turned without resistance. The door was not locked and it opened inwards with a gentle push. Sudden panic stopped her forward momentum and she tottered on the balls of her feet, uncertain about stepping inside. She looked suspiciously into her unlit hallway and round the door jamb and along the short corridor towards the bedroom. She was not sure what she was expecting to see, but instantly knew that someone had been inside the flat; and might still be inside. She heard nothing, not even distant noises of mothers shouting or children bawling, or other occupants somewhere else in the building. Or was that dripping, the sound of water? She removed her shoes in the hallway, leaving the front door ajar for escape if necessary, and inched her way sideways and silently along the inside wall across the wooden floor. The door to the lounge was wide open and she was able to peer round inside. But then she knew what it was that she had first noticed: she always left for work closing the doors onto the hall, she never left them open, for whatever reason, tidiness or habit, she always closed them. This time both doors off the hallway were wide open.

Outside daylight filtered thinly into the shadowy room through drawn curtains. Everything looked out of place, the old settee tipped over, drawers from the chest pulled out and emptied on the floor, magazines scattered, her pot of sweet-pea knocked over the table, half the compost tipped out. But there was nobody in there.

She moved soundlessly through to the adjacent kitchen, peeping around corners but they were all empty. The sink was clear, taps were off. She edged along to her bedroom. The trickling sound of water dripping from a tap became more discernible. The curtains were drawn to keep out the bright sunlight during the day, which was how she had left them. A floorboard squeaked as she stepped forward. Her bed was partially covered, the pillows disrupted, a pink nightie in a bundle, and in the middle was a pile of underwear, bras and smalls, an empty drawer from the chest discarded on the floor. The door through to the bathroom was open and the bright white neon strip-light inside burning. The shower curtain over the bath was pulled back and a sponge bag was lying on its side in the bath. The noise of running water was from the sink, the cold tap dripping steadily, water draining away down the open plughole. Two 2ml syringes and a broken glass ampoule were discarded in the sink; green headed needles still attached, tell-tale dark red blood in the nozzles. The bag in the shower had an unused syringe poking out and as Sophie bent low to inspect it more closely she saw it was filled with ampoules; she could read '*diamorfina*' on the labels. The bath itself looked clean, but there was a drop of blood, semi-congealed on the edge of the bath and another on the floor tile just below the first, still wet. She turned the tap off. On the shelf above, some bottles and make-up had been knocked over and there was a half discarded blister pack that looked unfamiliar: '*dexadrina*', white tablets, some pockets punctured. Amphetamines.

Sophie's sore eyes were screwed up in a worried frown, as a feeling of horror came over her. Injectable heroin and amphetamines. None of it hers.

Someone had broken into her space and violated it, finding her underwear, planting signs of intravenous drug use, had maybe even had a fix in the bathroom. And recently, like in the last hour, while she was being assaulted at Santa Clara by JR and his monkeys. The two events must be linked. That unfamiliar nervous feeling she had on walking in was biting at her, a sort of paranoia. Was she being watched, even now? Those ordinary looking people outside in the street, were they plants to look natural while they reported back her activities to someone else in control? Was JR behind all of this manipulation?

In sudden panic, she rushed to her bed, knelt down and found the old rug underneath disturbed. Pulling it aside, the loose floorboard was pulled up and her previous hiding place beneath was a gaping hole and empty. And she thanked the Lord that she had had the foresight yesterday to move the Baxwell money together with the zipped hold-all containing part of the heist's treasure up into the loft of the building. Whatever they were looking for, they had not found it. She retreated gingerly back to the lounge. She dared not touch anything, but became increasingly angry and bold, as she flung open the windows to clear the fusty smell and righted the upturned settee, closing cupboards. Back in the hall she put her shoes on and inspected the front door again. She was certain she had locked it properly on leaving that morning but it had obviously been picked from the outside. She would have to replace the lock and have a proper separate mortice fitted as well. She searched for a pair of kitchen gloves to inspect the sponge bag in the bath for more detail and then she wrapped everything in newspaper and walked down to the shared waste bins in the basement and managed to stuff the package deep into the bottom of one below lots of bulging black plastic bags. She returned to clean up in the bathroom.

This was a warning, that she could be found with evidence of drug abuse planted in her flat whenever JR wanted and at any time he could call the police to go round and she would be in trouble. Backing up what he had said earlier, the bastard. And what had he said about the merchandise they had stolen, the highway robbery. That was one of the questions that was bugging her: Robicalon said it was all his, not Baxwell's. He meant the stuff they found hidden in the bags of fertiliser and compost, she presumed, and the store of dollars in the secret under-floor compartment. How did he know that Baxwell's consignment was also in the Skoda? How did he know about the robbery at all?

She needed to see Roberto. She had little choice but to do what JR wanted: she would have to find the bid details from Baxwell and surely she would have to return all the stuff and the dollars. How would she know if it really was his? What was JR, a Town Council executive, doing with such quantities of marijuana, anyway? And how did he know Sophie had been involved, who had shopped her? Where did

Baxwell fit in with all this, how much had he really known, she wondered?

She had developed a headache and suddenly felt she could not cope. She had managed before under worse circumstances than these, she told herself. She made sure the front door was locked, she closed all the windows and drew all the curtains, blocking out as much light as possible. She found some painkillers in a kitchen drawer and made tea. She washed her face a little, inspecting the damage, the swelling of her lips and bruised chin. In the bedroom, she pushed everything off the bed onto the floor, promising to clear it away later, and slipped between the sheets still in her work clothes, suddenly feeling unbelievably exhausted.

Sophie woke after a few hours' heavy sleep, aware of outside traffic noise and raised voices, and rolled stiffly out of bed, aching and bruised. Her upper arms were particularly sore and her jaw felt as if she had been punched. There was discoloured drool from the corner of her mouth and smudged make-up on her pillowcase. She cancelled her evening shift at the Blue Ocean Club. She showered slowly in steaming hot water and gingerly washed her battered face, made instant coffee and returned to the bedroom to work on covering the tell-tale marks with cream and foundations: gone was the turquoise and smeared mascara, now fresh lashings of black eye shadow and a contrasting midnight blue that matched her dark eyes, and an orange fan that spread over her upper eyelids, curving under the heavy brows and undulating out over the high ridges of her cheeks. She dressed in black slacks and a ruby red blouse, gelled her hair into life and disguised her swollen lips with a matt oxblood, creating a sensuous confidence-boost ensemble of gothic appearance she needed to approach her friends.

Their meeting was billed as a simple catch-up with

payment, but now Sophie would have to bring more serious business to the table with her new information. The night was moonless and the backstreets dark, which gave her a sense of cover as she set off on foot for the waterfront at Puerto Pesquero, a little after ten o'clock, in a sleeveless black leather jerkin and ankle boots.

Although feeling pretty stiff, she was better for being on the move, in the warm outside air with its strong salty and fishy aromas. She darted up a side street, the Arturo Soria and then turned into a narrow concreted walk between a row of ugly brick and concrete blocks, mostly repair garages and storage. A short way along and between these buildings she found the non-descript battered metal door, with a huge air-conditioner unit chugging alongside. Tapping discreetly, she was admitted by Alfredo, a short rugged guy with a mass of curly black hair, and they hugged. Down a few steps into a capacious basement area, warmed from the open kitchen and oven, where the rectangular windows were blacked out. Once a bare concrete storage space under garages and a storehouse, it was now converted into an open living space with black-painted iron posts at intervals supporting a low ceiling, bare brickwork and bare boards, and some internal walls that created a few smaller bedrooms leading off. There were old soft sofas and chairs around the sides, a wood burning stove for the occasional colder winter evenings, and a large wooden table and benches in the middle. Always sharing with various local friends of uncertain number, Jamie lived a sort of commune existence, in which they all mucked in with house chores, the cooking and cleaning and collecting each other's benefits from the council offices on Ramon y Cajal. They were mostly university student drop-outs, enjoying odd jobs, like taking tourists out on the waters and fishing for their suppers, generally tinkering about on boats. They paid equal subs to Jamie every Saturday morning, after the last of the plates and cutlery from their weekly compulsory brunch had been cleared.

Jamie was there with his own welcome hug, with Sami and Lilly Belle and Alfredo, as they had all helped with the highway robbery, as JR had called it. Roberto, in jeans and denim shirt, clean-shaven for once despite his bruised face and swollen lips, was hobbling around with a pack of beers in hand, relating to the others his injuries and sacrifices he made for the team. Liz, in loose cotton slip-over and jeans, was sipping beer from the bottle, draped over a settee and was listening to him sympathetically, even if no one else was. She leapt up on sight of her friend and gave her a firm hug, complimenting her on her appearance. 'You look different: beautiful, babe. We were beginning to get worried you weren't going to show.' Her face was hot and shiny from being out in the sunshine all afternoon.

Sophie apologised for being late, as she went round hugging everyone; she avoided eye contact with Roberto. The whole area was wafted with powerful cooking smells, of steaming fish and oil. Lilly was on kitchen duty, perspiring over the hot gas hob under a slow churning fan overhead. They were having fresh bream and shrimp in oil with oven-cooked vegetables, and she would love Sophie to check the rice for her, while she prepared the salad. Everyone said how hungry they were as they settled around the rough-cut wooden table with a mound of cheeses and beers and wine bottles and a big jar of mayonnaise.

Lilly started serving, but Sophie sat on a couch apart from them for a while with a glass of wine, while counting out four separate piles of ten thousand pesos from her thick wad of notes in her bag, money that she had slipped out from Baxwell's bribe bundle before leaving. She kept running her tongue along her sore lower lip, although that only served to irritate it more. Across the room, Roberto continued regaling the others with tales of his bravery and Baxwell's anger on finding out that they had been mugged and everything had been stolen, the vehicle and all its contents.

Lilly had curly blond hair that framed her pretty face, as it draped to her bare shoulders. She wore a skimpy vest that perfectly outlined her curvaceous chest, leaving nothing to the imagination, as she leant over the others in turn, ladling generous servings of rice and fish. They all started to eat with noisy enjoyment while Roberto continued centre stage with his account of the night's adventure, describing how he and Bruce had managed to free their hands and then trudge the 25 kilometres back into town, a pretty rough walk in the dark. 'Those boys of yours, Sophie, were good, but they were rough. Fuck me. I have plenty bruises,' and, although they had already admired and commented on his facial bruises, he stood up and lifted his shirt to show them a variety of blue smudges over his back and side where the sticks and a boot had left their impressions.

'You don't have to tell them, Roberto, these were the boys involved,' laughed Sophie. All the others were smiling sheepishly.

'And girl,' piped up Lilly Belle, who had provided the long legs and shapely bottom. Roberto perked up and stared at Lilly's tight backside in short-cut rough jeans for confirmation, as she stretched far over the end of the table to place a salad bowl in the middle. 'We were told to make it look authentic, Roberto, sorry, mate,' said Alfredo. Lilly stared at Roberto's torso, grimacing in sympathy.

'You'll be fine, *esta bien*, he'll be alright,' encouraged Sophie stoically on his behalf, noticing Roberto's beady eyes scanning Lilly's chest and bare legs.

'We both had horrible blisters; Bruce worn through his black leather shoes. We got food and drink and sleep all day in my flat; Luciana there, she good. She switch phone off. Then we walk to Baxwell's, the shop and saw him in the office. To tell him what happen.' Roberto put on a pained expression, 'Ooh, he was ballistic. His face went purple, he lost his words. It was no joke, actually.' But he laughed outrageously, as he tried to imitate the facial appearance of Alex Baxwell on being told that all his valuable merchandise had been stolen. 'Must have been worth a lot, Roberto,' Jamie interjected, a bit under his breath, 'more than you thought.'

'Oh yes, we had double whammy, Baxwell's stuff from Ali Agra and the stuff that Bruce had?' Roberto was rosy cheeked and excited, soaking up their congratulations with sheer joy etched on his face. 'Baxwell, he say it was part payment by the General in Rabat, for his visit next week. This Ali Agra was his mule, supposed to deliver the car and then stay in Marbella for few days and return with The General next week. But he was scared and thought the Spanish police had it in for him, so persuaded this other bloke he met at Ceuta, Bruce, to take the stuff over for him. Our good fortune, eh?'

They all looked thoughtful, as they concentrated on eating. Roberto continued with comments about Baxwell's reaction: 'He went ballistic – *enfadado como volca,*' and laughed again with a full mouthful. 'He needed the merchandise, he shout, that it was already paid for, he was meeting some contact that day and needed the cash. How will he manage without this money, he need cashflow?' Roberto puffed out his cheeks and ballooned his belly against the table but only succeeded in making his bruises hurt more. 'He had already spent thousands on this week, put his neck out, he say. Was he to go and beg for time or give back the money for merchandise he had not sold? I confused, I admit. "You not understand, you dog," he called me. "You must have some idea who they were. What did they look like, what did they sound like? You idiot. All for the sake of a girl's bottom".' Roberto roared with laughter again, spraying bits of rice from his mouth and the others all joined in. 'He scream at me, he blue with rage. He shook me on the shoulders. His eyebrow twitching up and down. He hit me with newspaper. He was almost crying.' Roberto's normally rugged face with its lived-in look became quite comic in appearance, tears streaming over his red cheeks, choking as he tried to adopt the various expressions of Baxwell's repellent face, re-enacting all the various actions. Even Sophie smiled, secretly pleased that at least they had succeeded in making Baxwell's life uncomfortable, but, conscious of her own stiff jaw and puffy mouth, she remained cautious. She knew Baxwell would be at his most dangerous when angered and cornered. She quietly finished her food and emptied her glass in worried thought.

'Bruce, he good, he convinced, told Baxwell it not my fault, these were big bully boys with white Chinaman masks, very scary.' And as they all laughed even louder at that, Sophie raised her hand, looking at the faces around the table in turn, waiting for quiet, her expression one of concern.

'We need to keep a very low profile. Baxwell will be feeling cheated and very angry – he will be out looking for this gang, with his own men, he won't let this go. He'll hire some heavies, make enquiries around town with the contacts he has.' And she looked at Roberto, catching his gleaming eyes. 'I have two questions, Rob. First, who was the hash destined for, the stuff in the horsebox? And more important, who does Bruce work for?'

'He not say, but he was meeting someone – he was looking to find a source and flog it best he could. He was vague,' and Roberto shrugged and belched in satisfaction. He did not look concerned.

'And the money, the extra stash in the under-floor compartment, that was a surprise: half a million dollars, my estimation.'

Jamie whistled and smiled, 'That might come in handy.'

'Bruce talk about a racehorse he take back to Rabat in the

horsebox – that money was payment and he had to deliver the estate car and box and leave it – some industrial site on the north side.'

While the others were finishing their food with drinks aplenty, probably feeling pleased and imagining a fat pay-day at the end of it all, Sophie smiled at them and told them their money was ready. 'And thanks team, boys and girl, a job well done.' She hooked an arm around Lilly Belle and hugged her kindly. Tall and long-haired Sami wandered over to collect as the plates were cleared. There was general nodding and words of appreciation. Fruit and ice-cream tubs were placed on the table and cigarettes came out. 'Help yourself, people,' encouraged Lilly Belle.

Sophie leant across the table towards Roberto and spoke seriously at him, but for all to hear. 'Unfortunately, I think we may have bitten off a bit too much, I am not too sure,' and the others hesitated, glancing at her. She was tired and her face flushed in the warmth of the atmosphere, but she was in control and was ready to reveal something of what she knew, to help them decide on their next move. Jamie and Alfredo were blowing cigarette smoke up to the ceiling and Sophie took one that was offered.

In the pause, Liz jumped in and squeezed herself up to Sophie. 'Baxwell will automatically think it was an inside job, you know, the bandits finding his car in the middle of the night, too much of a coincidence. So he will batter Roberto again for information.' And here she looked hard into Roberto's blood-shot eyes with something resembling affection, that made Sophie flinch. 'I agree with Sophie. He will be watching all of you, us – so we need to be especially careful. He'll probably want to start searching our apartments, he will send round his heavies.'

'But Bruce was convincing, he believe him,' urged Roberto.

'Where is he?' Liz asked.

'Bruce, he in one of Baxwell's rooms in Casco Antiguo.'

'Well, I'm worried,' Sophie interjected. 'I was paid a visit by Mr Juanito Robicalon today. JR, he's known as around Marbella. Says he runs the place, controls the Mayor. I don't know whether any of you know him or have heard of him?' Jamie nodded slowly. Sophie was looking at Liz, 'He accosted me at one of our apartments. He knew about the car-jack and the robbery, that lots of hash and money was involved. In fact, he said, and this was a bit of a shock, he said the whole lot, the money and the hash, everything was his, and he wanted it back.'

'Wow,' said Jamie, exhaling smoke through his nostrils, letting his jaw drop a fraction. The others all looked at each other and Roberto was staring at Sophie. 'He do this to you?' and he had tender concern written all over as he stretched his fingers towards Sophie's face, almost touching her mouth. Sophie just smiled and closed her eyes for a moment.

'My God, you're kidding,' said Liz, coming closer to put her arm across Sophie's shoulders while inspecting more closely the dark patches around her chin and the swollen lips. 'This the JR man that you told me about, who wanted information about this property project bid of Baxwell's? Liz was recalling details of their conversation of Wednesday in the Plaza Los Naranjos. 'So soon. You said he would be back.'

'No, he tell you stories, cannot be,' Roberto murmured, taking an unopened beer bottle from the table. 'How hell he know about car mugging? And what, how can all stuff be his? Is Baxwell's, money for job and the hash been paid for.'

'But the main bulk of the stuff, in the bags in the horsebox, that's a shit load of stuff, that was Bruce's and it's by contract, you said as much. Who was buying? Baxwell is simply a middleman for someone else, he's not a drugs man, he knows nothing about the Marbella scene.' Sophie gained some confidence in talking about the details.

DEAD END

There was another gap in the conversation as some tired minds were accumulating the new bits to the story and trying to think of something reassuring to say. 'What if Bruce actually works for JR,' murmured Jamie, 'and he's reported what he saw, thinking it was all a set-up.' The others all looked on in puzzlement.

Roberto grunted, unconvinced. 'Maybe we interrupt something bigger,' he said, defiant, 'Bruce will know. He tell me nothing so far, but I find out tomorrow, I'm sure he will talk to me.' He gritted his teeth and snarled, 'I will make him talk to me.' The others looked at him with approval.

More glasses were filled, everyone sat around on the softer chairs and sofas, some smoking, a joint went round. Roberto had finished his third or fourth beer and went out the room for a pee. On his return he stood legs apart defiantly in the middle of the room in front of Sophie and his voice reached a higher pitch, as he asked: 'We in trouble, Sophie?'

Sophie hesitated. Nobody in the room knew about the two million pesos of Baxwell's bribe that she had already stolen, and nor were they going to. She looked around at her friends, dragging on cigarettes, sipping their drinks, Lilly Belle being hugged in Sami's arms, noting their young expectant faces and how they were all looking back at her for guidance, awaiting her answer to Roberto's question.

She blew a long smoke trail casually up to the concrete ceiling and turned a worried eye onto Roberto once again. 'Maybe. The question is: do we give back the stuff to JR, without telling Baxwell? That's if we believe him. That would amount to us admitting we took it in the first place. Or do we continue to play the innocent, know nothing of the hash or the cash, and hope JR directs his attention somewhere else?'

'Is the money and stuff safe?' Jamie asked sheepishly.

'Yes, I think so. As safe as it could be,' she shrugged, looking at Liz.

259

'Yes, my bag is stashed away behind the old freezer in my place.'

'Good.' Sophie continued: 'Whatever we do, JR is going to be hounding us, as well as Baxwell; he knows where I live and has already threatened me.' Sophie was fully aware that she needed to take a leadership role here to keep everyone on board and confident, especially as any one of them could be subjected to rough questioning, bullying, or worse, heaven forbid.

'Listen, I'm supposed to be exchanging a sample of the hash with Hsui Long Long later tonight; just a taster, to get his say-so, before hopefully organising a bigger deal. I plan to go ahead, without giving anything away. Perhaps I will find out some more, John usually knows what is going on.'

Later that evening, after midnight, when everything had been cleared from the table and washed up, and the surfaces wiped down, everyone doing their bit, and after a reticent Sami had guided Lilly away with him into an adjacent bedroom, peeling her from Roberto's persistent gaze, and Liz had left to find her way back home by car, Roberto fell asleep snoring on the sofa. Sophie tucked a blanket around him, and with Jamie and Alfredo, left quietly together, slipping along to the end of the alley to pile into Jamie's Opel van parked around the corner.

Jamie drove quietly along some of the darker backstreets off the town centre, finding his bearings among the many narrow and badly lit roads. Then the three of them walked in file along the backs of closed shops and dingy apartments, where a few battered cars and overflowing plastic bins sometimes blocked their way; the smells were of drains and cheap cooking, the paths strewn with rubbish, take-away boxes and discarded chips and plastic bottles and excrement. Along a short stretch of tacky neon lights flashing their offerings of strip joints and lap dancing, nudes and girls, gambling and take-away food, they found the back of The Peking Duck and two doors away The Peking Palace, The Magician's main 'centre of ops'. And there was Hsui Long Long, crouching in a doorway, sucking on a spliff with a couple of his mates.

Sophie hoped to have a chance to negotiate with the boss and she knew that his 'headquarters' were over the restaurant. John seemed happy and a little spaced out, but quickly reverted to a more serious demeanour as they pushed open a battered swing door into a shadowy corridor where a black-cladded oriental gentleman of considerable bulk listened to Long Long, who whispered Sophie's name a few times into his ear. A couple of other unpleasant looking heavies were watching from behind and then they all joined in with frisking the new arrivals, unforgivingly prodding under arms, into pockets, inside the boys' shirts and between their legs. Sophie had to open her blouse while a man scooped a long finger inside her bra cups and then knelt behind her and poked his hands along her trousers between her thighs and into her crotch. She gritted hard on her teeth and was almost ready to knee the man in the groin. They took her handbag off her and were then hustled down the corridor through a thick curtain into another dark hallway, where they waited with Long Long, glimpsing a bar and dance area, dark with seductive bass music and near-naked Chinese girls in high heels cavorting on tables. A few punters sat about pretending to be enjoying themselves. In semi-darkness someone else opened a heavy door behind them and Sophie was called through, with John, leaving her protection behind, locking the door behind them. They immediately climbed up some wooden stairs into a corridor that smelt damp and they followed the man into a smoky room, overpowered with the smell of sweet dope and tobacco.

Among other spaced out Chinese in sweat shirts and dark

pants gathered in groups around low tables, playing cards, Sophie noticed boards with stacks of money. The games were played in almost silence, everyone smoking. They weaved their way through to the back where in an alcove sitting cross-legged on a hard sofa was a nondescript Chinaman in white, sucking silently at a hookah pipe, the glass bowl of bubble hash standing on the floor in front of him. She could smell the wafts of flowery incense that surrounded him, and his head was tilted backwards, a satisfied swoon spread across his lined and gaunt face, his eyes closed, unaware of their arrival. She studied his elderly appearance; wearing white silk, open at the chest, a number of thin gold chains around his neck, and several piercings in each of his ears. He had a black moustache grown string-like to hang either side of his mouth, the ends reaching a foot below his jawline. His long greying hair was thin on top of his skull but gathered severely from the sides in a knot at the back of his head. His hands were at rest in his lap and he wore rather fetching silken slippers on tiny feet. A long serrated knife with a carved ivory handle was stabbed into the top surface of a low table and stood upright between them.

Standing opposite, Sophie coughed quietly.

The old man opened his eyes quickly and gestured Sophie to sit. Small cups on a little black tray were placed on the table. Still squinting through narrowed lids, he gestured again and Sophie politely reached for a cup, containing what looked like a clouded milky drink, but was more likely an opiate concoction with fermented rice. It tasted foul, but she managed to sink it down in one swallow, trying not to grimace.

The old man had closed his eyes again, smoking peacefully. Sophie was keen to start a conversation. John had told her to speak clearly in English and his father would understand. 'My name is Sophie. Thank you for seeing me. Can we talk about the deal that I offered you through Hsui Long Long – I spoke to him yesterday? As I explained I have access to a consignment of Moroccan dope, fresh over, the sort you people particularly like – the finest smoke. At very reasonable prices.'

Sophie paused and was watching for the old man's reaction. He seemed to mumble something, his mouth moving around the suction end of the pipe. Sophie looked from old man to John, hoping for enlightenment. He mumbled again and Sophie thought she heard: 'That is what you say – so be it.'

She looked at John for advice, not certain what to say next. She felt dry in the mouth and would have loved a proper drink, a cool beer came to mind.

Suddenly Ho Sup Ping sat up and came to life; for it was he, the all-powerful and wealthy ruler of his little southern Spanish empire in the wealthy tourist trap of Marbella, The Magician, mean and heartless by reputation. His slanted eyes gave a piercing look at Sophie through their cracks and his mouth became pinched and twisted as he poked his small head forward. He took the pipe away from his mouth. 'Except there is problem,' he growled. And spat a splodge of coloured saliva onto the bare floor below him. Sophie was taken aback, looked surprised and puckered her brows.

With perfect timing and without a sound, another little Chinese man appeared with plates of sweetmeats and rice, all in ornately decorated black bowls of mouth-bite size and replaced the tray already there with his before retreating backwards into the shadows of the room from whence he had come. John did not move from his position behind the old man. Sophie was about to reach forward to try something to eat, but then The Magician poked his angry head even further forward towards her with a meaner expression than before, the skin creased and stretched so tight around his face it looked as if it might pull apart. The puckering of his mouth comically made his shoe-string moustache dance a jig. 'Tell me, Missis, why we pay for stolen hash?'

There was a silence about them, which was disturbed only by the background rumbling of rhythmic music thumping somewhere far below. Sophie felt an intensity in the atmosphere, that the old man was about to explode with real anger. Clearly John had been warned and stood in silence showing absolute respect at his father's shoulder.

'I… I don't quite know what you mean. I am acting for my trusted customer in a spirit of honesty. He is from Morocco. I have a small sample with me,' she finished weakly.

The Magician settled back in his cross-legged position with his arms relaxed and hands turned outwards, to resume his smoking of the pipe, his eyes closed once again. Sophie noticed his long fingernails, sharp and claw-like. She was anxious for an answer and annoyed that he seemed to want to stay in his entranced position for ever. She became restless, looking around at the other men present. She motioned to John just when she thought he had nodded off completely, when suddenly the old man opened his eyes wide again with a jerk if his head. 'Hah; you lie to me, lady, and I rip your face off, ya?' He almost shouted, more spittle accumulating at his parched lips.

Uncertain whether that had been a question or just a random statement, she sought out John's expression for reassurance but he was grimacing as he placed a long restraining hand on his father's shoulder and then he said something in high-pitched Chinese, which sounded like reproach.

'I think she lie. My people tell me she lie.' The Magician was getting agitated, unfolding his thin legs to the floor and waiving his arms. He reached slowly for the knife on the table.

'Iwillnotbecheated,' he screeched in a single word in a

voice of even higher pitch than John's. He pulled the blade out of the table top, waved it at her once before hurling it with force into the wooden floor at Sophie's feet, where it reverberated menacingly for a while.

'No, father, she is friend, we trus' her.' John had come round from behind the sofa and had his arm on his father's shoulder.

'Who does Ho Sup Ping think the hashish was stolen from?'

But there was no reply, just an angry grimace on the face of the thin old man, who stood hunched and well short of Sophie in height. John now took Sophie's upper arm, steering her away to one side. 'We had contract to purchase at good price 350kg of hash resin worth a million dollars,' he was explaining, 'and the consignment gone missing. Money been paid, up-front, and The Magician he think we lose it, he cross, velly cross. Wants me to find it. He angry.'

'I can see that, I'm so sorry,' and Sophie wanted to thank Ho Sup Ping for his time, wanted to appear polite and did not want to depart with him still thinking she had cheated him, but John was pulling her back through the betting games room where nobody seemed to have noticed her or moved their positions and everything was just as it had been when they had first walked through.

Downstairs Sophie met up with the two boys and with John they sat disappointed at a small table in a dark recess of the club with some beers while the strippers on the far side carried on plying their trade.

'I find out, this negotiation with my father's team, for big consignment, not involve me, which odd. Must be something real special. Or somebody special, but I not know which. I will try find out. They will not be happy either.'

Sophie's worst fears were confirmed, it would appear. Not only had they stolen some big consignments, destined for some big deals, but behind them were some of the biggest boys, not some small-time punks who would roll over, but ruthless men and their organisations that would not take this lying down. She drank from a bottle of beer quickly to sake her thirst and thanked her friends for their support. Alfredo soon made his own way back to the digs. John promised her he would find out who was behind this deal, who his father had pre-paid for this consignment; he would keep in touch. He kissed Sophie on her forehead before he left. Some deep and natural belligerence within was keeping Sophie focussed at the moment, determined not to panic but to think this through.

'Fuck. We've got so far, I am not sure that I am ready just to cave in, not yet,' she promised Jamie, as they wandered arm in arm through the back alleyways again, towards the waterfront with its powerful smell of the sea, under a momentary bright moon that had emerged for the first time that night as low clouds cleared. Coming out between a row of garages and storage blocks onto a concreted promenade, they skirted along its sweeping perimeter to the secluded marina, pretty much deserted at that time of the night, although sounds of one or two boat people, obsessives or insomniacs most likely, tinkering around under torch light, coiling ropes or lashing lanyards to the masts or just ensuring everything was ship-shape for the morning, could still be heard echoing across the still waters from somewhere among the massed ranks of gently bobbing boats.

Jamie led the way to the end of a dry wooden jetty to where his boat was moored, alongside the repair yards and quartermaster's lodgings, a fat wooden skiff, a 34-foot twin-keel weekender that had seen better days. It was single masted, the sails down and wrapped, the covers on. He had spent many days in the summer giving it a new lick of paint, mostly white and blue, and the smell of paint and oil still hung around. They clambered across the side dropping into the hold, through a tight galley to the single cabin space, a couple of hanging lamps swaying from the low-ceiling above them.

They relaxed in the semi-darkness, the only light coming from the moon outside, sharing a joint and a bottle of dreadful white wine. Sophie's worries were never far away, but Jamie did his best at gentle encouragement and morale boosting, declaring that actually it was Roberto who should take full responsibility. The danger was that it might all get completely out of their control. Jamie countered with the point that nobody knew for sure that Sophie was in any way involved, or the rest of her young team – and were they not the best, he laughed. He even thanked Sophie for her support, the money and the fun involved. They nestled their warm bodies naturally and easily against each other.

Jamie aimlessly caressed the fine hairs and silky skin along Sophie's bare arms, while she countered with whispered love sounds. They kissed the wine drops off each others lips, their minds filled with blueberry haze. She pulled the clothes off his young body and expertly embarked on deliberately slow love-making on the solitary bed stuffed in the bow, where a pair of tiny port holes gave them obtuse views of the silvery moonlight twinkling eerily across the oily watery surface just a foot or two below them. Streaks of magic light played across Jamie's pretty face. There was a rhythm in the way the waters slapped under the boat to its gentle rising and falling that linked to the bobbing of her naked breasts like buoys on the open seas as she rode Jamie bare-back, while his large hands gripped the outside of her thighs. Her bruised body was complaining and tiredness slowed her, but their gentle appetites were readily sated. She slipped off, panting to lie face down beside him. Drifting into a pleasant sleepiness, she surprised herself with thoughts along domestic lines that she was unable to shift, wondering how much longer she would be able to keep the draw of male attachment away and when at some point she would succumb to someone's entreaties, Jamie's perhaps, to settle down, as her mother would have put it, to have a family of her own or something. She just needed some money to back up her ideas, allow her to move on somewhere else, somewhere safer and then she could think about it.

Sophie raised her head, casually watching silvery light playing across Jamie's sleeping features, his long hair matted in dark strands across his forehead, his chin rough with stubble, his young face in complete untroubled repose. She traced the curly hairs across his chest, reflecting how unnatural it was to believe in the tranquil aftermath of their climaxing that she could really be in trouble. She turned her back towards him and coiled her bare body into his lap and in his sleep he squeezed the flat of her belly, muttering something incoherent. She reassured herself that in reality their worries would all blow over pretty soon if they could all keep their heads down.

She was sure they would all be in the clear in a day or two.

7

Saturday August 30

Somewhere deep in the picture gallery of her mind, she was running hard through back alleyways dark and shadowy, her feet slipping on bits of rotten vegetables discarded across her path, a number of Chinese henchmen screaming in pursuit with long knives, which kept catching her, shredding her jacket, slicing cuts down her back. And just as she was shaping like a professional gymnast to leap hands first over a high wall into the unknown, across pitch black emptiness, her ankles were unexpectedly gripped, and she was pulled back. She was kicking hard as the sweet taste of dope filled her mouth and a sudden ringing swelled in her ears. She sat up suddenly, although raising her head off the pillow produced a dull ache behind her eyes. Only vaguely could she recall her weaving walk back to her apartment in the small hours of that morning, after leaving Jamie soporifically inviting her to stay. Nobody witnessed her staggering up the staircase cursing once again the broken lift, to flop spent and numb onto the top of her bed, just ahead of the rising of the next dawn.

Jamie was such a good lad, a pretty boy, what would she do without him? He was a relaxing outlet for her; he cared for her, she thought, but without placing demands or commitments, just two friends able to share intimacy when they needed to, without prejudice or jealousy. Jamie knew about her and Roberto, they had talked about it before but that knowledge was safe with him, he had no vested interest in spreading that sort of story; he believed in adults making their own decisions as it suited them. Sophie was also aware that other girls slept with Jamie. She could see his innocence in his gentle face in front of her now, the dishevelled black strands of hair curling over the forehead, his long naked limbs entwined around her. He pleased her, comforted her, responded to her desires without objection, without expecting anything in return, an undemanding freedom they both enjoyed. Eager though he was, he cleverly allowed her to lead him along her chosen paths. She could taste his faith, his love.

All she wanted now was to put her bursting head back down onto the pillow, prepared for the Chinese slaughter that she imagined was only a fraction away. But there was a persistent buzzing in the distance that she could not keep out. She was forced to prize her eyelids open letting in streaks of sharp sunlight that pierced through to her retina. She was wondering how it could be so light in the middle of the night and what day of the week it was. She squinted at the bedside clock, which seemed to show something around eleven. Had she slept through a whole day or something? Her thinking was still fuzzy but way in the far distance she was sure she could hear a doorbell buzzing.

The need to empty her bladder forced her up to stagger into the bathroom, where she sat heavily trying to orient herself. A glance into the mirror did not help: underneath the smeared make-up, her face looked pasty and ugly, with the dark bruises still in evidence; her chest sagged, her belly rolled obtrusively and she swore she would never indulge in alcohol and hashish again. She quickly washed her face and dragged a gown around her shoulders, passing through her bedroom towards the corridor as her doorbell buzzed again with urgency. Nothing had been tidied away; in the hall, she had to step round a pyramid of drying clothes from yesterday's wash, and she was aware the whole place appeared a mess, a bit like herself. She went to open windows in the lounge to encourage fresh air to relieve the stuffy atmosphere.

Through the peephole in the front door she recognised the distorted features of Alec Baxwell and her heart sank. What the fuck did he want? At this hour, on a Saturday? Then she panicked, wondering what he might have discovered and what else she had done wrong. She fell back against the door and grimaced, digging deep into her mind: he must have met the Mayor, or perhaps JR had had words with him, and concluded that she had indeed walked off with half his bribe money or was in with Roberto and the midnight car muggers. Had he found out about her futile attempt to sell Morocco's finest hashish to The Chinese Magician?

The doorbell was buzzing again; he was knocking and calling her name. She was surprised he had not woken the whole building and that Senora Sanita from across the landing was not outside in her rolled-up sleeves shouting at him to pipe down. She checked that she was covered up properly and the door was on its chain, pulled back the bolts, turned the main lock, and opened it a crack. Baxwell's pale blotchy face and pointed nose came into view, his foot sticking into the door gap, pushing it hard. 'At last. Open the bloody door, wench,' he hissed under his breath, 'we need to talk.'

'Such a polite start.' Sophie had no choice but to release the chain and pull the door open, acting indignant. Baxwell barged inside in a bluster. 'Good morning to you too.'

He was wearing a blue blazer, the buttons on the stretch around his middle, khakis and brown brogues, and was followed by a gangly black man Sophie had never met, in brown corduroy and a cardigan wearing a peaked cap. She thought charitably that Baxwell looked quite dapper, even though his bulging paunch revolted her, but in contrast the ultra-dark man from Africa who stepped forward gingerly and with polite reserve was something else altogether, a casual masculine hunk with broad pillowy lips and massive whites contrasting with the darkest of dark eyes.

'This is Bruce, from Morocco.'

She had to swallow and stare for a moment as he whisked off his cap, revealing a close-cropped rounded head, and stretched out a hand to Miss Sophie, which he warmly wrapped around hers. He gave a little bow and a slippery pink tongue mopped his wet lips like a cow's, behind a row of tombstone white teeth. Sophie could not suppress a welcoming smile.

'One time friend of Roberto de Salva,' Baxwell explained, as he paced into the lounge sounding angry and looked as if he had been up for hours. 'You won't have met, but I'm sure Roberto has filled you in with the all the gory details of his escapade the other night. The car they brought up from Morocco,' looking angrily at Bruce, 'with merchandise destined for me, should be safe in my garage just now. But it has disappeared, stolen by a group of motorway hijackers. Roberto mugged, can you believe, all for the sight of a girl's bottom. Trailing an empty horsebox, for some reason.'

He sat heavily, elbows on the table, hands waving in front of him, his voice rising and its Edinburgh accent becoming more pronounced, as he allowed his inner anger to surface. 'There were three of them, with face masks, unrecognisable, right?' looking at Bruce, who nodded. 'Except for the pretty blonde. You'd recognise her again, if you saw her?' Bruce gave a maybe expression and dipped his head humbly. 'They thumped Roberto across the back, beat him over the head, right?' checking Bruce again, who nodded. 'Tied his hands behind his back. And Bruce here, his hands tied as well. Left them by the side of the road, they managed to walk back from the highway to Marbella, what, twenty kilometres. The car gone, the merchandise and my money gone, damn it! And now to cap it all, Roberto has disappeared.'

Sophie, suddenly alerted, looked at Baxwell with something like mild panic in her widened eyes as her mouth opened to speak. But Baxwell charged quickly on, noticing her worried look, 'He was snatched by a gang of heavies, in the street outside Bruce's room, bundled into the back of a van. Bruce caught sight of them from his upstairs window but was powerless to do anything.' Like the other night, she thought, glancing at the black face of the African, who, still with cap in hand, had obvious subservient respect for the bumbling Scotsman.

Sophie's mouth was horribly dry and her eyes felt sore, waiting for the kettle to boil on the sideboard as she picked mugs out of the sink. Baxwell continued: 'Bruce called me, just now. I wanted to talk to you, to decide what to do.' Baxwell looked agitated and reached inside his jacket for a pack of Marlboro. Bruce stood nervously still by the door, moving sideways from foot to foot, with his gaze frequently directed at Sophie, while she in turn kept taking quick snatches of his good-looking chiselled face, disturbingly unexpected in a mysterious henchman from North Africa she suspected of working for that slimy toad, JR.

'So someone thinks Roberto's telling porkies about this mugging, and it was not me.' Baxwell was flushed in the face with anger and reached for a hot coffee mug. Sophie brought a plate of toasted and buttered bread slices over to the table and signalled Bruce to sit down. 'Help yourself.'

'So was it the Chinese, I ask myself? You know those Chinky fellows, used to work with them a bit, no?' Baxwell screwed up his eyebrows as he scrutinized Sophie for her answer. 'Or that bastard, Robicalon? Know him, now, you met him at the Mayor's, you said?' Baxwell stuffed a piece of dripping toast into his mouth and spooned heaps of sugar into his coffee, stirring noisily. Bruce sat respectfully taking small bites from around the edge of his toast and silently drinking from his mug.

He had not said a word since his arrival and Sophie was wondering whether he understood English. 'Poor Roberto, after his first beating on Wednesday night.' She slid onto a chair opposite, feigning ignorance but a mass of impossible thoughts bouncing around inside her head, from where the earlier muddle was only slowly clearing. The coffee was helping. She was thinking it must have been Ho Sup Ping's men, despite John doing his best, and she worried about what Roberto might be forced to confess. She needed to contact John as soon as possible.

Baxwell pressed on: 'You've seen Roberto since Wednesday night, have you? These two were driving along the motorway on the coast road and Roberto stops to help this girl with her car. What an idiot. She was pretending. But Bruce here tells me he was not totally convinced with the show they put on.' Again he turned his head sideways for confirmation to eye the Moroccan. Again there was nodding without smiling. 'There was something about the way he and the girl spoke, right, their body language, as if they already knew each other? Bruce thinks it might have been a setup, that Roberto had organised the whole charade.'

'But he showed us his bruises and his cut face. They looked pretty real.' Sophie spoke up quickly.

'So you have seen him?' Baxwell stopped and looked at her.

'Yes, on Thursday night, Liz and I met up with him; he showed us his bruises, he looked pretty hurt.'

'Well, he's a brave boy. But how else would they have known which car to ambush; how would they know that Roberto would fall for the girl in distress, you know, the oldest trick in the book. It all looks like a set-up, and Roberto must have known, I reckon, but I did nae want to believe it. He's been with me over ten years, he's always been loyal.' After a moment, Baxwell asked, 'Where did you get all these bruises, on your face, Sophie?'

'Oh, there're nothing. Just a rough man in the bar the other night. Anyway, Roberto, will he be alright, d'you think?' Sophie asked, conveying real worry, unable to look Baxwell directly in the eye.

Baxwell's anger was receding a little as he thought through his feelings. 'They drove the Skoda away without looking inside it – they must have known what was in there. And there was this horsebox, a trailer on the back, that was definitely nae in my agreement. Bruce is supposed to collect some horse and take the ferry back to drive it down to Rabat for a Moroccan merchant called El Mougrabi. There was a pre-arranged meeting point where he had to dump the car and the box, and then he had to collect twenty-four hours later. To me it seems like that it's Robicalon selling a racehorse to this El Mougrabi, who is a fanatic racer, has dozens of horses.'

Sophie is staring at Baxwell and then Bruce. 'How did you find all this out? Does Mr Bruce here speak English?'

'Of course, Miss Sophie. I explain it.'

Sophie almost laughed out loud, but restricted herself to a sweet smile with eyebrows raised in a little note of astonishment.

During a further short pause, Baxwell consumed more toast. Then he said emphatically: 'This was an inside job, Sophie. And what about Ali Agra, we've used him on and off before, he's always been OK. He wouldn't suddenly cry off.' It sounded as if Baxwell expected her to agree with him and that she knew more than she was letting on.

'And what *was* inside?' Sophie asked, innocently sipping at her mug.

Bruce exchanged glances with Baxwell, Sophie noticed, both of them looking uncertain as to who trusted whom, and who knew what. 'Bruce was unsure, but I was due about $30000 in cash from The General and 20kg of cannabis cake, finest Rif Mountain hashish, worth a few thousand pounds.'

'Gosh. And… and the rest, who was that intended for?'

Bruce was hugging his mug with his hands on the table and flicking his eyes across to Sophie's, leaving acres of glistening white spaces around his irises, that contrasted so spectacularly with their surrounding darkness.

'Never you mind, little darling. Supplying the Costa with what it wants, something you knew well in your day, eh? So what did you know about all this? Roberto must have said something, why he was travelling down to the docks, to Algeciras, what he was expecting to pick up.' Baxwell stopped slurping and trained his beady eyes in a nasty stare on Sophie again whilst she continued to feel her frontal headache and winced. 'Did you know what Roberto was up to?'

'No, of course not. Why would he tell me?' Sophie was in danger of blushing. At the same time, she realised Baxwell knew what had been in the horsebox, even though he was not directly part of that deal.

'Because you are his confidante, I've seen you two together sometimes. Did you know what was in the car?'

'No, I bloody didn't,' she stressed, feeling her cheeks definitely starting to colour. Baxwell was leaning forwards as far as his paunch would allow, pushing against the table edge, to reach for her chin with a clawed hand, rather like JR had done. 'If Roberto is responsible for this, I reckon you knew about it too. And that screwy blonde, Liz. If you're lying to me, Miss Sophie, I will…'

But he did not get to tell her what he would do to her if she was deceiving him, although it would undoubtedly have been illegal, because Sophie slapped his hand away and raised her voice: 'I'm not lying, quite definitely not. You bastard, how dare you,' rising from her chair, which scraped on the floor as she stepped back. She suddenly felt vulnerable and naked alone with these two big men, intimidating her. Bruce stood up too, probably from his sense of good manners and a little concern about Baxwell's aggressiveness.

'OK, Sophie, this is the thing,' Bruce interjected, in a cajoling sort of style, which surprised them all. 'Roberto has been beaten and taken away. Kidnapped by, we don't know.'

'The Chinese, do you think?' asked Baxwell, imploring Sophie to think about the problem, to give him the answer he seemed to want.

'Yes, possibly, but how would they have known it was Roberto? And why would they be interested?' She pulled her chair away from the table, sank into it, out of reach for the moment from Baxwell, as she tried to answer her own questions. 'They have spies everywhere in town, they might have picked up half the story, I suppose, and decided to get the truth from the man in the middle.'

'So we need to find him – where would they take him, Miss Sophie, do you think?' Bruce was asking.

'I really would not have a clue. I know nothing about this, don't you understand?'

'If the Moroccans have him, they will make him suffer,' Bruce added, in a rumbling sombre voice.

'Oh, no,' she exclaimed, leaning forward towards Bruce, 'that's terrible.' Through a wide v-shaped gap that had formed in the front of her gown, Bruce was able to ascertain that she was wearing nothing underneath; she quickly pulled the edges together.

'Yes, I am afraid so,' continued Bruce wringing his hands, 'if you have any idea where the money and hash may be, we need to know.'

Sophie nearly laughed, their ploy was so obvious. 'I know

nothing about all this.' She decided that if she played along with them, Bruce anyway, she might be able to find out more, but she needed to talk to him alone, without Baxwell there.

So all three of them sat quietly together for a while around the small wooden table in the stuffy room, looking straight ahead of themselves, with their various thoughts. Baxwell was brushing some ash from his trousers. 'If Roberto is in this, he must have stashed the stuff away somewhere, where might that be? His flat is a bit obvious. Or maybe he's just hidden the car somewhere?'

'I don't know, do I?' Sophie moaned again, sounding exasperated, reaching for her pack of Fortuna on the table, frantically tapping one out and fumbling with Baxwell's lighter. 'I don't look after him. He comes and goes as he sees fit. He *is* very loyal to you, as a matter of fact, has been over many years.' The deep inhalation of the tobacco smoke began to soothe her nerves.

'When he wants to be; till now. You're defending him, are you?' Sophie just frowned. Baxwell continued, 'But I think he's decided he wants out. He was asking me questions recently, about the future of his job and what he thinks he's worth. I was a bit suspicious.'

Roberto letting too much of his own feelings out, the idiot. But was this true, had Roberto really been kidnapped, or were these two playacting to make her confess. Baxwell resumed: 'Some powerful people have been robbed and will be upset. And when they are upset, they take revenge and can be quite ruthless. Roberto will be having a rotten time, I'm sure of that. I want to get him out of – wherever.'

'What can we do?'

'That's why we came here. I have alerted some of my boys and they have started some searching around, in the Chinese district, those hovels along the back of the hotels. Until we find the stolen stuff, I will be out of pocket big time. That amount of hash needs to be passed on, and then it will be obvious who's dealing. Roberto has some knowledge of the streets, but he would be looking for help, surely? That's why I'm looking at you, young Sophie. You knew these people.' His ginger eyebrows had sprung up his forehead and he cocked his head.

'The man who jumped me in the car that night,' said Bruce, 'was a short fellow in a white plastic mask, Chinese look, but he sounded Spanish.' Bruce looked thoughtful as he spoke with comfortable ease, nodding again at Sophie. That would have been Alfredo, Sophie imagined, responsible for the Skoda and with his baton and aggressiveness he had to prevent Bruce from running to Roberto's help.

'I could warn them to look out,' Sophie spoke slowly, 'the Chinese, but why would they cooperate? If it's good dope, they'll want to buy it and feed the market at their price. I could talk to Hsui Long Long, I suppose, but I couldn't guarantee he would tell me the truth.'

'We need to find Roberto, get him to confess to us, find out where he's snaffled all the stuff; get the merchandise to the rightful destination and then I get my money; and everybody is happy.'

Sophie was thinking what a complete tosser Baxwell was and how was she going to extricate herself from the fallout of all this. Baxwell would probably kill her if he found out the truth. Then she insisted: 'If Roberto is the victim here – and knows nothing about it…?' and managed some anguish in her voice which then trailed off.

'He's not. This was an insider job,' said Baxwell again, stubbing his cigarette out with venom and getting up. 'Roberto is the guilty one.' Bruce rose slowly, collecting the mugs and plates and stacking them on the side, trying to be helpful.

'Oh, you don't have to,' Sophie said, smiling feebly.

She followed Bruce to the kitchen area as Baxwell stood stretching by a window, holding a curtain back; he made some comment about how busy it seemed all of a sudden outside in Sophie's side street and at such a time. Sophie quietly reached for a piece of card torn from a cereal packet and found a biro on the side: she scrawled her telephone number on it and slipped the card between Bruce's fingers, placing a hand on his arm, while Baxwell's back was still turned. She mouthed at him: 'ring me later,' pointing a finger at his chest and then a thumb at herself. He smiled briefly showing his pearly whites, and nodded of course, but looked a little perplexed.

Soon Sophie was herding the two men out of her flat, closing the front door and leaning heavily against it as her legs began to buckle. She needed some fresh air to breathe. The early niggle of worry in the pit of her stomach had now become more of a deep pull of knotting and her headache was splitting.

After taking some tablets, her head was more comfortable but for the rest of the morning it was filled with worry, frustrated that their plans seemed to have back-fired, and so soon. And had put Roberto in such a horrible position. Even now he may have squealed to Ho Sup Ping and her dreams of Chinese henchmen with long knives screaming at her back was about to be fulfilled; they might be on their way over at that very moment. She must not let them in. She would call the *policia*. Find a hiding place; better still, get out of there.

How was it possible in such a short space of time for so many things to be going so completely wrong?

What would Baxwell really do when he found out about her role, as he certainly would? This was down to Roberto not playing his part well enough, not finding out more details in the first place, thinking it was all so uncomplicated; or Roberto spouting out something when inebriated in a club that a Chinese had picked up. They had a widespread network of watchers among the riff-raff, especially where drugs were involved, all feeding John with information. They liked to think they had the monopoly of the drugs trade in Marbella, which they probably did, and so controlled the street pricing; a new source flooding in would affect prices all round and that might hurt them. Perhaps the Chinese had heard that a big consignment of stolen Moroccan hash had arrived in town and that someone would be wanting to sell – at which point Sophie herself walks innocently into The Magician's lair trying to tempt him to buy the stuff, that he said was already his, pre-paid through some other contract.

And where did JR fit in? He knew all about the hijack – was that from Bruce? In which case it must be JR who has taken Roberto, not the Chinese.

She phoned Liz, to have someone else to mull things over with. And she would have wanted to know about Roberto; might be able to offer some ideas. She would also want reassurance that she was safe and that no thugs would be coming around her place looking for bundles of stolen money and marijuana.

'Baxwell has just been round here with that Bruce fellow. He's on the warpath. That's when he told me about Roberto. It was early this morning, Bruce saw him being bundled into the back of a van. Baxwell thinks it's the Chinese. I wonder whether it's JR. Somebody does not believe him and wants to extract the truth.'

'Poor Roberto, he *has* been in the wars. Maybe it was just some local ruffians,' suggested Liz, trying to sound consoling and to play it off as something less than it was, 'and they'll let him go soon, I don't know. Do you think he will be alright?'

'No, they're going to be beating the shit out of him, whoever they are. Somebody wants their money back. They suspect the mugging was a set-up, an insider job, as Baxwell kept saying. We'll find him and rescue the little sod. Baxwell's working on it.' As a quick afterthought she reminded Liz about the villa party the next day and how she would have the chance of seeing General Willie Whatsit close-up. 'We will need to concentrate on George and by then we will have Roberto back, I'm sure,' she repeated unconvincingly.

Sophie busied herself around the flat, tidying up, making the bed, washing at the kitchen sink, helping her to think straight and plan. She called Jamie who sounded completely in another world until the mention of Roberto being in trouble brought him back to a state of alertness. Sophie thanked him for last night and warned him to take care.

A little later she was out on her balcony to feel the sun and fetch some more washing in, when she noticed six floors below loitering in an entrance, two men in dark hooded jackets and dirty jeans close to a white van she had never seen before, with its near-side wheels up on the pavement. She crouched down out of sight behind the railings that were partly covered with shrubbery and clothes and watched the street for a while. The two men smoked and chatted but too far off for Sophie to hear anything. They wandered up the street to the corner with the main road and then back again rather aimlessly, and were joined by a third man after a while, before he drove off in the van, leaving the other two to carry on loitering.

Bruce phoned an hour later from a call box, said he had walked into town, was in the Parque de Alameda looking at the fountain and the tropical vegetation. Sophie asked him outright if he wanted to help her look for Roberto. 'Don't come here,' she said. 'I think I am being watched.' They agreed to meet in half an hour at the entrance to the park.

After applying a fresh face with minimal detail, cleansed and bright with shiny crimson lipstick, she left her block via the back stairwell, which was the fire escape that came out into a dingy lobby area in the basement which tradesmen used and where the cleaners had a cupboard full of their gear and the waste bins were parked. Through a solid wooden door that was never locked she stepped outside into a narrow concrete walled passageway to the back street, Calle Sierra Blanca which was used by the bin collectors once a week. Any watchers would have to have someone at the back, but Sophie noticed nobody particular that she could see as she emerged onto the pavement in front of a travel agent and opposite a tiny corner café. She had a cab driver waiting for her by his car, chatting to the passing old folk on the corner where the sun played across his back.

Bruce was sitting on a low wall watching a tramp with a dog in the shade of palm trees in the Parque. When he saw Sophie approaching in her white jeans, he whipped his cap off the top of his head and bowed a little as before. They set off at a leisurely pace towards the Chinese Quarter, talking in general about events. Bruce seemed perplexed. 'Do you think the Chinese were responsible for the mugging and robbery, Sophie?' he asked.

'Maybe. I think they might have heard something from Roberto, loose talk, you know, and jumped to conclusions and maybe they grabbed him – I'm hoping John, that's Hsui Long Long, can help me, I've known him for a long time and I think he would tell me if they were holding Roberto; or least help me find out.'

At The Peking Duck, they mingled with dozens of young workers in aprons who were hanging about in the dying warmth of the day and entered the restaurant through its rear alleyway; a few commie chefs were chopping vegetables and rinsing mountains of noodles along the row of steel sinks. Sophie was directed to an outside staircase and upstairs, in a smoky low-ceilinged room, they found John arguing with a couple of young Chinese lads, who he slapped several times across their heads.

Then Hsui Long Long waived them over to a hidden alcove where lukewarm tea on a tray was served by a tiny Chinese woman in jeans. Sophie introduced Bruce and the three of them sat together in a shared moment of companionship.

'I know nothing of Roberto. I not know Roberto,' Hsui confessed after hearing Sophie's story. 'We have not attack anyone. The Magician is velly upset. Consignment big, abou' 350kg cannabis cake, worth abou' sixteen mirron pesos; where it gone? Storen, by rivals, big worry on street. And The Magician a'ready pay about half that amount. Has he been douber-cross?' Sophie was amazed by the large sums involved. Hsui Long Long looked as bedraggled as always, unwashed dark hair streaking over the sides of his face, his drawn cheeks rough and unshaven. He had let his sparse chin hairs grow long and some of them were pulled together into a single twisted cord that descended down in front of his neck. He was chewing a stalk and spitting phlegm onto the floor, before he downed his tea from a small cup.

'Who was the hash for, John? Such a big amount, was that usual?'

'It was big consignment, unusual, but just happens sometimes after good crop. Paid for by Chinese market man, Magician nephew who had been to Rabat, he fly last month with lots money. I also find out that The Magician has to pay protection money, extra, this new, only this summer and he furious, lot of money and so we lift prices on street to try to pay, but this not so competitive. Trade fall off little and this not good. The Dutch they move in, some Inglish. The Magician now look faded.' And Hsui showed he had not lost his sense of humour, with a broad grin that showed his decaying teeth off at their worst.

'Who is the protection money paid to, John, do you know?'

'I think it is Mayor man, on City Council, that Robicalon Senor. They call him JR around town. He control much. He would run Chinese off streets without this.'

'Say again; which senor you talk about?' Sophie's mouth dropped open a little as the colour drained out of her face.

'JR – Robicalon.' Even Hsui Long Long, who had obvious difficulties with his 'r's, pronounced it properly and unambiguously.

Oh, dear God. The bigger picture and JR's potential role within it began to dawn heavily on Sophie and she swore inwardly. J-bloody-R was featuring a lot recently and his greasy paw marks seemed to be on everything. To find he was involved in a multimillion pesetas drugs haul that she and Roberto had unwittingly stolen, was almost enough to make her laugh but confirmed a few early suspicions. Naturally JR would be furious that his payday was in jeopardy if the hash haul was not delivered, and that's what Ho Sup Ping meant about giving her a price for hash that he had already paid for. And protection money, he must be coining it; all of which would have put the price up as well. As he had said himself, he ran this town and nobody did anything without his say so. Would he have kidnapped Roberto to get the information he wanted? Almost certainly, yes, that must have been JR's mob.

The tension in her mind was twisted one more notch and unnoticed by the others she helped herself to two more little painkillers with her green tea.

8

Sunday August 31

The early sunshine filtering through low-lying haze promised another warm day over southern England. Matthew Crawford, comfortably on course for his Sunday morning flight to Spain, relaxed in the back of his private taxi, conjuring up a vision of the woman who had been occupying much of his thoughts these past few weeks, his long-missed daughter. Stephanie had given him the photo of her taken some years ago that he had extracted from its frame, and he retrieved it from an inside pocket of his jacket, studying the face for the umpteenth time, fingering its stiff edges. He admitted to himself he was feeling quite excited, now that he was moving into action.

The driver asked him if he had heard the news overnight and seemed eager to tell him anyway. 'Lady Diana was killed last night. In Paris, in a car crash, along with her boyfriend.' It took Matthew a moment to focus, his mind clearly ahead of himself thinking of sunny coastlines and meeting Sophie for the first time. 'They were being chased at high speed by the paparazzi through the underpass system and the car hit a concrete post head-on at a hundred miles an hour.' Matthew was stunned; he could not believe it. Whatever the press and other commentators thought about Prince Charles's ex, he rather liked her, or at least sympathised with her, even if she was a self-centred attention-seeking bimbo. 'The radio reporter reckoned she was up the spout. Taken to some casualty department but was likely dead on arrival. Some French geezer did direct cardiac massage, opened her chest.' The pungent mix in the car of cigarettes and body odour did nothing to disguise the man's obvious pleasure in delivering such tragic news. 'Shame, really.'

Matthew sat pensive and saddened in the back for the rest of the journey and was quick to buy a newspaper at Gatwick's North Terminal. "Death Of The Princess" headlines were everywhere, on all the papers and TV screens. There was not much real detail of the overnight's events, plenty of blurred pictures of an underground road tunnel entrance and the front of the Pitie-Salpetriere Hospital. Most of the copy focused on her love affairs and Dodi Fayed and speculation over whether she was planning to marry, whether she was pregnant and whether her death was a conspiracy organised by the Palace, who secretly hated her, of course. He tried to put the story out of his mind when his flight number was called.

The Boeing flight Matthew shared with a pack of noisy tourists landed at Malaga Terminal 2 soon after midday. The queues for hire cars in the oven-hot basement area were moving frustratingly slowly. Matthew's pale perspiring skin made him feel self-consciously English and inappropriately dressed in an open-necked shirt and jacket with heavy shoes. In the clinging heat of the day he was dreaming of lazing in the sunshine, eating out and strolling the beaches. Everything was strange, having to adjust his watch to European time and finding the steering wheel of the little Renault on the left and the gear-change on the floor for his right hand. After the big automatic Volvo at home, it took him some while to adapt to the new car, all plastic and crisp, and the driving on the right side of the road. He let the windows down so that warm air rushed around him, ruffling his hair; he found a music station on the radio. As he followed the old motorway west with signs to Cadiz and Algeciras, the sun glared sharply into his eyes from high above on his left side, with glittering reflections sparkling over the sea.

He fumbled for his sunglasses and drove steadily among the hectic traffic, sticking to the A-7 coast road and looking out for landmarks, like the hospital on its commanding position near Santa Clara Golf, which he remembered from a previous visit. He took the slip road into Marbella, that looped round into Avenida Severo Ochoa and under the iconic arch of Marbella letters carved in white stone, and passed the BP garage on his right, which signalled that he was close. During the short ride, he was able to relax and smile inwardly as he tried to imbibe the atmosphere of the Costa del Sol coastline. Some of the recent anxieties about what he was doing, stepping into the unknown in a foreign country, uncertain as what he might find or what reaction he may have to face, were beginning to thaw with the rising temperatures and his spirits were lifted the closer he came to his destination.

With signs to follow, he easily found the Hotel Fuerte tucked away south of the main avenue, a large balconied block in salmon pink that paid lip-service to its Moorish influence, hiding behind tall firs and iron fencing. He drove off-street between little sentry-boxes and under a white barrier, and then parked in an open area. Through huge glass doors into a pleasantly cool lobby area of timber arches and marble tiles, he passed into an oasis of calm, far away from the hubbub of the town. The pretty dark-haired girl in navy suit and red silk scarf at reception was friendly and his third floor sea-view room was generous and comfortable, with its long drapes at the windows.

Despite some of the ominous thoughts that Maurice and

Annabel had shared with him before his trip, Matthew was in a positive mood and quite prepared to accept any outcome, as long as he was satisfied that he had done the right thing. He was going to be absolutely straight with Sophie and if she wanted to get to know Matthew as her 'new' father and some of his family and wanted to return to England some time, he would be delighted to have her stay with him; or if she wanted more time to think about her newly discovered circumstances, perhaps unable to return to the UK, she might prefer that members of the 'family' visit her instead, then Matthew was sure that could be arranged. If she wanted to have nothing to do with him or any of them, well, that would be disappointing but he would accept that too. He was happy to go along with whatever Sophie might want. He was prepared for her to be wary and maybe at first even less than friendly, in which case he would leave her with a contact number if she wished. But he needed to fulfil his desire to at least have made the effort and the rest would be up to her.

While dozing lightly on the flight, his head wobbling from side to side in the cramped seat, his fertile mind had him stumbling after Stephanie in her Fulham house, sharing food and laughter, and some perfunctory intimacy that involved them rolling around on the floor with a little Pekinese yapping into his ear and nipping at his side, before being abruptly interrupted by cabin service bumping along the aisles with their trolleys. As he drank his coffee he thought more of Stephanie, feeling at least they might be friends, although Richard whoever might not like the idea. He also found himself rethinking every aspect of his life, his job, where he lived, his friends, his relationship with his children. Maybe now would be a good time to retire from the University. His determination to face up to the past and accept it on his terms, before moving on, made him consider what he wanted from the rest of his life, what were his priorities. A new century beckoned on the near horizon, what better time for a major overhaul with an emphasis put on the important things.

Matthew had tried to contact Sophie from England on the telephone last week, but only managed to get an answer phone in Spanish at the number Stephanie said was a flat in town. The quality had been so poor and crackly, he was left uncertain as to whether his message had actually been recorded. He spoke slowly in English, saying he would arrive in Malaga on the Sunday and would be around Marbella in the afternoon, when he might come and look for her at her flat address. He dictated his London telephone number as clearly as he could, but he had heard nothing from her. However, as he stepped out onto a little balcony shaded by adjacent cypress and cedar trees that gently swayed in the breeze, overlooking a quiet swimming pool, he leant against the railing and caught site of the twinkling sea close by, and a pleasant if inexplicable sense of well-being came over him.

He was anticipating a jolly meeting with his long lost daughter, someone he was sure to find instantly attractive and interesting, who would be astonished but hopefully grateful in meeting him. He was determined to have some fun this week and all was well with the world.

He started to unpack, worrying whether he had the appropriate clothes. He chose a cotton pair of white slacks, coloured shirt and slip-on moccasins. On a table, he laid out a near-useless tourist map of the Costa del Sol he had picked up at the airport, with the little piece of paper that had Sophie's address and telephone number on and the name, address and number of the estate agency, Baxwell Properties. Stephanie had explained that those were the only contacts she had, although they were over a year old and she might have moved on since then. Anyway, they provided Matthew with his starting points.

His plans for the rest of the day were simple: he would look around the hotel and its immediate area, have a little bite to eat somewhere, take in some sunshine by the pool and perhaps walk down to the sea, adjusting to his bearings and the heat. He would find an outdoor restaurant for a lazy dinner later with a bottle of something and then get a good night's sleep before setting out on his quest tomorrow.

He strolled out of the hotel into the stifling afternoon heat wearing a wide-brimmed straw hat and wandered aimlessly along narrow streets picking up some cherries and oranges from a street-seller and soon found himself on the busy Avenida Ricardo Soriano, where he looked into some of the smart shop windows along with other tourists. By chance he had turned west and so after some minutes noticed across the wide road, the large double glass-fronted estate agency, Baxwell Properties, the name in hand-writing style on a green hoarding above. On a whim, he crossed over the road and strolled to the corner shop, which looked smart and not the pokey dusty little one-man band office that he had been expecting. Although it was a Sunday, the street doors were open and inside, with ceiling fans whirring overhead, a smooth-faced young man in dark-rimmed glasses was working at a flickering computer screen on his desk, with his name Alfonso Cesar printed on the name block. He earnestly informed Matthew in excellent English that all the rest of the staff were at a launch party for the opening of a newly-built villa complex along the coast not far from the office for the benefit of General Ishmail Nassif from Morocco, a major purchaser and investor who was in town on a celebrity visit. He handed Matthew a colour brochure from a rack by his desk.

'Senora Sophie Patek will be there. No doubt. With Senor Baxwell himself and many other staff members. They leave me here to hold the castle. Call at main gate, talk to security,

I'm sure Sophie would come and speak with you. Good luck.' Matthew thanked the young man profusely and scanned the other desks while he backed out of the office, thrilled to notice Sophie's name on one of them. '*Muchos gracias.*'

He returned briskly to the hotel to retrieve his car, with the street instructions retained in his head. He snaked along with the rest of the traffic the Ricardo Soriano, turning off across traffic down to Calle Ramon Gomez, bending round to the right and following the road five hundred yards to a left turning into Calle Velazquez. This was a narrow tree-lined road through a mature residential area, but it soon became more of a track, almost single file, sloping straight down towards the coast. With cars parked up both sides, he had to carefully negotiate through narrow gaps before finally arriving at what seemed like the end of the road, where vehicles were doubled up and left chaotically at all angles, with little space left to turn around. The new development, looking like a children's pile of giant red and white Lego bricks, rose up behind a long line of white hoardings that were plastered with Diamond Heights Complex signs and seemed to extend along the coast for half a mile. 'Just park anywhere you can find. There'll be lots of people there. Say I sent you,' Alfonso had called out as Matthew gratefully stepped out of the office back on to the hot street with a tingling sense of excitement. 'Or just squeeze yourself in, say you were family,' Alfonso added ironically.

* * *

The late afternoon party was in full swing. The last day of August and the sun was burning the bare flesh of sozzled guests outside on the terraces and around the kidney-shaped pool, where there was much whooping and screaming. A couple of young black lads had just bombed in, sending waves of chilly water over the edges and pushing those closest in their expensive outfits back with little screams, while business men in lightweight suits and adoring blondes on their arms observed the fun from safer distances, conceited smirks on their sun-drenched faces.

Skimpy-dressed Spanish and African waitresses had been darting around the guests all day with food trays and drinks, while the more serious investors and buyers were indoors out of the sun discussing pre-launch discounts, lease finance and off-market capitalisation. The guest of honour was Ishmail Nassif, The General, known to one and all as Willie because of his reputation, as Alex Baxwell described it to Bruce that morning, for freely and often with gay abandon "putting it about a bit." Laughing openly with Mr and Mrs Baxwell were at least two of The General's young Moroccan wives, with his numerous other hangers-on, attendees and advisers with bulging armpits, who had all retreated through the floor-to-ceiling windows to the shaded and air-conditioned environment of the main lounge, which delightfully overlooked the sea from its elevated position. The apartments were all lavishly kitted out with marble floors (from China), brass fittings (from Germany), gold-leafed lace curtains (from India) and soft leather upholstery (from Texas), with extensive self-cleaning slabs of glass window (imported incidentally from Denmark) in order to gain maximum advantage of the views in all directions.

Sophie, in a tight turquoise cotton-mix dress with elasticated bodice, had been pumping the punters all afternoon, giving her sales pitch to guests on tours around the complex, showing what was on offer, pressing on them brochures and sales prices and making sure they were all fed and watered. There was the usual spiel about booming local sales patterns around Marbella, the advantages of going with Baxwell Properties for all their needs and the poor service that the competition had to offer. They were always keen to hear about other local sights of interest around the South Coast, the shows they should see, where to shop for the best bargains and go for the best golf. When asked by an overweight African sweating profusely in a long white toga where he might find some nice girls to entertain him for the rest of the afternoon, Sophie advised equally discretely that he should ask his General whether he might have a loan of the services of one of his plentiful bimbo sycophants.

At one point in the busy afternoon, with dozens of people milling around the pool and the internal show apartments and Sophie working her hardest, when the noise levels of chit-chat were at their highest, she was bizarrely called down by a security guard to the main gate, where a man in uniform had arrived by motorbike, with a message on a card, typed. He had been sent directly by Senor Robicalon, he said and had an invitation for Miss Sophie Patek to attend the Mijas festivities this week, the main attraction event tomorrow afternoon, to be precise, which was the bullfighting. Sophie stood stunned for a moment, looking at the words written in ink on the card again ("I graciously ask for your forgiveness for my loutish behaviour and please be my guest at Mijas caridas extravaganza Monday. JR."); and she asked the courier to explain once again, which he did in rapid Spanish, stating who he was and who had sent him and that a car would pick her up from the office at midday tomorrow. (He also advised her to wear a wide-brimmed hat for the sunshine.)

JR must have known that she would need no inducement. With JR telling her that he was the main loser from the midnight car mugging and that he suspected her of being involved in it; and with JR being her first suspect for the Roberto kidnapping, she knew that she had to attend. With his threats the other day still ringing in her ears, her jaw still stiff from its mauling, she knew the invitation was an instruction, that she had to obey. He would put more pressure on her over the Baxwell bid and the mugging, although equally she might have the opportunity to find out the extent of his knowledge and whether he was bluffing.

She returned to the main rooms and stood with Liz, who had been helping out all afternoon with some of the tours and the sales pitches, in her best summer frock, quietly keeping her up-to-date with developments. 'I hope this will be a chance to find out something about Roberto.'

'I think we should talk to the police, Sophie, otherwise we may never find him.'

'Not yet, Liz, but I am going to see Hernandez tomorrow.'

'Ah, good,' and Liz smiled bravely at her friend, believing that to be a wise move. They had both been watching George Baxwell with surreptitious interest all the while, as he patrolled the party inside and out, moving confidently around the house and its wide terraces, wandering among the guests with words here and there and watching the activity in the pool below, checking on his comrades from time to time. A good-looking nineteen-year-old, Liz concluded, with a fringe of reddish hair that spilt over his pale forehead, he wore a clean short-sleeved white shirt with a black tie and a Baxwell Properties tie-pin. A pair of well-pressed black slacks, with bulging pockets and jangling bunches of keys attached on chains, were supported with a tightly-pulled leather belt that pleasingly exaggerated his prominent backside. He had been taking a few quick gulps of various alcoholic drinks, half left-overs, as he passed by trays and tables, when he thought nobody was watching. He was closely shaven and reeked of cheap aftershave. His bulging forearms were covered thinly in fine amber hair and after some hours on duty he had discarded the tie and relaxed with his shirt open enough to show, for those interested in such things, a studiously smooth chest. As the heat of the day continued without any let up, he was beginning to look weary, having been on his feet for most of it.

Liz quite liked the look of young George, his physique and standing, as she observed him from the other side of the lounge, by the loosely draped curtains. She had been drinking wine slowly, sipping with dignity so as not to get too inebriated and spoil her part in Sophie's plan. Her thin cotton front was unbuttoned for the plunging effect between her loose breasts that trembled delicately as she sidled over towards his side.

'Anywhere for a tired girl to go for a lie down round here, George?' she whined playfully into his ear, making sure her boobs made contact with his arm and that he achieved a good eye-full as he turned towards her. She managed a hang-dog expression. 'I mean, all this drink and excitement, goes to a girl's head, and then who knows where it might lead.' Her voice was oily smooth and suggestive, and George, for all his naivety, responded as expected with a childish twist of his mouth and a twinkle in both his little brown eyes. All previous thoughts and worries that might have been toying with his mind, about his job prospects, his debts, his dislike of his father or his parents' constant bickering, all these suddenly vanished as his eyes made a rapid scanning appraised of what Liz had to offer. He knew her from occasional meetings at the Baxwell house, but saw in her sharp blue eyes and shiny tanned complexion not an older woman beyond his normal sphere of interest and social standing, but an experienced object of desire ready to put his young prowess to the test, who admired him and was apparently available. Her unmarried status was a clear benefit. 'Show me where you keep your truncheon, why don't you,' she purred. Her scent beckoned, and the lascivious look in her eye challenged him directly to put his manhood to good use. What better way, Liz imagined him calculating, to lose the novice tag and to gain recognition from his comrades, than to experience a sexy middle class English woman of obvious breeding, who was feeling a tad abandoned and unable to score with her own set, eager for some young and firm flesh.

'Absolutely,' he sung in return, with a gentle Edinburgh slur, 'follow me, I'll show you.' George led the way into the hall, passing various people he knew with smiles and short comments, and Liz followed closely behind. They went along a corridor to a service lift that smoothly rose up through the house to the second floor, where the doors silently opened onto a marble floored corridor. George took one of Liz's hands and led her to the end, where he opened an unlocked door into an expansive guest bedroom, brightly lit through full-length windows overlooking the distant sea. A perfect king-sized bed with golden silk cover beckoned.

Liz put her glass down on a bedside table and lifted her hands up to his broad shoulders. 'You look as if you could do with a little lie down as well,' she sang, pulling his buttons apart and reaching for his chest through the open shirt. His body was warm and muscled. She could sense the pounding of his heart. With spade-like hands, he gently pulled her dress open to feast his eyes on her bronzed breasts, which he fondled as if testing a couple of loaves of bread for freshness. He started clumsily kissing her, around the neck and mouth. Liz, determined not to take things too seriously and to couch her role as sleazy sexpot with a sense of fun, saw straight away that she would have to do the leading and be sensitive to his inexperience. She explored his pouting lips and dry mouth with her clever tongue, while a cold hand slithered down inside his tight belt to his crotch, where she coaxed his soft spongy penis into something rather more generous. He looked flattered and bamboozled at the same time, but was determined to demonstrate that he knew how to handle women, how to satisfy them with all the appropriate tackle and technique.

Kicking off her strappy sandals, she quickly nipped back to the big bedroom door and pretended to turn the key that was in the lock. In the next moment they both had their tops bared. She decided to go straight to the meat of the matter and dropped onto her haunches in front of him, where she unzipped his trousers and hoiked his eager dick out of his Y-fronts before he could object. She was fascinated by his red pubic hairs and the admirable size and shape of his member, which like a leaping pink salmon, was standing out unaided. He glanced down with pride as Liz found its sculpted helmet, an easy mouthful, slotting it up inside the roof of her mouth. It tasted of warm salt and sweat and whatever else one might find dried on a young man's truncheon these days.

He was in a swoon, his desire to thrust overwhelming. He looked down at the top of Liz's head, moving rhythmically, the mass of blond locks flopping over her face and tickling his crotch. She pulled and sucked with skilful lips, using her tongue as a bombarding tool, while tugging his trousers with their bulging pockets off his legs and slinging them away across the floor towards the door.

He was in paradise, or at least the version he always imagined of it, and realised he had never been there before. And now he wanted to take control. He withdrew himself carefully, avoiding any snags on her big front teeth and pulled Liz up by her arms, twisting her towards the bed in one swift motion. He bent down to hook the bottom of her dress up over her back and literally ripped off her lacy briefs. Grabbing at her bared untanned buttocks with both his strong hands, he separated them, thrusting between them with newly found confidence, exploring the dark chasm from behind, while she tipped forward onto her arms and face on the bed, keeping her legs up as firm as she was able.

Although she was pretty sure, when she set out on this afternoon's adventure, with a hearty good luck and a quick kiss from Sophie, that she was not going to be taken from behind, by any man, the feel of this young blade, this engaging hunk, stretching his personal experience to wholly new levels of ecstasy by poking into her sadly underused and by now sublimely slimy passage, was pleasantly irresistible. Even if the Willie General himself had walked in, she would have urged this brave knight to keep to his task to the very end. However, she felt he was getting carried away, dreaming he was playing for Scotland at Murrayfield or something, because his powerful thrusting was starting to hurt. His pelvis slapped and hammered repetitively into her buttocks with all the subtlety of a machine-gun and he was grunting like an ox, exhaling noisily harder and faster. Her head was banging up and down on the mattress giving her a headache and she could not hold her position any longer, collapsing face down, with him left standing rigid, his arms raised up and fingers interlaced behind his head, his eyes closed, his enormous purple erection shuddering out in front of him. Liz twisted round and they both stared at this object, he with sheer amazement and she with admiration and the beginnings of respect, when suddenly a warm sticky white stream hit Liz's face, leaving some residual drops dripping from its source onto the bed cover.

'Oh fuck, little George, what's this?' And Liz squeezed more juice drops from him between her fingers, knowing that this hunky monkey had dumped his load early.

'Oh, shit. Bugger me.' George stood horrified, looking down at his fast shrinking treasure and quickly covered himself with both hands in a laughable moment of embarrassment.

'No, it's not shit, its spunk, and you've just come all over me, you little bugger. And I wish I could stay and lick it all off you. But I suggest you tuck yourself up and have a little sleep here, while I go and tidy up.' Liz stood up and bundled his underpants and shirt under the covers with him, as he curled up and rolled over to close his eyes, tired and oddly satisfied, his face buried in a soft pillow, where he would dream of his wild all-conquering exploits with the posh English woman with the pert frontage.

Liz retrieved what was left of her briefs and sorted out her crumpled dress and was in the bathroom, wiping and washing away the tell-tale signs of her tryst, regretting that they had not used a condom and that there had been no time for her climax. 'I hope he hasn't got gonorrhoea or something,' she mused, as she quietly closed the bedroom door and slipped away on tiptoe along the corridor to wait for her partner in crime and to find out how she had fared.

* * *

Matthew had little choice but to leave his small hire car guiltily where it was, blocking the way alongside the many bigger smarter cars already crammed there. He was feeling a little nervous about what their conversation would be like when, if, he found Sophie. He was hoping he would recognise her but took another quick look at the slim face in the photo, squinting into the sunlight, black spiky hair and leather jacket, to remind himself of her pretty features, before getting out of the car.

Diamond Heights, a busy packed collection of modern white-washed villas with terracotta tiled roofs on several levels, was certainly in a good spot, running along the edge of the sea that Matthew could discern rasping noisily over the shingle shore not thirty metres away. There was a chunky tower block of twelve stories at the far end, with luxury penthouses, which would command great views both ways along the coastline. The area was away from the main roads and would be a private and expensive enclave for its residents, with high walls around the plot.

Matthew walked through open makeshift wooden gates with a few others, noticing a uniformed security man slouching on one side, under a little hutch for sun protection, who signalled him to follow the path. Once inside he made his way through plush landscaped gardens towards the largest villa on site, that he could see covered in bunting and coloured balloons at the end of a semi-circle of smaller villas, as yet unoccupied with their blank windows, painted pastel blues and greens that looked almost artificial. The show villa, built in a Moorish style stacked over three floors with terraces and fancy balustrades, stone steps up to the front portico defined each side by pillars, floor-to-ceiling glass on all levels, underground parking, electronic gates, and tumbling bougainvillea in private gardens all around, landscaped with mature plants and bushes and palm trees was the bees-knees of smart villas, with private access to the beach, and must have been worth a pretty sum. Here like bees around a honey pot were dozens of smartly-dressed jet-set types, enjoying the party with its free drink, laughing and cajoling in the gardens, strolling around the terraces and slipping in and out of the front doors, glasses and brochures in hand.

A little reticently Matthew approached, trying to look casual and just part of the scene. He slipped behind a group of laughing young Greeks on the path, smiled at two young Spanish women in crisp white blouses, lipstick and heels whiling away the oppressive afternoon under a giant umbrella, and listened to Russian and German and French freely spoken all around as he joined the general drift of a milling cosmopolitan crowd towards the steps up to the double front entrance of the show house.

* * *

Seeing her best friend take on the pretty boy George, enticing him upstairs, Sophie had followed a little way behind. Listening at the door and timing her quiet entry to coincide with the heaviest grunting and thumping that she associated with rampant sex, she was astonished to see the two of them going at it with such fortitude and commitment on the side of the bed ahead of her. George was standing naked and erect, with arms aloft, head thrown back, as he rammed repeatedly and rapidly his magnificent beast between the upturned broad buttocks of her friend and confidante. Sophie crouched quite still on the marble floor with a perfect view from where George's taut and chiselled buttocks gleaming with sweat reminded her for a brief moment of poor Roberto's. She slid over the polished surface unseen and unheard, reaching out for the discarded pair of trousers; and then reversed out of the room, pulling the door gently closed behind her. In the corridor outside she found the leather covered key case, identifying the labelled bunch that worked the Baxwell office. She slipped the trousers back inside the room, her faint sounds completely masked by the dramatic physical activity going on without restraint on the golden silk bedspread, before departing unnoticed as quietly as she had come.

* * *

On stepping cautiously into the strange world of property development, Matthew was still pondering how best he might introduce himself. He presumed she spoke English, although sudden panic set in when he thought that perhaps he would have to speak to her entirely in Spanish, in front of all these people. At which point he contemplated turning around there and then, feeling it would be better actually to go back to the hotel and ring her tomorrow to offer to meet for a coffee or a private dinner; which would also give her a fairer chance to compose herself and prepare for the meeting.

Maybe he would just wander around the villa complex, now that he was there, have a drink, mingle affably with the wealthy and the good, and pretend to be a potential buyer before heading back to the hotel with his original plan in mind, a quiet dinner alone followed by an early bedtime. Just a cool drink and maybe something to eat would be nice, he was thinking, as he decided he was quite hungry. He started to climb the curving flight of steps leading up towards the front terrace, reminding himself to obtain a price list for these properties while he was about it, just to get an idea, in case he ever thought of retiring to the sunny south coast himself one day.

And then all of a sudden, he spotted her. Unmistakably.

Looking just as he had imagined: beautiful, slim and compact, purposeful and sun-tanned in a bright blue dress that was sleeveless and soft. It was the hair, the black spiky style setting off her petite face with their dark eyes that distinguished her among the crowd. She was at the top of the stairs, coming down in a hurry. He stopped in his tracks, one foot on the step above, and drew in a quick breath, his mouth open a fraction, his throat suddenly parched. He reached out slowly to form a hand-shake as he tried to mouth her name, but she skipped down the steps in clicking blue heels too quickly for him, passed him, barging if anything between him and some other shoulders in her hurry, before he could say anything. He watched her trot out through the gates he had entered, around the corner and out of sight. She was gone almost as fast as she had appeared and for a moment he wondered whether he had imagined her! He remained standing rigid with her name half formed on his lips, while others in the queue pushed at him from behind. He stared down towards the space where she had been, wondering what to do next.

* * *

Sophie drove with studied urgency from the complex back up to Avenida Ricardo Soriano, as she only had a little time before George would wake and want to be put his trousers on. She pushed the speed and parked in a shaded space around the corner. The low-lying sun cut crisp shadows along the street highlighting discarded rubbish, food cartons and cigarette packets, which the breeze was pushing around the pavement. A couple of dark green Baxwell liveried Seats were parked neatly outside and the place looked quiet. A bright strip of orange reflected across the central window display where some of the most tempting property bargains of your life were advertised. She approached with her grip firmly around George's bundle of keys. Alfonso had gone. She read the familiar warning signs written in both Spanish and English stuck on the inside glass that the premises were alarmed and that no money was ever kept in the shop. The toughened glass double doors required two keys, which senior staff member Sophie already had on her own collection.

She entered and the buzzer sounded once. Then the alarm beeping started up at the side of the door. She tapped a code into the keypad behind a small metal door on the wall and the beeping ceased. She worked her way between the desks to the back and then sprinted up the internal staircase to Baxwell's office. Now she needed George's bundle for the right key, which she found after a couple of tries. She moved to the back through an archway and found a light switch. On the floor was the solid metal safe about two foot by three, and Sophie crouched down in front of it studying the details. It had two bolt locks, key operated top and bottom, and that was easy; and then by twiddling a central circular dial, the correct eight-digit number would open the door. She knew Baxwell had written the secret number on the back of a notepad that he kept in the top drawer of his desk; she knew because she and his secretary Sonia had advised him together when the safe had been delivered last year, not to put the number in writing anywhere but to commit it to memory and had then watched while he did the opposite and wrote the number down on his pad after first choosing his code: his birthday in numbers backwards: 85918061.

She followed the procedure and dialled in the number. She heaved a mighty sigh of relief when she heard a satisfying clunk and the door swung open. She was looking for a black embossed folder, thick and shiny, with Alex Baxwell's name and Projecto Al Este De La Linea De Costa printed in gold lettering on the front cover. It opened like a book and contained bundles of letters and brochures, evidence papers and regulators' agreements, financing proposals, bank statements and balance sheet data that she had been partly responsible for collecting. And signed copies of Baxwell's bid details, ready for submission to the Mayor's council offices by Wednesday should also be there. The safe was stuffed to the brim, cash boxes and money bags, cash in bundles with elastic bands round, thick stacks of files and envelopes and papers and on the top shelf were accounting ledgers lying flat with dates in gold lettering along their spines, from the mid-eighties to 1996. There were other reports from surveyors, architects and various planners and an auditors' report of five years' of Baxwell business (1992-1997). But there was no black file for the East Shoreline Project.

Wearing cotton gloves she systematically turned everything out and just as carefully replaced everything exactly as she could, knowing that Baxwell would recognise immediately if there was anything different or out of place.

But the black file, Baxwell's most treasured application for what he saw would be the absolute pinnacle of his business, the making of his reputation and standing among the rich of Marbella, namely the East Shoreline Project, was not to be found locked in his safe.

'Oh. Shit.' Sophie was in despair.

She went weak and sank to the floor, deflated for a moment. Gritting her teeth and wanting to scream, she allowed the waves of annoyance to pass over her. She sat back on the floor against a wall, knees drawn up, head down, running her hands through her hair, while trying to think sensibly. She looked around the office, on shelves, on his desk, in his drawers (including one that was locked and immediately raised her hopes again when she found the right key on George's bunch), but eventually she had to come to the conclusion that it was not in the office; Baxwell himself must have the file with him, perhaps to work on at home before submission next week. She would have to return the keys and admit defeat to Liz, who would be devastated that all her hard sacrifice with George had been in vain. Realistically, Sophie had until tomorrow before JR and his thugs would be back on her trail.

9

Monday September 1

Matthew used the phone in his bedroom to dial through to the Baxwell office number. Somebody answered in rapid Spanish, which was disconcerting and he asked, in his clearest English, slightly too loud and over slow, for Ms Sophie Patek, *por favor*.

After a short pause, '*Buenos dias*. Baxwell's Properties?'

'Oh, hello. Erm. Sorry to disturb you, er, do you speak English?'

'Yes, I do. Can I help?' A cheery woman's voice.

'Oh, good. It's Sophie, is it? I'm Matthew Crawford.'

For a few telling seconds there was absolutely nothing positive passing through Sophie's mind to connect the name Matthew Crawford with anything or anybody that seemed relevant in her life right then. All she could think about was what bloody Baxwell had done with his black file, what ever could she tell JR about his project bid and where was poor Roberto? She searched her brain, thinking it must be a customer, who would be most offended if she did not recognise the voice, and so she said with enthusiasm: 'Oh, of course. How are you?' not actually knowing who the hell it was. She glanced at Clarissa, who had initially taken the call, questioning her with her face and pointing to the mouthpiece, whether she knew who it was, but received a blank signal in return.

'Oh. I'm fine, trying to get used to this hot weather. We don't get it so hot like this in September. Erm, I'm staying at the Fuente Hotel, which is nice actually and I was wondering if we might meet up, some time?'

Ah, that Matthew Crawford, the one in her mother's postcard, now she remembered; some old codger from her past who wanted to meet her for some unknown reason and he had arrived in Marbella. Great!

'Yes, that would be nice. I am a bit busy today. How long are you here for?'

'Return flight Saturday, so we have a few days.'

'I'm going to the bull fighting this afternoon, actually. I'm working at the Blue Ocean Club tonight but I finish at ten o'clock. Not too late, is it? We could meet in the lobby of your hotel after that? It's close. For a drink.'

Sophie felt she was being generous with her time and was not sure why; for her mother, she supposed. Matthew was delighted, Sophie sounded friendly and easy to talk to, and his worry that she would only speak Spanish was dispelled. And he had broken the ice, at least. He was feeling more positive and had the whole day ahead of him to enjoy the town and the weather before their meeting. He might even take a walk down to the beach, take his shoes off, feel the sand between his toes, dip them into the sea.

* * *

The feria at Mijas, with its full programme of bull-fighting every afternoon, was always in early September, when the days were still hot and the level of expectancy high. Although bullfighting could be found on local television screens any night of the week, all year round, every loyal supporter, whose inner feral feelings were stirred by the smell of warmed bodies and sweet blood, would swear that nothing could replace the thrill of it all, the rich colours and the noise of the braying crowds, happening before their own eyes. Mijas would have a week of partying and street celebrations that this year would culminate with the star attraction of El Apariceone the elder returning from semi-retirement to perform for his home crowd that had witnessed the glamour of his greatest triumphs over a twenty-year career, together with his teenage son, the new people's hero, taking on the finest bulls Andalusia could find. It was also rumoured that this might be the final time Mijas would host bull-fighting as, like many other areas of Spain, in response to the general mood in the country, it was contemplating hanging up the red capes for the last time.

'There is long and admirable tradition to bull-fighting on the South coast, but, sad to say, there is big senior audience, as you can see around you.' This was part of JR's explanation to an innocent Sophie about some of the rudiments of the sport. 'But you make the whole afternoon so much more exciting,' he added with charm oozing from every pore of his hot face, 'with your young age and beauty.' JR in turn had the look of an elegant matinee film-idol, and the more powerful for that, in his light suit and silk tie, sunshine glancing across his distinguished features and reflecting off his thickly creamed black hair. 'The number of fights is falling steadily and the shows in these small towns not make the profits they used to.' Sophie feigned a sadness about that and continued to cheer as enthusiastically with everyone around her as another thundering black bull was felled and dragged out, and another red faced and flushed matador bowed towards the Mayor's stand for special acknowledgment.

At around midday, Sophie had been picked up by a driver in an official black Mercedes and driven smoothly up through the mountains to the high plateau above Fuengirola, where they weaved slowly through the walking crowds along narrow decorated streets to the Playa de Tores of Mijas, in the old town market square of some historical note. A bubbling crowd was dancing and cheering to the sounds of a brass band playing triumphal marching tunes nearby, among the smells of frying peppers and meats. On stepping out in a tight black number that showed some cleavage and clutching her wide-brimmed black straw hat as advised, she was ushered through the arched entrance by two uniformed officials, and then into a marquee decorated lavishly with masses of flowers in full bloom, pink and white bougainvillea and rich-smelling lilies, where Senor Juanita Robicalon was waiting with an entourage of flunkies and aides, all looking at their youthful best in flamboyant colour and designer chic, in close attendance.

He welcomed Sophie with a warm handshake and a glowing smile, rather like a long-missed friend, and thanked her most profoundly for finding the time to attend as his honoured guest. He led her with a firm guiding hand at her elbow to a reception area that was cool out of the sun, where drinks were being served by waiters in white gloves, with lots of ice clinking in buckets. She could feel the excitement that buzzed around the spectators, recognising the faces of some local celebrities while mingling with officials from the Town Hall. And there was Senor Nestor, surrounded by smartly dressed young women showing flesh and bosom, lasciviously sliding towards her with his hands clasping hers. Thankfully she was spared his attention for too long as he was called aside to meet some other dignitary and she was left in the only marginally safer hands of JR's flunkies, all attractive dark haired, dark skinned Spanish beauties, attentive and thoughtful, asking in English questions about her life in Marbella, and wanting to know about her time in England. After Sophie had downed at least two glasses of expensive Rioja that had been thrust into her hand, JR led them along a dipping narrow passage of whitewashed stone that was cool and shaded, out into the bright sunlight that filled the arena, which was by now overflowing with over-dressed, over-excited spectators.

The bullring at Mijas, one of the oldest in Spain, was also unusually oblong and small, with a capacity of only about four hundred people, clustered mostly in two groups at either end. Seats were found reserved at the highest part at the back of a small VIP area which was under some coloured awning for sun protection. Sophie found herself sitting between JR on one side and the Mayor's wife on the other. Senora Nestor, filling comfortably a lovely full-length black silk dress edged with lace and ribbons, immediately confided in whispered English while fanning herself vigorously that she hated these events with so many people making such a noise and that bullfighting was not really her cup of tea and that Sophie may call her Isidora, if she wished. Behind her were JR's female team, whose duty included offering anything she needed and to feed her with helpful comments about the spectacle in front of them, in case she was less than familiar with Spain's national sport.

The early contests involved two up-and-coming local matadors, looking pretty in their bright silks and sashes, both of whom, according to the written programme that Sophie clutched in her hands, had been under JR sponsorship over the last two years, supporting their training and career development, and he clearly took pride in their performance. The two, adorned in JR's colours of canary yellow and orange with a narrow contrasting purple stripe that stretched from left shoulder across to right waist, were no more than teenagers, seventeen year-olds, but had already learnt how to milk the crowd of its adulation that they so obviously craved. *Bravo*, the Mayor called, clapping wildly at their every pass; *excellente*, JR intoned.

As a spectacle, Sophie knew what to expect as she had attended a bullfight in Madrid once, but she had never quite acquired the taste or fully understood the passion in rejoicing at the torment and slaughter of the poor bulls. She knew that the capes were red, not because bulls were singularly attracted to the colour, but because the inevitable spilling of blood would be less conspicuous to the crowd on a red background. She asked JR at one point: 'Why call it a sport when obviously the bulls have no chance of winning?' but he seemed not to hear her, his expression remaining fixed with sheer pleasure at the sight of the third or fourth young beast cut down and dragged out of the arena. The picadors, who busily ensured the continuity and flow of the entertainment, were elegantly dressed in blue with white stripes and had their own red capes that they brandished with schoolboy flourishes, making sure that all traces of spilled blood were brushed over with sand as quickly as the dead creature was removed from sight.

'Well, good point,' JR murmured a little later, with an admiring twist of his mouth. 'The newspapers *El Pais* and *El Mundo* both put their bull-fight reports in the Culture section rather than the Sports Section, so maybe, Miss Sophie, you are right,' he smiled just a touch, with the neat line of his moustache doing a worm-like quiver at the end.

The crowd became rather subdued during the heat of the day as the ritual slaughter continued with occasional flourishes and, as the shadows from the lowering sun stretched taut across the sandy arena in a curved arc, Sophie had to hang on to her hat with a hand as a welcome gust of wind blew a little air across their faces. During the mid-session comfort break, for more champagne and canapés, for raucous small-talk and back-patting, for stretching the legs and emptying the bladders, while sharing the queue with a familiar local TV presenter that she could not quite name, Sophie saw across the marquee crowds The Magician, Ho

Sup Ping, with two of his Chinese women, looking at odds with his surroundings in a western pin-striped two-piece. He was drinking tea as he observed the good and the wealthy all around him, with an entourage of unhappy-looking dark suited thin Oriental bodyguards. She was certain he had seen her, although they both turned away rather than acknowledge each other. Sophie wondered whether he was here to spy on her or on JR. But soon everyone was returning to their seats with a show of further excitement as the build-up for the highlight of the afternoon on that the first day of the feria approached. Jose Luis Rodriquez del Almo, a maverick star and wealthy celebrity, which explained the high ticket prices for the day, himself recently returned to the ring after a short spell in jail for not paying his taxes, was to perform against one of Andalucia's finest bulls, groomed and prepared for just such a special occasion by none other than JR himself, or at least the Robicalon ranch, as he eagerly explained and for which he had been admirably rewarded.

'You are about to watch the slaughter of one of your own animals, that cannot be a pleasure, surely, you must be feeling some sorrow, some guilt.' Many in the crowd had turned towards the VIP box and were applauding Robicalon with raised arms and cheers, quietly calling his name, when they heard the announcement over the tannoy.

'Absolutely not. This is privilege and honour for which any self-respecting bull would give his hind legs, to be dispatched in front of adoring crowds by Senor del Almo!' And he laughed outrageously.

The bull gives his life, let alone his hind legs, you idiot, was the essence of her thoughts at that moment and Sophie would have shared these out loud with the women behind her if the crowd had not all suddenly risen to their feet as if on a signal to applaud and scream their appreciation of what they were about to witness. 'What a bastard,' she mouthed to herself.

Jose Luis del Almo had just entered the arena. Orchestral music was climaxing over the sound system, as the great man strolled stiffly in tight trousers into the sunshine towards the centre of the arena. Encouraged by an almost hysterical crowd, he held his head back, his arms aloft and twirled theatrically for all to get a good view of him. His flowing black locks, tied with a scarlet sash around his forehead, caught the breeze in the glancing sunshine, as he settled himself, his arms still, his deep ruby cape draped flaccid beside him. Suddenly there was quiet, everyone hushed in awe and expectation. A magnificent black beast with sturdy horns and glittering eyes appeared through a wooden gate that closed behind it. It stood solid and threatening, snorting and pawing at the ground. It started to trot forward slowly at first but with its head down gathered momentum and speed across the sandy ground towards the shimmering red cape. It brushed past del Almo, who stood almost motionless and unflinching, tall and majestic. Within moments the first few passes were over, two or three quick turns, sand kicking up and the crowd cheering at each. The sweating beast was beginning to show signs of its frustration and confusion. The first of many banderillas was stuck into its neck as it passed, each one cutting through the muscles and weakening him, so that his neck was lowered and more exposed. Its pain and anger were increased, its thunderous charges becoming more reckless. Roars of approval went up with each stab and spurt of blood, as del Almo demonstrated his increasing dominance over the mighty creature. The bull stopped for a moment and was staring at its adversary poised for another determined charge at the red target. The hushed spectators started to lean forward in anticipation. As the end-game approached, the bewildered and frustrated beast, trapped inside the ring with nowhere to hide, was reduced to kneeling with exhaustion, defeated and humiliated, while the gloating del Almo taunted it by touching its head, goading it.

He turned away from the animal and selected his weapon of death, delivered to him by his second, a young fighter whose expression showed his obvious idolization of his master. The narrow hipped matador held the long glinting sword drawn slowly from its sheath skywards, like a priest with a sacred cross. Stepping towards his victim, with its head down on the sand, stumbling, blood streaming from both sides of its neck, del Almo placed the sharp point just behind the great ridge across the bull's massive skull, and with his left arm fully poised away from him pointing to the sky, his right arm at full stretch with the sword, the crowd suddenly hushed once again, he applied his full weight to the easily found target, sinking the shiny steel fully to the hilt, severing the bull's spinal cord. The crowd went mad, ecstatic with joy and love for that man. *Maravilloso*.

During the loudest cheer of the whole afternoon, Sophie decided she had witnessed an appalling charade of pointless slaughter, and given a choice would side with growing public opinion and the animal rights groups that demanded that this tradition and tourist attraction of Spain should be banned. The bull was done for from the start, it rarely hit back or gored any human in response. This was not sport, it was gruesome entertainment, and for the wretched bulls it was criminal and tragic.

'You must come out and see me at the stud farm, you'll be impressed. Do you ride?' asked JR, once again pressing his face close towards Sophie's, so she could hear him over the noise of the crowd.

'Ride? Bulls?' she shouted back, with a faint smile.

'Horses. I have some fine locally bred stallions, some champion racers. We run a riding school, in the mountains beyond Benahavis; we have a villa there and all the facilities. Please come out this week. I am selling a racer to a Moroccan Lord, for a large sum of money, I want to hear what you think of him.'

He was almost pleading and a hand was placed across her lap, the tips of his relaxed fingers touching her, making ticklish contact with her thighs through the cotton of her dress. Sophie had no choice, although she was uncomfortable with the thought that he was beginning to control her and that she seemed willing to bend to his wishes. She found he had a certain charm about him, was good-looking, wealthy and powerful, enough to turn any girl's head and she had to admit that in other circumstances, she would probably find him irresistible. Although at that moment she actually thought she was going to be sick and had to swallow a horrible taste from her mouth. She nodded at him with a strained smile, before excusing herself for the ladies' room.

She was looking for an opportunity to question JR about Roberto but there were always people close by, grabbing him to talk to or introduce to someone else, everyone ignoring her. He accompanied her back to the guest enclosure and pulled her to one side, gripping the flesh of her upper arm with a heavy hand wrapped around her shoulders, which made her feel extremely small. He spoke firmly about her duties to him and the Council. Sophie was at a loss at first as to what he meant but then he directly asked if she had found out anything about his lost merchandise, stolen in the car mugging incident and the information he needed about Baxwell's bid for The Project. It was at that moment that it suddenly dawned on her, the dollar stash they found in the hidden compartment of the Skoda must have been payment to JR for his bloody racehorse that he said he was selling to a Moroccan lord.

Jesus. Is this getting worse or what? 'I have seen the books and I have written Baxwell's bidding price on this.' Sophie calmly reached inside her shoulder bag for a small piece of folded paper that she had prepared earlier and held it up for JR. He snatched it eagerly and unfolded it with his long fingers, unable to wait. Glancing quickly at the figure Sophie had written in ink across the middle (a number she had plucked out of thin air), his eyes almost popping out with apparent shock, he stuffed the paper into an inside suit pocket. 'Are you sure? This is big.'

Sophie nodded, said she had heard it from Baxwell himself.

'As to the other question, I have no idea where the car is or the contents. A friend of mine has disappeared. In fact, the man who was driving the car you say was yours from Morocco that was mugged on the roadside. Roberto. He knew *absolutely* nothing about the plans for a robbery, he was quite hurt by his beating.' She stamped her foot and spoke with even more urgency: 'Have you heard anything about him?'

'Now what makes you think I would have anything to do with that scoundrel?'

'More to the point,' Sophie spoke in a hoarse whisper, as several guests and spectators were shuffling past them in the direction of the complimentary drinks bar, 'where is he? He was snatched in the street and taken away and... well, that was most unfair?'

'Little lady, how am I to know what low-lifes like your friend Roberto get up to. Who is he anyway, your lover perhaps?'

She raised her eyes to heaven and smiled sourly, glancing up at his shiny face, noticing the bundles of black hairs in his nostrils. 'That's the second time you have accused me of having odd lovers. He is a friend and works closely with Baxwell. He would never mean anyone harm. If you know where he is, I want to know,' she demanded, trying to sound threatening, but JR was holding her wrist strongly and pulling her closer.

'Forget this man, he's not important, I want you to be my lover, Miss Sophie,' he exclaimed with urgency in his whispered voice, speaking into her face, his intense black eyes boring down into hers and once again she could feel his hot breath on her cheeks. 'You are so strong and beautiful. Think of all the wonderful shows and performances I could take you to and the things I could buy you, you would never be short of lovely things to wear and places to visit.'

Sophie firmly placed two straight fingers across JR's lips, feeling the wet spittle between them. The warmth of his body closely pressing hers felt horrendous to her. 'Enough. You have said enough, stop before you make a fool of yourself.' She wriggled out of his grasp just as two of his female assistants placed hands on his shoulders from behind and told him he had some more duties to perform. There would be a fireworks show later in the arena and a dinner he was attending with awards and traditional dancing. It all sounded like a perfect ending to a fun day and very Spanish; and in any other circumstances Sophie would have loved to stay, but she was now eager to get away. She thanked JR for his invitation.

'It is the presentation Wednesday at the Council chambers. So come out tomorrow to the ranch, we have some demonstrations and exhibitions, other visitors, like an open-day, it will be fun,' he persisted, 'and we could go riding, it is lovely there.'

Sophie shrugged. 'I will try. I might bring my Moroccan friend, he came over this week and is interested in stallions and racing.'

'Fine. Of course, but we may have to dump him in the woods.' He chuckled as he presented her with a small white card from a pocket.

'I'll drive out about midday, then, all right?' she checked, reading the writing on the card before slipping it into her bag: it seemed like a secret exchange, except that lots of people around them must have seen it happen.

JR was nodding, a lascivious expression across his face,

like the Mayor's, as he backed away with his women. 'Good, good. We can have some lunch. I insist.' He bowed in her direction before turning, to be swallowed up in the swirling melee of people inside the marquee. Sophie squeezed her way through the moving crowds outside and around the entrance, wondering why she seemed to attract such despicable men, and found a taxi cab for the ride back down the steep slopes of Mijas to Marbella in the slowly dying sun.

JR had been trying to charm her, in such contrast to their previous meeting when he had threatened her. But that was mere technique: he would always have an overarching plan, bigger than she would have contemplated, and it would probably involve crushing her and spitting her out when he had finished with her. She needed to see his place though, it might give away some clues and she had to carry on trying to find Roberto, for all their sakes.

* * *

Matthew spent the day exploring the tourist attractions of Marbella. From the marina and promenade, he turned up the steps of the pedestrianised Avenida del Mar, between well-appointed apartment blocks. He admired the numerous weathered bronze works of Salvadore Dali, on permanent display and then up to the Parque de Alameda. Crowds of wandering tourists with their ice-creams and cameras were strolling around the lovely fountain with its coloured pictures depicting old religious scenes on the outer ring and its generous central water display surrounded by smaller sprays.

He emerged again on the main avenue, the Ramon y Cajal and found a small café for a sandwich and coffee. He crossed over to the Old Town, climbing steadily through narrow paved walkways full of little boutiques for shoes or clothes, tobacco and food shops; the locals had their wares on displays around their doorways and haggled over price with the passers-by. There were a few dusty cafes on the corners and he found Naranjos Square full of people sitting under orange umbrellas, taking drinks or tapas, while the late-flowering geraniums drooped from the old balconies in the breeze. Just off the square in a forgotten corner was a deserted church, its outside façade decaying with age and beating sunshine, a dilapidated carved crucifixion hanging on the outside wall over the open doorway. It was delightfully cool inside and his soft footsteps echoed up around the shadowy rafters overhead. A handful of white candles in a row on a ledge in front of the altar burnt forlornly and Matthew sat at the front on a tiny wooden chair lost in his own personal thoughts that had little to do with Christ or the Holy Catholic Scriptures. After a few minutes' rest he left and returned steadily downhill the way he had come, back to the hotel, for a drink in the shade outside by the pool, where he absorbed himself with a book.

The slow evening passed pleasantly enough with another quiet dinner alone in the hotel, a couple of beers on the terrace at the back looking out over the sea and watching the sun go, and later lazing on the soft couches in the lounge, reading newspaper stories still buzzing with controversies over Lady Diana's death, before heading into the lobby at ten o'clock. He waited patiently staring excitedly at every person who walked past, or came out of the lifts or attended the desk for checking-in even at that late hour. Matthew had caught some sun during the day, his forehead and nose feeling sore, despite generous cream; and the effects of the heat and the wind along the coast and the beers had made him feel sleepy.

Sophie was late. Just as Matthew's eyes were beginning to droop, a young woman in fashionable black, leather, tight trousers and silky blouse, dashed in through the revolving glass doors at the front, alive and real, standing at the centre of the black-and-white tiled floor, like an actor making her entrance, looking a little out of breath. Her eyes darted from face to face of the people moving about from reception to the lifts and stairs, to the restaurant entrance or the bar area at the back, with its windows overlooking the gardens behind, to the line of telephones on a far wall and to the concierge desk, where a little man in uniform sat with his brochures and keys and little blackboard. She did not at first see Matthew half-hidden behind a spiky rubber plant in a Grecian pot beside a pillar and slumbering deep in a leather armchair. But he suddenly opened his eyes and stood up, stepping gingerly out from around the pot and with a hand outstretched, called her name. Sophie was consulting her wristwatch when she turned towards him, looking into a face she felt she had seen before.

'Hello. Sophie?'

She looked flushed but smiled suddenly. 'Yes. Hi, you must be…?'

'Matthew, Matthew Crawford. I called…'

'Yes, lovely. How do you do?'

They shook hands a little stiffly. Sophie's was cool, his was hot. She slipped her leather jacket off her shoulders and wandered over towards the bar. He could not help but notice her tight blouse, buttoned under strain, showing the edges of her black bra and some exposed plump pale flesh.

'Sorry. Hope you haven't been waiting long, I was working down at the Blue Ocean Club, in the bar,' she laughed, and he could detect the smell of cigarettes and alcohol about her.

'Do you feel like another drink? Or a coffee, perhaps?'

'Yes, a coffee. That would help. I have to meet someone soon, an important matter. Sorry. He's an old friend, a police officer actually.'

'Oh, nothing serious, I hope?'

'No, oh no. It's about a friend who has disappeared. It's a long story, but I need to talk to him and I'm expecting him here later. But, come on, let's find a table and then you can tell me what all this is about.' She sounded friendly, showing him a nice row of teeth. Her lipstick was a glossy blood red colour, which he liked.

They settled on opposite black chairs around a tiny table, Sophie facing the outer door, Matthew noticed, occasionally looking at her wristwatch. They ordered and continued with small chatter.

'How was the bull-fighting?'

Sophie was tempted to give this man her deepest held feelings about the entertainment of the afternoon but decided against. She pulled a face, 'Oh, colourful, interesting, the people, you know. A bit gruesome.'

'I've never been to one, don't think I want to.' Matthew decided to stride on: 'I used to be a friend of your mother, I met her the other day. She sends her love to you, by the way'.

The room was dimly lit and smoky and at a subdued level in the background the familiar song 'Dancing In The Street' was playing, Matthew trying to remember who the singers were. Sophie gave a small smile and nodded.

'I realised she only lived a few miles from me across London.'

'Fulham. It's quite nice there, isn't it?' Sophie was wondering where all this was leading while keeping an eye out through the glass doors into the lobby for Hernandez. After such a busy and hot day, what with all the crowds and the tensions with JR and then an evening in the heaving and noisy Blue Ocean, she was justifiably tired and would soon be ready for her bed.

'Your mother actually went to a finishing school in the country near where I was at school, many years ago it was, in Worcestershire, a long way from home and we met at one of the social events, Sunday afternoon tea. It had all the usual school rules applied and sounds pathetic now, doesn't it, but it was our thrill of the week. It was the only time we were allowed to meet girls.' Recounting the long-ago events that were so germane to him, Matthew wanted to sound modern and up-to-date with this lovely woman before him but was embarrassed to appear so old-fashioned. 'Martha and the Vandellas,' he said. 'The song,' and he pointed vaguely up at the ceiling speakers to indicate the music. Old fuddy duddy, she was probably thinking.

Still he was her father. When was he going to have the courage to tell her, outright? He needed to ask her to speak about herself so she would become comfortable talking to him.

'So you work as an estate agent?'

'Yes, Baxwell Properties. They have five offices along the coast, I work in head-office here in Marbella.'

He was tapping his fingers on his thigh to the Four Tops, realising that she probably had never heard of them. 'And you work in a bar?'

'Yes, I do two or three nights a week; it's fun, I know lots of the people, and the money helps,' she laughed easily, the tiniest of dimples, her eyes soft under her dark brows and he thought she looked much younger than thirty. He liked her voice, darker than he imagined. She reached for her cigarettes and glanced towards Matthew, her brows raised a touch, offering him one, but she knew somehow that he did not smoke.

'So how long have you been out here?'

And Sophie began to chat quite easily about her life in Marbella, her jobs, a mention of Alex Baxwell, where she lived and so on, it felt like she was confessing to the Mayor again.

Matthew noticed she lived alone and no mention of boyfriends. He took advantage of a pause as she reached for her coffee. 'Back in 1967 your mother and I actually went out together, you know, we were boy-friend girl-friend.'

'Really,' sang Sophie, with a curious lift of one brow.

Matthew looked suitably sheepish, as if he had said something silly, but quickly added: 'Well, only for a very short time,' and shook his head, smiling at the memory. 'She had to go back to Switzerland, with her parents. I think they divorced shortly afterwards.'

Sophie vaguely recognised the background story of her mother's youth, but was only half listening, distracted by activities around the bar and figures moving about in the lobby. When she brought her attention back to Matthew, a handsome kindly face, she thought and lovely hair, it was his appearance that more interested her, deciding his hair needed a closer trim and some designer grizzle around his chin would make for a softer modern look.

'Her sister was quite fun, did you ever meet her, your Aunt Daphne? She was into clothes design and the Carnaby Street scene then, it was quite exciting, really…' and Matthew tailed off.

'Yes, I can remember some holidays in the mountains with Mum and Dad and my aunt, and cousins, there were three of them, I think. We would cycle in the summer and toboggan in the winter.'

'So actually what happened was that Stephanie and I became uh, and the thing is, she erm…'

'*Hola,*' called Sophie, raising her arm.

'*Hola,*' called out a swarthy man lolloping over towards them. He pulled up a chair and sat hunched between them with a confident blustering manner, just at the point where whatever Matthew had bursting to let out was on the tip of his tongue. In a flappy raincoat and worn-down black shoes, the man looked every bit the stereotypical policeman, in his late thirties with his dull tie loose and a dark day's beard growth. He spoke to Sophie in Spanish, kissing both her cheeks and then offered his firm grip to Matthew on his introduction as an old friend from England visiting for a few days with news about her mother.

'All well, *bien*, I hope?'

Sophie finished her coffee, Matthew sipped disconsolately at his, the three of them chatted about nothing in particular and after a few more minutes Sophie and Hernandez left with apologies, needing to talk in private somewhere else. Matthew watched them pass outside through the front doors of the hotel, thinking that maybe they were a couple and wondering when on earth he would be able to meet Sophie again to tell her his news.

10

Tuesday September 2

The sun had been relentlessly warming the back of Sophie's apartment block for a few hours by the time Bruce ambled along as instructed to the rear service area, where the untidily parked wheelie bins were beginning to smell. He had walked twenty minutes from the apartment Baxwell had found for him in the northern district and arrived excited at seeing Sophie again. Unnoticed, he took the stairs three at a time to the sixth floor and waited a few seconds before pressing the bell.

Yesterday evening Sophie had had a conversation over the telephone with Alex Baxwell in which she argued for the day off today, as she was planning a visit to JR's ranch, where she hoped to find out more about his role in the car robbery business.

'I've had no news at all about Roberto,' confided Baxwell. 'It's been more than two days now and no one has seen him – it's like he has disappeared off the face of the earth. But my boys picked up a rumour from the Chinese chatter in town that Robicalon is muscling into the drugs scene and demands huge protection money to allow any of them to operate, the Chinese, the Dutch, the Moroccans, any of them. The Chinese seem livid just now, feel very hard done by, and on the warpath. So be careful, Sophie. That JR is dangerous.'

'Yes, I know. Thank you for your concern. All set for Wednesday?' she asked to humour him.

'Aye, should be a grand affair. Make sure you're there, chance to meet the dignitaries. Look, I could have one of my men detailed to you, for security, be with you all the time, if you would like – means you can still be free to move about without the worries, eh?'

'Do you really think that's necessary?' Sophie asked, not especially concerned. 'Anyway today I shall have Bruce protecting me.' And the thought rather excited her.

Sophie's plan was to take a short visit into town to help Bruce buy some clothes, to replace the miserable rags he had arrived in and was still wearing over a week later. The zip jacket and brown corduroy trousers had definitely seen better days. She would lend him some money, as he had not received any funds since his car with its potential source of income had been mysteriously stolen. Sophie sympathised with him without admitting anything, although Bruce's circumstances were beginning to make her feel guilty. He seemed so lost in her Spanish world, and yet she found him to be a naturally easy-going man, so broad shouldered and cuddly, with his grizzly beard turning grey, although she supposed he was only thirtyish. In return for her generosity he had agreed to accompany her to JR's out-of-town ranch she was visiting later, and she guaranteed him a sight of racehorses in training.

'I like racehorses,' he said and smiled broadly, like a schoolboy saying he liked sponge cake. 'Perhaps this is same ranch that my contact is working for, what you think?' His big eyes seemed to open wider.

'That would be a bit of a coincidence … but now that you mention it, I would not be at all surprised if you were right. You really don't know the name, of the ranch or the man you were collecting this racehorse from?'

'No, I don't know,' he shrugged. 'I had to just take the

vehicle and the horsebox with Nabil to this address,' and he showed Sophie a bit of paper: the road name Trapiche was written at the top with a crude line drawing of roads coming together at a junction, next to a dual carriageway that she took to be the Autovia, and a curvy arrow pointed to the middle with a 'P' sign in a box. There was a string of numerals scrawled along the bottom looking like a phone number. 'Do you think Roberto might be there?' he asked innocently.

'This looks like a road junction, on the Camino del Trapiche, where it goes over the motorway and it's pointing to a car park,' said Sophie looking doubtful and trying to figure out the map. 'I would think this is just a drop-off point. Have you tried this number?'

'Yes, it made no connection.'

'And you have not been up to this site, this P on the map? To look round?'

'No, without the stuff, without the horsebox, I thought I'm just going to get myself beaten up. I backed away, I'm afraid, no courage,' and he shrugged with a small display of shame. Sophie could see his point, but if he was working for JR, he would have been advised to keep out of the way.

'I wonder how Roberto is standing up to his ordeal,' Sophie mused. It was more of a comment and Bruce knitted his own brows at her expression of concern. 'You and Roberto are lovers?' he asked, and those big brown eyes scanned Sophie's tender face, looking for a reaction.

She flashed a smile, averted her eyes and turned away. 'No, oh no.' She knew she was not going to blush from embarrassment or guilt or whatever, and brought her gaze firmly back onto the African's face. 'Just we have known each other for ages. Look, I need to nip upstairs to get something from a storage place in the loft, I won't be a minute. Get yourself a drink or something.' She let herself out of the front door, put the lock on its latch and darted up the stone stairs to the next floor landing. High up above her head in the ceiling was a hatch, a metal door that dropped open on release and gave access to the plant room on the flat roof, where water tanks and air-conditioner units were found. Nobody ever went up there, as far as she knew, except inspectors occasionally or when there was a leak. A long wooden pole with a brass hook on the end was clipped into the corner wall and using it skilfully she was able to reach up and push on a clip, which released the trap door downwards, allowing a folded lightweight step ladder to slide down towards her. She pulled it down the full distance section by section, until two black plastic feet touched the floor; she shimmied up the almost vertical flimsy structure.

She poked her head through the opening, hearing the sounds of dripping in the big plastic tanks. The only light she had came through the gap from the landing below. Stepping up onto the next rung, she bent at the waist to lean further into the hot dusty space, feeling along the wooden floor for the hold-all zip bag that she had slid deep into the darkness beside a tank a couple of days ago. Bruce, fascinated by Sophie's spontaneous and kindly nature and her athletic beauty, had quietly followed her out of the front door and up the stairs to the landing. He heard the rattle of the ladder and was now standing below it, staring intently up at Sophie's lower half, perched on the ladder above him, her legs bare and her bottom too, while her top half was out of sight stuck through the roof opening. At full stretch Sophie heaved the bag towards her and felt inside the zip opening for the packet she wanted. She pushed it all back after a moment and retreated backwards down the ladder, a wad of peso notes in her palm. She noticed Bruce gawping upwards with wide eyes and open mouth, a picture of the naïve schoolboy catching sight of something forbidden, the school nurse in the showers without any clothes on, perhaps, and now transfixed with amazement. She feigned surprise and tugged her inadequate dress down and between her legs with her free hand, realising she was only wearing a skimpy thong underneath. Descending awkwardly one handed and still all the way under the watchful eye of the fascinated African, she whispered, 'Cheeky monkey,' when she had straightened herself and her dress at the bottom, and standing on tip toes, her feet together, she spontaneously sprang up to plant a kiss on Bruce's cheek. 'You can put the ladder away now,' she called over her shoulder, as she tripped back down to her flat, where she waited with a thumping heartbeat for Bruce to return.

'So what were you looking at, exactly?' she laughed, dimpling her cheeks, when he came back inside. He looked suitably embarrassed and could not find any words. Sophie put her wad of pesos down where she would not forget it and finished tidying other things around the flat, folding all the washing away in her bedroom, before changing. Again she mentioned the watchers on the ground outside she had seen earlier and they both carefully looked through the lounge curtains: the white van was still there, although parked further away, but it seemed to be empty, nobody inside or hovering around nearby. Still suspicious, they left by the back stairs and the rear entrance, finding her car a few streets away. She stuffed the wad in the glove compartment.

In the man's store El Bruno Roches, they found underpants and socks and slacks, a couple of T-shirts, jeans, another shirt and two pairs of soft loafers in suede. They were looking for a jacket and Bruce was trying on different ones, disappearing behind a screen and emerging each time with a different pair of trousers on or a different shirt, smiling sheepishly. Sophie liked him best in a green blazer. Lastly they bought a bright multi-coloured travel case with wheels attached, to put everything in and Sophie paid with cash from her purse, about thirty-four thousand pesos. Bruce was so pleased that he would not stop humbly thanking her for her wonderful generosity until they had descended back to the street, where he dropped a bundle of his old clothes into a bin. 'My poor mother will be amazed when she sees me, in all this finery,' and his big smile showed all his white teeth. They rested in the sun for a few moments in the Parque, where they glanced at the various sculptures glinting in the bright light while sharing a coffee and an ice cream. Then they walked casually side by side, two tourists out in the city on a hot afternoon, his height and bulk such a contrast to her diminutive figure. Back to the underground car park, Bruce's case stowed in the boot of her car, they set out to enjoy the drive along the coast west to Benahavis, never bored with the twinkling sea views.

Sophie encouraged Bruce to chat about his life, living in Rabat with his mother, who made the most delicious bread, he said, baked twice a week. His father had never been there, worked in the ports, slept away a lot, drank a lot and then one day years ago upped sticks and left his mother and nine siblings to fend for themselves. She took in washing for extra, but money was always short and there was never much to eat. Bruce the eldest had to be the bread-winner of the house, always sending money home whenever he earned anything, which was never much. The courier job he had managed to get was paid in cash but only after fees, commissions and bribes were paid first, leaving precious little in the pot. It was not surprising that the drivers and couriers often turned to stealing and trickery to make ends meet. His brothers mostly worked the land for the old folks; his mother relied on them for little extras.

For her part, Sophie talked about working in the agency for Alex Baxwell and life on the Costa del Sol. From the car they watched the sparse traffic speeding along and lowered the windows to get some relief from the heat. The humidity did not seem to bother Bruce too much, but Sophie found herself perspiring excessively and her legs were sticking to the seating. She was in tight white slacks, a sleeveless top in crimson cotton and decent underwear, but the closeness of the husky black man was making her nervous. His manner was relaxed and easy-going, accompanied by an unfamiliar charm that she found alluring. Despite his size, his movements were supple and fluid and he was always showing off his big white teeth with his generous smile, using his eyes to express much of his feelings. Sophie liked all that.

He had brought a map with him, opened out on his knees, and was trying to follow the route she was taking, turning off the A7 onto the Carretera Benahavis and following the road heading north through the outskirts of town. They were running away from the urban sprawl over flat wasteland and rough ground towards the mountains and soon entered a lush valley, running alongside the Rio Guadalmina, the narrow road clinging on to rough hewed granite on one side with a thin barrier on the other where the gravel sides dropped steeply to the river. The road climbed and wound around the granite outcrops to the Benahavis roundabout, skirted the town and then headed straight out to climb more rapidly into the hilly wooded areas, to the north and west. Winding over ridges and around hairpin bends, twisting this way and that, mostly on a narrow concrete strip that was sometimes gravel, they travelled forever higher for over twenty minutes. Eventually they came out onto flatter terrain, ahead of a valley completely wooded on both sides. A small sign had been nailed on a stake and driven into the ground at a wobbly angle just where an easily missed track ran to the head of the valley among thick clumps of cypress trees. A few wild goats stood munching off overhanging branches.

'"South Andalucía Stud Farm and Riding School",' Bruce shouted, seeing the sign and pointing left. Sophie whipped the

Renault off the main road and they ran on a neat black strip of tarmac that wound its way round the jagged promontories of the mountains and passed through more wooded and wild areas, a feeble stream running alongside them at one point. Soon strips of neatly cut grass were bordering the road on either side and a sturdy well-built stone wall appeared on their right bordering the road for hundreds of yards. Behind it there appeared to be an estate of well-planted trees among undulating greenery, with paths laid out, contrasting with the untouched wildness of the land beyond. On rounding a long right hand bend, a gap appeared with a grand entrance, brick pillars and large wrought iron gates that were swung open inwards. The road was lined with cars parked along the edges, up on the verges and a few people were freely wandering in and out of the estate entrance.

As they cruised past, Bruce excitedly called out '"South Andalucía Stud Farm – The Robicalon Estate",' pointing to the entrance which Sophie had actually spotted. She parked some yards further along on the right-hand verge. 'Seem to be lots of people.'

'It will be fine, we'll have a look round and leave after an hour or something. OK?'

Bruce nodded. He seemed easy.

Walking through the open gates, where a couple of men in caps and dark uniforms were turning cars away, they joined other visitors on foot. Sophie spotted the CCTV cameras on posts just inside, as they ambled up a gentle rising brick-laid roadway, lined neatly with trimmed grass and white fencing. At the summit of the entrance path, the road curled around an ostentatious fountain, cherubs and lions sculptured in stone, with water arcing from their open mouths and up from several layers, the central spray rising thirty feet. The main villa commanded a position straight ahead, set back into a hillside, with its own sweeping drive, three floors of whitewashed frontage with pillars on either side of the front entrance, dark grey tiled sloping roofs, balconies and big windows, surrounded by perfect cut green turf, wild craggy mountains as a backdrop. Ahead of them the land sloped down into a wide valley of pastures where several brick outbuildings nestled at the end of gravel paths, behind pines. There was the riding school, with two rows of solid brick and oak-doored stables seen through an arch of blooming crimson bougainvillea; and the indoor riding school next to it, and several paddocks, where grazing ponies were on view; then an outside training circuit covered in honey-coloured sand, surrounded by more white fencing. And everywhere the lawns were manicured, the hedgerows trimmed, the plants at their most colourful; flags were fluttering against white poles and all along the bricked pathways were lighting posts.

Behind them, the fencing that lead up from the road shielded a wooded area that gave way to wild grass sloping up towards a row of ageing two-storey terraced cottages, with white rendering and coloured doors, partially hidden by a newly planted row of thin pines and conifers, and its own loose stone roadway marked with a *privado* sign on the side.

Down by the training circuit plenty of well-dressed on-lookers around the perimeter were watching a bare-headed woman on foot, in jodhpurs and black boots and a flowing white shirt, using a long flexi-whip, barking commands at a frisky bare-backed stallion as it bravely trotted round and round on a single bridle and lead. A white marquee was erected nearby and people were crowding around with drinks and food, sitting at the tables arranged outside. A narrow track bordered by palms and firs, between the riding school and the indoor arena, led deeper across the valley towards a thickly wooded area, where a sign indicated the way to the Robicalon Stud. The whole landscape was beautifully planned and laid out with neat borders and gardens everywhere, looking their best in the September sunshine.

The Mayor referred to Senor Robicalon as the most powerful man in Marbella, by which of course he meant the richest. As Sophie was taking everything in, she came to realise the wealth of the man and the world he inhabited, that was oceans away from hers. And here his wealth was on show by the bucket load. Bruce was totally in awe of his surroundings as well, and lost for words. He dutifully followed in Sophie's footsteps in the direction of the riding school, shuffling along between a rows of wrought-iron chain fencing, listening to lots of chatter in various tongues among other visitors. They arrived at the stable blocks, in rows facing each other with a cobbled courtyard between, and inquisitive nodding heads of some fine stallions and ponies poking over their half-doors, chomping and snorting. A few girls were working there with long forks and brooms, with wheel-barrows of hay. Some were brushing the hides, others leading horses out with saddles and bridles for eager little girls waiting to swing themselves up onto them for their precious hour long riding lesson.

Sophie made out Senor Robicalon at a distance, bare headed and distinguished-looking in riding jodhpurs and dark coat with a crop in his hand. She felt instinctively that he was her adversary, wisely remaining wary of him. She was still aware of the twisted pain he gave to her chin, her sore upper arms and the bruise on the back of her head. Yesterday he had generally been quite charming and she was not so afraid of him that she would not confront him, certain that he knew a whole lot about Roberto; it was more about timing, and with this visit she hoped to be able to talk to him alone. She had told Bruce that she would seek JR out and that Bruce should feel free to wander about the estate. She caught JR's eye and he raised his arm and waved his crop.

'You ride, Sophie; you want?' he called, pointing to two

magnificent brown stallions being saddled up. Sophie came over hesitantly shaking her head, 'No, not me. I'll watch you.' And proudly JR swung himself up onto one of the horses, while the other was mounted by an impeccably dressed female rider. They walked their steeds over the cobbles, clopping loudly out into the open ground and then into a covered school barn of flat sand and striped jumps, where they demonstrated the horses to the watching spectators. JR looked a competent rider and controlled his horse perfectly as they trotted one behind the other, cantered along the straights and looped across from one corner to the other in a figure of eight and the crowds clapped occasionally. Someone watching commented the two stallions were being auctioned at the end of the afternoon with reserved bids already placed at ten million pesos each.

It was more than an hour before JR was able to break free from the attention of his visitors, who wanted to talk business or sport with the great maestro, hearing him wax lyrical about horse racing and the rewards of running a stud farm, and stroll out of the school entrance still in his riding boots and jodhpurs over towards the main house with Sophie, chatting about the excitement of his day. A minion dressed all in black brought round his new vehicle, an open-topped Jeep in fetching camouflage green. Donning his sunglasses, he drove her out the front gates at speed and then even faster along the outside road passed the surrounding brick wall, to a sudden turning off the main tarmac onto a gravel track that veered off across rougher terrain. JR was clearly having fun at off-road driving and he was smiling widely as they bumped up to a peak on the hillside, from where they were able to look down over his estate in the distance, the sedate looking buildings and neat patterning of the pathways laid out like a map. Even though they were a good mile away, Sophie could clearly make out the activity around the white marquee, the adjacent sandy ring circuit and several horses grazing in the paddocks.

JR's dishevelled black hair was flapping untidily in the wind. He purred with pride and delight, pointing out the various sections of the estate, with a permanent look of smug satisfaction on his hot and tanned face. 'We employ several racehorse trainers and have over twenty jockeys who ride under my colours,' he shouted across to Sophie over the engine noise. 'Which is good.' They drove on over rising ground, over bumps and round sudden twists, as the track became more and more vague and loose. The vegetation and fine grasses thinned to just a few spindly wild olive trees, where brown and white goats scuffled in the dry earth and pulled at tiny leaves on low hanging branches, taking no notice. After a steep twisted climb, they emerged on the top of a promontory of craggy rock that jutted out over a vast valley that stretched far away and below them. JR brought the Jeep to a halt and switched off the engine.

There was not a single cloud in the sky; they sat squinting into the high sun that was beating down on their wind-swept faces. From a cool-box on the floor between them, he pulled out a couple of cokes, dripping with freezing water. He had a small towel to dry their hands and the drink tasted delicious to both of them.

'This is one of my favourite spots; I come up here for some peace and time to think. I ride here sometimes and then we go down that way,' and he pointed southwards over towards the edge and a twisty path that meandered down through a rocky ravine. 'It leads off towards the coast, and sometimes I ride out along the beach, in the evening especially when most people have gone.' He sat back and smiled in sweet satisfaction, slurping more of the drink. He hoped he was impressing his young companion. Sophie was prepared for what came next.

'Think what you could have here with me, Miss Sophie, you could live in luxury. Just be mine, be my lover, and I will let you in to share this.'

The surprising thing was how serious JR sounded and convincing too. Sophie risked a quick sideways glance at the suave face, smooth shaven, thin line of moustache so neatly trimmed (by a manservant, Sophie imagined). She had heard that JR's wife had died a few years ago, a riding accident apparently, and he had lived alone since, throwing himself into the activities on his estate and the work of the Town Council, which included training race horses, breeding stud, real estate and property development. And the drug protection racket, if Hsui Long Long and Baxwell were right. He also had a lecherous reputation but for some reason many women found him irresistible; Sophie was not one of them.

'I'm not your type, Mr Robicalon. And only a couple of days ago you attacked me, accused me of being a thief and a drug addict, remember. Do I ignore that?'

'Oh Sophie, I was angry. I am sorry, I did not want to hurt you. But I have to show my boys that I will be tough. So they respect me.'

'How's that man's foot, by the way?'

'Flavio – he'll be fine. He is hopping around at the moment.' And JR smiled a big smile. 'You are strong woman, I like that. You could be good, for me, for my life. I did not mean hurt you. Please, call me Juan,' he sang softly and twisted in his seat to reach across to touch her shoulder, casually laying a hand around the nape of her neck as if the most natural thing in the world. Sophie stiffened, feeling repulsed.

And just as Sophie was beginning to imagine all sorts of unpleasant scenarios that might have developed with JR in the back of his Jeep, and to her enormous relief, the sound of distant horse hooves approaching fast drew his attention away from her. Clattering up into view behind them was one of Robicalon's men in black, sweating hard. He pulled up short of the Jeep and called to his boss. JR stood up in the car and twisted round, calling impatiently '*Que pasa?*' He sounded more than a little irritated.

He jumped out and walked over to the rider who remained mounted but leant down low to talk urgently into JR's ear. Sophie picked up something about a man who was injured, who was not well; it did not sound good. JR was wanted back at the ranch to see what he thought.

He returned to the Jeep, with a thunderous look, and avoided her eye. 'I fear we must return, earlier than I had hoped.' He jumped into the driver's seat, looking uncomfortable, but remained polite. 'I am so sorry. I cannot leave these idiots for more than five minutes. Something important, one of my men, not well, they want me to take a look. Sorry.'

'Oh, no problem, not to worry,' sounded Sophie, suppressing her obvious feelings of relief.

He started up the engine again, reversed jerkily, skidded the Jeep round to race back along the track over the bumps and craggy dips and twists back to the main road, jamming frantically through the gears, with the man on horseback only just keeping up behind. It was a hair-raising return ride and Sophie was relieved when they slowed and turned into the drive. She felt sick and jolted by the time JR screeched along the riding school cobbles and juddered to a halt. He had not said a word all the way back. 'Please, Sophie, just mingle again with the people and 'ave some refreshments while I go see what the trouble. I will see you later, yes? Please,' as he touched her elbow and she climbed out of the Jeep, feeling queasy. He still had a look close to horror on his face, but maybe it was the dishevelled appearance of his hair, which he started to plaster down with the palms of both hands. The man in black had dismounted and jumped into the back of the Jeep, as JR reversed and spun round to head out of the school and back up to the roundabout at the entrance. Sophie walked a little shakily behind them at first, watching carefully as the Jeep rounded the spraying water fountain with tyres squeaking through the puddles and drove along the side road she had seen earlier marked private, that took them up to those terraced houses, that she had assumed were the living quarters of many of his staff.

Sophie needed to find Bruce straightaway. Something about the whole episode of the rush back with JR made her feel suspicious. This was no ordinary worker who was not well, surely. She rushed over to the training circuit and turned toward the marquee fifty yards on. Bruce was lazily slumped under a tree in the shade with a bottle of beer in his hand, eyes closed, legs stretched out in front of him, pretending to be asleep.

'I not asleep, Miss Sophie, I only pretend,' he protested at her reprimand.

'Yes, yes. Come. I want to follow JR up to those cottages. Something about a man of theirs being injured and not well. JR was shocked and angry.' And she pointed the way, pleased her ankle boots only had one inch heels which were comfortable to run in. Bruce dropped his beer bottle under a tree and loped along behind her in his new sneakers, soft soled and suede. They reached the circular road, almost running over wet bricks by the fountain where the wind had blown water beyond its surrounding well, and strode unstopping up the side track that lead towards the line of cottages, marked *privado*. As she approached the buildings, she could see that there were six narrow houses, with small windows and coloured painted doors, but in need of attention, looking a bit neglected, the glass less than shiny, the roofs sagging in their middles, some tiles slipped. They were set well back from the road and all seemed quiet; there was nobody about at this time, no workers or inhabitants, presumably everyone occupied with their jobs in running the estate on this open day with so many visitors. An empty pick-up truck was parked in front. There was no sign of JR's Jeep.

Sophie could see that their pathway ran past the end of the cottages, a plain stone wall without windows, and wound around the back of them and that was where she felt the Jeep must have gone.

'Come on.' Sophie led the way along the gravelly path and Bruce followed, through a broken wooden gate, up to the corner of the first house, where a brick wall about Sophie's height jutted out, conveniently for them to slide behind. Sophie peered gingerly around the edge while Bruce was able to look over the top. Across a broad open space of waste ground and gravel overgrown with tall weeds behind the back of the cottages, an area that was well out of the way of visitors, they both took in JR's open-topped Jeep parked at an angle in front of another building (that was not at all visible from the estate), a dirty stone and dilapidated granary store or some such, which stood apart fifty yards back, facing them at the edge of a thick copse. There was no sign of JR or his side-kick. An old tractor and a pick-up truck stood alone over the far side, and rusted pieces of metal work, a plough, a broken wheel barrow, used black tyres, half broken bales of straw and other rubbish were strewn about. The building had a wide open garage at the front with sliding wooden doors and tiny filthy windows on the upper floors. It looked dark inside, but Sophie was fixed with amazement on the rear end of an estate car that was parked in there, front first, a light green colour covered in dust, with an MA sign stuck on the back and the plate obscured but unmistakably Moroccan, with a number that she recognised: 4889–45|2.

Once Sophie had regained her wits, she indicated to Bruce by sign language that she wanted to get a closer look. So in an uncomfortable crouching position they both made a dash around the perimeter of the open ground to duck behind an ugly rectangular metal tank the size of a truck, probably for oil storage, that stood forlornly on its concrete base to one side of the granary building. Although quite why, as they would have made perfect targets whatever way they ran, had there been an armed guard on duty anywhere with a rifle and magnification sights. But there wasn't, so they arrived safely unseen and crouched down on the dirt ground behind the rusty tank, catching their breaths.

'That is car we have driven,' Bruce whispered. 'What's it doing here?'

'That is what I was wondering,' murmured Sophie.

They heard male Spanish voices, and by lying flat on their stomachs were able to observe the garage entrance from under the tank, among the dried nettles and weeds. Three men had emerged from the darkness inside, edging past the estate car, and stood outside in the glancing sunlight for a few moments. JR was looking agitated and was wiping his mouth and nose with a handkerchief. He sounded angry on turning to the other two and indicated they should close the garage, and one of them should stay there on guard and let no one through. '*No deje pasar a nadie, comprendido!*'

They waited, watching JR and his man in black hop back into the Jeep and skid off at speed over the gravelly ground, around the end of the terrace and out of sight. Sophie wanted to look inside the garage building. She whispered to Bruce: 'We need to get rid of him,' and pointed in the direction of the one man left behind to stand guard, who was noisily tugging at the old wooden gates to get them across the garage opening. Bruce nodded and they watched for a while, until the guard had given up and settled himself on a low brick wall the other side, where he sat with one elbow on a raised leg, his head on one hand, looking bleakly across the wasted forecourt. Bruce and Sophie moved away from the tank and skirted quietly and quickly around the back of the building, keeping close to its walls, hopping through loose undergrowth and long grass, glancing through darkened windows although they were unable to make out anything within. There were plenty of signs of neglect, water leakage off the roof, a few broken tiles grounded and rotting window frames. A long line of sloping stone steps, worn and mossy, led up to a wooden hatch like a door the height of a man half way up the side of the building, which looked jammed and unused for decades. Above was a substantial cast iron bracket and pulley bolted through the upper wall on hinges that was once used to heft heavy bags of grain in for storage.

They sneaked along to the last corner, checking where they placed their feet over the unkempt ground. And there they recognised the old horsebox, tilted forlornly out of sight against the sidewall of this remote building, both its tyres flat, its rear door swung open and inside empty. They gave each other knowing looks and nodded agreement. Up ahead no more than thirty feet sat the slouched figure of the guard, his back curved towards them, his bulging holster attached to a thick belt and only half covered by the tail of his shirt. Bruce slowly removed his own belt from around his waste, threading one end a short way through the buckle and holding it out in a loop in front of him with both hands as he advanced on tiptoes around the horsebox. Sophie peered after him, watching anxiously with her heart in her mouth, a hand held over her lips, almost unable to imagine what Bruce was about to do.

Somehow without making a sound he stalked along the wall, creeping steadily closer towards his unsuspecting target until he was a mere two strides behind him, when he made a sudden leap forward, throwing his looped belt over the man's head, gripping and heaving on his end, pulling tighter and tighter with all his might, while at the same time dragging the poor man backwards from off his seat on the wall. He fell heavily with a grunt onto the hard ground on his shoulder, as Bruce twisted him away face down and then placed a sharp knee into the small of his back. Bruce was bigger than him, heavier than him and was on top of him, perched like a giant vulture on his prey, his large hands forever tightening the leather strap around his neck, choking him and blocking off circulation. The struggle did not last long, the man's hands scrabbling hopelessly at the constriction around his neck, unable to get a grip and unable to grab Bruce's wrists. After a few moments of jerking, there came a stillness, the man's flaccid arms collapsed out across the ground on either side, his legs bent, a lone black shoe pulled off.

Bruce relaxed and let the strength drain from his arms. He felt for the man's pulse in his neck. Then he pulled the heavy duty Luger from its holster and standing up, hurled it high and long into the woods behind them. Satisfied, he looked across at Sophie. 'He'll be out for a while, twenty minutes maybe, but should recover.' Sophie looked relieved, thinking that Bruce might have killed the man. 'I learnt that in army, back home,' Bruce explained modestly.

They dragged the body away from the wall to hide him behind the horsebox. Bruce fed his belt back through the loops of his trousers and followed Sophie round to the front of the building, where she was heaving against one of the wooden doors. Once inside they sidled around the car in the half-light, confirming that it was indeed the same Skoda estate that she and Liz had found abandoned in the McDonald's car park that night, still filled with tacky Moroccan souvenirs in broken cardboard boxes. The inner door panels were stripped off and the hidden compartment in the floor behind the driver's seat was exposed and empty. 'How *did* this get here?' Bruce repeated in a high-pitched voice of amazement, his eyes popping out.

But Sophie knew the answer and was moving with

increasing apprehension towards the back of the garage where she had spotted a steep wooden staircase leading up into a dark void. Although she moved unhesitatingly up the steps, she knew she was not about to find anything pleasant. It was probably the smell that alerted her, which explained JR's reaction with his handkerchief over his mouth when he had come out, a blend of body sweat and excrement and something else, that gave her a sickly sweet sensation in her dry mouth: blood.

Rather than there being two floors above, she passed through a rickety doorway into a large shadowy space that spread across the whole building and reached high up to the sloping rafters of the roof, as hot as a furnace in the late afternoon sunshine. Natural light had been prevented from penetrating inside by blankets nailed over some of the windows or paint sprayed over the glass. The bare wooden flooring was rough and blotched with unspecified stains and the very air seemed rotten and musky with years of collected dust. There was nothing in the way of furniture, this was not an inhabited room but an occasional store place, she supposed, just a few piles of old sacks and some broken wooden crates.

Something instinctive directed her forwards towards the far end where she saw a blackened hump lying towards one corner, body shaped and immobile, covered by a blanket. Oddly there was one narrow shard of light, emerging through a tiny strip of glass in the roof above that had been missed by the spray, that was sadistically playing across a human foot that poked out from one end of the hump, dirty and twisted.

Sophie moved bravely closer to the dark shape, where flies buzzed low, bending down but almost revolted by the odour that caught physically in the back of her throat. She coughed and felt the sensation of vomit rising in her chest. With a hand clamped over her mouth, her thumb and forefinger squeezing her nose tight, she eased off with her other hand the covering blanket, with its wet stains and stiff filth in places, and peeled it toward her, revealing the near naked male body underneath, bruised and beaten, and dead. A swarm of flies became over-excited, frenzied activity around the face and eyes. There were dried faeces stained down the legs and the mouth was horribly swollen, the eyes too, but there was no mistaking Roberto, with his black curly hair. There were plenty of cut marks, razor sharp and clotted, over the arms and shoulders, and a sustained bruise spread over the left side of his abdomen. A thick smear of congealed blood across the floorboards had shoeprints smudged in it and she noticed other blood marks chaotically printed about them. Around his neck, connected by a long chain that curled away across the floor towards a fixture on the far brick wall, was a metal halter that had cut through the adjacent flesh in places. A coil of heavier chain lay in a pile just beyond his head, which was wrenched awkwardly to one side. Hands clamped behind his back, with metal cuffs around the wrists, were connected to yet more chains. Sophie looked up at the roof above and could just make out screwed into the woodwork a large pulley system and crank handle with an industrial-sized steel hook suspended above her head and she made the presumption that the chains were once hanging from the ceiling with Roberto attached. Now he was dead, a twisted neck, a mass of body blows and cuts, blood loss, internal haemorrhaging, whatever.

Carefully she stepped nearer, bending to place a finger on his cold neck just under the sharp curve of his jaw, but quite why she was not sure, as he was as obviously dead as it was possible to be. She took one last look at his face, as tears sprang hopelessly to her eyes and her chest heaved. She tottered over to the side of the room and spilled some of her stomach contents down the brickwork, adding to the mix of pungent odours that she could no longer tolerate. Her chest heaved some more, she wanted to cry out. She started panting and her turmoil emerged in grunts. Bruce was standing apart transfixed, his eyes staring in shock at the torso that he recognised as once his recently acquired comrade. He also had his hand over his mouth and nose. The noise of Sophie's retching awoke him to the reality of the situation and he moved to put an arm around her shoulders and help her back down the stairs. They shuffled out into the fresh warm air and he directed her sensibly away from the entrance and to the side of the garage, once again to crouch down on the ground behind the rusty oil tank, so that they would not be seen by anyone returning to the scene of the torture. They both knew they could not stay there long as the unconscious guard might come awake and start shouting for reinforcements. Their own lives would be in danger if found to have observed the scene upstairs. They needed to leave and soon.

Sophie wiped her eyes and her mouth with some tissues, spitting out foul-tasting debris onto the earthy floor. She straightened up and fought back tears of anger and tears of despair.

'Did you know about this? Did you?' she shouted with venom in an urgent whisper direct into Bruce's innocent looking face. 'Did you inform JR, tell him about Roberto?'

Desperately Bruce grasped her by the shoulders, almost shaking her to listen. 'No, no. I am so sorry for poor Roberto. I have never met JR. I was put in place to protect the merchandise and horsebox, but a terrible job I did of that. I assume it was JR that I should have reported to, but I never seen any of them, I kept out of the way since the mugging.'

'I need to get away – if JR finds me, he'll cut me up too. Bruce, I'm sorry, I didn't mean…'

'Miss Sophie, that all right, you are upset. This is most horrible.'

'Why don't you stay, Bruce and deflect him a bit. He'll

probably listen to you. Say you think I left the estate a while ago, after enjoying the horses. Or something. Be casual. You could get a lift back to town with someone later, couldn't you? There's bound to be some taxis. Here…' Sophie found her leather bag on its thin strap was still around her shoulders and from it she extracted some peso notes for Bruce. 'OK?'

Bruce was nodding, trying to understand what all this meant, while Sophie held onto his arms looking ashen-faced and shocked, and although she still had her doubts about Bruce and his role, she could read a degree of trust in his honest features. She wanted to say sorry that she had involved him in all this misery.

'I need to get back to town. I will go to the police. And I will need to talk to his wife; and Baxwell. Oh God. Take care, Bruce.'

They moved hastily away, again around the back of the granary store building, keeping close to the brickwork, glancing only briefly at the still body of the guard lying face down in the dirt by the wall as they had left him. Sophie moved off through the wooded area which would take her down to the fencing that lined the entry road and her exit point, while Bruce moved round to the front of the terrace and across the grassy slopes leading down to the paddocks and the horses once again, where he could lose himself among all the people still there and find himself a lift back to town later. Forcing herself to adopt a normal walking pattern on the driveway, she calmly left the Robicalon Estate through its open gates, giving a dismissive smile to one of the security men. She hurried along the roadway to her car, which had been steadily heating up in the sunshine. Once she had turned it around in the narrow road and was heading back to town on the only route available, checking repeatedly that there was no one in pursuit, she could contain herself no longer and allowed a flood of tears to erupt over her cheeks and drip onto her lap.

With the windows wide open and warm air rushing through the car, she returned to Marbella in a state of agitation. She had been gripping the wheel tightly to stop the trembling, and her arms were aching. She could hardly remember the journey itself, but found herself dashing along the back alleys, sprinting up her cold stairwell three steps at a time and inserting her key into the front door. Dry tears had crusted around her eyes and she had smeared mascara and make-up out over her cheekbones, had dark smears on her fingers. She needed a drink and downed a glass of wine almost in one go. She wanted time alone, time to shower away the dirt and the stains and the smell, to erase the image of Roberto's tortured face that kept wavering across her mind.

What the hell has JR been doing? Kidnapping the man was one thing, but to allow that torture to happen, to kill him, surely that was a mistake. No wonder he looked so angry. JR must have wanted information desperately and he had been slighted, sorely treated and robbed; he would have needed to show the drugs community that he had everything under control, that he was not a push-over. But what was it that had made him *so* desperate that he would have someone killed, was it just the money? Why did Roberto not tell JR what he wanted to know and get himself released, surely he would not have held out to his death, even if he did persuade himself that he loved Sophie, surely he would have revealed the truth of last Thursday night and who was behind it, to save himself?

Of course, once JR and his thugs had committed themselves to that kind of task, it would have been difficult to extricate themselves, so to release Roberto, even if he had told them everything, would have left them open to inquiry and investigation once he told his gory story to the police or worse, the press. JR had looked angry when he came out of that garage building, presumably because of the idiocy of his henchmen that they had brought Roberto there, that he was on his estate during their open-day with so many visitors. And with the important auction that day, why would he have taken the risk. Arrogance. Or maybe JR was not aware that Roberto was being held up in that loft, until the rider in black came out to tell him, when it had gone wrong. Anyway, for whatever reason, they had brought him; and there he had died by the look of things, that very day, unaware that his lusty love-partner was nearby on the same estate enjoying the hospitality of his ultimate murderer.

Before leaving, Sophie, in two minds, had stared at the black handset in her lounge for twenty minutes before plucking up the courage to make the call she wanted, to Hernandez Cagigas, the deputy police chief. But he was out of his office and she could only leave a message for him to call her back at the flat in two hours' time. She had decided to first visit Roberto's wife, Luciana, who was not someone she knew at all really but to whom she felt a strong obligation; and then to see Baxwell in his office with the news (and she knew she would have to tell him the truth); and finally she would go to see Liz when she was back from work. A round trip, to be back in two hours. She quickly did her face, a little lipstick and dressed in old jeans, a blouse and a loose denim jacket and left, with her small shoulder bag, again taking the dingy back stairs to the service lobby.

Just as she emerged from the narrow back alleyway of her block into the Calle Sierra Blanca, whilst she was thinking that she could try for Hernandez in person at his headquarters in Velasco, she found herself unexpectedly hustled by a couple of ugly Chinese youths with untidy long hair, chewing gum. They had appeared so suddenly that Sophie was quite taken aback. She stepped sideways to avoid them, but they blocked her way, their faces smirking, menace in their eyes. She turned round on her toes ready for flight, but a third older man, with bare tattooed arms, blocked her way behind. He had a shoestring moustache draped over his flat mouth and he smiled slowly at her, showing his few stained teeth and then spat a gob of phlegm onto the concrete at her feet. He was holding a black cloth of some sort in one hand. Sophie was hemmed in.

The older man reached out with his left hand and gripped her neck, as she immediately went through a re-run of last week's assault at the hands of JR, thinking he was up to his tricks, but the chewing monkey blocking her way was definitely Chinese. One of the youths behind was pressing into her back, a hand at her elbow and he whispered through her spiky hair, his salivary lips wetting her ear. 'You come with us, Miss Sophie, no trouble, yes, you come. We go see The Magician, he want you.' And he stabbed her in the small of her back with his fist, pulling her away from the passageway over to the road. Sophie caught a look of satisfaction on the older man's face, just before she turned away from him and in that instant, broke free of the grip on her and darted forward with a swing of a fist to catch any of them she could. She dashed full pelt across the road without considering any traffic and, having adopted the posture of a short-distance sprinter, covered the distance to the far kerb and then more, veering off into another passage between high-sided concrete walls with the three Chinamen in frantic pursuit, when for some reason that she could not understand, she decided to vault over one of the sides. At a junior school back home sometime in the long distant past, she recalled how she used to excel at high jump, and she must have considered that with an athletic leap she could make it to the top of the wall and roll over out of their grasp. But that was then and this was now.

She grappled with the sharp edged brickwork along the ridge of the wall, which was considerably higher than she was tall, her arms tensed, one leg thrown over the ledge to help with leverage while pulling herself feverishly upwards over the last couple of feet, but unfortunately her trailing leg was grabbed by two Chinamen at the same time and although both were relatively lightweight, they were sufficiently strong to pull her down, tearing some skin off her palms and a knee, and ripping her jeans. She landed painfully on the concrete path seven feet below on her elbows and knocked her forehead, although much of the fall was cushioned by landing on the Chinamen. But still she fought and struggled and tried to shout out, as the three men grabbed whatever bit of her they could get hold of and dragged her and lifted her still kicking back along the path out onto the pavement where around the corner the back of a van was open and waiting. She was upside down when one of them hit her in the crotch with his fist from above, hard between her buttocks, which was so painful she wanted to scream but had already used up so much of her breath, all she managed was a fearful gulping followed by a feeling of sickness. She was hurled into empty darkness with a crash, landing on her back. She received another punch in the belly and a smack across her face, before being squashed face down with a knee wedged into her back and her arms wrenched behind her, where they were firmly taped around the wrists. Then the older man who had clambered into the van after her pulled what was a black hood over her head and tied the strings around her neck. She remembered hearing the crash as the back doors were slammed shut, but the light had already gone out.

* * *

Matthew had thought about ringing Sophie that morning from the hotel, maybe at her office again, but hesitated, feeling a little embarrassed or shy, he was not sure which. He had lain awake worrying that he had over-played his hand already and that she was not interested. He was gladdened by her resemblances to Stephanie, reflected beautifully in the line of her jaw, the dimpling smiles, the determination of character. He recognised next to none of his own features in her pixie face or her voice, but that did not matter to him, he was sure of his ground. She certainly seemed to be a busy young lady with lots on her plate and her mind preoccupied, it was just that she did not seem to want to bother about some old geezer from London, past flame of her mother or not. She was in control of her life, self-determined. He could not decide whether her obvious familiarity with that swarthy policeman last night was a good thing or not.

Late in the afternoon, determined to find the block where she lived, he took the car west along the main avenue, had difficulty turning left across the traffic and then struggled along the narrow back streets to find anywhere to park: there were so many one ways and no entries, and cars lining every available space, across kerbs and entryways, making the roads even narrower, then blocked by delivery vans stuck in the middle, that amid all the tooting and shouting and awkward reversing, Matthew wished he had walked from the hotel. After a hot and irritating while, he was able to nip into a space vacated by another car in front of him, somewhere along Calle Alonso de Bazan. He took a guess in which direction to start walking, reading out almost aloud the names of every street as he came to junctions, with Sophie's address written on a piece of paper that he carried in front of him.

His vague plan was to try her apartment in the hope that he may catch her in a more receptive mood. He stopped at a tobacco kiosk on a corner and tried to ask in his best Spanish but the sun-tanned man with the leathery skin and thick drooping moustache did not understand him or the writing on the paper and he had to retreat in a muddle, thanking him. As he moved away, a group of three thin Chinese men loitering on the next corner caught his eye; they were smoking, chewing and looking surreptitiously up and down the road; they glanced his way and for a moment Matthew thought they were sizing him up for a quick mugging, but they suddenly darted down a passageway and out of sight by the time he passed.

He eventually found her apartment block, in the adjacent sloping street, stretching half its length, in a rather tatty looking building painted cream with shops along the ground floor fronting the pavement. It was six or seven stories high, really in three blocks each with its own communal entrance at twenty yard intervals along the street, and he did not understand the numbering. There were long green-painted balconies to every floor, and pot plants, washing on racks and upturned bicycles adorned every spare space, as far as he could see. On a first floor balcony, an elderly couple lay asleep on deckchairs end-to-end, head to head, with one large straw hat placed over them. A smelly fish shop on the corner was doing a good trade.

He found the glass-fronted entrance with numbers fifty-five to eighty-one indicated and on the wall next to the door, a panel of little aluminium bell stops with a space beside each for a name in rows, and a small speaker cover. The heavy glass door was locked, but he did not have to wait long before a departing resident opened the door, allowing him to slip through, murmuring something about losing his key, into a dank entrance hall with stone steps spiralling upwards. Some engineers were working on the elevator. Matthew took the stairs, arriving on the sixth floor out of breath; he found number sixty-four easily and rang the buzzer without hesitation, twice but no one opened the door. He rang the apartment next door and a well-built middle-aged woman answered, admitted to speaking only a little English in reply to Matthew.

'Sophie, not in. No,' she said, looking sorry, wiping large

floury hands on her white apron. 'She go out, I hear her go out. Just now, five minutes. Only five minutes. She always working, always busy, nice woman.'

Matthew looked confused, only because he must have just missed her by a few minutes and he was unsure whether to go after her or to wait. 'I'll leave a note,' Matthew said, 'thank you.' He had already written on a card his name, the hotel, his room number and hotel phone number and so at the bottom he added, while standing by her closed door, leaning against the wall, watched carefully by the neighbour: "May I take you out to dinner one evening this week, so we can share the news that I have?" And he signed it clearly, Matthew Crawford. He slipped the card under her door, turned to the woman in the next doorway and smiled, nodded and called '*Gracias*' as he rapidly descended to the street once again, feeling disappointed.

As he meandered back towards where he thought he had left the car, he was crossing at a corner of Calle Alonso de Bazan, when a battered blue Transit van, its tyres squeaking and gears crunching, appeared at speed from between rows of parked cars from the road behind Sophie's block, and crossed right in front of him, so close he almost felt it, he had to stop abruptly in the gutter. The front windows were open and the Chinese faces that craned to see if any traffic was coming round the corner looked familiar. The van jerked forward, with its engine revving noisily, and turned sharply in front of an approaching car, which had to brake, with horn blaring. Tyres squeaked again and the Transit wobbled a bit as it raced away with blurting exhaust. Matthew watched it disappear from sight around another corner.

* * *

Sophie lay still, whimpering with pain and fear, short of

breath. Her world had become a nightmare and images of Roberto's tortured and bloodied body kept welling up from the deeper recesses of her confused mind, only for her own half-naked self to replace it, twisted and in distress. She was jolted by the movement of the van, her head bouncing up and down on the metal floor, above the grinding of the drive-shaft as it bumped along, stop-start through the city traffic to goodness knew where. She felt sick and more tears welled up and stung her eyes that she could not wipe. She wanted to scream but her bruised abdomen would not let much out but a strangled groan. Behind her back her hands were stinging where she had cut them on the brick wall.

After an interminable time that might have been ten minutes or sixty minutes, she could not swear to it, the van came to a stop and amid the sound of car doors slamming and shouting voices outside, the engine was switched off. Then the van doors were opened and she was dragged out by her ankles, strong hands gripped her arms unkindly, until she was standing upright again feeling the warmth of the day around her for a moment, before being made to walk. Commands were barked at her from behind amid background noise of muffled voices, Oriental and foreign. She tripped over a step and the air was suddenly cooler; then she was stumbling down some stairs, lots of stairs with twists, and she would have fallen but for the clamp-like grip someone had on her. It was probably two flights down, must be underground, and then she walked some more, before being shoved forward and left to stand. She dared not move; she tried to hear what was happening, but there were only some muffled voices far away. Her face was hot breathing the same stale air inside the rough hood.

Someone was prizing her boots off her and she nearly fell over. She was about to complain about her treatment but was pushed in the back again. She shuffled forward, feeling the hard floor with her bare feet. A door closed and a key was turned in a lock. All had gone quiet and she was sure she was alone.

Her arms were aching horribly, but her wrists were taped tightly behind her back and there was no give. She waited, turning slowly as if she was looking around, but could see nothing. Not knowing what was coming next, intermittently holding her breath and then breathing fast, she wanted to panic and call out. '*Hola*,' she ventured into the darkness. 'Hello,' a bit louder. Nothing. She moved her feet forwards, inches at a time, one then the other, her body in a slight crouch, thinking she was heading towards the way had come in, where she thought the door was. She wanted to reach out with her hands, to feel her way; perhaps she should go backwards. So she decided to shuffle sideways, less painful hitting something with her shoulder, a wall or piece of furniture, rather than her nose. Still nothing, after several shuffles. Perhaps she was in a huge room and would never reach the walls. Instead she sank to her knees, trembling, close to defeat, thinking should she give up. 'Oh God, please help me,' she whined.

Not being a believer, she inwardly saw the weakness of her plea. She assumed when the Chinese came back they would want her to tell them about the robbery and the truth of her part in it and above all where the hash consignment was. She was ready to tell them, tell them anything to get herself released. She would immediately leave, get the first flight out of Malaga, to anywhere, it did not matter. Liz might come with her. She had not played her hand well and for her own survival she had to leave, cut her losses.

She would have to make it up to Liz; she had used her without much consideration for her safety. She would have to tell the Chinese about the money bag in Liz's place. She was so sorry. Sophie's punishment, their punishment, was

Roberto's tortured body, his bruises, his broken neck and the pain he must have gone through. That was all her fault, she should never have listened to him in the first place and taken on the heist, what a stupid girl. She said it sounded bonkers, how right she was.

She screamed as loudly as she could into the woolly material of the hood, for a good five seconds. And then she flopped awkwardly onto her bottom, using her hands at the back to help her balance, with her finger tips pressing onto a smooth floor, of linoleum perhaps. In that way she started to edge backwards, sliding on her rear, her knees bent, pushing with her feet. That felt safer; progress was a little faster. She was perspiring heavily and she wiped her upper lip with her tongue, tasting the salty sweat. Then all of sudden her curled fingers knocked against cold masonry, a wall, and she gingerly leant back against it and stretched her legs out in front of her along the floor. Her body perspiration began to evaporate and she shivered, feeling cold all over, except inside the hood where her face was burning still and her scalp felt itchy. Any relief she felt was temporary.

She had never felt so hopeless or foolish, in all her life; so out of control. And so alone.

She was alone for a long time, several hours, it was hard to tell. She listened intently for any sounds but there were none. She became so stiff, leaning against the wall, her bottom so sore on the hard floor, she seemed to lose all feeling in her feet. She tried stretching her legs and her body, only to become even more conscious of her stiffening bruises and joints. At some point she became aware of the need to empty her bladder and she repeatedly called out, increasingly angry at the lack of response. She tried deep breathing, eyes closed, head against the wall and her thoughts directed somewhere else, but the nagging persisted. She tried to sleep, her lids heavy. She rolled over off her bottom and crouched on her knees but that was not sustainable for long. She stood up slowly, wobbling and leaning against the wall for support. She called out again in despair and tried stamping her feet. Then she started cautiously to move along the wall, feeling with her hands at her back and after many paces she hit a corner. She turned through ninety degrees and scraped along with her back and hands against a dusty brick surface, deciding she would try to work out the shape and dimension of the whole room, which would fill in the time and take her mind off her desperate need to pass water. But then the side of her head hit sharply on something hard and metallic, that seemed to be sticking out of the wall, and that hurt. She moved away from it, screwed up her eyes tight, holding back the tears. She wanted to rub her forehead, but could not. She stood still for a while, too frightened to move, feeling a slow warm trickle on the side of her face, suddenly completely scared of what else might be in the room. Her urge to urinate became more desperate. She slid down the wall, calling out urgently and with venom in her voice, descending onto her sore bottom, knees bent up; she tried holding herself, squeezing her thighs together and up against her belly, but the pressure became beyond her control. She helplessly voided, a warm drench inside her jeans, and the strong smell reached her senses almost immediately. She was sobbing as she slowly tumbled over sideways in despair, feeling so tired. She lay her forehead on the cold floor and after a little while her eyes closed and she dozed fitfully.

She had no idea how much time had passed, how long she may have slept for, whether the day had passed into night, or beyond, before she became aware of someone speaking in Chinese: two women's voices. Hands touched her and helped her up into a sitting position. The ties around her neck were loosened and the hood was slowly pulled upwards over her head. She pulled eagerly free and screwed up her eyes at the mercifully feeble strip light. She looked about, terrified, but a feeling of freedom and optimism rushed over her with the fresher air, suddenly breathing easier without the heat and smell of the hood. Two Chinese women, in loose fitting white cotton and plimsolls, were bending over her. One had a cup in her hand and was pushing it towards her mouth. Sophie looked up into their faces, searching for friendship.

'Drink. Water,' one of them said. She tasted and then gulped keenly, spilling some down her front as the woman tipped it between her lips and the cool water tasted of heaven. The other woman had a damp face flannel that was warm and she wiped Sophie's face and neck. She pressed the side of her forehead where there was a cut to soothe it, showing her the red stains of blood on her cloth. Sophie murmured her thanks and even managed a smile. She was aware of the pungent smell and tried to apologise for wetting herself.

It seemed that she was in a darkened cellar, the size of a double garage, with black painted walls and ceiling, no windows, all brick and rough concrete, with a dull lino floor. There was a single door in the far wall and a small strip-light above it, the only source of light, and a flat low ceiling not much higher than her height. Next to her, fixed to the wall was a wrought iron contraption with arms on great hinges and a wheel like for an old-fashioned carriage, and above it there was a rectangular opening in the ceiling that had been boarded over, but Sophie concluded that once this was part of a lift system, feeding up into the building above. It reminded her of Roberto's chains and his torture.

'Where am I? What is going on? Do you speak English, Spanish?'

But they said nothing. One of them went outside and brought in a wooden chair that she placed almost in the centre of the room and they both helped Sophie up onto her feet.

Then the tapes around her wrists were cut free and she was able to slowly agonisingly bring her arms to the front. She screamed and tried to hug herself but both arms felt so weak. Her wristwatch had been taken off, she noticed as she rubbed her sore wrists, trying to get the feeling back in her hands. The two women removed her crumpled jacket, leaving her in the cotton blouse. Then they unzipped her and wriggled the clinging jeans down over her bottom and pulled them off, the knickers too, as she hopped from foot to foot. She was so unsteady, it surprised her. They wiped her legs and then sat her down on the cold wooden seat.

They withdrew without a word, closing the door, and Sophie heard the key turn in the lock. She was left alone again, but with the dim light on and no hood, her hands free and a chair to sit on, she felt things were definitely improving, even though she was now half naked.

Again she had no idea how long she had been sitting there, it felt like an hour or two since the women had left, when, without warning, a big man in bare feet barged into the room, kicking the door closed behind him. Sophie had not heard the key turn in the lock and she looked at him in surprise, her hands crossed over in her lap. She had never seen him before. He looked unpleasant, older than the others, heavy and stocky, brimming with rounded muscle. He wore grey baggy trousers tied with a cord and a dirty white singlet vest, his bare arms well-tattooed. He was a comic figure in some ways, with a thin droopy moustache, cropped black hair and a scarred face. He had a fat roll of tape and a black hood in his hands and he circled around Sophie a few times, staring maliciously at her face. Behind her, he suddenly grabbed her arms and wrenched them backwards, hurting her and taping around the wrists, as before. She moaned but could not resist, she felt too tired. The man circled around her again, taunting her, and from behind her again, he pulled the black hood over her head firmly, although she shook her head vigorously and shouted; the ties were tied. Once again she was in the dark.

She heard the closing of the door, the clunk of the key in the lock and had the impression that the light had been switched off. The hood was a fresh one, it did not smell like the first one. She could breathe more easily in it and it was not yet as hot, although she knew she would soon warm up, the woolly material being sucked into her mouth at every inhalation. She flared her nostrils and worried about her oxygen levels and the more she worried the faster she breathed. Panic could so easily set in, and she told herself to calm down. Her body felt cold which probably kept her awake, but after a while she dozed off, in her sitting position, her head lolling forwards, until it jerked suddenly back, awakened by the stretching pains in her neck.

As far as she could tell, she was alone again for several hours, although she knew that it was common human habit to overestimate time periods, even when not disorientated, and especially when idle. The more time that passed, the harder it became to judge, only she was ready to relieve herself again when she heard the women's voices return and she was so thirsty. They removed the hood slowly and once again, she felt a sense of joy at that small freedom. In the dim light she took deep gasps to fill her lungs. She was led across to a corner of the room where a plastic bucket had been placed; the two women made signals that she should squat as one of them lifted the tails of her blouse out of the way. She tried to balance herself over the plastic ring, but she needed support under her arms to steady her and in that undignified position she half-filled the bucket with ease. The tinkling noise and accompanying smell were enough to embarrass her but she was rapidly losing any remaining dignity.

'I want to sleep, I want to lie down,' she moaned, trying to indicate with her eyes closing and head lolling towards the floor, but they did not understand, placing her back on her chair. Her wrists were still taped but the hood was left on the floor. She said she was cold. But after giving her some more sips of water, which she gulped at, the women went away again, switching the light off. She felt hungry and still thirsty and started to weep. It was dark in her dungeon, but without the hood on she felt free to walk around the room, remembering to avoid the iron torture device. She also tried not to kick the bucket – and was amused at her own sense of gallows humour. She tried the door handle, when she could find it, but nothing moved, the door was solid. She lay down close to the wall opposite the door, with her bucket close by for when she might need it, and dozed uncomfortably for short bouts, before waking with a start, shaking, her head and neck stiff and sore, her limbs screaming complaints.

The routine must have been repeated again, but she lost count. The same two women would return to offer her some water, wipe her face and encourage her to use the bucket. Her wrists were left taped up and the hood remained in a bundle on the floor. The reason for leaving her cold and hungry with just a blouse on, was for humiliation, she supposed. The hood and the darkness added to the disorientation. After one such visit, the big muscleman returned, looking fresh enough, his long black hair tied back in a pony-tail. He was carrying the tape roll again and a leather belt. He kicked the door closed with a bare foot and meandered over to her by the far wall. Bending down he lifted her bodily in one movement and dropped her sitting on the wooden chair in the middle of the room, the seat feeling cold to her bare bottom. He hooked her arms painfully over the back and used the belt in addition to strap her tightly in place. Then he bent down and taped each of her ankles to each of the two front legs of the chair. She screamed at the top of his head: 'What are you doing, you fucking idiot?' in English and then in Spanish, to no avail. The man stood over her, looking down on her, his face impassive. She screamed at him again and he suddenly slapped her face with his open palm, once and then twice and each time she felt her teeth jar and it hurt.

'Shut,' the muscle man said viciously, before pulling the black hood over her head, and tying the strings around her neck. 'No, no, please,' she moaned but he started shouting at her through the hood, on one side and then the other, close up blasting sounds into her ears, Chinese expletives mostly. She understood nothing, except he was venting his anger and making her feel scared and vulnerable. Her cheeks were stinging, made worse by the slow flow of fresh tears and she knew that her time was only going to get harder.

11

It seemed like many hours later, after she had been left alone as she was, trussed up to the chair in the darkness, when her hood was yanked off suddenly and as she blinked herself awake, she saw a new face staring at her in the shadowy light. A short man of typical Chinese appearance, narrow eyes and pained grimace, sunken cheeks and a wispy collection of long hairs wiggling freely from his upper lip, that seemed to tremble with anger. He looked seriously mean. He was in baggy whites and bare feet and carried a short whip like a riding crop with a tuft of cut leather strips at the business end. And he used it, once or twice thrashing it across her shoulders and outer arms. It produced a stinging pain, sharp, like a knife and Sophie screamed each time. He was asking her questions in a faltering English and she was obviously not giving him the answers he was looking for.

'Where is Moroccan hash?'

'What Moroccan hash?'

'Where is Chinese money?'

'What Chinese money?'

He whipped her across her bare thighs and the sharp stinging made her tremble and scream: 'Shit. OK. OK, damn it!'

The man leant forward so his face was close to hers and

spoke succinctly for once, controlling his temper. 'Skoda car carried money and in horsebox was hidden hashish from Moroc. The best. The drivers ambushed on road from Algeciras last Wednesday night. You responsible, yes? Your friend Roberto has confessed, everything. Now you tell me where money and hash is hidden and we let you go. No more pain. We get merchandise and you walk away. Yes?'

With agony etched across her young face, perspiration wetting the nape of her neck, Sophie slowly raised her eyes up to meet the mean Chinaman's tired black eyes. He stretched his mouth out sideways in a sort of smile, his teeth showing behind the screen of thin black hairs and he was nodding. He smelt repulsive. And God, she was tempted, either to reveal everything to this cruel monster or to spit in his face, one or the other. 'Look, the money was in my apartment, but I was broken into, the money was stolen. It was JR, Robicalon and his men. He told me. JR has all the money and the hash.'

Sophie was pleading, tears welling up along her lower eyelids with the continuing stinging pain.

'Roberto dead and you be next,' he dripped, the words squirming out of one side of his mouth like so much spittle. He snorted through his nose and gobbed the lump of phlegm from the back of his throat across the room to hit the wall behind. And he swiped his whip across her thighs again. She screamed and strained at the tapes, shaking the chair, making its wooden legs rattle on the floor, shaking her head and body from side to side. She watched as violacious weals appeared in lines across the skin of both her thighs. 'Bloody hell, that hurts, you pig,' she screamed, tears spilling over.

The Chinaman stepped back calmly, staring at his cowering victim with a measure of contempt and little sympathy. Sophie was rattling at the chair, trying to bounce her legs up and down to relieve the agony. Her head was bowed, eyes screwed up tight, she was willing it all to end.

The thought that if she told them the truth, told them where the money was, where the horsebox and the hidden hash was, she would not only put Liz at risk, and maybe Jamie too, but would then be disposed of anyway by the Chinese mob, who would have no further use of her. She started to sob, with the pain, the indignity and the thought of dear Roberto lying twisted in his own shit in that dark room. 'It's JR, Robicalon – he has the money and all the hash, ask him,' she screamed again. JR and the Chinese must be working together, how else would these people know all these details? Why would JR tell them? She was confused and she was close to beaten.

* * *

During a relatively quiet morning at the Baxwell Properties office, Matthew strolled in with his smile and sunny disposition, as he had done on Sunday, and observed several unfamiliar uniformed staff at their desks, but no Sophie Patek. The overhead fans were whirring away noisily and the computer screens were flickering, and a few customers stood around staring at brochures and advertisements. Sophie's desk was actually being used by someone else, but he walked over there anyway, to start his enquiries. Apparently Ms Patek had not been in to work yesterday or that day so far; she and Mr Baxwell were expected to be at the Town Hall presentations later. She was probably preparing her stuff at home. Matthew accepted the offer of a quick word with Mr Baxwell himself if available and was soon ushered up the back stairs to the gallery office.

The little rotund red-faced Scotsman was in a fine Italian suit with shiny black slip-ons and was standing lumpen behind his desk. 'Hello. Can I be of any help?' he drawled, putting on a forced smile.

'I am an old friend of the family. I was hoping to just have a quick word with Sophie, but she is not here. Thought I'd just introduce myself, Matthew Crawford.'

'Ah, an Englishman, over from …?'

'London, flew from Gatwick on Sunday. Here for a week. It's jolly hot, isn't it? Don't know how you stand it all the year round.'

'It jolly well is, yes, I don't like it too hot myself, as a matter of fact, but it certainly attracts lots of people and they all want to spend lots of money here and that's fine by me.' He smiled and offered Matthew a cigar from a box on his desk. 'So you know Sophie from England, well, do you?'

Matthew shook his head to the cigar and then nodded. 'Her mother and I go back a bit. I have some family business with Sophie, so I really wanted to talk to her soon. She was not at home yesterday afternoon, I went round to her apartment and she has not answered her phone all morning.'

'Look,' Baxwell confided, blowing thick and smelly smoke up towards the ceiling, looking worried. 'I am a bit worried about Sophie myself; as it happens, I've not seen her since Sunday afternoon and one of my employees has disappeared, was killed, actually, so things are a little difficult just now. We have to be in Malaga this afternoon for a presentation, four o'clock, a very important bid for a planning and development licence worth a considerable amount of money, I may say and guess who's the favourite to come out tops?' Baxwell beamed with pride although he was obviously nervous too, fiddling with his buttons, flicking imaginary dust off his sleeves. 'But I need Sophie, out front, you know. She's crucial.'

'Well, I saw her Monday night, she met up with a police inspector in the Fuente Hotel where I'm staying; she said there was some business to talk about and that a friend of hers had gone missing.'

'Roberto, yes, he's the fellow. I only found out last night. Sophie was talking to the police, apparently. And I have in addition lost a great deal of money, some sort of robbery, but that's bye-the-bye.'

They both stood for a moment more, lost for words.

'My guess the person you might like to talk to would be Liz Harris. Elizabeth, she's Sophie's best friend in Marbella. Knows Roberto. Knew Roberto, I should say. I phoned her this morning; she was a bit distressed, said she didn't know where Sophie was – but she is most likely to know where to find her. I'd go and see her, if I was you,' finished Baxwell with a quick glance at his wristwatch and a dismissive look at Matthew as he turned back to the paperwork that was so preoccupying him.

Matthew walked out, with a promise to call in again before he left for home, and with the address and number of Sophie's best friend Liz written on a tear-off piece of note paper. And if he did see Sophie he promised to remind her not to be late for the presentations, Town Hall, Malaga, four o'clock sharp.

* * *

In the dark, Sophie, trussed and hooded, was slumped on the chair. All her stinging weals across the soft skin of her shoulders and thighs were playing an unremitting tune of burning and screeching in a fluctuating cycle, as her own awareness drifted in and out along the ill-defined border between wakefulness and sleep. Whenever her neck stretched too much or her head drifted backwards, she would jerk up straight, blink and squeeze her eyes shut, willing her nightmare to end.

Had there been further visits from her two minders, she vaguely thought there must have been? With help onto and off her bucket, sips of water pressed to her cracked lips when she would take gulps and spill most of it down her shirt?

She remembers a mouthful of rice at one point, barely able to swallow more than a few grains. Her muddled mind was plagued constantly with fears of more thrashing and more pain. There had been at least one more such visit, she could recall, that came without warning, her Chinese torturer creeping unnoticed up to her hooded head and suddenly shouting Chinese obscenities into her ears, first on one side then the other. He would hoik some phlegm from the back of his nose and spit it out onto the floor somewhere. Then he would demand to know where she had hidden the Moroccan hash and all the Chinese money. Her poor answers were followed inevitably by a smack across her face and a whip across her bare legs or ankles. She would grit her teeth and screw up her eyes, unable to scream; she would hold her breath and jerk her legs up and down against her restraints; she would squeeze the last drops of tears from her eyes as the stinging pulsed through her body. She would shout her own obscenities, 'Motherfucker, go to Hell.' The mean Chinaman swore The Magician himself would be coming down to cut her tongue out of her mouth. Once she made the chair wobble over and she fell backwards cracking her head on the floor, which only served to make the desperate torturer angrier and he left her there, on the cold floor until after some minutes her two faithful women returned to lift her back upright again, removing the hood and wiping her sweating agonised face clean.

She had lost her grasp of time. The women were moving around her, unbuckling the strap and cutting loose the sticky tape around her wrists and ankles. They slowly worked her onto her feet, but she could barely support herself, her limbs so feeble and numb, like a new-born calf. They tried walking her slowly around the room, one woman on either side, while she tried to tell them to be careful of the Chinaman's gobs of phlegm over the floor. She used the bucket and then they were pulling a pair of clean underpants up her legs tucking them in place, baggy cotton things that made her laugh, even the two women smiled at each other, but she was grateful for them nonetheless. She sat on the chair exhausted and in the dim light could see the angry-looking weals across the top of her thighs, some deeply cut and clotted, where the skin had broken. One of the women pressed her warm flannel kindly over them, trying at least to be helpful. The other woman wrapped a sheet around her lower half to cover her up with a brief gesture of sympathy, before they both shuffled backwards in their slippers to stand aside by the door.

Much to her absolute surprise, the door opened and closed to admit Hsui Long Long. She could not believe it, thought he must be an apparition, until he bent down in front of her, putting his bony hands on her covered knees, and looked straight into her face with concern etched across his young features. His face was scrubbed and shaved, but for a few straggly black hairs that remained over the outer reaches of his upper lip. His hair was newly gelled, combed back from the pale forehead and he wore a clean white shirt with his stained and ripped jeans. There was a thin string of beads around his scrawny neck and the usual coloured strips tied around his wrists.

'John!' Sophie exclaimed. She nearly cried for joy at the sight of a friendly face and tried to raise her arms to hug him, but she could not get her heavy limbs to move. Her hopes of an end to her torture soared, her eyes widened and she tried to smile her dry lips. 'John, it's so nice to see you. I've been so scared. What is happening? Where am I?' Her chest heaved as she made loud sobbing noises.

John ignored her questions. He was there on a mission. 'Sophie, so solly. You, like this. Not good, not what we want. The Magician, he want justice, he want what is rightfully his.' She imagined Ho Sup Ping telling Hsui to smarten himself

371

up, wash his hair, comb it nice, put on clean shirt and go persuade that dreadful woman to tell him truth. There was nothing but grim determination on Hsui's thin face, as he balanced in his low crouch, which told her things were not too easy. 'The Magician think you work with JR to rob him. He already pay for big consignment of Moroccan hashish, but now no delivery.'

Sophie's eyes opened wide as she shook her head. 'No, no, I am not with JR, I hate JR, he attacked me and robbed my apartment.'

'You and JR are lovers, perhaps?'

'For God's sake, no, John. Why does everyone think every man in Marbella is my lover? It's ridiculous.'

'The Magician see you with JR, at bullfight in Mijas. You close, he say.'

'No, John, JR invited me, he fancies me. But absolutely no, he gives me the creeps. JR has the money and probably your hash consignment. You know, he kidnapped Roberto, he tortured him, killed him. Rob's dead, you know?' Her face wet, Sophie tried to speak and lick the tears around her lips at the same time.

'Yes. Yes, I know. Solly. Bad business.'

'I don't want… please, John, help me. Persuade your father it was not me, JR has the hash and the money. Please.' She was reaching out to her old time friend, clutching at his sleeves and pleading into his eyes, but Hsui had turned away and would not make eye contact.

'I see what, I will try.'

'John, can you get me a telephone, so I can call some people, I need to talk to Liz and Baxwell.' And Hernandez, she thought: God, he will be thinking she has let him down. Maybe he called round to her place, found her gone, not returned for over a day, nor appeared at any of her club venues to work or see friends, nor been at the Baxwell Properties office for work. He would have been to see Jamie and they would almost certainly be scouring the streets of Marbella at this very moment. Bruce would have got back to town to tell Baxwell about Roberto, Liz would know. They would both be looking for her, wouldn't they? Her car should still be there. Her keys had been in her bag that the Chinese took, maybe they've found the car and searched it without finding anything. They would have searched her flat, confirmed the empty space under her bed, but would never have been up to the attic.

'John, where am I?' she pleaded.

Or maybe no one has even noticed that she was not around. Jamie and his friends will be keeping their heads down, Liz wondering whether she should go see the police, Baxwell will be fuming with anger; and they all hate her anyway for what she has done. And Bruce will be confused, bless, he won't know where his loyalties lie. Or has he been the link with JR all along?

'I will try. You in factory, edge of town,' he whispered. He smothered his own quick smile and stood up. The women still hung back respectfully against the wall and had not moved or said anything during this time.

'Water, for Miss Sophie.' Hsui Long Long backed out, 'I will see. Wait,' and hurriedly left.

They brought her water in a plastic bottle that they left with her; and some food in two bowls, a little warmed rice in one and a few small pieces of dry chicken in the other, which she consumed ravenously without any taste. She was left alone after that, a whole day it seemed, with the light on and no hood or restraints. She used the bucket herself and tried to sleep on the hard floor or on the chair; occasionally she would rise to walk slowly a few paces around the room. Her basement cell became increasingly hot and stuffy like a sauna and she sweated profusely, which was no less unpleasant than shivering in the cold like before.

She noticed the one peep hole in the middle of the door and looked more carefully around the rest of the room, for cameras or two-way mirrors but found none. The little neon strip above the door was protected behind a mettle grill and the switch must have been outside the room because she could not find one inside. A few hot pipes painted black ran through the room at ceiling height from one side to the other. The steel gantry with its pulley and wheel that she had bumped into was positioned over a rectangular cut out in the concrete floor, and sank a few feet below, but was boarded over like the rectangle in the ceiling above and she imagined there must have been a lift shaft there once upon a time.

She moved her chair to a corner position on the same side as the door, so as to avoid the line of any watcher, and then stripped off her damp and dirty blouse, wiping off the perspiration over her face and chest, before tossing it over the chair. She sat in her black bra, her lower half draped with the sheet; being so naked made her feel even more vulnerable but she needed to cool down. She slept as best she could in the chair with the walls for better support, her head nodding against the rough masonry, or sometimes sitting on the floor with her arms for cushions on the seat of the chair.

The stinging across her shoulders and thighs had not subsided and at times she wanted to scream with the pain. She felt bruised and stiff in so many places. Her eyes were heavy, her head musty, she craved to lie down properly, to rest her head, a soft pillow would be heaven. And as if by magic another Chinese woman she had never seen before came in with the turn of the key, carrying a rug and a blanket, as if answering her dearest wish. Sophie wanted to hug her. She helped her arrange the rug and blanket as a mattress and pillow against one wall and she lay face down with her head supported and her arms folded under her chest for comfort, remembering lonely nights during her childhood, when she would cuddle a soft teddy bear that her father had given her just before he left. A sense of relief coursed through her veins and she was almost asleep and dreaming before the door had been closed and locked again.

* * *

It was after six o'clock and Matthew was waiting for a while at the door, just up one flight from the lobby off the Calle Juan Alameda. It was the busy rush home time and the street noises seemed to have followed him in. A child was screaming along the corridor somewhere wanting its dinner and at the top of the next landing two women with sleeves rolled up were having a conflab and complaining about something in demonstrative Spanish. The apartment block, like Sophie's, was white-washed, clean and utilitarian, certainly not luxury, and was long and narrow, about six or seven floors, with balconies heaving with plants and greenery. Liz was on the first floor and her front door opened straight from the landing, where lots of sunny light poured in and geraniums by the balustrade flourished in terracotta pots. There were the usual strong smells of cooking and garlic.

The door was opened by a tallish blonde woman with a nice tan and stunning blue eyes, who peered suspiciously around at Matthew, who introduced himself and apologised immediately for disturbing her. Without any make-up, her hair unkempt and dark lines around her eyes, she looked a touch gaunt, but Matthew saw how attractive she was. She wore a shirt and jeans and was in bare feet.

'I am a friend of Sophie Patek's, we spoke earlier on the phone?'

'Oh, gosh. You've caught me…' and she ran her fingers through the swathes of thick untidy hair.

'Sorry.'

'Erm, you are…'

'I'm Matthew Crawford, Sophie's father, erm, friend of her mother's, actually. From London.'

'Of course, of course, come in.'

Matthew looked anguished that he had tripped himself up and revealed the truth to a complete stranger, like something private had just dropped out of a pocket on to the floor for all to see, although Liz gave no indication of recognising what he had said. With a glance up at the two chattering women on the landing above, who were staring down at them, she invited him in and said she'd put the coffee on. 'I am looking for her, wondering if you might have heard from her or know where she is,' he continued following her into the hallway. 'Alex Baxwell told me he had not seen her for a while as well and was worried and he gave me your address, I hope you don't mind.'

'You go in there and sit yourself down, help yourself to a drink and I won't be a minute.' Matthew was directed into a bright sitting room, with views over the road to other apartment blocks and rows of small shops, a French window open onto the outside balcony at the front and a nice cool breeze drifting in carrying the subtle smells of the sea that Matthew so loved. He looked around at the soft furnishings, the colourful rugs, small television on the sideboard, pictures in frames, nothing special. A copy of *El Mundo* lay open on a cushion, with headlines about the English Princess with dozens of photographs depicting the life of Diana Spencer. There was a half empty bottle of Bombay Gin on the side with some glasses and it looked as if Liz had been drinking already: there was an empty glass with melted ice and a sodden piece of lemon at the bottom.

Liz returned after a few minutes with her face on and fresh lipstick and called through the open door that she had coffee and pastries, if he would like. Matthew was staring down at the outside traffic, mesmerised by the random movements of people and cars below at street level, while deep in his own recurring thoughts about how Sophie might react when he told her the truth. They sat at a low settee and although the room seemed overly cluttered and untidy, he was suddenly taken back to Fulham and Stephanie's house with its rugs and old leather sofas and smell of coffee and cake on a tray. Liz had brushed her hair and wore a neat pink top, clean slacks and a pair of silky slip-ons. She had a bottle of white wine in her hand and two glasses that she filled almost to their brims, handing one to Matthew. 'I think I would prefer some alcohol at his stage, wouldn't you?'

She carried a plate of fritters with cream. 'These *pestinos* were from yesterday, but they're still fine, quite creamy, if you like.'

'Sorry to hear about your friend. Mr Baxwell mentioned something about him disappearing and now he has been killed, I understand?' The question came with undisguised concern, sudden worries about Sophie's own safety coursing through his mind. He took a hurried sip of wine and looked across at Liz's face, where anxieties were etched around her eyes, her brows lowered and knitted. Matthew bit into a crispy pastry, tasting the sugary cream inside.

'Yes, Roberto was grabbed off the street a few days ago, and disappeared, it's a long story, but Sophie found out that he had been killed, on Juanito Robicalon's estate. He's a powerful man in Marbella, ex-police chief now Council organiser, has the Mayor in his hands. Roberto had been involved in stealing a car, which was carrying drugs and money from Morocco.'

'Oh, my God, really?' Matthew was horrified.

'He doesn't normally do that sort of thing; this was the

first time, as far as I know,' Liz added quickly, answering Matthew's inner question. 'Typical, it turns out to have been a special consignment for some big people, and they have been pretty angry and I think these gangsters were getting their revenge.' Liz was sipping away at her glass, trying to find courage, he supposed, and then she reached for her pack of cigarettes and flicked a lighter on. 'Have one?'

'No thanks.'

'Sorry.' She blew a line of smoke towards the ceiling. 'Well, this place was turned over on Sunday afternoon when I was out, with Sophie actually, at a Baxwell villa party; they picked the lock or more probably bribed the caretaker to supply a key – it was a bit of a mess inside but they found nothing. I had a store of stuff in a bag behind the freezer, but they didn't find it.'

'Gosh, this is awful. Were you involved then? Was Sophie…?'

'Yes, she was, I'm afraid; she organised it.'

'Oh, dear. That doesn't sound too good, does it? And have you heard from her – I mean since she found out about Roberto?'

'No. We were last together at the Baxwell party at Diamond Heights, on Sunday. She was going to the bull fighting at Mijas on Monday and she phoned me that night to say that JR had invited her to his estate the next day. She promised she would feedback afterwards. She was hoping to find out something of Roberto's whereabouts – which she did, but no one has seen her since.'

'This is a worry. Something must have happened to her – she would have contacted you if she could, surely?'

'Yes, I agree. I last spoke to her on the phone on Monday. Today she should have been at the presentations in Malaga, with Baxwell, but I haven't heard anything.'

'Does Sophie have a boyfriend, or anyone she lives with?'

'No, not properly, that you would call a boyfriend. She and Roberto had it off a few times, I can tell you, but she had other male friends. No commitments, though, that's Sophie.'

Liz looked pleased at her own summary of her friend's character, not giving too much away but generous at the same time, as she took a large bite of her sugary *pestinos*.

'Oh, really?' Matthew was beginning to sound repetitive, as he started to think he might be getting out of his depth. 'She would be especially upset at Roberto's death then?' His pale face looked horrified.

'I mean, she kept it quiet, she didn't flaunt it. But there must have been something there, you know.' Liz was drinking freely now and Matthew wondered whether she was jealous, whether there had been some rivalry between the two, over Roberto perhaps. 'I love Sophie, don't get me wrong, best friend and all that. This was Roberto, seducing her, leading her on. He's married, you know, to Lucy, Luciana. She's a bit of a lump, really, but he was being a naughty boy.'

'So do you think Sophie might be in some sort of trouble?'

'Yes, she could be. Or she's dossed down with another one of her boys. She had an affair with a police inspector a few years ago, as well, they still keep in touch.'

'Ah, that must be Senor Cagigas, Hernandez?'

'Hernandez, yes, precisely.'

'And you have no idea where she might be now?'

'No. I've been tearing my hair out, asking around, ringing around. But I can't go to the police, not about the robbery, it might land Sophie into even more trouble. I need to go see Luciana as well, commiserate, offer her some help.'

Her cigarette was finished and so was her glass. Matthew felt it was time he left and pulled himself up straight, took a deep breath in. Liz jumped in before he could say anything: 'So did you say you were a friend of Sophie's?' Liz stood up slowly, considering pouring herself another glass.

'Well, yes, her mother and I were friends many years ago and I wanted to come out to meet Sophie.' Matthew sounded rather feeble, he thought. 'I had never met her before.'

'What, you have come all this way, from England, from London, to meet someone in the family you had never met before? Oh, you poor man, to find all this aggro. What unfortunate timing!'

'Well, yes, it's just coincidence, really. My daughter was married a few weeks ago, I gave her away, and it got me thinking...about my first daughter, my first daughter was Sophie, nearly thirty years ago and I had never seen her. Felt I ought to, felt I should.'

'Oh wow, you're what, her father? Christ! And does she know this, have you told her?'

'No, not exactly. You're the first person I've told here, actually.' He gave rather an embarrassed laugh.

Liz put her arms up to Matthew's shoulders, spilling some wine down his sleeve, and kissed his cheeks, one after the other. 'And you've arrived in the middle of such a fucking crisis, you poor man. God, what a mess!'

* * *

During later periods of half wakefulness, her mind was tormented by intense feelings of fear, of pain, of humiliation, fear for her life. She would sit up and try to think of Hsui Long Long doing his best for her, before drifting back into a frustrating sense of boredom. She discarded her bra which felt dirty and tight, and wrapped herself in the sheet. Once she was roused from a deep sleep by the Chinese couple who were fussing around her, and she found a bowl of thin soup and a plate of noodles left on the floor next to her. She slurped carelessly from the bowl and sucked in the noodles in her half sleep and drank some more water from her bottle.

The plastic bucket had been emptied and she was alone again with her fears.

She slumped back onto her blanket on the hard floor, exhausted, but so grateful to those women for their help and little acts of kindness, yet all part of the process she imagined. She was awake suddenly when the red-faced angry image of Alex Baxwell came to mind and she remembered about the day of the presentations at the Council Town Hall and that it must have happened, without her. Was that today or later, she did not know whether it was day or night? JR and Baxwell would have been there, Baxwell angry at her absence, no doubt. Plus many other powerful people from the council, from businesses and the public in the galleries, it would have been quite an event; she actually felt sorry to have missed it. She wondered whether Baxwell was celebrating now or looking for Sophie to commiserate with or to strangle. The sum she had shown JR on that piece of paper, claiming it to be Baxwell's bid, was astronomically high, at twelve billion pesetas (about sixty million pounds at the exchange rate at the time), and she would have at least forced JR to beat that level unnecessarily or risk losing the battle, to Baxwell, of all people, which he would have found unthinkable. She warmed to the idea that JR would have had to go into severe debt to fund his bid, which was some sort of revenge, but she knew Baxwell would be apoplectic.

12

Thursday September 4

Sophie could not grasp the true passage of time. She began to feel as if she had been in captivity for a week or more, forever even, but it was probably only two days. At one point she was pacing slowly but steadily around the room and her inner clock was telling her it was daytime and she felt hungry. Later she sunk into a fearful trembling state in a corner wrapped in her sheet, her wounds smarting. She did not know how long she had been crouching there or whether she had slept at all, but sometime when she was helped up by her friends, her bottom was completely numb and the rest of her body so stiff, she cried out when they tried to get her to walk again.

The two women helped her onto the bucket and gave her some water from a bottle, without speaking. This time when they stood her up, they had some clothes for her to put on, a pull-over cotton shirt and loose baggy trousers with a cord to tie at the waist. And a too small pair of slip-on shoes. And Hsui Long Long, her loyal John, appeared soon after, watching her and pitying no doubt her state of helplessness. Silently he came to her on her chair and whispered to her. He talked about an exchange being planned for later tonight after dark, she must not worry. She was uncertain whether she had understood him. She just stared at the old leather jacket he was wearing that was too big for him. His shoes were different too, big laced-up hiking boots she had never seen him wear before. He looked different, ready for some sort of action. Sophie felt confused and was prone to crying. 'What, what you saying, John? Am I going to get free. Back to my friends?'

The women had left, pulling the door closed and John was helping Sophie to practise walking in her unfamiliar attire around the room. She was leaning an arm on his, as he supported her weight, and pleading into his face, smelling him, a cloying mix of weed and soy source. 'So you mean I am being exchanged for the hash? Is that what? Are you going to hand me over to JR, while he gives you the hash consignment?'

'Yes, I sorry. It is best I could do.'

'He will kill me, John, JR will not spare me, he will not trust me to leave him alone. I need to escape. John, you've got to help me. I need to phone, maybe Jamie, he will find a way.' She turned to face him, grabbing his collar with both hands. 'Where is the exchange, John, where will it be?'

'I have told enough, Sophie.' They walked some more, but her legs were stiff and weak and she was trembling with fear, a hollow sickness in the pit of her stomach. They had arrived back at the chair and she collapsed on it, in a heap. But he leaned in towards her and whispered close to her ear again: 'It will be at the stud farm, JR's farm.'

Sophie was shocked, she could not believe it. 'What! Why there? You will be playing into his hands, he has an army of men working for him, he will set a trap, for you.'

She was sounding desperate, she felt desperate; she wanted to run for the door, see if she could make her escape. Hsui Long Long sprang a twisted smile across his face and narrowed his eyes even more as he crouched against Sophie's legs. 'The Magician, he has surprise for JR, don't you worry, ha.'

'Oh, God, Hsui, I *am* worried.'

And then he fished out from the front of his heavy jacket a portable telephone, a chunky Motorolo with a stubby aerial. He also had her shoulder bag. She managed to raise her aching arms around Hsui's neck this time and squeezed him hard with genuine affection, while kissing his cheek: 'Thank you, John, I love you, you have been kind.' He said she had ten minutes, no more, he could not guarantee the reception down there, so make it quick. He stepped out of the door and she heard the key turn. In her bag remarkably were her car keys and her little book of contact numbers.

* * *

Matthew had had a late breakfast, just coffee and lots of it. He had slept poorly during the night, too hot and his mind thinking too many unpleasant thoughts and possibilities concerning Sophie, so he had got up for a drink and then when he returned to bed he slept heavily passed his eight o'clock alarm. He got up needing a shower at half nine. He had read some of the papers in the lobby but returned to his room needing to be close to the telephone. Liz had promised yesterday to ring around friends and to talk to Hernandez, if she could, after visiting that poor Roberto's wife, and she would phone him, she promised, at his hotel later in the morning with any news. 'Let's not get too worried,' she had said, 'I am sure there'll be a simple explanation.'

When the telephone did ring, he was enjoying the sunshine on his face sitting on the balcony reading a Jeffrey Archer novel, and he nearly jumped out of his skin.

It was Liz.

'Sophie has just phoned me,' she shouted down the line, before Matthew had time to finish saying who it was. 'She's in the hands of the Chinese, she said, doesn't know where, she's exhausted and confused, but alright. Poor dear, she was crying. Said something about an exchange tonight, a swap at JR's stud farm, didn't know what time. After dark, she said. The line was awful, I could hardly hear her – then it went dead.'

Liz sounded desperate, but at least she was coherent. 'That Robicalon, the Town Council man. I knew he would be involved, he's evil that man. I would not trust him an inch. Sophie said JR will cut her up if she is given over to him. She said something about Hernandez, leaving a message for him. I didn't really get that.'

'What shall we do?'

'Christ, I don't know, I don't know. We don't know where she is. Right. Stop, think, you silly woman.' Matthew could imagine Liz standing herself upright, pulling her shoulders back, chest out, smacking her own wrist. 'Come on, get yourself together,' she goaded. 'We should get the police. We must go find Hernandez, yes, he'll help. They used to be, you know, lovers once; he'll want to help. He's deputy police chief. But where the fuck do we start to find her, Matthew?'

'Where is the police headquarters?'

'At the top end of the park near me, in Avenue Arias de Velasco.' Liz was speaking in increasingly excited tones. There was no pause. 'Come over here again and we'll go together, it's not far.'

'OK, good idea. I'll come, I'll drive, we may need the car.'

'I'd be happier if you came. Thank you, Matthew. Listen, in the meantime, try and find Bruce, he went to the stud farm with Sophie on Tuesday, so if we have to go out there, he'll know the way. Ring Baxwell, he'll know how to find Bruce. You've got his number?'

'Yes, yes, here. I'll do that, Liz, well done. We'll find her. We will. Give me an hour.'

Matthew stood stricken, his mouth agape, and leant

sideways against the wall for support, with the phone still limp in his hand. What the hell have I walked into here? His beautiful lost daughter kidnapped and her life at risk. 'The Chinese, the bastards,' he said out loud. 'What have they ever done for us?' Matthew felt bewildered. He did not understand about an exchange: who was exchanging what for what? Sophie for money, was that it? And this was Liz's simple explanation?

* * *

For the remainder of what she presumed was the day, Sophie mostly sat forlornly on her chair, staring into the distance, transfixed by anxieties. She wandered around the small enclosure sometimes, trying to get some strength back in her legs, but her reserves seemed to be at rock bottom, so sleep-deprived, hungry and thirsty and so much of her body aching. Her thighs were marked horribly with bright red weals that she was sure would leave scars forever. Images of violence and unpredictable disaster crashed around inside her muddled head, so certain was she that everything would end in tears, if what Hsui said was true and the Chinese were planning some sort of surprise for JR, when almost certainly JR would have set them up for a beating, given half a chance.

After unaccountable hours of relentless and complete silence, during which she was more than ready to cry for mercy and forgiveness, she suddenly heard the key in the lock turn. She whipped round to see the door slowly opening and her two familiar helpers entered ahead of two hefty Chinamen, one the big muscle man with the tattoos who had been the first to beat her up, the second of similar appearance and looks, only slightly smaller, who she had not seen before; they could have been brothers, both lacking much in the way of facial expression, or manners, for that matter.

Sophie flinched at sight of them and backed away but the two women fussed over her, straightening her tunic and trousers, tying the cord tightly and hung her bag round her neck.

Muscle man said: 'Shoes on. We go.'

'I need the bucket, better have wee-wees before we go. Please.' She felt terrified as she moved over to the corner with the two women in attendance and pointed the others towards the door. The two men reluctantly turned away and stomped back after a few minutes. Shoes on and tidied, the men yanked her towards them, one of them taping her wrists together in front of her. 'Oh no, not again,' she pleaded and started to tremble. The black hood was pulled over her head from behind, before she could say anything else, the strings tied loosely around her neck. She shook her head and stamped but was told loudly in her ear to shut up.

She was marched out of the room a little too fast for her exhausted legs to manage, a Chinaman gripping her on either side. She stumbled at the wooden stairs and was half-dragged, half-carried up with several turns, her arrival journey in reverse. They dragged her outside and she felt warmer air fluttering her loose clothes but perceived no daylight through the hood. There were murmured sounds of male voices and she was quickly pushed forward and helped up onto a ledge that clanged as she fell onto it, cold and ridged and she knew she was back in the van again. The two doors were banged shut, crashing one after the other, and she felt enclosed. She was sorry not to say goodbye and thank you to her two minders, who had at least shown her some sympathy. The engine was started and the van rattled and juddered as it manoeuvred its way. She was being thrown about by the sharp movements, the stopping and starting, but there was someone else in the van with her, a man with unfamiliar voice, who grabbed her arm with a harsh grip mumbling under his breath Oriental words of reassurance, before placing her hands on what felt like a wooden bar, that she could hold on to. She gripped tightly, in a half crouching position, and was still trembling and ready to scream or cry, so uncertain she felt of what was to happen.

The space in the van was smelling strongly of diesel fumes and Sophie felt disorientated and uncomfortable. After a short period of time, the ride became a little smoother and faster, the noise of the engine louder, as she imagined the van on a motorway. Despite her state of fear and trepidation, her hunger and her discomfort from the bruises and whip marks and stiff limbs, her eyelids responded to the rhythm and rolling of the vehicle and the droning of its engines by drooping; and surprisingly she dozed against the side panelling of the van on and off, her head uncontrollably lolling from side to side. In the complete darkness and inside the hood she felt hotter and hotter and then there was more lurching and twisting and she had to grip harder again to stay still. She was feeling vaguely sick by the time the vehicle jolted to a stop. She heard raised voices and the van was manoeuvred around and went in reverse, and then stopped with another jolt, the engine switched off. The juddering and body shaking had ceased; silence and stillness for a few precious seconds.

The man inside the van made her stand up and he removed the hood. She was able to stretch almost to her normal height, just having to bow her head slightly. She was in the dark but could make out that the man with her was the smaller of the Chinamen brothers. She started to breathe more easily but still the smell of diesel fumes was overpowering and she couldn't wait to get outside. She was also conscious of the stale smell of her own body. After a while the back doors were opened together. The immediate rush of night air was such a relief that she almost sighed, as she gulped at it while she could.

Outside was blackness, but in the feeble moonlight

she could make out a few Chinese figures in baggy whites standing on a pathway in front of her. She was edged forward towards the opening and stood still on the sill above the back bumper, looking out along a bricked pathway that sloped upwards and was lined with neat white fencing that Sophie recognised. In that instant she wondered if Roberto's body was still rotting in that granary storage building or whether it had been disposed of, and shuddered at the thought. In her mind she began to incline towards the continued protection of her Chinese 'friends' than the complete uncertainty of what otherwise lay ahead in JR's vicious hands. She told herself to breathe and to stay calm.

Suddenly a beam of white light burst out from a high point to her right, and then another to her left, search lights aimed down and along the pathway towards the back of her van and Sophie was centre stage. She was blinded at first and felt awkward in her unfamiliar clothes, embarrassed by her unwashed appearance and disgustingly lank hair.

The Chinese Transit was parked in between the wide open wrought iron gates of the stud farm, reversed into the driveway at the entrance, with a clear escape route to the main road if necessary ahead of them, while fifty yards up the slight incline of JR's nicely paved brick driveway, just at the rim of his bright lights, his armed Spanish team had reversed their van and parked it, with its back doors open facing down the slope. Its position obscured any view she may have had of JR's preposterous fountain beyond; nor could she hear its trickling water spays, although perhaps it was turned off at night. Some shouting between the two sides followed and then two older looking Chinamen in dark suits, white shirts and ties came forward out of the darkness and were lined up below her on the path. As her eyes accustomed themselves more to the light, she could make out the dark figures of two of JR's thugs shining torches into their van and pulling out two soft cases onto the paved ground which they unzipped and then stood aside to allow them to be seen. She recognised their tight black suits and bulging waistlines and their familiar tough bully-boy attitude.

There was more shouting between the two sides across the short divide and then the two suited Chinamen started to edge forward up the inclined pathway, from the Chinese side towards the home side. They wanted to check the merchandise first, Sophie realised and were sending two marijuana experts carrying a traditional set of brass weighing scales to inspect and to report back. A ten-minute delay ensued while they fussed about and fiddled with their equipment, rummaged into both bags on the ground removing packages, placed them on the scales, conferred, and repeated the procedure a few times. In the end, they nodded a lot to each other and towards the watching Chinese, crowded about Sophie's van. The merchandise was satisfactory apparently, so 350kg of the finest Moroccan hashish, worth thirty million pesos on the streets of Marbella (about a hundred and forty thousand pounds, Sophie presumed, but would fetch three times that in London), that had been hidden in the fertiliser bags in the horsebox of the Skoda and which she part-organised to have stolen, was all there in the Spanish van, just waiting. Roberto must have revealed its whereabouts to JR before he died, poor sod. Leaving everything as they had found it, the two Chinese experts slowly shuffled themselves back on their return journey down the incline with their brass scales and soft rubber shoes.

The exchange was imminent: out of the Chinese frying pan into the fire of the Spaniard's revenge.

Sophie was urged to jump down from the Transit, but she could hardly stand, her legs felt wobbly. Suddenly Hsui Long Long appeared from the darkness to help her down onto the driveway. Was she relieved to see him, and there she was thinking that perhaps he had abandoned her? 'John. Don't do this,' she whispered into his face, a look of desperation on her gaunt features, 'JR will cut me down. I need to get away.'

'Come, you come,' he said, trying to force a smile, leading her forward, away from the open doors of the van. She could make out the movement of Chinese men just beyond the reach of the light beams in standing and crouching positions lining themselves along the pathway on both sides, matched she was sure by equally well-prepared armed protection and deterrence activity on the home side. Until the moment they released her into JR's hands and the bags of hashish were safely in Chinese hands, when each side would be satisfied.

What could possibly go wrong?

More shouting and nodding took place, by men that Sophie could not see, but the 'Let's do it,' from the Spanish side was a deep baritone that she recognised belonged to JR himself, hidden in the shadows somewhere but watching her intently, she imagined. And licking his chops too, because she felt certain he was not going to let the Chinese walk away with that stash of hash, even if they had paid him for it: the opportunity to break the Chinese over this would overwhelm his planning.

Two dark shaven-headed Spaniards were now lifting the bags from the ground and were starting to walk down the slope towards the Chinese end at the gates. Hsui pushed Sophie in an uncertain and reluctant walk forward toward them up the incline and the idea seemed to be that the two parties would cross in the middle, where the bags would be handed over to two Chinese men scuttling along behind Sophie and Hsui, and Hsui would hand Sophie over to the two JR henchmen. The two teams would rapidly return to their vehicles with their prizes and depart in opposite directions with haste and no further ado.

Sophie was half-minded to turn and run back to the safety of the Chinese Transit, which at that moment seemed marginally more inviting than the potential of JR's unwanted attention.

At a point where only a few strides separated the two missions, when Sophie's sense of panic was about to reach fever-pitch, thinking for certain that the Chinese had everything to lose and JR everything to gain, and that her God had really deserted her this time and if ever she were called upon to give Him a character reference she would definitely hesitate, she stopped walking and stumbled, her legs crumpling under her in a way that could only be attributed to a sudden sense of wishful thinking, when she thought she picked up the faintest distant sound of squeaking car tyres on the road outside, or was it her desperate and exhausted mind playing tricks with her at this late hour? Hsui bent to hold her up around the waist, to encourage her to stand. Instead, after another faint squeaking of rubber tyres chimed in her ears, nearer than before, she stretched both her arms up around his lightweight neck and allowed her full weight, not that there was much of that, to hang around his less than substantial frame in the hope that both of them would topple onto the pathway, thus delaying for a few more precious moments further progress. The two cropped Spaniards in black suits with their heavy bags of merchandise also stopped, as they eyed the near-by play-acting with obvious suspicion and mentally went through a process of considering the best timing of drawing their own weapons from their bulging hips to fire off a few rounds. Did she just hear the slam of a car door?

A kerfuffle broke out at the gates, loud voices, angry calls, people shoved aside and Sophie distinctly heard an Englishman speaking with authority and saw with true amazement her mother's friend from London, who she had met once (and had completely forgotten about), striding with purpose past the Transit she had been in and up the sloping drive into the bright search-lit area. And equally amazing was the glamorous blonde trying to match the man's stride for stride in her heels, the incomparable and lovely Elizabeth. For a quite bizarre moment Sophie thought she must still be in one of her disturbed sleeps, in a weird dream.

'Excuse me, I am sorry to interrupt the fun, but I am looking for a Miss Sophie Patek,' said the clean-shaven smart Englishman in a confident voice. 'I believe she is here against her will. I am here to take her home.' And indeed it was Matthew Crawford adopting a commanding pose in his neat summer suit and pink striped silk tie, with a hand shielding his eyes against the piercing lights, searching for the man in charge. An astonishing moment of silence that lasted a number of definitive seconds then followed, during which time, nobody and nothing moved. The only sound was the distant hum of the emergency power generators supplying the overhead search lights. Two bald thugs in sombre suits were midstride hauling canvas bags of stolen hashish, a bedraggled Chinese waif with off-putting stringy hair and a pathetic physique was bending over a young woman in baggy pyjamas who was crouching uncomfortably on her knees under him and both were staring wide-eyed at a well-dressed be-suited Englishman with a foppish mane of blond hair and a tanned glamorous companion close behind; all caught in a freeze frame, their sharp-edged black and misshapen shadows picked out across the patterned driveway waiting for somebody to give the signal to move onto the next frame.

A crisp shot rang out and Hsui Long Long's gangly body spun acrobatically away out of Sophie's grip, a spurt of warm blood splashing across Matthew's jacket and blue shirt, and Liz's face. Sophie stared at the twisted heap lying motionless arms akimbo five yards away, his mop of black hair soaked in a spewing dark puddle spreading across those nice paving stones. She clapped her hands onto her astonished face and tried to scream: 'No, no,' but she just could not make a sound, somehow it was all trapped at the back of her throat, tasting of vomit. Liz looked on with astonishment and wiped at her face. Voices were raised, other shots rang out, the two Spaniards retreated backwards uphill as rapidly as they could with their weighty bags and their reaching for their holsters, but each one was pierced simultaneously through the chest with a bone-crunching thud by six-foot-long hemp darts that poked horribly blood-stained through their backs and that sent them unceremoniously to the ground in adjacent piles.

Standing fully exposed in the bright light, turning slowly round and round, Sophie looked for danger or for safety and a way out, somewhere to run to, as sounds of shouting and shooting and of men grunting in pain filled her head. She could hear truck engines revving, doors slamming and the metallic crunch of vehicles colliding. She felt dizzy and sickly. She kept seeing shocked faces turning in confusion and indecision. Her horrified eyes were obscured by streaming tears. Suddenly the lights faded out; the instinct to start running overwhelmed her, but she could not make out a secure path. She twisted this way and that, still in her malicious nightmare re-enacting her escape, cut short by strong arms clamping around her ankles and pulling her head under a faeces-stained blanket to suffocate her in the foul smell. Someone up the slope urgently called her name, a deep baritone voice. She saw the blue and yellow lights of police flashing down the pathway and commands rang out as a buzzing engine sound overhead added to the noise. Armed men in bulky black outfits were crouching in formation in the shadows, swarming up the drive and taking up kneeling positions at intervals, heavy machine guns at the shoulder and night vision sights flashing dot-sized red markers around the crowded scene.

Somebody guided Sophie away, a hand firmly keeping her head down and she heard Liz calling her to run and then it was Bruce with a protective arm around her, his hand under her armpit to lift her clear as her tired legs failed her. She floated above the cacophony of crazy noise on saving wings, cushioned from the mayhem of gunshots and falling bodies towards the high-pitched electric screech of the sirens that nearly split her ears. They stumbled past the Transit van which was rammed into the side of an empty patrol car, its windscreen shattered, a wounded man hanging head-first out of an open side-door. Her one-time swarthy lover, the implacable deputy police chief, Hernandez de Cagigas, was running the show with impressive command and she reached out a hand to his cheek as they passed and he called; '*Rapidamente*, go, take care.'

As they hurried through a *Policia* cordon, past three armoured vans and two further patrol cars, there was a heaving and forceful suction of the night air as a nearby explosion threw coloured flames and smoke into the sky, reverberating late with an impressive thump. Sophie looked back towards the estate, over the outer walls, seeing bursts of black smoke billowing upwards beyond the woods as they reached Matthew Crawford's hire car further up the road.

Through the darkness of the night, they bounced and twisted back to the coast road, Matthew driving with studied concentration and Liz next to him quietly giving him the occasional direction. In the back Bruce remained silent, stroking her hair, as Sophie slipped down across his lap with her eyes closed, unable to wipe the sights of Hsui Long Long's head burst open and Roberto's broken body from playing weird patterns across her troubled mind or to prevent herself weeping in periodic spasms, leaving wet patches on his new trousers.

Matthew pulled up at Sophie's block for Liz and Bruce to dash up to her flat to collect a few things: some clothes, Liz knew what would be essential, and a handful of jewellery, and her British and Spanish passports, all packed into a travelling case. Bruce went up to the top floor and pulled down the attic ladder to scamper up and put his head through into the loft, and under instruction, remove the remaining Baxwell bribe money in Spanish pesetos. Sadly, the bag with JR's five hundred thousand dollars was best left behind.

Once more on the road, Matthew called out quietly: 'Say goodbye to the Golden Mile and the Costa del Sol, everyone,' as he headed for Malaga and the port.

'Where are we going?' sleepy Sophie asked from the back seat.

'Away from here, Sophie darling, for the last time.' Liz was looking back at her friend, with relief and something close to love. The forty-two minute drive through to Malaga east along the coast road, was uneventful, only sparse traffic and no police cars or other interruptions to worry them.

Just before they arrived at the docks, Liz leant over from the front seat and touched Sophie's shoulder. 'Are you all right, little one?'

Sophie had fallen asleep again and just managed to open her eyes, looking at the pretty figure of her friend, her blond hair splayed out in a thick bunch, caught like a flashing halo in the intermittent background street lighting. 'I am now. I was so scared.' She whimpered. 'I thought you might not come. In time.'

'Hernandez, he's a good man. We must thank him, somehow.' And then as they joined a short queue of stationary cars and trucks waiting to board the most unprepossessing of ferries, *La Dignidad d'Espana*, bound at one am for the southern Spanish islands, Liz again turned round. 'And your... Matthew here has been an absolute treasure and booked ferry tickets for us to Majorca and then we fly to London via Paris, first thing tomorrow. We can do your hair and shower at the airport and tidy up then. It will be for the best. It's what you wanted.' Sophie heard her distant words of comfort only vaguely as she drifted in and out of sleep cradled in the safety of Bruce's gentleness.

At the dockside, while they awaited the formalities, Sophie had woken for long enough to want to stretch her stiffening legs and she moved tentatively away over the vast reaches of sea-sprayed tarmac. She was wearing a big jumper that Liz had brought and a waterproof, eyeing the turbulent skies overhead and staring out over the watery blackness ahead. A thunderous downpour of rain looked imminent. Howling winds were rattling the flagpoles and the salty tasting air made her lips sting. Standing close by, Bruce edged closer toward her and then reached for her round the waist. He held her close for a moment, bending his great head down, landing a kiss tenderly on a wet cheek while wishing her well. Then he ambled away, with his colourful suitcase on wheels and a backpack, and when he reached the metal barriers at the far exit a hundred yards away, he turned and waved to her. He said he would find a room for the night and then return to Marbella tomorrow. He needed to go back to his home in Morocco where he had responsibilities to his family and that he would not fit in, in England or Spain or anywhere else Sophie might want to travel. Sophie had smiled and said she understood, but was unable to hide her heavy sense of disappointment.

Later on board, the three of them shared some coffee and a sandwich in a dimly-lit canteen with a low ceiling and blackened windows all around in which their decrepit appearances were reflected back at them. The sea and the wind were thrashing against the glass at the bow and the boat was heaving fairly generously, but Sophie was hungry and thirsty and tucked into her bread and hot drink with enthusiasm. She kept her hood up to shield her face from prying eyes. Liz touched her scabbed forehead and noticed her swollen jaw and cracked lips. Sophie looked shocked, her eyes having a vacant look. She wanted to lie down, her head felt heavy, but on the other hand the dawning realisation that her previous nightmares were over, that she was in safe hands, and that she had gained some moments of sleep in the car, all seemed to give her a stimulus to stay awake. Plus, the stomach-churning lurching of the ferry as it fought its way through a north Mediterranean storm would have prevented her anyway from getting any rest.

Sophie looked directly into Liz's eyes, as if to ask whether she looked too bad. 'We'll have a good clear up in the airport,' she reassured her friend kindly. 'Matthew was the real hero today, Sophes,' Liz was explaining in her quiet perfect English. 'He shepherded me around, found Bruce, took us to Hernandez and helped plan the rescue, which has delivered two vicious gangs of drug dealers to the police all in one go.' And she finished with a big smile while Sophie concentrated on watching every movement of her friend's lips to grasp all that she was saying. 'Most important of all, we have you back safely.'

Matthew, with Hsui Long Long's dried blood still stained across his jacket despite his attempts in the toilets to wipe it clean, was sitting back, his hands on the table, contemplating the reality of his daughter and her beauty, reliving his own frightening memories of how close they had been to losing her.

'Matthew was telling me something very interesting about you two.' Liz sipped at her coffee with a twinkle in her eye, looking across at Matthew.

'Was I?' he prevaricated, uneasily. 'I'm not sure now is the time really.'

'Oh, I'm sure it is as good as any other, given the various shocks and surprises we have all had in the last few days. Another one won't be so bad – anyway this is nice news.' Liz pulled Sophie close to her with an arm round her shoulders for comfort and Sophie looked innocently from one to the other. 'What are you two talking about?'

Matthew swallowed hard. He had to raise his voice to be properly heard against the background clatter of the staff behind the counter, the wind rush outside and the surrounding engine growl. 'I was telling Liz why I had come out to Marbella. Why I wanted to meet with you. About when your mother and I had been good friends, years ago as teenagers. Back in the Sixties.'

Sophie interrupted him, 'You told me, you were her boyfriend for a while.'

'Yes, but I did not get to the best bit. How Stephanie had got pregnant; how she had to return to Switzerland with her parents. I was banned from seeing her again by her mother, so I never saw her baby. She had a baby girl, born on the sixth of May, 1968.' Sophie glanced up with her brows deeply knitted and caught the slight glisten of moisture in Matthew's eyes, but he dipped his head to hide his emotion and she could only look at his hair flopping over his forehead.

But then he leant forward on his elbows and had the confidence to look directly at Sophie's damaged face, with its bruises and scabbed patches. 'And I had never met that girl, and I felt a strong desire recently to meet her – that woman. When my other daughter was getting married.'

It was as if Sophie's eyes had just been switched on: their cloudiness seemed to fade, focus returned as they enlarged and came alive; in complete surprise or a dawning realisation, Matthew was not sure. Their colour deepened, hardened, and they were the exact same shade of navy blue as Matthew's. But then signs of growing panic appeared, as she looked from Matthew to Liz, to Matthew and back to Liz again, with a knitted brow, as if to ask her whether she knew what Matthew was talking about. Then her eyes drifted off to the middle distance across the canteen, as if something far away had caught her attention, and slowly she forced herself up onto her tired legs, using her hands to push up from the table, and she pattered away to a side-door, which led out onto a wet and windswept deck, where she stood heroically hanging on to the railing, overlooking the crashing seas below, a ridiculous figure, bedraggled in baggy trousers and a plastic waterproof. She liked the cold feel of the wet spray across her face. She stared out at the dark void of endless black sky and turbulent sea, fascinated by the way the vessel rode the swell of the ocean, the rise and the fall. Normally rough seas and extreme movements would make her feel sick, especially had she stayed in the stuffy hold, but out there, standing defiant against the elements, the wild freshness of the salty wind thrashing against her complexion, she felt awake and knew that she would come through.

That Matthew Crawford had probably saved her life, she was in no doubt. He had appeared suddenly, unasked at the very moment of crisis in her life and assumed the brave role of white knight. He had taken an exceptional interest in her welfare and now she knew why. But was that possible? Not Georgio, the father she had been brought up with, at least for a few early years before he left, the man her mother had treated as her father, without another word of anyone else. Would her mother not have told her something about this before now? Was her break from her mother so severe, or was the break just a symptom of their loose relationship. They had not shared much affection to be honest, over the last few years. She had been travelling her own road, hustling here and there, getting on with life as best she could, thinking she knew who she was and where she stood in her world. Then she screws everything up with Roberto for the sake of her greed, when all of a sudden, out of the blue, comes a handsome sophisticated man on his white charger to save her. And to tell her that he, not the affectionate Georgio of all those years, but that he was her real father?

Maybe that explained her uncommitted life, never to settle for too long in any one place, to keep moving, meeting different people, keeping the predatory males at arm's length. This was a pattern of behaviour of someone insecure in the world, uncertain of her place.

Like with Jamie. Or Roberto. Heavens, was she ever going to want to settle down with any man? How was she supposed to react to this news, what was Matthew Crawford expecting? She knew nothing about him. She needed to talk to her mother, to get some clarification, confirmation, reassurance, to hear her point of view. Still bombarded by images of flies buzzing around Roberto's lifeless face, of Hsui Long Long's head ripped apart, tormented by grief and guilt, she blinked desperately to clear her vision. Knowing that her sobbing sounds and wet tears would be lost in the wind and spray, her wretchedness disguised by the storm brewing around her, she felt uninhibited. Suddenly she wanted to cry and wanted her mother.

After an interval, leaving her alone to think her own thoughts, Matthew stepped outside to find her and went to lean over the wet railings as well, standing beside her, gripping on tight. He had no coat or wet protection and he felt the cold. 'I'm so sorry, Sophie, I did not want to spring this on you. But it is true, I am your father.' He had to really raise his voice out there, almost to shout into her face to make himself heard. 'Not that I want to take anything away. I didn't want to interfere, I just wanted the chance to get to know you. And then I walked into this turmoil; I don't know how you got yourself into such a mess, but I will help you any way that I can, obviously.' He tailed off, not sure where the conversation should go. After a minute, during which they both stood as still as the shifting deck allowed, staring at the churning waters below them, Sophie turned to Matthew with a pleading look, her eyes and mouth reacting with a sort of bemused confusion. 'I need help,' she sobbed, but it was lost in the wind. She wiped the fingers of one hand severely across her eyes, trying to clear her vision of spray and tears, still gripping on to the railing with the other, and moved nearer, to close the gap between them. She tilted her head against his nearest shoulder. She had a view of the tormented sea below and watched a group of gulls being carried up in the swirl and whipped back high over the rigging, landing some way back in the ship's wake, she supposed, snagging their catches as best they could.

She shouted loudly into Matthew's neck. 'You saved my life, Matthew, you were so brave. I am so grateful. If you are my real father, that is the most amazing thing I have ever heard.' Matthew heard her words, or nonetheless understood the sentiment of them and hugged her. And she could no longer hold back the heaving of her chest, the uncontrollable sobs, her nightmare, her fears, her relief and her exhaustion all combining to break down any internal control of her feelings that she possessed. 'I love you,' she whispered.

Dead Ending

1997-July 2007

1

One thing Matthew Crawford had promised himself, shortly after that questionable speech at Annabel's wedding, when he had revealed to one and all that he had had a first love in Stephanie Patek at the age of seventeen and that she had had a daughter by him and that he was determined to find her; and that was, that he would never want to make another family speech quite like that again. Not any time soon.

He had gone on to find his Sophie and what a revelation she turned out to be: feisty, single-minded and clever. A natural beauty, a woman any father would have been proud of. But she was seldom far from trouble, it turned out. She had revealed to Matthew only in the briefest of outline some of her activities in London before she had decamped to the Costa del Sol, and had painted a picture of hard work and fun in southern Spain, only occasionally referring to some less salubrious aspects, but Matthew invariably interpreted anything that Sophie confessed, especially if it showed her up in a less than favourable light, as being her poor luck, more about being in the wrong place at the wrong time. He would never accept that she was willfully dishonest or had planned to make extra money through theft and deceit, these were traits forced on her by events or by some of the company she kept. Being influenced by the wrong sort of people, like that character Roberto she talked about with sorrow and some affection; could happen to anyone.

Like two recovered trophies following a foreign campaign, Matthew returned from Spain rather earlier than planned with Sophie and Elizabeth, to settle back into a routine of working life as best he could. Looking back over the last decade, following his bold rescue of his long-lost daughter, he wondered many times whether there was anything else he could have done, the family could have done, to prevent or prepare for the disaster that ultimately befell his lovely Sophie.

Matthew and Sophie had sat together on the half-empty early morning flight to Paris from Majorca during which he painstakingly repeated his story for her to digest, explaining how he and Stephanie had fallen in love during a short interval at school in the summer of 1967, and how she had been forced to go back to Switzerland with her family, where she had her baby; and just after, married Geogio. And how Sophie had been brought up there in Zurich for her first few years. 'Your mother was feeling guilty, I think, that she had never told you any of this before, but she did what she thought was best for you. She knew she would never see me again. She wanted you to have a good relationship with Georgio. But unfortunately they divorced after four or five years, you were quite young. And she brought you to England. And then I popped up at her house from nowhere after thirty years – and we discovered that we had been living within a few miles of each other, actually for about the last ten years or something.' They both had been amused by that.

Sophie, now washed and a little cleaner, in jeans and blouse, had drifted in and out of sleep with her head lolling against his shoulder, dreaming of the two Chinese women dressing her in those ridiculous baggy underpants and pyjamas. After their in-flight breakfasts, she had been able to describe some of her experience in captivity and the torture she had suffered. She had rolled back her sleeves to show Matthew the skin abrasions around her wrists and the cuts on her palms. Matthew had related his visit to Marbella, how he had followed her around the town, always one step behind her.

Matthew could recall how she had laughed and apologized. 'I wish I had met you earlier in my life,' he remembered her saying.

She had described to him her two Chinese minders who had shown her some kindness. 'I felt they were concerned for me, but they did not speak English so I couldn't find out anything from them. I was so scared, in the dark for hours, not knowing what was coming next. I was confused about time, it felt like I had been there forever.' She had a look close to panic as she relived some of the details for him. 'And then all that shooting; the noise and the chaos, it all seems such a wild dream. Poor John, Hsui Long Long – I've known him for a few years, we worked together, we learnt about street life together. He had always been good to me.'

'He deserved better than a bullet through the brain.'

Sophie had started to shiver with the memories and then she said she just wanted to sleep and sleep and wake up much later to find all that nastiness had gone. Matthew had reassured her that they would go straight to her mother's in Fulham, where she could sleep in nice clean sheets for as long as she wanted, and she had nodded like a little girl, which was how he had begun to think of her, his little girl.

'Don't worry, Sophie,' Matthew had reassured her, 'the memories will soon fade. You're safe now.'

A week after returning to England, with Sophie moving into her mother's house, Matthew was invited round to

Fulham for a meal. It was only the second time he had seen Stephanie and Sophie since his return. Richard was there in the kitchen wearing a blue and white striped apron, oddly doing the cooking, a steaming bowl of stew on the hob. There were some wine bottles opened in the lounge. It was a balmy evening, mid-September and everyone was relaxed.

And Sophie looked so much brighter, rather as she did when Matthew had first caught sight of her outside the big show villa, when she brushed so hurriedly passed him. Her hair was wonderfully gelled and spiked, her eyes painted in orange and navy blue, her cheekbones softened by an array of autumn colours; her lips pastel peach, her nails a match. She wore a tight fitting cream skirt and a slinky green patterned blouse, and Matthew thought she looked irresistible. She was moving with freedom, she seemed more confident and she was obviously comfortable in her mother's house. When she stood close to Stephanie the likeness of mother and daughter struck home powerfully – the same hair colour and slightly olive skin, the high cheekbones and narrow mouths, with their unique twists and curves along the upper lips and their husky voices – and when they smiled the little wrinkled lines that appeared along their noses were identical.

Sophie hugged him with affection at the door, clearly pleased to see him. To her, Matthew was the man who turned up in the nick of time to intervene brilliantly, leaving the villains in the hands of the *guardia,* saving her from the vicious Chinese on the one hand and the indescribable Robicalon on the other. Her hero. Not forgetting the role of Hernandez, of course, pitching up with the cavalry with perfect timing.

Sophie rather fussed around Matthew, treating him more as a long-lost uncle, with whom you might joke and fool around, rather than her father, but she would come round and get used to the new facts. 'So how are you settling in,

Sophie?' They were in close discussion on a settee together. 'So different from life in Marbella, eh?'

'Sure. Oh, sure, you would not believe. I cannot believe I am here sometimes.' And she raised her eyes to the roof and did a little dance before taking up a cigarette that was smouldering on a nearby ashtray and sucking deeply. 'I feel I am in a dream still. A few days ago I was trapped and stuffed in a dark cellar, not knowing what was going to happen, and then all that shooting and screaming, and suddenly I am running and dashing in a car and then I'm on a boat in a storm with all that sea spray; and then we are on a plane, for hours and moving through airports and onto another plane, and then finally a car brings us to Fulham – and my lovely mother.' She waved her hands about to illustrate the chaos of it all. 'It's all such a dream,' she laughed. Stephanie smiled too and Matthew noticed how the two looked at each other with affection. Some of Sophie's infectious bounce and energy was playing off others, which was good, and Stephanie looked definitely happier as well. Matthew remained uncertain how Richard fitted in exactly.

They continued to chat and share experiences and Sophie filled in with some more news. 'I have spoken to Liz. She is staying with friends in Stanmore and she sends her love, by the way. I spoke to Alex Baxwell on the phone two days ago. I rang him at the office. It was weird. But he told me that life was going on, even if he had lost a great deal of money over the events. He was sorry about Roberto. He said they have not found his body or arrested anyone for his murder. The police are investigating, Mayor Nestor is suspended. He thinks JR will be arrested any day now.'

'What about that development project that was so important?'

'Well, the East Shoreline Project – he said it was not awarded, as the Mayor's office were investigating irregularities in the process, and then the whole thing was cancelled. Baxwell sounded furious but at least he has his business. He will carry on just as before.'

Sophie raised her hand over her mouth, her eyes suddenly welling up, her face crumpling. 'I can't forget Roberto's face and all that shit – the smell.' Matthew took her hand and gently pulled her closer. 'And then poor John, he was doing his best. He did not deserve that.'

'I know, he was a good friend, from what you have told me. Poor boy. And it's a shame Bruce could not come with us, I think he was a good bloke, really.'

'He was, except it was Bruce that betrayed us to JR originally. I mean he didn't mean to, but I forgave him; he wanted to change sides once he saw what sort of a man JR was.'

'This JR sounds like a monster,' Stephanie cut in, sounding incredulous and finding some tissues for Sophie. Sophie and Matthew were nodding. 'What will happen now, over there, do you think?' Sophie used the tip of a little finger to poke and smear along her lower eyelid, hoping to dab away a tear without smudging the mascara.

'Hernandez arrived just as the Chinese were killing JR's men,' Matthew said. 'So the *guardia* prevented a slaughter. That explosion we heard was a storeroom, the old granary building that was stuffed full of hidden hashish cakes and contraband, blown up and destroyed by charges set by the Chinese. At least that is what was in the papers yesterday; details were slim. The Magician, he was the head honcho Chinese man, he was arrested two days ago. Hopefully JR and the others will be charged pending further investigations, which will probably take ages.'

'Come and sit down everybody,' Richard called out on arriving with his heavy bowl of steaming goulash. 'Supper is served.'

Later in the evening when they were finishing a lovely coffee tiramisu, and were relaxed with the wine and warm conversation, Sophie whispered to Matthew. 'I worry that they will catch up with me, somehow, sometime.' And she tried to stop her trembling by hugging herself tightly, before drawing heavily on another cigarette. Again Matthew comforted her with an arm around her shoulders. 'You're fine here, nobody knows you're here. You're safe, Sophie.'

How much did Matthew come to regret those words?

A few weeks after Matthew's triumphant return to England, several guests were invited to his Chiswick house for an afternoon of quiet welcome, so that Matthew's newly-discovered and long-lost daughter could have the chance to meet some other members of his family and *vice versa*. Annabel and Douglas were there, so were Roger and Alison, and Matthew's sister, Jennifer, whom he rarely saw, some other friends of Matthew's including Maurice and Pauline of course, and they had even managed to get his mother Minnie down from Welwyn to join them for tea on the lawn, the weather being kind to them even in mid-October. Annabel was at first reticent, her role as first-born daughter usurped by another late in life not easy to accept; but Matthew soon observed how she was drawn into Sophie's cheery approach and attractive personality, and her generosity shone through, soon making arrangements for some Christmas shopping together in town later in the year. Sophie became the centre of attention, narrating tales of life on the Costa del Sol among the wealthy celebrities, the bawdy late night parties, working for seedy estate agents, and being serenaded by the unscrupulous twister Juan Robicalon, now preparing for his incarceration in a Malaga jail while awaiting trial, not forgetting the wandering hands of Mayor Nestor. Her audience were fascinated and intrigued, but Sophie wisely kept some distance from the absolute truth.

Stephanie came without Richard, Matthew was pleased to see, and they all made their own introductions and drank and ate with measured politeness, while Matthew and Stephanie shared some private moments in his study. The window onto the garden was open and they could hear the quiet mumblings of the guests outside and everyone seemed to be getting on fine, which was what civilized people did.

'I've had this photo of you on my desk for many years now, I really should have a more up-to-date one.' He handed the frame across and Stephanie reached for a small pair of gold-framed glasses to see the picture properly.

'My word, I remember when that was taken.' She laughed.

'Sophie seems to be settled in.'

'Yes, but she's restless. She has met up with some chap she used to know. She wants to get a job and move to a place of her own.'

'Is there anything I can do? Money, or anything?'

'She's trying to get her money from her account at the Bank de Sol in Marbella; her account there is quite full she says.'

Later Matthew saw some role reversal as Roger related his many stories of student life and Sophie became a keen listener, during which they laughed easily together, with Alison frequently butting in jealously. Stephanie and Annabel had been in deep conversation about Annabel's mother, as well as wanting to hear about her wedding and honeymoon holiday. Annabel confided in her father at a later date how she found Stephanie to be so elegant and she loved the way she dressed, quietly displaying her obvious beauty; and Matthew came to understand that she liked her and that respect between them was growing.

Matthew was determined to stick to his promise, the one about wedding speeches. Unexpectedly on a Sunday just after the New Millennium Year celebrations, when he was dozing quietly in his study, a coal fire burning itself out at his feet, Roger had phoned him to tell him that he and Alison had finally decided to take the plunge and get married. Something to do with Alison being pregnant, Matthew came to realize. Normally it would be the bride's father that would give his daughter away and make the appropriate clichéd speech. Except that Ronald Blunt was long dead, a frightening spell of depression that had ended tragically when Alison, poor dear, was only a young teenager. So Roger had gallantly suggested that Matthew would be the perfect substitute. Matthew immediately suggested someone more along the lines of senior family member on the male side such as Uncle Frederick.

Alison was an attractive girl, intelligent, rather single-minded, a bit pushy for Roger, perhaps but Roger seemed to be delighted with the idea. Alison was going to have a baby, so marriage seemed the obvious direction. They had known each other for a few years, indeed had been living together for ages, although Roger was still apt to appear naïve about women. Maybe fatherhood would change all that. No more late nights on the town with the boys or all-day trips to Twickenham for rugby internationals with pub crawls home, or weekends away shooting in the Highlands. Roger was a big boy, quite capable of assessing their own suitability for each other. Annabel told Matthew over the phone that she rather approved, she thought Ali was a steadying influence on her sometimes wayward brother.

Matthew replaced the phone on its cradle with feelings of warmth for his children. They were both interesting and intelligent and so full of life. Annabel was the sensible one, steady and loyal, but Roger was perfectly capable of emulating those characteristics if he put his mind to it, and so maybe this was a defining moment for him. Matthew meanwhile was going through one of those periods of low mood he had experienced lately, when everything slowed down, and the desire to do anything waned. He had found himself at weekends often just sitting in his armchair, staring out into the garden, or reading a book under the glow of a lamp in the evenings. He always felt buoyed by listening to Annabel, her natural cheeriness was infectious. Three years had passed since her wedding and she and Douglas had had two children in quick time, so Matthew was well used to the Granddad idea. He had taught himself to list carefully birthdays and other important family landmarks in his diary so that he could take his senior responsibilities seriously. He sometimes drove up to Yorkshire for a weekend with them, and they would ramble over some remote Dale or trample around Harrogate, before ending up at Betty's for tea and cake. A family wedding in the autumn of 2000 would be an event to enjoy, and he was sure he would manage to get Stephanie along with Sophie, successfully bringing them on board.

Alison had been in teacher-training for a while but was then working for a well-known publisher in London, with unquestioned ambitions for her career which she might have to temper a little with an offspring in tow. And Roger might find himself heavily involved in domestic duties so that she could work near full-time. That would be good for him, Matthew had thought.

He looked at the framed photo of Stepanie Patek, the gangly teenager, that still had its place on his desk, and thought for the umpteenth time how he should have obtained a more up-to-date picture by now. Feelings of desire, of need for someone to share his life with, to give it some new purpose, still nagged him.

The wedding of Roger Crawford and Alison Blunt took

place on a damp Saturday in May in south-west London,
near the deer park in Richmond, at St. Marks Church on
Ham Road and afterwards in a small hotel for the reception
and sit-down lunch. There had been quite a gathering of
old folks and young upstarts, to enjoy the speeches and he
was glad he was not involved in any of them. Matthew was
polite to everybody, even the crowd from Roger's university
days, who dominated the conversation at his table with
dull and predictable talk, mostly from the world of law and
accountancy. He moved places for the dessert to be nearer
Bel, who had left her two little girls for the afternoon with
a friend nearby so they could enjoy the occasion more freely,
and she was happy to chat about her job and how Douglas
had just returned from West Africa and was looking for a
more permanent UK appointment.

He would have had more fun had Sophie been there, but
she had apologized at the last minute, busy with her new
work, as the house manager of an up-and-coming boutique
hotel in Camden Town. Matthew felt disappointed that he
had not actually heard from Sophie for a few months, but
some chap had appeared on her horizon apparently whom
she liked and they were going out.

Sadly, Alison lost her baby early on with a miscarriage and
had never fallen pregnant again. Which might have been
one of the reasons that after just three years the couple
divorced. Matthew was saddened, although not too surprised,
as, unlike Annabel, he felt they had little in common and
Roger's wayward spirit had not dampened any, nor Alison's
career ambitions lessened any. They had simply drifted apart,
although, Matthew learned later, Alison had found someone
else in the media industry who worshipped her and had
effectively prized her away.

After so many years Matthew still had the problem of acceptance, Roger supposed. Since losing Rachel, he had never really readjusted sufficiently to find complete happiness. He had friendships among other women but had not found someone he could spend more of his life with and he remained closed and private. Despite new projects and challenges with change of Governments and funding upheavals, he found himself unable to throw himself fully into something, scared of displaying any weakness that he might be prone to, not having Rachel by his side; he still spoke to her, but she was not there to bolster him as she once did. By the turn of the year 2007, University funding was being squeezed, even more than usual, and he found himself thinking more about retirement, as he was sure he lacked the necessary vigour for the greater strife that he foresaw lay ahead.

Apathy and boredom were beginning to creep up on him, compounded by a sense of loneliness, so retirement both attracted and frightened him. He wanted to write and travel, although he was not sure what about or where particularly. Historic essays perhaps with visits to Peru and inner China, commenting on little known civilizations from the past. Retirement from the university would give him the time to do those sorts of things, but would there be any joy in doing them on his own? What he craved more than anything was a confidante, a travelling companion, to share his experiences with.

Secretly he still wondered whether Stephanie would ever become more of a friend. Richard, who was some years older than her and an intellectual type with his head always buried in papers and heavy reference books, with his steel wired glasses perched along his nose, seemed happy living with her. Matthew was never clear what exactly he was involved with. He travelled a bit and was not always around, but when Matthew saw them together, they had the outward appearance of a loyal and comfortable couple. Matthew dared not ask her directly what was happening, but he still found her to be such an attractive alluring woman, with her reserved elegance. And whenever he was close by her, so many of those aching memories of that wonderful summer would flood back.

Just before Christmas 2006, Matthew was invited to Stephanie's for a party and there was Sophie with a handsome black guy called Rufus, a couple of her neighbours and a work colleague and her sister, Daphne, now hugely overweight, and with Jonathan from all those years ago, but no Richard.

After a fun evening catching up and sharing family stories, Daphne particularly being in good form, Matthew was able to whisper to her out of Stephanie's hearing: 'Do you know what's happened to Richard?'

She did not hesitate. 'Gone, darling, her Majesty had had enough. Out he went, a couple of months now I think. For the best,' she wrinkled her nose and nodded, and then stabbed him in the ribs with an elbow. 'Maybe Matthew's time is yet to come.' She winked and roared with laughter as Stephanie returned with a tray and immediately asked, 'What's so funny?'

'Oh, just reminiscing, little sister.'

Matthew felt suddenly elated, his senses picking up a variety of messages, and however unrealistic his thoughts about a reunion, he was still optimistic that he might make a breakthrough one day. He was hoping that Sophie might help him. He needed her to be on his side. They got on together all right, talking as adults and she still called him Matthew rather than Dad, but as the years had passed they did not see much of each other, naturally, with Sophie developing her own life, her own friends, even picking up with some of her old acquaintances from earlier years.

'The hotel job is a big one for me, I have to manage a few people front of house and I have some budgetary responsibilities,' Sophie explained to him once when he asked her. She was doing well though, it would appear, and perhaps had found her niche.

By Spring 2007, Matthew had started to settle reluctantly into a new and unusual retirement mode and a slower pattern to life, as he continued to do things with his circle of like-minded late-middle-aged friends. He and Stephanie had been out together, to the West End theatre and a private showing at the Royal Academy and a few private dinners and were comfortable in each other's company, which pleased Matthew but he had remained slow at making any other type of approach.

He found he was more prone to tears these days. Even sad news on the TV, a disaster perhaps, a moving play on the radio or someone they all knew well passing away, he was apt to brim over, needing a small wipe of his nose to recover. If he ever thought of Rachel, and he thought of her a lot, he was liable to need to sit down – quietly on his own and stare out into the garden imagining her there deadheading the rosebushes, or to take a walk along the river tow-path at the Strand-on-the-Green and stare forlornly at the passing Thames. Even at low tide when the smell from the flotsam on the exposed riverbed gave hints of sewage, his love for the site and his ability to commune deep within the recesses of his mind with his long-missed life-partner, his lovely Rachel, dead now these past twenty years, were not dampened.

2

Now we are at the start of a damp English summer and it's 2007, ten years since Matthew returned from the Costa del Sol with his rescued little girl in tow. It will be Sophie's birthday in a few days' time and plans for a party have been made. She will be forty and Matthew can hardly believe it. Coming downstairs almost at first light, he wonders what had woken him. Checking his watch, he sees it is barely six o'clock. Empty bags are piled in the hall for today's shopping venture and he notices a small brown envelope on the tiled floor by the front door. There is no longer a cat to rub around his ankles and he concludes it was the guard flap on his letter box that thumped and must have disturbed him.

In the kitchen he switches the kettle on for a cup of tea, having decided that he is awake and unlikely to return to bed. Perched on a bar stool, he looks at the rather crumpled envelope, with his name in hand-written large letters across the middle, no address, with Matthew spelt with only one 't'. He is curious and opens the envelope with a knife cutting along the top. Inside is a folded white sheet of lined note-paper. On opening it, he sees a lot more of the same large handwriting in biro, a little smudged in places and not level on the lines or written with any confidence.

As he starts to read the words, shock makes him stumble

and misread, and his heart immediately takes a sickening dive. He starts again and forces himself to go slowly line by line:

> *"I need to see you, private, urgent.*
> *You must come alone – and if you want*
> *to see me alive it must be soon. Tell no one.*
> *Sophie*
> *The canal path River Lee Navigation,*
> *south from Hackney Wick, past the lock"*

There is no date on the page, no timing, no indication when it was written. It had been pushed through his door early this morning by someone on foot who knows his address. He thinks he recognizes her writing, but it is as if written under strain, the lines wavering, the letters uncertain. Matthew panics, a deep empty feeling in his gut.

What, now? When, Sophie? What is happening?

He stares again at the letter, but can make nothing else out of it, there are no other clues, just the feeling that Sophie was in grave danger and was demanding Matthew come to some strange venue over Stratford way. He pulls out an A-Z from a shelf and searches for the River Lee Navigation and the Canal, finding Hackney Wick Station and seeing the path that would lead him there. He identifies the Old Ford Lock about half a mile south along the towpath. It is not so far from where she lives in Leyton, but nevertheless it is out of the way, remote. Surely this is a trap. He is being lured out, into unfamiliar territory – by whom? What for?

He reaches for his phone and dials Sophie's mobile telephone number but there is no dial tone, with a 'failed contact' message on his screen. Should he phone Stephanie? No, she would be shocked and he would be unable to reassure her. If she was aware of something she would have contacted him by now. He thinks about just phoning her for a chat to see what she talks about and whether everything is alright, but so early in the morning would be ridiculous and his voice would croak with panic and he would give himself away. The note said tell no one. Perhaps he should call Maurice and arrange for him to walk the Lee Canal from the south, from Pudding Mill Lane and they could meet halfway. If it was some kind of hoax then no harm done, but if there was someone there running away down the path when he, Matthew, approached from the north end, he would have to pass Maurice who at least would get a good sight of him. If Sophie was in trouble, Maurice would be a help. But all that would take time, Maurice might not be around and would he believe him? More likely think Matthew had gone off his rocker.

He should go, now. He hurries back upstairs to get dressed and then returns to a drawer of his desk and takes hold of a brass knuckle-duster that his father had handed down to him years ago, a war-time relic: supplied to all ambulance drivers during the Blitz in London, although how he was supposed to defend the country from the Hun with such a thing, he had never been sure. It is heavy and ribbed and fits neatly into Matthew's right-hand grip and he slips it into his jacket pocket. He puts on a pair of heavy walking boots, grabs the car keys from the hall table and rushes out.

Driving half-way across London over to Hackney, his mood waxes from composed anger to begging ineptitude. He cannot imagine what is going on, although his gut feeling is that Sophie is quite truly in danger and has been kidnapped and whoever is involved will want a large amount of money for her release. He has stuffed two hundred pounds' cash from his desk into an inside pocket, in case that might help although he doubts such a feeble amount will cut the mustard.

He parks near Hackney Wick in an unobtrusive side road

and walks rapidly, half running the unfamiliar back streets towards the canal crossing.

The skies overhead are fittingly gun-metal grey with gloom and the canal path is deserted, end-to-end slabs of concrete. Grass and moss and wild weeds grow freely along its edges, spilling over to the water level. Breeze block walls are daubed liberally with colourful graffiti and obscene instruction. Plentiful dog excrement, fag ends and domestic litter are strewn along the path, newspaper and plastic blown up by the wind against the metal fencing running along the left hand side. Heading south, the still waters of the Navigation Canal, once the small River Lee, lie inert on his right side, one foot below the level of the path. The surface is coated in green algae and blue oil streaks, and broken branches, cans, plastic bottles and several half submerged supermarket trollies are trapped in this silent backwater. Not even an occasional barge seemed to pass this way, to disturb the dilapidated serenity and inertia of a once active method of transport.

Matthew is anxious and makes his way reluctantly, glancing frequently over his shoulder, gripping his brass weapon in his pocket for comfort. A disused industrial warehouse and park is half-hidden by the fencing and an ugly block of council flats at some distance across the canal looks as bleak as any communist state building. A handful of old cars seem to be abandoned alongside a back alleyway and he is observed by no one and sees no one. Up ahead he catches sight of the Old Ford Lock, with its steel bridges straddling the gap with their white fencing. On the left side hidden among abundant trees and greenery is the Old Lock Cottage, dirty and closed up. A battered long barge in fading green and red livery occupies one of the locks, but its hatches are battened down and there is no sign of life within; it floats abandoned in its brick-sided trap. Caught on the water surface around it are frothy suds of white fluffy detergent, yellowing like nicotine stains an old man's sputum.

He walks past keeping to the left side to where the path comes to an end. He stands at the middle of a Y-junction, the main River Lea opening out into something wider straight ahead of him, a basin and past mooring for long boats, now crowded with a clutch of more abandoned barges, before draining off southwards. A narrow steel single-section plank with white-painted rails bridges the twenty foot to the towpath on the far side of the River Lea tributary, and he steps onto it, a forbidding level of uncertainty playing on his mind. Ahead, he can either continue south along the main river course which he can clearly see curling around a long left-hand bend; or take the smaller left hand path that runs darkly and overgrown along the smaller tributary. His eye catches sight of something unusual, a bunch of clothes or materials hanging from fencing some fifty or sixty yards ahead, which must have been blown by the wind and caught in the wire, appearing in the shape of a cross. It is hard to make out at the distance, but it seems to be down the left hand subsidiary path and after a little hesitation, he crosses the bridge and hurries left, to at least satisfy his curiosity. The path begins to peter out into a narrow sandy track hemmed in by the overgrowth of bushes and weeds with ivy rampant, and he feels he is coming to a dead end. But he persists for a little way further, alongside a seven-foot high fence that surrounds a building merchant's yard beyond.

And in a sudden moment Matthew will come upon what he had been coaxed out from home to discover. At first it looks like just a bundle of old clothes, black cloth, white cotton, caught on the barbed-wire of the high fence, as it had caught his eye back at the lock, hanging from the top and loosely fluttering in the breeze. But as he nears, his eyes not deviating for an instant from the object, it grows in size and shape, to become human and fleshy. Matthew breaks into a stumbling rush towards the figure, wired to the fence with its arms spread out as in a crucifixion, the body hanging vertical, heavy and immobile. The head is hooded in black, a white cotton blouse ragged and blood-stained barely covers the female form within and the bare legs, blue and mottled and caked in clods of sticky grume, with her small white feet not quite reaching the ground.

His instinct is to hurl himself to the rescue, grabbing at the wire mesh, trying to get a foothold to reach up and to pull off the hood. Stripped and beaten, he can see the throat has been deeply cut on both sides and, as the dark cloth thick with coagulant slides messily over the head, the short spiky black hair that is revealed is unmistakable.

Matthew moans loudly at the sight of Sophie's white beaten face and furiously blinks away the prickling tears. He stares horrified and weak, until a feeling of nausea forces him to turn away and cough up some vomit over the pathway, where he sinks to his knees, his eyes screwed up tight to obliterate reality and to try to change it for the better.

But he returns to look at her thin body, caked like mud down the sides where her life-blood has drained freely and coagulated on its course and then pooled and thickened on the ground beneath her. Her head lolls forward and as he looks up into her open eyes, pale and vacant, her skin feels slightly warm to his touch and Matthew feels sure that she has only been dead a short while.

He whips round to scour the path and surrounding vantage points, feeling suddenly vulnerable and certain that someone somewhere will be watching to confirm his arrival, that their mischief is complete with his discovery. But he sees nobody and slinks down onto the grass verge again, facing the canal, dropping his forehead onto his bent knees. Perhaps he might have rescued her had he arrived earlier. His weeping is silent but the jerking of his sobbing chest is obvious. A paper-boy on his bike riding the path comes upon the scene a few moments later with alarm and halts, just after the steel bridge over to the lock, nervous to proceed. Matthew spots him and calls out. 'Can you ride very fast to the nearest police station and tell them there is a dead woman on this canal path who needs cutting down from the fence. And an ambulance would be nice,' he finishes. The boy is temporarily transfixed and stares uncertainly, wondering no doubt whether Matthew has done something horrible. But then he turns and shoots away peddling fast, calling, 'OK. Quick as I can.'

Matthew is distraught, but he knows he has to tell Stephanie. After the police have held him for questioning for six hours, he is allowed to return home. A driver takes him to his own parked car in Hackney from where he slowly drives back over to Fulham, and arrives in a numb state at Stephanie's house without warning. The bright flowers in pots along the street, verbena and petunia, and the trees in blossom offer him no respite. He notices the cracked paintwork around her front door. The house looks tranquil as usual. The doorbell sounds softly inside and the dog yaps a couple of times.

In the slightly dim doorway Stephanie stands surprised, a rather tired enigmatic expression on her face. At that moment Matthew recognizes her smile of old, her 'come on' looks, in her school bedroom urging him on, throwing her top off and playing with Matthew, knowing he would be drawn along with her, whether he wanted to or not. She was beautiful then and she is beautiful now, her looks preserved in their place as she gently ages.

'Hello, Steph. Sorry I didn't phone or anything. I've got some bad news, I am afraid. Awful. About Sophie, can I come in?' He is going to have trouble controlling his voice, he knows, he feels ready to collapse. He looks in pain, worried lines deepening around his mouth and unlike his usual appearance, he is unshaven and disheveled and his hands are dirty.

'Of course, come in. What is it?' She closes the door after him, a note of concern in her croaky voice, and follows Matthew who has headed for the lounge. He stands over by the windows looking out into the tiny patch of garden, with most of its colours still to emerge. Without turning, Matthew speaks quietly, with a slight break in his voice. 'Sophie is dead.' There is an anguished and disbelieving noise from behind.

'What!'

'I found her this morning, after a note had been posted through my front door – she was over Stratford way, along the canal at River Lea. She had been murdered and tied to a fence there, for me to find. The note was anonymous, possibly written by Sophie under duress, I don't know, but there were no other signs of anybody anywhere near – so I've been with the police these past few hours. They will be investigating.'

Matthew is gripping his own hands as if for support and only lets the tension go when he turns to face Stephanie. She is shocked, wide-eyed and silent, her fists clenched either side of her face, staring at Matthew. She looks confused and frightened.

Matthew continues: 'She was hanging from barbed wire fencing, her arms tied with wire out sideways like a crucifixion. She had not been molested or anything, nothing sexual, the police thought but she was covered in bruises. Her throat,' Matthew stalls a moment and he has to swallow and his chest heaves as he tries to suppress his sob, placing a finger across his own throat, 'had been cut, both sides. It is likely that she had been fixed up there first, and then she bled to death. She died on the fence. I thought she was still slightly warm when I touched her; the police thought it happened within the last twenty-four hours.'

It is the vengeful purpose of the killing that is obvious to him, and the nasty way they made him discover her to achieve the additional message that he himself might not be safe. These points he discussed with the police, in the shape of DS Wilson, who seemed interested in the possible Chinese link from the events in Spain a decade earlier, but otherwise was not much taken by the randomness and felt it was most likely a local gang, a drugs feud. Matthew felt horrified at the slur but had no answer to refute the accusation; he had already come to accept that poor Sophie had been misled before down that pathway and those things never ended well.

He sinks onto a chair, leaning forward, his face in his hands, sickened by the memory.

Stephanie is uncertain what her reaction should be. She feels numb with disbelief. She cannot really take it in. She keeps asking which hospital she was taken to and she wants Matthew to take her to see her. She knows she should be screaming with anguish, but a rift had developed between her and Sophie long ago, and much of their emotional links had faded with time, rather like the way strong daylight repeatedly saps the colour out of clothes left in the sun. She is instantly saddened because it is her daughter that has suffered and horrified at the mode of her death, but she cannot summon up the floods of tears that others might have expected.

Matthew puts his arms around her shoulders when she sinks next to him and pulls her closer. 'Come, sit here.' Her head rests across his shoulder and quietly she wipes her cheeks with a handkerchief. 'She is in the morgue at Hackney Road police station. I have identified her, but I thought you would want to see her and the police will want to question you. I promised that we would be in later today. I know its five o'clock or something but I can drive you over.'

Stephanie is silent. 'Let me get you a drink, a small brandy, maybe?' He steps over to the side cabinet, finding some bottles, and reaches for a brandy and two glasses. He hands her one and remains standing.

'How horrible. Why, why? What had she done?'

'We will have to wait for investigations and forensics. They had not found a murder weapon. Her bag was near-by, emptied, no purse, no money or cards, if there had been any inside they had been taken; a lipstick, a packet of tissues, you know the sort of stuff. They had no idea immediately of motivation, but to me it looks like a revenge killing, picked out and murdered as an example, the sort of things gangs might do to leave a message to others. You know, do not mess with us, or something.'

'It does not make any sense; what harm was she to anybody?'

Matthew had only vaguely told Stephanie about what Sophie had been up to in Marbella and he was not inclined to expound on those things at that moment. 'She was part of a drugs theft, involving the Chinese gangs in Spain, in Marbella; and there was trouble with a powerful estate owner and drug-dealer there, you heard her mention Juanita Robicalon. In the end Sophie shopped them both, both sides were caught red-handed and the leaders were imprisoned eventually. The Mayor was disgraced, caught up in property fraud, corruption and jailed. The lead Chinese man, The Magician and this JR fellow, both were imprisoned for drugs dealing and money laundering, sentenced to ten and twelve years. The Mayor was released after five years and The Magician died in prison apparently, but JR was released early on good behavior in January of this year, and I think that is the link. Either party could have organized a hit squad to find Sophie and kill her. As an act of vengeance, both JR and the Chinese had lost a lot of money, their reputations; a warning to others.'

Police investigations found no sign of sexual assault and

never found the murder weapon. In Detective Inspector Forrester's opinion, there was little to suggest a random mugging, this was an execution, a deliberate act of retribution for something, some hurt or bad thing that she had done to someone; somebody had deliberately brutalized her for revenge, settling a score, that was his view anyway. The coroner eventually returned a verdict of misadventure. No culprit was ever found for her murder and the investigation, even to this day, remains open, unofficially.

Matthew was fifty-eight years old when he found Sophie dead, alone, hanging from a fence close to the canal at Stratford; he had been forty-eight when he found her alive, in southern Spain, caught in a web of danger, partly of her own making. Matthew understood who was responsible. Sophie had told him most of the details of her Marbella story, and had said, on more than one occasion and half jokingly, that if JR or The Magician ever got out of jail and found out where she was, one of them, or both of them, would kill her. Matthew came to realize that she lived with that fear all the time, however irrational it might have seemed in the apparent safety of anonymous life in East London in the twenty-first century.

Nobody was prosecuted for Roberto's murder, his body apparently destroyed in the explosion at the granary on JR's estate and so no forensics could be found to be helpful.

A few weeks later on a warm weekend afternoon, long after Sophie's broken body has been buried at a miserable service in Fulham Palace Road Cemetery, when the hullabaloo has largely settled, and both Matthew and Stephanie have come to terms with Sophie's fate; when they are taking a deliberate walk along the north river towpath under Hammersmith Bridge, and are thinking of going into The Blue Anchor for a drink; when they are leaning against the old brick wall, watching the forceful swell of the river carry seagulls along and two single oarsmen resting in their sculls are passing the time of day, Matthew speaks quietly, looking down at the murky water, his hair lifting in the breeze: 'You left me once, Steph, to have your baby, our daughter. Without explanation. I was devastated.' After a short pause, he turns to look at her, squinting against the light, 'Don't leave me now.'

Stretching her arms around his shoulders, Stephanie pulls him closer to her. He feels the comfortable fit of her body against his, even through their coats. She presses her cheek against his and he senses her warm breath on his ear as she whispers:

'I won't, Matthew. I promise I won't leave you.'

Unsure whether he believes her, he hugs her tightly, suddenly feeling seventeen again.

THE LONDON SNIPER

DANIEL PASCOE

ALSO BY THE AUTHOR

THE LONDON SNIPER

Arthur Chigwell.
Grieving father of a son brutally beheaded by Iraqi extremists in 2004, desperate for revenge on all those he holds responsible.

Jarvis Collingwood.
Ex-Army sniper, his own brother gunned down in front of him in Iraq. Cold, calculating and willing.

Leon Deshpande.
Specialist security adviser and investigator, used to getting his man, especially if the price is right.

Naomi Lonsdale.
Young and naive, easily taken in and horribly used.

The London 2012 Olympic Games closing ceremony. Dotted around the vast stadium: all of the gunman's targets, enjoying an evening of spectacular celebration, little knowing how the night – or even their lives – will end.

The London Sniper is a chilling contemporary thriller exploring the ultimate revenge.

Find this book and more available at:

www.bookguild.co.uk